Praise :
Ramble and Roar

"A debut that blasts out of the gate with all the exuberance of the Roaring Twenties, *Ramble and Roar* is a joyride of a book. Charged with the sinuous power and passion of 1920's New York City, this story vividly portrays a world where mobs rule the streets—and once you're in, there's no getting out. A prodigal tale that speaks to rebels without a cause, drawing them back to the truth with gentle hands. Catie Cordero is an author to watch, and this book is going on my keeper shelf."

~Heather Day Gilbert, award-winning, bestselling author of *The Vikings of the New World Saga*

"Catie Cordero has written a rollicking, spirited tale that will capture readers from the first chapter. Danger, suspense, and true love are all part of this coming-of-age story of talent, dreams, and finding what really matters in life. Readers will leap into this tale with Cordero, who has a unique gift for entertaining readers and challenging them to think beyond the story to their own lives."

~Ann Byle, book reviewer and author of *Christian Publishing 101*

"It's a great pleasure to read a book that is as full of life as Catie Cordero's *Ramble and Roar*. From the first page, I was entranced by the characterization, delighted by the bantering dialogue, and wholly engaged with the plot. Cordero has done her due diligence in making history come alive, peopling her story with characters who feel as familiar as a best friend. The reader cannot help but experience the full tension between innocence and corruption, tradition and change, fatalism and hope that characterized the Roaring 20s. And all throughout this rollicking ride with Eliza, Hugh, Warren, and Mattie, the reader finds echoes of our own time."

~Susie Finkbeiner, CBA bestselling author
of *The Pearl Spence Series*

"Richly laced with historical detail and fine-tuned dialect, Ramble and Roar brings 1920s Manhattan to blazing life. Catie Cordero's energetic debut will delight fans of the genre."

~Katherine Scott Jones,
author of *Her Memory of Music*

"Meticulously researched and deftly written, this work of historical fiction brings both the grit and glitter of the Roaring Twenties to life. Timeless themes of love, loyalty, youthful ambition and passion are woven seamlessly into layered storylines, making for a captivating read. With *Ramble and Roar*, Catie Cordero has made a laudable debut as a novelist."

~Todd J. Wiebe, Research Librarian and
Associate Professor, Hope College

Ramble

And

Roar

A 1920s Novel

CATIE CORDERO

FLYWHEEL
BOOKS

Published by Flywheel Books, Zeeland, MI. www.catiecordero.com

Printed through CreateSpace, Charleston, SC.

Per public domain, this book features songs, *There'll Be Some Changes Made* published by Harry Herbert Pace (Black Swan Records) and *Give It To Me Good* published by Okeh Records.

Summary: Eliza Belcourt flees to the sleepless streets of Manhattan to fulfill her destiny but every sparkling dream comes with a price, and the Irish mob is ready to collect.

ISBN- 13: 978-1985377622

For my husband, Jonathan.
My greatest supporter and friend.

ACKNOWLEDGMENTS

I have dreamed of this book for 10 years. It started as an idea in 2008, which led to stacks of library books on my kitchen table. It's been a long journey of learning, writing and reading to reach the place I am now. On the journey, I've had help from family and friends. Life is always better with help.

Thank you to my faithful critique partners and content readers, Jonathan Cordero, Cindy Overbeek, Connie Alvero and Janna Vanderveen. You sweet people have read this manuscript more times than can be counted on two hands. God bless you.

Jean Gilson, my newfound friend from Dundalk, Ireland. Thank you for your assistance with phrasing and capturing the essence of everyday Irish lingo.

Heather Gilbert, you have taken time to teach and train me in the ways of indie publishing. You have shown such generosity with your time and knowledge. I'm grateful.

Ann Byle, you believed in this story at its beginning stages, when it was rough and needed improvement. Thank you.

Susie Finkbeiner, my dear friend whose beautiful writing has mentored me, and her friendship has helped me grow as a writer and person.

Kelly Petroelje, thank you for taking my characters and bringing them to life. The cover is a testament to your keen eye for art and painting.

Thank you to my husband and children, for your love and support. You are amazing.

And to all my other family and friends, thank you for your prayers and encouragement on this journey.

Last but far from least, thank you God for sitting with me each day as we write together, dream together, and imagine the possibilities. I love you.

AUTHOR'S NOTE

America stood as the eager bride—waiting.

With her eyes open, she allowed the veil to be pulled away. Thus she began her new life. She was no longer the innocent America of the nineteenth century; she had entered a new world of possibilities, eager to experience all of life's pleasures. She was now in the "roaring twenties."

She learned new words like research, impulse, and desire. She developed a new consciousness in literature, politics, music, social atmospheres, and perhaps above all, the opposite sex.

In an attempt to limit this emerging America, a constitutional amendment was put into effect on January 16, 1920. It was called the Volstead Act, which prohibited the manufacture, transportation, and sale of alcoholic beverages. But this attempt failed sorely as certain entrepreneurial spirits, also known as the mob, saw an opportunity for new businesses such as bootlegging, breweries, and speakeasies. The mobs, both Irish and Italian alike, fought for control in all the major cities. Money never accumulated so fast and neither did the dead bodies.

And then on August 26, 1920, a victory was won for the female population with the signing of the 19th amendment. Women were finally given the right to vote.

America found herself in a completely new arena. Changes were unfolding all around her. New innovations like the vacuum cleaner, the washing machine, and public radio broadcasts were introduced. Fashions became more daring as the female hemlines inched their way up the leg. Commercial airlines and the affordable automobile revolutionized transportation. These changes molded and shaped America into the new modern age.

And now, it was July of 1925. Calvin Coolidge was president, the stock market was booming, and consumerism was in all its glory as it bewitched the people through advertising. America was in a time of the "new" and "improved." The trouble was that not everyone wanted new or improved. It appeared that America herself had become divided into the traditionalists versus the liberalists. Tradionalists were greatly opposed to the emerging youth who bucked restraint and rebelled against the former ways of the proper, American lifestyle. And the liberalists…well they didn't really care what anyone said. Fueled by post-war cynicism, they lived for the next thrill. Life was calling. It was time to answer.

CHAPTER ONE

I wasn't looking for death. It found me. That's what I tell myself.

But I know the truth. I made the choices that led me here. I chose this path. And now, death lurks a step behind. Ever a step behind. Waiting until the sun goes down. Darkness is good at concealing evil.

I wonder if anything can save me now.

One word echoes faintly in my conscious: hope. It's been so long since I've courted hope. Yet, it beckons.

Death and Hope.

Both reach out, but only one can win.

~Warren Moore

CHAPTER TWO

July 4, 1925
Saturday, 9:30 PM

"You kissed me." Eliza Belcourt leaned back, eyes wide.

"My sincere apologies." Hugh Whitmore gestured to the ornamental rug below his patent leather shoes. "I tripped."

"Are you saying that you *accidentally* fell on my mouth?"

"A most advantageous accident." Dimples surfaced with his smile. "Your lips broke my fall like a pillow."

"Your hands are still around my waist."

"Just trying to regain my balance. Thank you for your help."

She waited.

His hands didn't move.

"Have you found that balance yet?" She arched her right eyebrow.

"I didn't realize I was still hanging on." He motioned again to the rug. "Beautiful rug, but a terrible hazard."

"Hazard indeed." She crossed her arms. "Admit it."

"I beg your pardon?"

"Admit that you didn't trip."

He put a solemn hand to his chest. "A confession would mean that I seized this moment alone in your parents' library and kissed you on purpose. And *that* would be improper. So I insist that I tripped. By any chance, did you feel fireworks?"

"Are you referring to the explosives outside or the kiss?"

"Both?" He sounded hopeful.

"Neither."

"That's a shame."

She grinned for a moment and walked toward the camelback sofa. It sat beside rows of mahogany bookshelves filled with French classics and pretentious words. "The greater shame was my performance in the ballroom ten minutes ago." She sank onto a cushion. "Quite sobering. I made a fool of myself, didn't I?"

"On the contrary, I thought your song was lively and unique. What were the lyrics again?" He paused, then snapped his fingers. "Ah yes. 'Give me that jazz. I want that jazz. Give me that wind me up, pull me down razzmatazz.' The song did seem to resonate with the crowd. Many a gent looked plenty wound up, much to the chagrin of their wives."

"Much to the chagrin of my parents, too." She sighed. "I felt it only right to stand throughout the song, but they would have preferred I sat on the piano's bench."

"And preferred that your hips hadn't kept perfect time with the rhythm."

"It happened so naturally."

"But the real shocker," he lifted a finger, "was probably the kick of your heel near the end."

"I admit, I got carried away." She frowned. "My mother hid her face behind her fan, and father had the baby grand rolled away almost as soon as I bowed."

"Yes, the turn-around was impressive." He sat on the opposite end of the sofa and hitched up a shiny black shoe, resting it upon his other bent knee.

"It was humiliating."

He waved his hand in dismissal. "It will be forgotten by morning."

"I won't forget. I wrote that song, Hugh. Me." She pointed her finger toward her chest. "I put my heart and soul out there, in front of all those people, and no one gave me any applause." She raised her voice in frustration. "Even Geraldine, my supposed bosom friend, didn't give a single clap. She allied with the majority's silence."

"You seem to forget," he countered calmly, "you did have one person who applauded."

She rolled her eyes. "You don't count."

"How is that?"

"Because you don't have to prove yourself. You're the envy of most bachelors and the desire of every eligible lady. Nevertheless, despite how popular you might be, no one joined your exuberant clapping and whistling." She leaned her head against the backrest. "Hence my retreat from the ballroom."

"It's true. I am well-liked." He smoothed a hand down the front lapel of his tuxedo. "Regardless, I think you fail to see yourself clearly. You are Eliza Belcourt. It doesn't matter one whit what those people think of you."

She fidgeted with a pearl button on the wrist of her white glove. "I should have done the song my father had selected."

"It wouldn't have been nearly as entertaining. So, what possessed you to disobey the *great* Hector Belcourt?"

She laid her hand on the rolled armrest, considering how to answer. When she opened her mouth, the words came out only above a whisper. "Have you ever swum naked in a pond?"

His posture straightened. "No. Why?"

"I've done it. Once." She glanced at his face.

He didn't look offended.

She dropped her eyes and continued. "It was the pond at the back of our property. I've never felt so free in my whole life. Stripping off my clothes was like tearing away the bonds holding me down. As the coolness of the water touched every part of my skin, I felt every fiber of my being relax. It was simply the water and me. No one watching. No one judging."

She lifted a fervent pair of baby blues. "I tell you, it's the most exhilarating thing in the world. You must try it. Those minutes in that pond opened my eyes to how trapped I feel inside my refined household with all the rules and etiquette. I need to rid myself of the shackles. Music is my ticket to that freedom. That's why I disobeyed my father tonight. That's why I've disobeyed him quite regularly since that evening swim." She paused. "What do you think of that?" She held her breath, waiting for his response.

He didn't answer or make eye contact.

She shifted on the seat, trying to decipher his expression. She feared he disapproved. Merciful heavens, what if he told her father? "Hugh. Please say something."

He folded his hands and nodded. "Yes."

"What?" She crinkled her brow.

"I'll do it."

"Do what?"

"Swim with you."

She gasped. "You thought I was asking you to swim with me?"

"You didn't?" He now looked utterly confused.

"No."

"But you told me I needed to try it."

"Yes, but not with me. On your own."

"You want me to swim naked, alone?"

"Yes."

His eyebrows pinched together. "No man in his right mind would do that."

"Ugh!" She threw a hand in the air. "Why do I bother with you?"

"For pity's sake, Eliza." He rubbed a hand over his forehead and spoke in a low voice. "You told me you were swimming *naked.*"

"The point of the story is freedom." She shook her head. "I can't stand much more of this stifling life. I need to go some place where people will applaud me. I read in *Radio Stars* that Marion Harris recorded her songs in New York. People love her."

"New York?" He inclined his head. "You want to go there?"

"Yes, Manhattan." She spoke the word like it was a dream world, full of every good and glittering thing.

"I have heard that it's a prosperous city, but I don't think it would be wise for you to go alone. It could be dangerous without a chaperone."

"My father won't offer a chaperone. He won't allow me to go. I will have to make other arrangements. But somehow, I must get there." She gazed ahead, adrift in her thoughts. "In New York City, I will record my own music and become the next Marion Harris. Then everyone will see. Then," she paused, "I'll be something great."

He slid closer, resting a palm on her fisted hand. "You already are."

"Maybe to you, but for everyone else, I have to prove myself."

"No, you don't." He tipped up her chin. "You are Eliza Belcourt. You are perfect just the way you are. If you try to please others, you will risk losing yourself."

She felt her throat constrict. It didn't happen often, but sometimes, Hugh surprised her. Tonight, he was on a roll. He toggled between egocentric and heart wrenchingly genuine with complete ease. The latter stole her breath away. She told herself they were just friends and must remain so, but goodness, she was struggling to remember why. Involuntarily, she leaned toward him.

Stroking the outline of her cheek, he kissed her without an ounce of accident.

She wound her arms around his neck and returned it.

Lingering only a moment more, he drew away. His dimples resurfaced with a wide smile. "Eliza Belcourt, you're positively devious."

"I beg your pardon?" She tried to catch her breath.

"You practically fell on my mouth."

She huffed. "You must be dreaming."

"Well if I was…" He rose to his feet and bent within inches of her ear. "It was a very pleasant dream." Strolling through the library's double doors, he disappeared around the corner.

She had anticipated certain proceedings for tonight's party, but none had included Hugh, the library, and—she touched a hand to her lips—that. A blush set into her cheeks. It was Independence Day, and she definitely felt fireworks, but they weren't the ones her father ordered. Pressing a palm to her heart, she closed her eyes. She couldn't fall for him. She had to stay focused, regardless of how good that was.

"There you are," said a male voice.

She jolted as her father stepped through the door. His disapproving expression made her cringe.

"We've started the firework show." Hector gestured to the hallway that led out to the garden. "I thought you might want to see it, unless you're too ashamed to show your face after that disgraceful performance."

"Actually, I'd love to see the fireworks." She stood, hastening to leave.

He held up a hand, halting her mid-step. "Tomorrow, you will write a personal letter to each of our guests apologizing for your indecent choice of song."

She chewed the inside of her lip. "What if I'm not sorry?"

"You should be sorry. Your mother and I were humiliated. Such words. Such mannerisms. A shameful display."

"I wrote the song."

The muscles in his jaw twitched. "I will pretend I didn't hear that. You will write the letters or your fingers won't ever touch a piano again." He turned sharp and left.

Anger slithered through her veins, setting her cheeks on fire. Instead of joining the guests, she strode up the stairs into her bedroom. Hell would freeze over before she apologized.

CHAPTER THREE

July 5
Sunday, 7:00 AM

"Are you pretending to be ill?"

Eliza's mother didn't have to speak. Her heavy gardenia perfume preceded her arrival. "Hello, mother." She cracked open her eyes.

Katherine Belcourt hovered at the side of her canopy bed. "I noticed you didn't come out to see the fireworks last night."

"My stomach feels awful." She added a moan for effect.

Katherine placed a hand to her forehead. It trembled.

"Are you anxious, Mother?"

"You're not feverish. Did you start feeling sick after your…" Katherine's lips thinned, "performance?"

"No. Can you ring the bell for Neville? I need her to bring me some tea."

"She is ironing your shawl. You do realize that today is Sunday; we must leave for mass in one hour." Katherine patted her arm.

She understood the silent message of her mother's gentle tap. It didn't mean, "I'm sorry you're ill," but more, "please snap out of it like a good girl." For years, she had played her role as the obedient child, but it had achieved nothing. "I can't go to mass today."

Katherine dusted an invisible hair from her sleeve. "We can't have people thinking that you're avoiding confession."

No doubt the gossip had gone into full circulation since her song, but she refused to confess sins she wasn't the least bit sorry for. She suspected that her parents' church attendance was more for pretense than passion. Her mother obsessed over appearances: appear thin, appear young, appear happy. She stared at her mother's waist. The fact that the maid had squeezed her into that yellow taffeta dress was a testament to miracles. She pulled the quilt over her face. "I'm too sick."

Katherine tapped her foot, thinking aloud like she usually did. "I suppose I could tell Father Andrews to add you to the list of prayers. Then people won't speculate about your absence." She stopped tapping. "I'll have Neville bring up some chamomile, along with parchment and pen. Your father said that you have letters to write our guests."

She shoved back the bedspread. "You want me to write those letters?"

"It must be done, dear."

"Why?"

"Because you dishonored everyone last night with that song."

The words pierced her. "Mother, it wasn't just any song. I wrote it."

"*You* wrote *that?*" Katherine sank onto the edge of the bed like a wilted daffodil. "Gracious Lord." Her eyelids closed as her fingers grazed the strand of white rosary beads that hung around her neck.

"Yes, and I'm proud of it." She lifted her chin. "I've written many songs."

"But those lyrics. And the tune. I saw your hips sway."

"When I sing, I feel free. I come alive." She fixed her gaze on her mother, beseeching her to understand. "Singing my own music makes me happy."

Katherine's reserved expression faltered. She looked down at her hands folded in her lap. "You have a beautiful voice, and you're very talented, sweetheart. I've always thought so." A wistful smile curved her lips. "You play the piano better than I ever did."

"You taught me how."

"You were easy to teach. A natural talent."

"I remember when you had the piano imported from London." Eliza spoke with a dreamy tone. "It was beautiful, and you loved it. I saw it in your eyes every time you looked at it. But the only time I ever saw you play is when you taught me lessons. I have never understood that."

"Every sophisticated young lady should learn to play the piano, so I taught you. Though after last night's performance, I have some doubts. Why couldn't you sit and play the song your father had chosen?"

She rolled to her side, staring at the long drapes framing her window. She used to pretend they were curtains on a stage. When she was eight, she had emerged from behind them, singing for the world to hear until her father arrived to the show. Shaking his head with disdain, he had said, "If only you put half as much gusto into your studies as you do singing, perhaps I wouldn't be forced to pay for a tutor. Before you, there wasn't a Belcourt who needed academic assistance. An unfortunate humbling, I guess." She had sung quieter after that and worked harder in school, though it didn't avail much. She still earned lower marks on her studies than the other girls in class. Her parents' disappointed scowls stuck fresh in her mind, and the pain lingered. She spoke in a hushed tone. "I want people to embrace me for me."

"Darling, they will embrace you, but not if you behave poorly. We are Belcourts. We have a reputation to uphold."

"Yes, I'm a regular hussy." She mumbled into the quilt.

Katherine leaned closer. "What did you say?"

"My stomach is feeling fussy."

"I can imagine why." Katherine propped a hand on her hip. "You will not attract a proper suitor with brazen behavior. Oh, the embarrassment. I think I'll ask the priest to make a house call. A confession is definitely in order." She walked to the door and stopped. "Neville will bring the paper. I expect the letters to be written today, stomachache or not." With a prim spin on her heel, she exited the room.

Glaring at the closed door, Eliza flung off her covers. "I won't write a single word of apology. I did nothing wrong." She had anticipated today for the last three weeks and nothing and no one would ruin it for her. Tiptoeing to the door, she listened for approaching footsteps or voices.

The hallway was silent.

A sneaky smile lifted the corners of her mouth. "They haven't seen nothing yet." With a bounce in her step, she hastened to her dresser and yanked open the top drawer. She dug under the stack of cotton nightgowns for her hidden music sheets. Pulling them out, she read the title of the first page. Her heart drummed to a faster rhythm. Tonight, everything would change.

———

Hugh couldn't erase the smile from his face. The kiss with Eliza had replayed in his mind at least a hundred times, followed by daydreams of swimming together in a pond. He knew he should control his thoughts. It was Sunday, after all. Fastening the top button of his collar, he shrugged on his suit jacket and nodded at his reflection in a wall mirror. Heads would definitely turn in his direction.

Strolling out of his bedroom, he walked through the wide hallway paneled with wallpaper, exhibiting an extravagant bird and flower motif. He never knew Eliza had such a rebellious streak. One thing was for sure, if she truly intended to go to New York City, she could not go alone. She needed to be watched over, protected. And for that, he had a plan. Rounding a corner, he glided into his parents' dining room, where his father and mother sat at the end of their oval fourteen-chair table. "Morning," he greeted his parents as he settled into a chair.

Vivian paused in stirring her coffee and smiled. "Good morning, son."

Daniel nodded to him while he read the paper.

A maid entered the room with a plate and silverware and laid it out before him. "Good morning, Mr. Whitmore. Can I pour you a cup of coffee or juice?"

"Coffee, please." Studying the silver breakfast trays, he selected several slices of bacon. With a glance at his father, he asked, "Have you talked about our plans with Hector yet?"

Daniel didn't look up from the page. "Awful early to be thinking of business."

"It's a matter of urgency."

"What do you mean?"

"Did you tell Hector that we want to dissolve our partnership?"

Folding the paper, Daniel set it down. "I only told him that I have been contemplating the future of the steel industry, and perhaps a larger city would provide more success. To which he replied that we've built a great foundation here and going elsewhere was asinine. I said it's something I've considered, but no decision has been officially made. He looked skeptical. I'm sure he would have said more had we not been interrupted."

"If it weren't a Sunday, I'm sure he would have already called."

"I'm surprised even that stopped him," said Daniel. "I expect a call first thing Monday morning."

Hugh buttered a piece of toast. "I want to request that you hold off on severing our partnership for now."

Daniel's forehead creased. "Why is that?"

"Because I fear that if we end it now, Hector will not give me his blessing to marry Eliza."

Vivian exchanged a surprised glance with Daniel. "I didn't know you were officially courting."

"We haven't exactly voiced it. However, at yesterday's party, Eliza made it clear that we are in a relationship."

Vivian leaned forward. "What did she say?"

"It wasn't so much what was said, but what happened."

Daniel's fork clinked to his plate. "What happened?"

"She kissed me." A sly grin tipped his mouth.

"*She* kissed you?"

"It was mutual."

Daniel's expression grew stern. "It was only a kiss, correct?"

"Of course."

"And you intend to propose?"

"I most certainly do."

"Well then," Daniel's shoulders relaxed, "good."

"I'm simply amazed." Vivian studied him with wonder. "This kind of impetuousness is so unlike you."

"When I'm with Eliza, I feel like I could do anything."

Daniel arched a brow. "Keep it within reason."

Vivian ignored her husband. "I think that's wonderful, son. Risks oftentimes lead to new opportunities. I dare say Eliza is a risk taker. Her song last night definitely showed spirit."

"Spirit." Daniel tilted his head. "That's one way to put it. Did you catch the looks on Hector and Katherine's faces during her performance?"

"It was clear that they disapproved." Vivian's shoulders lowered with a sigh. "I should have applauded her. I was proud of Hugh for clapping. In the old country, we had a saying, 'The greatest mistake you can make in life is to continually fear that you will make one.' Eliza has gumption. I'm glad she's drawing that out of you."

His mother's praise broadened his smile. "She does make me come alive."

"She's lovely." Vivian reached for his hand. "I believe she will make an excellent wife."

"I would marry her tomorrow if I could." He turned to his father. "Do you think Hector will give me his blessing?"

"I'm sure he will agree that you are a suitable match. Of course, I will wait to cut our business ties because Hector will probably hold that against us."

"I assumed the same."

Vivian sipped her coffee. "I wonder what will be worse, being Hector's business partner or family member?"

"If we're in New York, we won't have to see much of him."

"The distance might help," said Daniel. "I thought you had reservations about relocating. Has something changed your mind?"

"Not entirely. I'd rather stay here, but I do believe it behooves us to see if New York City can offer better business opportunities." In truth, he liked his cushy life in Elkins Park and the envy of his peers. However, a month ago, his father had deemed him the heir to the Whitmore estate and accounts. It had taken five years for his parents to accept that his eldest brother, Frederick, was gone for good. He had vanished with a brief note saying that he needed a fresh start. His father had spent countless dollars to locate him, but to no avail. The pain of Freddie's departure had greatly depressed his mother, and she had begged Daniel to move somewhere new. So they had left Pittsburgh with all its memories and had moved eastward to Elkins Park. It was here that Daniel met the rich aristocrat Hector Belcourt and became his business partner. Persuasive and confident, Hector had led them to believe that he owned a thriving steel company, but within months of signing the agreement, Daniel had uncovered the truth. The Belcourts were nearing bankruptcy. As a man of his word, Daniel continued with the partnership and helped the company turn a profit. However, it had been four years and Daniel and Hugh were weary of Hector's less than honest tactics. "As long as Eliza is with me, I don't care where I live."

"Don't forget, she has to say yes first."

Hugh turned to his father. "Do you think she'll deny me?"

"She is one of the most eligible ladies in this city. I'm sure you have competition."

"Competition?" He waved his hand in dismissal. "Eliza adores me." He recalled their secret kiss in her parents' library. She had an effect on his heart like no other. When she entered a room, people noticed. Her poised elegance contrasted beautifully with her wild ringlets of black hair and her blazing blue eyes. When she stood close, his temperature rose. He longed to hold her, kiss her, and love her forever.

"When do you plan to propose?" asked Vivian.

"Soon. But first, I must speak with Hector."

"Good luck." Daniel reopened his newspaper.

"I don't need luck. I will, however, need money to buy the ring." He wiped his mouth with a napkin. "I think a thousand should do it."

Daniel's fork hit his porcelain plate.

"Fiddlesticks," said Vivian. "I saved your grandmother's ring for such a time as this."

"You want me to give Eliza *that*?"

Vivian looked struck. "It's an heirloom."

He turned to his father, his expression earnest. "Please, I need to buy the right ring. My future happiness depends on it."

"Oh all right. You can have the money. We'll make a trip to the bank tomorrow." Daniel shook his head. "I sure hope she says yes."

CHAPTER FOUR

Sunday, 10:00 PM

The six-foot gate loomed before Eliza like an iron prison. All of Belle Vue Manor, her family's estate, sat inside the protection of the barricade. Each night, the entrance was locked, meaning that her escape involved a hearty climb. She hiked up her dress and tucked it into the back of her lacy bloomers.

Like all the previous times, she jumped to clutch the top rail. The two-inch-heels of her Perugia pumps scuffed on the metal as she hefted herself to her chest and swung her leg over. She straddled the fence like a horse jockey in stockings, hoping that her neighbors were not witnessing the sneak preview. Hauling over her other leg, she fell to the ground with a groan. She looked down Ashbourne Road and noted the soft glow of her taxi's headlights. Hurrying past the other private estates, she tapped on the cab's window.

The driver exited the car and opened her door. "Took a little longer tonight."

"Sorry, Hank. Thanks for waiting."

"No trouble, Miss Eliza. Are we heading into the city?"

"Absolutely."

"Good choice."

The fences and mansions of high society faded into the background as they drove south on Old York Road. As they entered the bustling streets of downtown Philadelphia, a light rain peppered the windshield.

Hank pulled to a stop beside the curb of Shakers Nightclub. Electric lights beamed through the club's windows, dancing over the taxi.

Adrenaline rushed through Eliza's veins. She tucked a few coins into Hank's palm.

"Have fun and take care of yourself." He tipped his newsboy cap.

"As always." She grinned.

Stacked bricks propped open the club's heavy wooden doors. Swinging music poured out of the club and into the streets. An overflow of smoking patrons crammed below the awning to avoid the rain. It didn't matter that the floor tiles had cracks and only half the overhead lights beamed. Shakers possessed an atmosphere that stripped away worry and saturated the soul.

Eliza squeezed her five-foot-four inch frame into the crowd, tasting the humidity and thick smoke in the air. Against the back wall was a small stage. Her heart raced inside her chest. In twenty minutes, she would be standing there.

Currently, a four-piece band scrunched together in a semi-circle and played a hopping tune. The pianist thumped the ivory keys on his upright, joined by a bass player plucking his strings. A beam of light radiated upon the singer's ebony skin as she stood center stage. She was the money of the show. Her name was Flora Gray, and to Eliza, she was an angel.

"Eliza!" The club's director lifted his hand and waved her over.

She hastened to meet him at a table, right of the stage.

"Jeez doll, where've you been?" He opened his pocket watch. "It's 10:40. You're on in twenty. I was about to pull your spot."

"I'm so sorry. It won't happen again." She stroked a sweaty curl off her brow with a shaky hand.

"Better not. You got a good voice, but I've a club to run. I need to know you'll be here."

"Of course." She nodded emphatically. "I'll arrive much earlier next time."

"If the crowd likes you, you'll get another shot, but if not," his shoulders shrugged, "that's the end."

Despite her internal apprehension, she maintained a bright smile. "Then I have to make them love me."

"Exactly." He patted her on the back.

As she stared at the stage, fear whispered in her ear. What if you fail? Maybe you aren't good enough. She swallowed down the rising emotion. No, she had to get this right. She had to succeed.

While the saxophonist played a solo, Flora Gray descended the steps and walked toward her. "Tonight's your big debut. You ready?"

"I don't know." She hoped Flora didn't note the tremble in her voice. "But I'll give them my best."

"Atta girl. What song you gonna do?"

"*Give it to Me Good* by Virginia Liston."

"Liston, huh? Well, all right." Flora grinned. "See I knew there was soul in you. You give it to them good, Liza girl. In the truest form you got."

"What if—" She fidgeted with her gloves. "What if I don't know the truest form I got?"

Flora looked her over with a sideways glance. "Take out the bun."

"What?"

"Let your hair fall."

"Why?"

"Your hair is attached to your proper life. But you ain't in Elkins Park no more. You in Philadelphia. So you gotta let that hair down. 'Cause when that hair falls, so do all the other inhibitions."

Sweat already soaked her scalp. With her hair down, she would perspire more. It seemed completely undignified. Her mother would send her straight to confession if she saw her hair down in public. Although when she had swum naked in the pond and the water flowed between her loose tendrils, she had experienced sweet liberation. "Okay. I'll do it." Bobby pins clinked on the table, one by one, until her thick curls dropped around her shoulders.

"Yeah." Flora put a hand on her hip. "That's it."

Eliza checked over her shoulder to see if anyone was staring. "I feel scandalous."

"Good. Now go sing your song."

The club's director stepped on the stage. "We got a new act tonight by the name of Eliza Adrienne. Put your hands together in a warm welcome."

Drying her palms on the side of her satin dress, she joined the director on the platform. She curtsied and clutched the microphone stand between her fingers. While the pianist clunked the keys and stomped his foot to the tempo of one-two-three-four, one-two-three-four, she looked at the crowd.

They stared back with blank expressions. They probably wished Flora was still singing.

The note that she was supposed to sing came and went.

The pianist glanced at her, mouthing, "try again."

Another measure of notes, and she pushed out her lyrics in a trembling voice. "I'm happy. I'm so happy. I've got the sweetest man there is in town."

A couple seated at a front table frowned.

She swayed but her quivering knees made the movement look jerky instead of attractive. "And he's a dandy, just sweet as candy. There ain't another one that can be found."

Groans filtered through the crowd.

"Get Flora back up there," a man hollered.

Eliza gripped the stand tighter. "My lovin' sweetie, my lovin' sweetie, he sure is hard to beat."

More boos rumbled through the crowd.

"And when he kisses me so sweet…" She choked on her words and looked down at her shoes. *They hate me.* She stopped swaying.

"Don't stop, doll." A male voice called over the crowd. "You're doing fine."

She looked up. In the back corner, a tall figure stood wearing a dark coat. The smoky air and dim lighting shadowed his face, but she could perceive a stark white ribbon on his bowler hat.

"Keep going," he called again.

"Sing it, baby," echoed Flora.

Hope welled inside her chest. The man in the hat, whoever he was, wanted her to finish. By golly, she would do it and do it well. "Why every day you'll hear me say." Pulling the microphone off the stand, she walked toward the edge of the stage with a hand propped on her hip. "Give it to me, give it to me good."

"All right," someone called out.

"Just like a sweet daddy would." She rocked her hips from side to side. "When we're strolling through the park, I'm happy as a lark. I'm lovin', turtledovin', he can't be beat." She wiggled her fingers like she was calling them to come closer and dropped her tone lower. "So give it to me. Give it to me good. I say, sweet daddy, won't you, give it to me. Give it to me good."

Several patrons whistled.

She cupped a hand beside her cheek and tilted her head to the side. "When I die upon my grave, I want these simple little words engraved." She grinned. "Give it to me. Give it to me good. Oh, sweet daddy won't you, give it to me, give it to me good."

When the last note played, she swung an arm behind her back and bowed.

The man in the hat whistled loudly. "That's what I'm talking about."

A smattering of applause and cheers went up.

"Thank you. Thank you." The club's director re-appeared on stage and motioned to her. "Eliza Adrienne, everyone."

She smiled as she bowed again. Descending the stairs, she wondered if her feet touched the ground. It had been tense, and she needed practice, but oh, to hear that applause.

Flora came to her side. "You did it, baby. You got through your first performance."

"It was rough."

"Yes, but you finished strong. That's what matters."

"It was that man in the crowd who kept me going. Did you see his face?"

"No, it's too hazy to see anyone's face unless they're directly in front of your nose."

"I have to see if I can find him and thank him for helping me out."

"You do that." Flora patted her arm. "I'm looking forward to seeing more of you."

"Thank you. I hope someday I can be half as good a singer as you."

"Just keep singing, baby. That's all you gotta do."

Eliza shuffled through the crowd, shaking hands and receiving praise. Reaching the back corner, she searched the tables for a man wearing the bowler hat with a white ribbon. "Did any of you see that man who cheered for me during my performance?"

A lady pointed her finger toward the door. "I saw him, but he headed out almost as soon as you got off the stage. He might be outside the club."

"Oh, thank you." Hastening toward the exit, she shoved her way out the doors. Aside from the lampposts, the dark sky hindered the visibility along Broad Street. She walked the sidewalk, searching for the hat. How could he disappear so quickly? She looped back toward the club when she noticed the bowler's stark ribbon. The man strode on the opposite sidewalk, about three car lengths away. "Sir!" she called out.

He paused, turning toward her call.

She waved her hand like flag. "Sir, please wait."

As if startled, he hurried on.

She darted between a Chevy and a tin Lizzie. "Please, I want to thank you." Her heels clattered as she chased him. She hugged the sidewalk's curb, trying to steer around a herd of people hogging the path. One of the men threw back his head, laughing. Stumbling to the side, he collided with her body. She fell over the curb with a yelp. Her purse popped open as it hit the pavement, spewing her handkerchief, watch, and coins. The road's moisture seeped through her dress. She looked around, mortified.

The man offered a slurred apology.

She scrambled to collect the contents of her purse. Glowing lights approached. A furious honk sent her reeling backwards. Mud and grit sprayed from the car's tires. She screamed as it squirted her face. Wiping her cheeks with the back of her hands, she suddenly stopped. Her eyes widened in horror. Her favorite handbag rested inches from her shoes, displaying a new design of tire tracks. "No, no, no." She scooped it up like an injured bird. Likely unfixable. Sighing, she looked down the sidewalk, hoping to see her mystery man, but he was nowhere in sight. One look at her filthy dress told her she couldn't go back into Shakers Nightclub. Cradling her purse to her chest, she trudged over to a white-checkered cab. "I need a ride to Elkins Park."

The driver leaned against the side of his cab and flicked ash from his cigarette. "Rough night, sweetheart?"

"It had its moments. Can you drive me?"

"That's over thirty minutes. It'll cost you."

"I can pay."

"Very well." Opening the back door, he assisted her into the back seat. He glanced over her dress. "Wanna tell me what happened?"

"No." She stared at her dirty lavender dress. No amount of Fels-Naptha could clean it. Mud speckled her skin like polka dots. Curls stuck to her neck with sweat. And a car nearly hit her, but all was not in vain. She had succeeded at Shakers Nightclub. Tonight, they applauded her. Things could only improve from here.

———

Hugh parked his car in his driveway at Rosemont House. Pulling his black hat off his head, he rubbed sweat from his brow. Never in a million years had he expected to witness the events of that night.

Earlier, he had been in his bedroom rehearsing the speech he would give Hector when he saw headlights outside his window. Peering between the curtains, he observed Eliza approach a taxi. He raced downstairs, grabbed the keys to the Rolls Royce, and followed her cab to a nightclub. His surprise only grew when he watched her take the stage with her hair down, no less.

Her parents would be furious if they found out about her rendezvous in Philadelphia, but to expose her secret would mean losing her trust. An expedient marriage would be most advantageous. The sooner they married, the sooner he would help her achieve safer ways of pursuing her dreams. Perhaps he could arrange a few recitals or a performance at an upscale restaurant. Anything would be better than that low-class club.

In his rearview mirror, he caught a glimpse of headlights shining behind him. He turned to see Eliza exiting a taxi at the end of his driveway. His eyebrows shot up. What happened to her? She looked like she'd been trampled.

Eliza waved to the driver as he turned the taxi and departed Ashbourne Road, and then proceeded to walk toward Belle Vue Manor.

Cracking open his car door, he followed at a distance. He stuck to the shadows of their lamp-lit street even though the wet grass would leave streaks on his polished shoes.

She stopped at her family's gate, stared at it for a few seconds, and then looked down at her soiled dress. Heaving a sigh, she yanked off her shoes and tossed them over the top.

His eyes nearly jumped out of his head when she yanked off her stockings.

Wadding them up, she sent them sailing over the rail. She cast a quick glance over her shoulder, then scaled the fence like a jungle cat and sprang onto the grass on the other side.

Her agility impressed him. He waited until she vanished behind the house before turning to head home. He couldn't allow her to go back to that nightclub. It was too dangerous. Somehow, he had to find a way to protect her. Reaching into his car, he plucked his hat off the seat. "She's going to be a handful," he muttered to himself.

———

Eliza eased the back door open with skillful precision. She crept down the hall, careful to sidestep the squeaky floorboard. Stopping at the staircase, she paused. It felt like eyes were watching her. The hairs lining the nape of her neck lifted. A scan of the hall and living room showed nothing. Everything appeared still. Releasing her breath, she ran a hand along the smooth oak rail as she tiptoed up the steps.

A fated footstep creaked below.

She froze, waiting for his voice. When it didn't come, she ventured a look behind her. Not five feet from the banister loomed her father's shadow.

"Come down here, young lady."

Heart pounding, she hedged down the stairs and came face to face with him.

"Where have you been?"

She couldn't force the words past the lump in her throat.

Grabbing her by the arm, her father ushered her into the living room and parked her into a stiff upholstered chair. He snapped on the lamp; his brows leapt in surprise. "You're filthy. Where have you been at this ungodly hour?"

She shoved her soiled stockings behind her back. "What hour might that be?"

The vein beside his temple protruded. "It is one in the morning, Eliza Adrienne Belcourt. Where have you been?"

One? He should have been fast asleep by now. She nibbled the inside of her lip and considered telling him that she went to Geraldine's house and fell in a puddle. Instead, she lifted her chin, meeting his harsh stare. "Philadelphia."

"What were you doing there?"

"I went to a jazz club."

"A club?" His voice was loud enough to reach the Whitmores. "I cannot believe my ears or my eyes for that matter." He gestured from her muddied face to her bare feet. "I cannot begin to fathom the foolishness of your actions or the danger you've encountered."

"I was careful."

"Your appearance is proof of that. Have you forgotten that we are Belcourts? We uphold a prominent reputation. Nightclubs are improper institutions for a lady of your caliber. Furthermore, I'm dismayed that you purposefully deceived me by sneaking out of this home. I am beyond disappointed."

Hot tears burned in the corner of her eyes. "It's not the first time I've disappointed you, and I'm sure it won't be the last."

His thick brows pulled together. "Are you back-talking me, young lady?"

She knew his water was boiling, but she was tired of the charade. She sat up straighter in the chair. "I've never tried to disappoint you, father. All I want is to make you proud of me. But no matter how hard I try, I never succeed. The one thing you want is the one thing I can't change. I'll never be the *son* you hoped for. Perhaps you should ask God why he failed you instead of blaming me." She didn't see the back of his hand coming until it connected with her cheek.

"Enough. I will not tolerate your insolence. It's time you stopped acting like a spoiled child. You are eighteen years old. A woman your age should be married. I'll hear no more of this *jazz.*"

Tears broke from her eyes. "I love to sing. It's all I think about. If I could just—"

"Singing is a hobby. It appears I have been too lenient with you. Tomorrow, I will begin the search for a proper suitor. It's time you learned your place as a woman." He exited with a stiff stride.

She wilted against the chair. "I don't want a marriage. I want my dream."

CHAPTER FIVE

July 6
Monday, 10:00 AM

"Me lady, yer father has requested yer presence in his study."

Eliza looked up from her magazine to see Neville in the doorway of her bedroom. "Do you know what he wishes to speak to me about?"

"I don't. He said to bring ya at once."

Flipping the page, she frowned. "I think I'll finish this first."

"I beg to differ. We'll head on this minute or I'll be out on me tod."

Her maid's thick accent and amusing phrases brought a grin to her mouth. Neville was one of the many Irish immigrants employed at Belle Vue Manor. She couldn't be more than three years older than Eliza, but the creases on her forehead and near her eyes said she'd lived more life. "Very well." Folding the corner of her page, she set it on the end table.

With a glance over her shoulder, Neville stepped closer. "C'mere till I tell ya, it might have somethin' to do with the early visit this mornin' from Mr. Hugh Whitmore."

"Hugh?" Her eyebrows rose. "What did he want?"

"I couldn't say, me lady, but Mr. Whitmore left grinnin' from ear to ear."

"It could have been business talk." She followed Neville through the hall. "Maybe my father offered him a promotion."

"Perhaps. Unless, it does be in regards to ya?"

Her throat constricted. "Me? Did you overhear something?"

A sneaky glimmer flickered in Neville's gaze. "It's not me place to be sayin'." She knocked on Hector's office door. "But I think yer about to find out."

"Send her in."

She walked inside. Her father sat at his enormous merchant's desk while her mother perched on a small sofa to the right of him.

Hector gestured for her to sit.

She lowered herself beside her mother.

"After your escapade last night, I determined that I would find you a husband." He signed a document. "That problem solved itself this morning when Hugh asked me for my blessing to seek your hand in marriage. I have agreed and estimate that he'll be proposing within the week."

Her mouth dropped open. "Hugh wants to marry me?"

Katherine patted her knee. "It came as a shock to us as well."

"But we haven't even courted." How did he jump to such a conclusion? Her mind returned to the evening of July fourth. Sure they had kissed, but she didn't intend it as a gesture of marriage. It was an impulse in the heat of the moment. Unfortunately, Hugh had viewed their interaction differently.

"You've known each other for years." Katherine flicked her wrist. "Your father and I are willing to overlook the slight breach of etiquette to ensure this great match."

Her mind whirled as she looked between her parents. Somehow, she had to undo this mess. "Hugh is a fine enough man, but I don't wish to marry him."

"I beg your pardon?" Hector's forehead creased.

"I don't want to marry him," she repeated.

Katherine's eyes widened. "He is the most eligible and respected bachelor in all of Elkins Park. Even Pennsylvania for that matter."

"I'm not ready to marry anyone right now."

"You are eighteen," said Hector. "You are plenty old."

"I have dreams for myself, besides being a wife and a mother."

Hector's fingers folded on his desk as he gave her a critical look. "You will follow your duty and marry. You will not shame our family with your antics. Nothing rivals that of a good match."

Eliza saw the by-product of "good matches" firsthand with her parents. Her father didn't care about her mother's happiness, or anyone else's. He only cared about himself and his standing in the community. A marriage between Hugh and her benefited him, hence his quick blessing. What better way to further strengthen his business partnership than with a marriage? Her frustration mounted. "Men are allowed to have dreams. Why shouldn't I?"

"I'll hear no more of this."

She rose to her feet. "Don't you even love me? Am I just a commodity to be bartered and sold? Are my dreams worthless? Don't you even care what they might be?"

"I said enough." He stood to his full height. "This is not up for discussion. You will do as you're told. You will marry Hugh like a proper young woman."

She gritted her teeth. "And if I don't?"

"Then you will be responsible for the collapse of our family business."

The force of his words rocked her back a step. "What?"

"When Daniel became my partner, the Belcourt Steel Industry was on the verge of bankruptcy. He turned things around for us, and we can't afford to see him go. Recently, he's been making comments about wanting to branch off. Without his business expertise, I don't know how the company will fare. However, if you marry Hugh, I doubt Daniel will part ways. His continued involvement in our company will guarantee our financial stability."

"Why should this fall to me?" Eliza spun on her mother. "Mother, say something."

Katherine stroked a nervous hand over her rosary. "Perhaps we lived too extravagantly, for too long. Those beginning years were hard. We dipped into our savings in order to keep up appearances."

"Then you should've stopped buying things! Why did you continue to entertain and host parties? Why did you insist on having things imported?"

"Don't stoop to judge what you cannot possibly understand." Katherine inhaled a sharp breath. "We are Belcourts. We are leaders in this city."

"What if I refuse Hugh?"

Katherine shifted her gaze to Hector.

"You will not refuse. Your mother and I have enough money to live comfortably but there isn't an inheritance left for you. Hugh is willing to marry you without a dowry. No other man of status would do that. A marriage to Hugh solves everything."

The pain of inadequacy pierced her heart. Since she wasn't a boy, she couldn't carry on her father's name. To him, she was useless. He had invested her inheritance into his sinking company. She stood between her parents, feeling utterly abandoned. Even her mother, whom she thought would defend her, had deemed her own need for luxury and comfort of higher importance.

"A marriage between you and Hugh is necessary," said Katherine. "Daniel will not leave the company if you marry his son. You are our only child. I'm sorry it's come to this, but we cannot undo what is already done. We need you to marry Hugh. This is your opportunity to carry on the family legacy."

Hector studied Eliza. "The decision is already made. You must accept his proposal. Hugh is a good man and will make a fine husband. In time, you will see that. Are we clear?"

Wrestling back her tears, she nodded. "Is that all?"

"For now. You're free to go." He waved his hand in dismissal.

She strode from the room with poised, even steps, determined to appear strong. She climbed the staircase and entered her room. Neville stood by the closet, hanging up a gown. She looked over with raised brows, ready for good news. "Neville, if you don't mind, I'd like to be alone." She said in a stiff tone. "I have a terrible headache."

Blinking a couple times, Neville sprang into action. "Yes, of course me lady." She closed the closet doors. "Would ya like me ta close the drapes?"

"No."

"Shall I bring ya some tea?"

"No, I just need to lie down."

Neville hurried to the bed, turned back the blankets and exited the room.

When the door closed, Eliza pressed a hand to her mouth and ran to her bed. Collapsing on her rosebud quilt, she wept, feeling a weight so large she thought it might crush her, or at least her hopes of ever leaving. When her tears ran out, she gazed through her window that overlooked the back yard. In the distance, she could see the pond. She had tasted freedom in those waters. It had inspired her to sneak out, sing at Shakers, and write glorious jazz. But now, everything would be for naught if she married Hugh. Her efforts would all die with *I Do*. She would be nothing more than a wife, and then a mother. She was forced to carry on a man's legacy instead of creating her own.

CHAPTER SIX

July 8
Wednesday, 11:00 AM

Eliza pressed her fingers to her throbbing temples. "My head feels like its being tortured for a crime."

Neville drove another pin into her scalp, fastening her heavy black tendrils atop her head. "I apologize, me lady. Ya have a lot of hair."

"It doesn't matter how many bobby pins or clips you use, a few curls always manage to break free. Perhaps if my mother didn't insist on all these elaborate arrangements, my head could have a rest."

"Don't ya like havin' the pretty styles?"

"I guess, but sometimes I wish I could let it hang around my shoulders."

"Well, I suspect today yer gonna want it fancy. Mr. Hugh Whitmore be waitin' fer ya in the parlor. Yer mother's instructions to me was most adamant that yer hair be perfect."

She stiffened. He must be here to propose.

"There." Neville clasped a jeweled barrette. "My word and willywigs, don't ya look grand."

Observing her reflection in the vanity's mirror, she had to agree. It was Neville's best work yet. Her mother would be pleased. Everything about her appeared shiny; all but her eyes.

"Must be an important visit."

"Hugh's going to propose," she replied in a flat tone.

"Oh, me lady. Amn't I the happiest fer ya. If ya don't mind me sayin', ya must be the luckiest girl in Elkins Park."

"I'm sure that most ladies would share your sentiment." She sighed. "If only I did, too."

Neville tilted her head to the side. "Does ya not want to marry him?"

"It doesn't matter what I want." She pushed herself off the vanity's bench. "My father makes my decisions." Ignoring Neville's stricken expression, she left the room. Her feet felt heavier with each step toward the parlor.

Waiting beside the fireplace in a three-piece suit, Hugh turned to see her. "Eliza." His brows rose. "You look lovely."

"Thank you." She noted his meticulous appearance. His trousers exhibited a precise crease in each pant leg, and Brilliantine oiled each strand of his brown hair in its proper place. "You look thorough."

"Thank you." A crinkle formed on his forehead as he processed that compliment. "I haven't seen you wear that dress before. It matches your blue eyes."

"I didn't know you paid such close attention to fashion."

"I don't. Only yours."

She averted her gaze. "My mother recently had the dress imported."

"Really? Where from?"

"Somewhere in Europe." She waved her hand. "She is always importing something: clothes, furnishings, linens, tea. Mother says, 'Any ordinary person can buy from regular stores, but we're not ordinary. We're Belcourts.'" She exhaled a slow breath. "It's exhausting."

"Are you saying you don't like the finer things?"

"I don't deny that I like them, but my mother's materialism is excessive."

He scooped her hand. "A woman like you should have everything money can buy and more."

"That's nice." She slid her gloved hand out of his grasp.

Unaware of her retraction, he continued to smile like a schoolboy in love. "I wondered if you would accompany me on a walk today. I thought perhaps we could travel Belle Vue's gardens."

A perfect setting for a proposal. She inwardly grimaced. "It looks a little cloudy. I think it might rain."

"I predict that the skies will brighten." He offered his arm.

She took it with a frown, wondering if his weather prediction was literal or metaphorical.

He led her down the hall and out of the sunroom's exterior doors.

Roses and lilacs welcomed them into the garden. The clouds had parted, allowing the sun to warm their cheeks.

Rhatz. A perfect setting and perfect weather.

"I remember the first time I saw you," he said. "It was four years ago at the Piersons' ball. You entered the room with your parents." He shook his head. "I was mesmerized at the sight of you. I'm sure every woman present envied your dress. It was an ivory gown with gold braiding. You looked like royalty mingling with the commoners."

"I remember that dress." Her inheritance paid for it.

"But what really piqued my interest was when Bertram Lonsdale placed a kiss on your gloved hand, and you rolled your eyes when he wasn't looking." He chuckled.

"You saw that?"

"I certainly did." His dimples surfaced. "I loved it."

His forwardness made her cheeks flush. She rubbed a nervous hand by her throat. "Before Bertram kissed my hand, he said to me, 'I would like to offer my assistance to you in any way that I can.' Such a presumptuous comment necessitated the rolling of eyes."

"A correct assessment." Hugh continued along the brick

path between the sculpted topiaries. "Seeing that you had spunk made me want to meet you even more."

"As I recall, you didn't speak to me the whole night. You seemed plenty occupied with all your dance partners."

"Were you jealous?" His right eyebrow arched.

"Not at all. I was too busy dancing."

"Yes, you were the belle of the ball. I tried to get to you that whole evening."

"Is that right?" She cast a sideways glance at him.

"Indeed." He stopped walking. "I learned an important lesson that night. If I want something, I must go after it with everything that I possess, because hesitation could mean I'll lose my chance. The dances that followed, I made sure my name made it on your card."

"That you did." She looked down at the path. Between the bricks a weed squeezed through a crack. Little white blossoms grew at the top of its stem. She stared at it. That weed had been determined. It needed to reach the sun so it had strained and pushed until it broke free. She understood this kind of striving. Bricked in by a male-dominated society, she found that reaching her own freedom was nearly impossible. Yet if this little flower had survived and found the sun, then maybe she could too.

"There isn't another girl like you in this city. Since the first time I saw you, I knew we would be a great match. I have spoken with your father, and he has given me his blessing. He said this is what he hoped for." He reached for her hands. "It's what I hope for." He shifted his weight, ready to sink upon a bended knee.

Her heartbeat quickened. "Wait."

He froze.

"I need to ask you something."

"What is it?"

"Remember the night we talked at my parents' Fourth of July party?"

"Vividly."

Heat filtered up her neck. Good gracious. If only she could go back in time and erase that kiss. "Specifically, do you remember me saying I want to become a jazz singer?"

"Of course, and I fully intend to help you with that. I will arrange some recitals and perhaps organize a few social occasions where you'll be able to sing."

She inhaled a frustrated breath. "I need more than that. I want to make records and be known to the world."

"You are my world." He patted her hand. "The important thing now is starting a new dream together." He extracted a black velvet box from his coat pocket and sank to one knee. He landed directly on top of the small weed.

Her eyes widened in horror.

"I love you, Eliza. Will you marry me?" He opened the lid to reveal a three carat yellow diamond circled by white baguettes, propped on a gold band.

She stared at the gaudy ring and then at Hugh. The beating of her heart had escalated to a neurotic tapping. She had spent the last two days hoping that he would change his mind and not propose. But here he knelt, while her parents waited inside the house. The garden that once felt unfettered now hemmed her in. Escape seemed impossible. Her fate had been decided. With her hopes crushed, she nodded her acceptance.

"I knew you would say yes." Beaming, he stood and removed the glove from her left hand. Sliding on the ring, he admired his prize. "A perfect fit. Let's go inside and share the news with your parents."

As he guided her toward the house, she glanced back at the crumpled little blossoms and splintered stem. Soon, it would brown, wither, and die. When the next strong wind came, it would blow away as if it never existed.

CHAPTER SEVEN

July 11
Saturday, 7:00 pm

Eliza lay on her bed, thumbing through sheets of lyrics. She had written so many songs, which now might never be given their debut. Hugh's pathetic promise to arrange a few recitals only proved that he didn't plan for her to pursue a singing career. "Marriage will only transfer me from the control of my father to that of Hugh." Tears trailed down her cheek onto the page of a song entitled, *I'll Break Them Down.*

She reread the lyrics of her song. "I've been taught, oh so very well. How to sit, to stand, and act so swell. They got me doing circles. I'm sick of all these hurdles. But some day, I'm waiting. Gonna take my chance, and then I'll break them. Those rules ain't gonna bind me no longer. I've grown up, and I'm now stronger. So I'm gonna break them. Yes, I'll break them down." Shaking her head, she gave a sad chuckle. What a joke. She hadn't broken anything down. The walls only climbed higher.

A light knock sounded on the opposite side of the door, followed by Neville's voice. "Me lady, can I come in?"

"Just a moment." She tidied the song sheets into a stack.

Hurrying to her dresser, she opened the top drawer, shoved them under all the nightgowns, and closed it with a thud. She wiped her cheeks with her hands and grabbed a powder puff off the vanity's desk. Patting her face, she looked in the mirror. A red rim outlined her eyes. Rhatz. She picked a magazine off her nightstand and settled on the divan under the window, pretending to read. "Come in."

"Goodness, thought I heard cattle racin' in yer room a moment ago, but now I see yer only catchin' up on a bit o' readin'." Neville grinned.

Pretending to be oblivious, she shrugged. "Just passing the time."

"*Good Housekeeping* is one of me favorites. Plenty of tips fer any woman."

She nodded and flipped a page.

"The guests be arrivin' soon. Yer mother asked me to check over yer dress and hair to make sure everythin' be tightly in place."

Setting the magazine aside, she slowly stood but kept her chin lowered to hide her red eyes.

Neville retied Eliza's sash in the back of her gown. "So tonight's yer big announcement." She came around to face Eliza, straightening a pendant on the top of her dress. "How does ya feel?"

She clamped her quivering lip with her teeth, willing her emotions to remain in check, but her tears disobeyed.

"Dear me." Neville hurried to the vanity's drawer to fetch a handkerchief. "Didn't mean to make ya cry."

She sank on the edge of her bed. "I feel trapped. I didn't choose this marriage. My father did."

Neville pushed the handkerchief into her hand.

"I have to get away." She mumbled into the cloth tissue. "I need to go to New York City."

"Not sure I be hearin' ya right. Ya want to leave all this?" Neville gestured toward the closet of gowns, the rows of shoes, and cases of jewelry.

"If it would mean that I could finally be loved and valued for being me, then yes, I'd leave it all in a snap."

"And what would ya do there?"

"Become a jazz singer." Her shoulders drooped with a longing sigh. "It's been my dream for years. I want to sing for audiences. Have my voice heard on the radio. I tried to start my career at a nightclub in Philadelphia, but my father ended that." She clenched the handkerchief in her fist. "Do you think I'm foolish for wanting such a thing?"

Neville stroked a loose black curl into Eliza's French twist and fastened it with a bobby pin. "The Irish have a sayin'. 'Ya got to do yer own growin', no matter how tall yer father was.' Yer father do be a strong man, but yer a keen woman too. I watched ya sneak out in the mid of night, I know about the song sheets hidden under yer nightshirts, and I heard ya sing at yer father's Fourth o' July party." She paused. "Ya have true talent, me lady."

"You really think so?"

"On me honor."

"There's only one way that I will ever be discovered." She whispered in a solemn tone. "I need you to do something for me. It must remain a secret. I want you to call Broad Street Station and find out if they have any departures heading for New York City before 8:00 AM tomorrow."

"Lady Eliza, ya don't plan on goin' there on yer lonesome, does ya?"

"Nothing is decided, but I need those times. Please, can you do this for me?"

"Ya don't know what yer askin' of me. Yer father be waitin' fer ya the last night ya snuck out because Mr. Barrett heard ya leave. He woke yer father to tell him. Mr. Barrett and Mrs. O'Daly watch over Belle Vue like a couple of foxes. If I get caught placin' that call, I will lose me job."

"I won't let that happen. I promise." She glanced toward her closed door. "I knew my father was tipped off. I wouldn't have gotten caught if it weren't for that nosey butler."

"Aye, but that's why the favor yer askin' is mighty steep. The telephone is in the kitchen. How are ya gonna get all the staff outta there while I place the call?"

She drummed her fingers atop her knee. "I will gather the staff for an announcement."

"And if they notice me missin'?"

"I will make an explanation for your absence."

"I don't know…."

"Please." She took Neville's hand.

Her maid's eyes grew large at the personal gesture.

"You are the only person I can trust. This means everything to me."

Withdrawing her hands, she nodded. "O'right. I'll do it. When does ya plan to make this diversion?"

She shifted her focus to the vanity's mirror. Picking up the powder puff, she dabbed her face. "Right now." She waved for her maid to follow her into the hallway. "I will ask Barrett to gather the staff in the parlor, that's when you must slip into the kitchen unnoticed."

Neville fidgeted with the edge of her apron. "I understand."

Spotting their butler in the foyer speaking with the head housemaid, she lifted up a hand. "Barrett. A word, please."

He gave his last instruction to Mrs. O'Daly and hurried over. "What might I do for you, Lady Eliza?"

"I would like you to gather all of the staff so that I might give them some important instructions in regards to tonight's party."

His forehead creased. "Is something wrong? Your parents already informed me of their wishes for the evening and the guests are to arrive in less than forty minutes."

"I'm sure their directives are fine, but tonight's celebration is in honor of my engagement, and I would like to add a few thoughts of my own. If you would graciously indulge me and collect the staff into the parlor, I will not keep them long."

Giving a hasty nod, Barrett hurried to do her bidding.

She waited in the parlor as the staff trickled in.

Barrett ushered in the last of the staff, including Neville who looked at Eliza with wide apologetic eyes.

Oh no, he forced her to come too. She looked at her polished shoes, contemplating a solution.

"We're all here, Lady Eliza," said Barrett.

"Wonderful." She looked at her gloved hands. "Neville, would you kindly do me a favor? I actually wish to wear my other white gloves tonight. They need to be pressed. Please attend to that matter."

"Of course, me lady." Neville bowed.

"Thank you." She watched her slip into the hall leading to the kitchen and trained her eyes upon the waiting staff. "Thank you all for joining me at this last minute. Tonight my father will be announcing to our closest friends and relatives my engagement to Mr. Hugh Whitmore." She paused while the staff offered soft applause and congratulations. "Because this is an important night for both me and my fiancé, I wanted to share a few thoughts I had. First, I would like to use our gilded Haviland porcelain with the rosebud print."

"That is the same china your mother has selected for this evening," replied Barrett.

"Ah, well. Splendid. Second, I would like to have the cake served before the cheese and fruit platters. I feel cake is finer than fruit any day. Don't you agree?"

A few staff chuckled their agreement.

She glanced toward the hall but caught no sight of Neville. "In addition, I would like Hugh and myself seated on the right side of the table with my mother on my left and Hugh's father beside him."

"Actually, your father mentioned that Daniel was to be placed left of him."

"Well, my fiancé would like his father next to him and that's how it shall be done." Regardless of the lie, she straightened to her full five feet, four inches to show her sternness on the matter.

"Very well, my lady." Barrett nodded. "Is there anything else?"

Before Eliza could answer, Katherine walked into the parlor. "What's going on? Why have you called a meeting?"

"Hello, mother. I felt it acceptable that for my engagement party I should be able to make a few requests of my own."

"The guests are due to arrive shortly." Katherine looked at the ornate wall clock. "My goodness. It's already 7:30. Are you nearly finished?"

Her throat tightened. Where was Neville? "One more thing." She hedged, scanning her mind for some further instruction. She noticed a residue of sweat on Barrett's forehead and a frown on her mother's face. "I would like three bouquets of roses from our garden set on the table. It is my favorite scent."

Katherine brushed an agitated hand across her rosary. "Eliza, I've already arranged for flowers to be set on the table."

"Roses?"

"Yes, roses along with irises and lilies."

The last word sent a shiver along her spine. She hated lilies. A memory resurfaced like it happened yesterday and not twelve years prior: she danced barefoot in the garden, twirling and singing to the birds in the air, while she picked a bouquet of flowers. When she spun again, she found her mother staring at the place the lilies once grew. Her face looked stricken. "Eliza Belcourt, what have you done?"

"I picked flowers for you," she said with a hopeful smile.

"My lilies." Katherine touched the torn stems still planted in the ground. "You picked all of them."

"You always put fresh flowers on the table. I thought you would like them."

"These lilies are special. I never pick them. They are all I have left to—" Her forehead creased with pain. "How many times have I told you to ask before you take something? Don't you ever listen?"

Her chin quivered. "I wanted to surprise you."

Katherine snatched the bouquet from her hand. "You crumpled the petals." Shaking her head, she tossed the flowers onto the ground. "I can't display them now."

Eliza never picked a lily again. She despised the sight of them and the failure they reminded her of. She squared her shoulders with resolve. "I want only roses."

Mrs. O'Daly looked between Katherine and Eliza. "We already have the vases of flowers on the table. Should I take out the irises and lilies?"

"That won't be necessary," said Katherine.

"It certainly is necessary." She cast a sideways glance toward her mother and then looked once more to the hall.

Neville snuck past with a slight nod and tiptoed up the stairs.

"The irises can remain but not the lilies. Their smell gives me a headache. Thank you. I believe that's all." She clapped her hands. "You may get back to your duties."

The staff trickled out of the room.

Katherine remained behind. "It hardly seems appropriate to make changes so close to the arrival of our guests."

"Since I wasn't asked for my opinion in advance, I decided to give it directly myself."

"I felt my choices suited the evening fine."

"Considering that you and father chose the man I would marry, I feel at least I deserve to pick my dishes and flowers." She stepped past her mother and walked away.

———

At precisely eight in the evening, all the guests were ushered into the dining hall. Eliza settled into a mahogany chair next to Hugh.

He leaned close to her ear. "Everything here looks lovely, but nothing is as lovely as you."

"Thank you." Her reply held little enthusiasm.

Hector rose at the head of the table.

The sixteen guests perked up in their chairs, eager to hear his words.

"Welcome and thank you all for coming on short notice. It is a pleasure to have you join us in celebrating our exciting news. As our closest friends and relatives, we wanted you all to be the first to hear." He glanced at Eliza and Hugh with a smile of approval.

Her stomach twisted. She knew better than to think the gesture to be genuine.

"Most of you know that Daniel Whitmore and I have been partners for several years. Together we made the Belcourt-Whitmore Steel Company a success, and now we are going to be united by a new partnership. The marriage of our son and daughter."

The room erupted in gasps and applause.

"Three days ago, Hugh came to our home and asked Eliza to marry him. I am privileged to share her acceptance of his proposal. They plan to marry this November."

Daniel and Vivian clapped along with the other guests.

Hugh took Eliza's hand, radiating with admiration.

Fighting the urge to pull her hand away, she plastered on a smile.

"Tonight is a night of great joy," said Hector. "I propose a toast to Hugh and Eliza. May they be fruitful. May their happiness abound, and may their love last forever. To Hugh and Eliza!" He thrust his glass in the air.

The guests followed suit.

The kitchen maids arrived with the first course of onion soup. They set a bowl atop a gilded china plate in front of each guest.

Appearing at her elbow, Neville slipped a piece of paper under the rim of her plate. She covered the paper with her hand.

The delivery was not lost on Katherine.

Hugh, oblivious to the note, grabbed his gold spoon and scooped in a bite of soup. "This is delicious."

"Belle Vue has always employed talented cooks." Eliza slipped the paper below the edge of the table, unfolded it, and read. *5:15, 7:15*. Closing it, she stuffed it into a hidden pocket of her dress.

"Once we purchase our own manor it will be imperative that we get a good cook and this recipe." He lifted his spoon.

"Of course." Unless she boarded a train and left.

Katherine leaned toward her and whispered, "What did Neville deliver you?"

Eliza flinched. "Appointment times for a bridal store in Philadelphia."

"Is that right?" Her mother's eyebrows lifted. "I didn't know that you had a store in mind. What's it called?"

"Madalene Perren Boutique," she swallowed. Luckily she frequented Philadelphia enough to know a shop name. "It's for Tuesday at half past one. I wanted to inform Mrs. Whitmore so she could join us."

Katherine studied her and then nodded. "Very well. We'll speak with her about it tonight."

The meal progressed through the courses: salad, garnished meats, and smoked fish. There was always a plate—either with food or without—before each guest at all times.

"Eliza, do tell us how Hugh proposed," asked her grandmother.

"Oh…of course." She dabbed her mouth with her napkin.

Everyone's attention turned to her. Hugh appeared the most eager to hear the story of how he proposed.

"He came early Wednesday morning, looking dapper as usual and not a hair out of place."

A good-natured chuckle filtered around the table.

"He recited a beautiful proposal. I was overcome with happiness and accepted." She saw a couple frowns at her lack of detail. "I am a lucky woman."

He smiled at her. "Trust me, I'm the lucky one."

Meeting his eyes, she realized that he meant it.

"Congratulations, darling." Vivian spoke to Eliza. "We are thrilled to have you as a part of our family."

"Hugh has chosen well," said Daniel. "We couldn't ask for a better daughter-in-law."

She nodded in thanks. If they only knew she was forced to say yes.

"We couldn't ask for a better husband for our daughter," Hector said to Daniel.

"November is only four months away," said Katherine. "We'll need to work on the invitation list immediately."

"It will no doubt be a long list," said Hector. "We are connected to so many in the community."

The maids cleared away the finished courses and laid out fresh plates and silverware. As they distributed the cake, Hugh whispered to her, "If it was up to me, I'd marry you tomorrow."

"Our mothers would feel robbed. Look at how happy they are discussing the wedding details."

"Yes, it's a special night for all of us." His eyes lit up. "Only one thing could make this night even better."

"What is that?"

"A song by you."

"Really?" She straightened in her seat. "You'd like me to sing?"

"Absolutely." He tapped his fork on his glass. "Might I have everyone's attention, please? After dinner, I request that we all gather in the parlor so that my beautiful fiancée can play the piano and sing a song."

Hector paused with his fork stabbed in his square of cake.

Eliza watched his jaw clench. She hadn't written the apology letters. For this she congratulated herself.

"I'm terribly sorry Hugh, but we've already created an agenda for this evening. Following the meal, you and Eliza will be opening your engagement presents."

She looked at Hugh, willing him to fight for her.

His brow knitted, then released. "Another time then. We can't miss opening those presents."

Her hope that he might support her vanished. If he couldn't defend her now, he never would.

CHAPTER EIGHT

Saturday, 1:25 AM

Eliza retired to her room, glad that everyone had finally left. She threw the glove sheathing her right to the ground. Hugh had placed a kiss above her knuckles as he'd departed. She glowered at the offending glove. "He doesn't love me. If he did, he would have demanded that I sing for our guests. He didn't stand up for me in order to appease my father, and that's how it will be the rest of my life if I marry him." Kicking off her shoes, she sank onto the edge of her bed. "I need a man who will fight for me. Someone who will believe in me. Someone who will love me for who I am, not who they want me to be."

She pulled out the paper Neville had slipped her and read the train departure times. 5:15 and 7:15. She snatched her pocket watch from her nightstand and popped it open. It said 1:27 AM. If she left now, she could catch the train to New York City. This was her chance. Her pulse sped up. In ten swift steps, she reached her closet. "In New York, I'll be free to live my own life." She opened the luggage on her bed and went to work, packing music sheets, three nightgowns, underwear, four dresses, panty hose, one extra pair of shoes, and a bag of hygiene products. "Soon, my voice will be heard on the radio, and my name will be spelled in lights. I'll be a star, loved by all."

Clasping the suitcases shut, she turned to a shelf of hatboxes. She couldn't carry more than one box along with her luggage; she'd have to limit herself to a hat on her head and the other in hand. With a wistful farewell to the others, she selected an all-occasion garden hat and a white travel bonnet, which she wore.

Tiptoeing to the stairs, she stopped beside the banister. Shadows danced around the hall and parlor, cast from the remnants of the fire burning in the fireplace.

She sucked in a shallow breath. Please, Barrett, be asleep. Tonight, she couldn't get caught. Creeping to her father's office, she edged open the door, switched on the dim light and hastened to the desk. She retrieved two sheets of paper from a drawer and scrawled a note for her father on the first. After writing the second note, she folded it into an envelope and tucked it into her pocket. She glanced toward the door.

Darkness shifted in the hall.

She ducked behind the desk. Was that a person? Maybe Barrett? She strained to hear footsteps. When none came, she reached beneath the desk and felt for the secret drawer she had discovered as a child. Scooping her finger under a carved notch in the wood, she pulled it open. Her father's stash of gin, cigars, and legal documents lay stacked on top. Digging further, she found the envelope of cash he kept for emergencies. A triumphant smile curved her lips. Got it. She stuffed the money into her purse. "Thank you for funding my trip, Father." She left the drawer open and hurried out of the office. Hurrying to the south wing of Belle Vue, she tapped on the second door in the servant's corridor.

Footsteps approached, and it opened.

Neville wiped sleep from her eyes. "Me lady, what's the matter? Why didn't ya ring yer bell?"

"I agree with you. I have my own growing to do." Her words rushed out in a hasty whisper. "I need you to call Hank at the Checkered Cab Company. Tell him to bring me to Broad Street Station." She shoved her hand into her pocket and removed the note along with her engagement ring. "I need you to deliver this to Hugh tomorrow."

Neville blinked, looking confused. "Yer actually leavin'?"

"I'm taking the 5:15 train."

"I encouraged ya to stretch yer wings, but I didn't mean fer ya to run away." She stole a glance over her shoulder at her roommate, who luckily still slept. "Mr. Whitmore seems like a good man. Won't he help ya?"

"Hugh doesn't understand my passion. I'm certain he never will. I know you're worried about me, but I have to go. I promise to write you when I'm there."

"Lady Eliza, I done been to New York City. It has a dark side. Not sure it would be safe fer ya."

"I can handle it." She clutched her maid's hands. "The only way that I can live my life is by leaving. Please, I need you to help me."

Neville's shoulders slouched. "O'right. I make the call, but promise that ya be careful."

"I will."

"God be with ya, me lady."

She smiled sadly. "I skipped mass. He might not grant that request."

———

A hand shook his shoulder. "Master Hugh, there's a woman at the back door saying it's urgent that you speak with her. I've tried to send her away, but she's quite adamant."

Hugh blinked trying to adjust his eyes to the oil lamp shining in his face. "Walsh, what's the meaning of this?"

"My apologies, but the woman says it's in regards to Lady Eliza."

The name wakened his senses. He sat upright. "Has something happened to her?"

"I'm not certain."

Pushing off his bed covers, he hurried after his head butler to the back foyer.

A younger woman dressed in servant's attire bowed as he entered. "Master Whitmore, I do be Neville, Lady Eliza's personal maid. I apologize for this intrusion, but I had to tell ya that me lady be headin' to the train station at this very minute."

"I beg your pardon?"

She shoved the ring and note into his palm. "Read this."

He ripped open the envelope's seal and pulled out the single sheet of paper.

Dear Hugh,

My parents forced me to accept your proposal as a means of keeping your father as a business partner. You are my friend and I don't wish to hurt you, but I must break our engagement. It's time that I live for my own heart. I am going to New York City to become a singer. I wish you the best. I hope that you will forgive me.

Sincerely,
Eliza

He ran a hand through his disheveled hair in disbelief. "She's leaving?"

"You still have time to stop her before she goes. She is taking the 5:15 train at Broad Street Station. If ya hurry, ya might be able to talk her out of it."

His brow furrowed. She had only accepted his proposal to appease her parents? That seemed impossible. He had felt the emotion in her kiss. Perhaps she was confused, and due to her parents' manipulation, she felt the need to flee. Why else would she leave? He told her he would help her sing in Pennsylvania.

What could New York offer her that he couldn't?

"Please go after her," said Neville. "I've been to New York City. Lady Eliza thinks it's a land flowin' with milk and honey but it's not. There's another side, a dangerous one. I worry fer her. I worry somethin' fierce."

Hugh stared at the maid and then at the ring in his hand. He abruptly turned to his butler. "Get me my keys."

Thirty minutes later, his car squealed to a halt outside of Broad Street Station. He left it parked at the curb, racing through the entrance. In a swift arc, he scanned the lobby. Patrons sat on benches while others stood in line at the ticket office. A woman in a white hat moved nervously forward in line. He exhaled a slow breath. *Eliza.* For a moment, he stood indecisive. Should he impede upon her decision? If she wanted to leave, he couldn't force her to stay. But if he let her go, she could encounter danger. His mouth dried. Spotting a newsstand along the wall, he deposited a nickel and retrieved an Evening Public Ledger. He walked closer to the ticket line, sat on a nearby bench and opened the paper.

"Next," called the ticket agent.

Eliza approached the barred window and set her leather suitcases on the floor. "Do you have any 5:15 AM departures for New York City available?"

"Yes ma'am. Would you like first, second, or third class?"

"How much is a first class ticket?"

"Is that round-trip?"

"No. It will be one-way."

"That will cost $2.55. Would you like to purchase it?"

"Yes, please."

He stamped the time and date on a yellow ticket and scrawled a few details in ink.

Eliza paid her fare.

"You will board at platform four." He handed her the ticket. "Train is running about ten minutes late."

"Thank you." Grabbing her luggage, she turned toward a

solid marble staircase that led to the second floor.

Hugh gripped his paper tighter. He couldn't believe it. She was going to board that train. He followed her, at a distance, up the stairs and into a general waiting room.

She paused, reading the signs.

He noticed her tremble as she stood. She was nervous, as she should have been. And probably afraid, as she definitely should've been. He sank onto a wooden bench, peering at her from behind the newspaper. And he still hadn't stopped her. As he should have.

With a nod, she walked out of the waiting area.

Hugh continued after her, passing through a lobby that overlooked 15th Street and into an expansive train shed with paved platforms.

She strode 12 feet ahead of him, unaware of his presence. Stopping below a sign that read Platform Four, she sat on a bench.

He sat on one a few feet from her, shielded behind his newspaper. His foot tapped. She deserved to be confronted. She ought to see her commitment through. He exhaled a frustrated breath. Why did he have to fall for Eliza Belcourt? Why couldn't he have fallen for an ordinary girl with ordinary dreams? But as he studied her from behind the Public Ledger, he knew why. She wasn't commonplace. She swam naked in a pond, snuck out to sing at a nightclub, and now planned to run away from a life of privilege and an engagement to *him* in order to become a singer. Though he couldn't understand why she'd do something so stupid, he had to admit that she was brave.

A train howled before it hissed to a stop at the platform.

Eliza rose to her feet.

He knew he had to move now if he wanted to stop her.

Hefting her suitcases, she approached the train's porter, who checked her ticket and punched it.

The porter pointed to her luggage. "Would you like me to bring your cases to the baggage car?"

"No sir, I'd like to keep them with me."

"Of course, ma'am. There are overhead racks in your compartment. Might I carry them for you?"

She nodded, handing over her luggage.

They walked along the train.

The porter stopped at a first class car and helped her up the steps into the carriage.

His heart sank. She hadn't even paused. She was definitely leaving.

Other passengers boarded the train while baggage handlers tossed suitcases into a rear car.

Lowering the paper, he watched her compartment. He would never force a woman into marriage. Sadly, he thought she had wanted to marry him.

A final bell signaled its departure. The wheel rims squealed as they grinded against the steel rails.

He caught sight of her one last time as she looked out her window. She turned in her seat and for a moment appeared to stare directly at him.

The train pulled ahead.

He stared after her. "I'll come for you, Eliza Belcourt. You might be leaving me now, but I'll win you back. Somehow."

CHAPTER NINE

Eliza twisted her soft leather gloves between nervous fingers. Never, never, never had a Belcourt lady run away from home, stolen money, boarded a train, and rejected the hand of a wealthy, suitably matched man.

Until today.

She looked out the window as the train chugged over the bridge, crossing the Schuylkill River. Taking slow breaths, she tried to calm her rapid pulse. She had succeeded without being caught, but she couldn't shake the feeling that she had seen Hugh at the station. Of course that was impossible, but the image of him appeared real. If he had been there, he would have stopped her. She grimaced, after he read her letter, he would be livid and humiliated. In truth, she didn't want to hurt him, but she had no alternative than to run away.

The rhythmic clicking of the steel tracks coaxed her body to relax into the plush seat. Her eyelids grew heavy, and she allowed them to close. Sleep silenced her anxious thoughts, leaving only one: *they can't stop me now.*

A whistle hollered from the caboose.

She sprang upright.

The train slowed, hissing to a stop at another station en route to New York. A sign swinging on a metal beam read Trenton, New Jersey.

Eliza's carriage door slid open and a porter tipped his hat. "Good morning, ma'am. How's your ride been so far?"

"Smooth and quiet."

"Glad to hear it. You'll have another passenger joining you shortly. Should keep you company for the rest of the trip."

"That will be nice." As the porter exited, she leaned forward to look out. People passed by on the platform speaking in hurried voices. A child cried as he dropped his wooden car and the wheel broke. His father scooped up the toy, promising to fix it. The child smiled despite his wet cheeks. She lost sight of them as a male passenger stepped into her car with swift nonchalance.

The porter spoke from behind. "Have a good trip."

Meeting her eyes, the gentleman called back to the porter. "I'm sure I will."

Her breath caught inside her lungs. My goodness, this man was gorgeous. His broad shoulders strained against the fabric of his tailored, charcoal gray suit. A striped fedora hat tipped over one eyebrow, partially obscuring one of his extraordinary aquamarine eyes.

"Hope you don't mind me sharing this compartment with you." He spoke with a husky ease.

"I didn't pay for a full carriage. Only a seat."

"I suppose I'll select one of my own then." He pulled off his hat to reveal a slick head of chocolate hair.

"You have a few to choose from." She motioned to the empty, floral-patterned cushions.

His gaze swept over the small space. With fluid, deliberate steps, he strode to the seat directly across from her.

An alluring scent of spiced musk rolled past her nose. She breathed in the rich cologne. He smelled delicious.

"I think I like this one." He peered at her. A glimmer of mischief crossed his eyes. "Is that all right with you?"

Her heart fluttered. "That would be fine."

"I hoped you'd say that." He lowered to the seat and rested his elbow on the armrest.

She bowed her head to hide the rosiness surfacing on her cheeks. Was he flirting with her? She stole a glimpse in his direction.

He stared at her.

She tipped her head back down, and her cheeks reddened more. He had caught her looking. Should she say something? What would she say? She supposed she could introduce herself. Or would that be too...

"Where are you heading today?" He interrupted her thoughts.

"Eliza Belcourt."

"What?"

"New York City—I mean—my name is Eliza, and I'm headed to New York." She tasted the stupidity saturating her tongue.

"I'm pleased to meet you Eliza-headed-for-New-York. I'm Warren-Moore-headed-there-too," he grinned.

Her heart failed to pump a beat.

A bell rang out.

She jumped. Without a warning, the train lurched forward, offsetting her balance. Her face plunged into Warren's chest as her hands grabbed the top of his thighs.

"Most ladies demand a date before embracing, but this works for me."

She scrambled backward, her eyes bulging in horror. "I–I–I am so sorry! The train moved so quickly that I lost my balance and I—"

He held up his hand. "Don't apologize. You may sit on my lap for the duration of the trip if you'd like."

Her mouth dropped open. She knew her eyes looked like saucers.

"I'm only teasing. But I have to say," he leaned forward, "you are adorable."

She managed to sputter a thank you.

"Any time." He winked.

Her mind muddled beneath the allure of his charm. She fidgeted with her gloves. Below her lashes, she saw him tilt to the side. His eyes traveled up her long dress, over her hips, and paused above her midriff. She straightened with a huff.

He met her eyes. "Nice ankles."

She gasped.

He opened his hands in surrender. "I'd compliment more, but that's all I can see."

She gasped again.

"I mean no offense. I simply wanted to appreciate the beauty before me."

She didn't know if she should be angry or flattered. His boldness was entirely unsettling and, well, exciting.

"Do you live in New York City?" he asked.

"I'm going there today for the first time." She inhaled. "Do you?"

"I do. I was visiting a *friend* in Jersey."

She thought she heard a hint of sarcasm when he said the word friend.

"Are you visiting someone in Manhattan?"

"No. I'm going to pursue a career as a singer. I want to cut a record and perform."

A throaty laugh burst from his mouth. "You? New York City has pretty rough edges. And most debs are lost as to what—"

"I might be a debutante, but I'm not incompetent."

"I'm not trying to insult you, baby, but New York is no playground. Sure, it's a land of opportunity, but you've got to know where to go and where not to. Besides, you're gonna stand out."

"What do you mean?"

"Look at you." He indicated with a wave. "Long dress. Gloves. Hair stuffed in a bonnet. Don't get me wrong, you're a doll. But Manhattan girls aren't like you. They wear short skirts and smoke like chimneys. I'm not sure you can handle it."

She faced the window, chewing the inside of her lip. What if it was too dangerous? She didn't know anyone or anything about New York. Goodness, how was she to live? Her back leaned deeper against the seat. But if she went home, she would be stuck forever. She would wither like that little weed in the garden. Her eyebrows pinched together. No. She refused to be crushed. "How dare you judge me? You know nothing except what you see on the outside. I'll do better than survive in Manhattan; I'll be great in Manhattan. I will sing and perform. No one and no city can stop me."

"Quite spirited for such a little doll." His voice held a hint of humor. "You're right, I did judge you. I apologize. With that attitude, you'll do fine."

"I'll do better than fine." She crossed her arms.

His eyebrow arched. Leaning forward with a hand on his knee, he spoke in a low tone. "You sure will. I think you're going to like New York City."

Her anger thawed under the heat of his stare and tantalizing cologne. She smoothed her palms over the front of her dress and gave a dignified nod. "I will."

A defiant curl slipped from her bonnet and swung forward in one buoyant swoop.

He reached out with a tender stroke, brushing it back into place. His fingers lingered too long upon her cheek to be considered an accident.

His audacity necessitated a slap, but for some reason, she let it slide. The coolness of his touch was electric. It sent a rush of adrenaline through her veins. She hated the fact that something as simple as a small touch could do that.

The smile ran away from his face.

They looked at each other in silence.

Breaking away from her gaze, he faced the window. "We're about to enter the tunnel." His voice was coarse. "This trip has taken long enough. I'm practically turning gray."

His sudden change in demeanor caused her to pause. "I think it seems to be going relatively fast."

"Not fast enough."

Her forehead crinkled. Goodness, what happened? Did she do something wrong? The train traveled below the ground into a dimly lit tunnel running under the Hudson River. She gripped the armrests of her seat. "Are we completely below the water?"

"Yeah." He stared at the concrete walls outside the windows. "There isn't anything to worry about."

She stared at the walls passing her window, feeling anxious about the eerie tunnel and Warren's reserved tone of voice. Emerging from the concrete tube, the train rambled up a hill bordered by dense trees and underbrush. She exhaled, relieved to be above ground and see the blue sky.

The caboose released another long bellow before the train entered the sprawling shed of Penn Station. Sunlight poured through the skylight windows of the lofty ceiling, illuminating other trains, tracks, and platforms. Marbled stone walls and industrial steel archways outlined the room.

"We're here." Her breath rushed out in a stunned whoosh.

"Welcome to your new home."

"Do you mean that?"

"I do." His eyes were solemn. "Forget what I said earlier. I'll be listening for the radio announcer to introduce Eliza Belcourt."

"Thank you." She smiled. "My stage name will be Eliza Adrienne. It doesn't sound quite as debutante."

Creases appeared at the corners of his eyes. "I like it." He pulled her baggage from the racks and handed it to her. "There's a swanky hotel a couple blocks from the station. It's called The Gregorian. I want you to stay there a couple of nights on me." He tucked a twenty into her hand.

"I can't accept this." She tried to push the money into his palm.

"No, I want you to have it. I wish I could take you there myself, but I have an important meeting."

"I shouldn't accept this from—"

"Take it. It's my way of saying sorry for insulting you."

She sighed. "Thank you."

"Don't mention it. Once you exit the station, grab a cab, and they'll take you to the hotel. And after you've done that, make a trip to the City Diner. It's not far from The Gregorian. They've got great breakfast. My friend, Mattie O'Keefe, should be working. Perhaps she could give you some advice."

"I appreciate your help." She stuck out her hand. "I guess this is goodbye."

"Guess so." He shook it.

"Maybe we'll run into each other sometime."

"Maybe. I wish you the best on your journey."

"Thank you."

He paused as if to propose an idea. Instead, he tipped his hat and left.

She followed passengers from the train. Climbing a large wrought-iron staircase, she walked through a concourse into the main waiting room. It was the largest room she had ever seen. Crowds of people milled around her. Men in fedoras read their newspapers while women clicked along on the gleaming floors in their T-strap high heels. She clutched the handles of her luggage and spun around, taking in the room. Her shoes rose off the floor with a little jump. "I did it." She turned to a nearby gal. "I'm actually here. I'm in New York City!"

The lady didn't look impressed. "Wanna medal?"

She chuckled. "Where is the exit?"

"Up there." The lady pointed to a flight of steps.

"Thank you." Up the stairs, Eliza passed through a hallway flanked with shops and cafes. The aroma of fresh pastries wafted past her nose. To have a station this glorious, Manhattan had to be special.

A set of glass doors towered ahead.

She took a deep breath. Clasping her luggage tighter, she marched into the summer morning of New York City. Glorious buildings shot up to the sky. Cars streamed up and down the streets. Explosions of color filled her vision: electric lights glittering on buildings, girls in bright dresses, men in pastel shirts and polka dot ties stopping to buy their paper from the newsboy shouting, "Extra, extra, read all about it." The city's fast-paced energy dazzled her. "I'm going to love it here."

CHAPTER TEN

Sunday, 7:15 AM

Warren spotted Eliza on the street's curb waving for a taxi. The graceful sway of her wrist matched her proper demeanor. She was pure as, heck, he didn't know anything pure. In his line of work, attachments were never good.

After ten months of struggling to make a living in New York, he had met Julian O'Keefe, a member of a lucrative Irish mob known as the McKennas. Seeing the opportunity to gain power and recognition, Warren had convinced Julian that he should be added to the gang, but the mob boss was skeptical. He didn't know if the "new guy" could hack it. So they put him to the test. He had to steal a crate of bourbon from a rival gang's warehouse.

Julian gave him a gun and a word of advice. "Be quick or be dead."

Parking twenty feet from a dingy warehouse, he scanned the building. No windows. He flicked on his flashlight, walking to the door. A few twists of his jackknife and the lock clicked open. He hedged into the dark. The smell of old whiskey moistened the air. He shined the light around the room, surprised to find it so bare. On his right were two rusty Fords.

In the middle, a stack of crates loomed under sheets. That had to be the bourbon. He pulled off a sheet. The crates were empty. He yanked another sheet. Empty. His pulse sped up as he uncovered the rest. They were all empty.

A door at the rear of the building opened.

Moonlight poured into the room along with six angry Italians.

Pistols cocked.

He'd been set up. Running for the Fords, he dove onto the packed floor. Dirt rammed under his fingernails as he hit with a thud.

Bullets clanged along the rusted metal cars.

He calculated his chances of reaching the door without being shot. Six men and only six bullets. He was gonna die.

The entrance was at seven o'clock and the guys were moving in at twelve.

He had to force them to spread out. Clutching the cold revolver tight in his palm, he lay on his side and pumped a shot under the car. It missed the target, but drove the men to take cover behind the crates. He leapt up and ran. A bullet grazed his arm. Running diagonally, he shot twice at the crates. Gunfire pounded in his ears. A bullet ripped through his shoulder as he dodged out the door. Dropping behind his car's front tire, he glanced around the side.

Five men emerged from the warehouse.

"Looks like you ain't gonna make it, Patty."

He fired his gun.

A man laughed. "You missed."

He fired again.

The man fell to his knees.

"How about that time?" He shouted.

The other men shot back, now running toward him.

He fired his pistol. *Hit.* He pressed the trigger again. *Click.* No bullets. Time was up. Gunfire filled his ears. He closed his eyes, knowing this was the end. Then the shooting ceased. Was he dead? He heard loud footsteps approaching. Perhaps it was Satan.

"Ya made it." Satan's voice sounded oddly similar to Julian's. "Open yer eyes ya crazy plonker."

He didn't know they were closed. His eyelids rolled up. Julian towered over him. "Thought fer sure ya'd die in there."

Warren touched his shoulder. Blood wet his fingers as it leaked down his jacket. "You were watching me all along?"

"Course we were." Mob boss, Lonan McKenna, knelt beside him. "We tipped 'em off that ya were comin. Since ya made it out with yer neck, ya passed the test. Yer worthy of a place in the McKennas."

He glared at Lonan. "If I had one bullet left, I'd put it through your skull."

"That's the spirit." Lonan offered his hand. "We best get ya to the hospital 'fore ya bleed out."

As furious as he was, he felt proud. He made it. There was no going back.

His life changed that day. He told himself it was all for the better. Most of the time he believed it.

He spun his black Model T into the parking lot of a distinguished brick building known as Club Fianna. It served as a nightclub and the headquarters for his gang's meetings. It was also named after Lonan's young mistress. The boss could have anything he wanted with the application of force or charm. The latter of which, he used to hang on to both his wife *and* his mistress. He plucked the keys from the ignition, stepping from his car as a yellow Cadillac sped to a halt just shy of his shoes.

Julian stepped from the Caddy, flinging his door closed. "See my new breezer?"

Warren lit a cigarette. "I've seen it twice. Your drinking is affecting your memory."

"Liquor is an Irishman's medicine. It can cure anything."

"Can it cure your ugly face?"

"It can cure a woman's eyesight, so."

Warren laughed.

Julian rubbed a hand over the bumper. "I traded in my old Jalopy." He cast a look of disapproval at Warren's Ford. "Ya can trade in yer old gal fer a breezer like mine. They have all sorts of colors."

"I'm keeping my tin Lizzie. She's the only gal I won't trade up."

"At least ya have yer priorities in order."

He smirked. Opening the club's door, he motioned to Julian. "After you."

"Watchin' yer back?"

"Somebody's got to."

"Ya don't have to worry 'bout me."

"In our line of work, you never know."

They entered the company's front office to find receptionist, Kiki Jones, lounging at her desk with the latest copy of Vogue. Looking up from her magazine, she smiled. "Good morning, Warren." She winked at Julian. "Morning, Jules."

Warren tipped his fedora. "Looks like you're working hard."

She pulled a wine glass from below her desk and took a sip. "It's tough, but someone's gotta do it."

He smirked. His gang couldn't have hired a better receptionist for their phony brokerage. Every good mob needed a good cover. They operated under the guise of real estate. Even though the gang never showed a house, they appeared legitimate with business cards and a sign on the door. Kiki was the icing on the cake. She answered the phone and took messages. When a male customer or cop walked into the office, she gave them a card, light conversation, and a little show of leg. They always left with a smile on their face.

The guys walked across the room and down a hall to a pair of tall, ebony double doors.

"Kiki was making eyes at you." Warren elbowed Julian.

"I didn't notice."

"You should look harder next time."

"She's a grand bit of stuff, but I don't be interested."

"Maybe if you took the car for a test drive, you'd find it runs pretty smooth."

"Are ya speakin' from experience?"

"Not personally, no. But I heard from a good source that she's got plenty of horsepower."

"I think someone's feedin' ya a pile of cac."

Chuckling, Warren pushed through the double doors into the spacious club. It smelled of cigarette smoke and Brilliantine hair oils. Nine Irishmen sat around one of the many tables. Stuffed ashtrays, bottles of gin, and beer mugs cluttered its top.

Lonan looked up from the deck of cards he shuffled between his fingers. A moist Cuban dangled between his lips. "About time yous fellas showed up."

"Wasn't easy." Warren ambled to the long marble bar lining the back wall. "Takes half a day to pull Jules' lips off his car."

"Shove off," muttered Julian as he joined the gang at the table.

Quinn "Red" Caheny wiped a slosh of beer from his scraggly red beard. "I fer one like yer new breezer."

Julian nodded to him. "Always knew ya were a man of good taste."

"Have ya seen his wife?" asked Lonan.

Red scowled.

Walking behind the four-foot bar, Warren viewed the wealthy supply of spirits. The club's floor-to-ceiling shelves housed whiskeys, wines, gins, and beers. Customers could name their poison and have it served up in a shiny glass or teacup for the sophisticated ladies. Nevertheless, he stuck to his drink of choice. Selecting a crystal decanter, he poured himself a glass of scotch.

Red counted out stacks of black, red, and white chips to each player. "I be cuttin' this twice." He grabbed the deck of cards from Lonan. "Always seems the hand comes out in yer favor when ya do the shufflin'."

"The cards never lie." Lonan put his hand over his heart. "And neither do I."

"Ah here now, ya lie so much yer startin' to believe yerself, so."

"Cuts me deep, Red." Lonan slid two cards to each man. "Now I be takin' yer money."

Red glanced at his cards. "Not on this hand ya won't."

Warren lit a fresh Chesterfield. Tilting his head backward, he blew out a stream of smoke and checked his cards: ace of hearts, jack of spades. Good hand.

Burning a card, Lonan laid three in a row: four of hearts, Queen of diamonds, and ten of spades.

The players anteed their bets.

Red started the round. "I fold."

The next couple of guys threw in white chips, the ten-dollar minimal bet.

"Twenty." Julian tossed in a red chip.

Bet came to "Big Mel" Muldoon, a man whose bags below his eyes sagged as badly as his gut. He wiped the sweat off his brow and pushed his cards toward Lonan. "Fold."

Warren smirked. Mel folded. What was new? He shuffled two red chips between his fingers, set them down, and tapped his index finger on a stack of black chips. "Any story since I've been gone?"

"Had a peeler come into the club last night," said Lonan.

"That right? How'd it shake out?"

"He looks at the booze and asks, 'Who's the guy in charge?' 'Me,' says I. Then he pulls out his badge and gun and tells me I be under arrest fer sellin' illegal alcohol. Told him I beg to differ. We yanked him outback and gave him a little schoolin'. He won't make that mistake again."

"Wished I'd been here to see it." Warren took a slow drink and tossed in two red chips. "I call twenty and raise twenty."

Several cards dropped to the table with the murmurs of fold. Lonan and Julian were the only players to match the bet. The next flop revealed a Queen of clubs.

"We gonna get any food in here?" Red crossed his arms on the table. "I be so hungry, I could eat a nun's arse through a convent gate."

"Yer hardly wastin' away," said Julian. "Yer chin has sprouted a twin."

Red grumbled 'maggot' as he lifted his beer.

"Kiki is bringin' sandwiches around noon." Lonan set his cigar on an ashtray, turning to Warren. "How ya do in Jersey?"

"Tommy 'The Quick' Francello wasn't so quick this time." He flicked the end of his cigarette. "He's taking it nice and slow at the bottom of Colonial Lake."

Lonan nodded in approval. "Serves him right. No one hijacks a McKenna shipment. That'll be a lesson to his partners."

Warren relished the praise. Since he had joined the crew, he felt like he had more to prove than the others. He was only half-Irish. His mother's family had emigrated from Ireland to Pennsylvania before she was born. She married his American father when she was sixteen. However, his quick wit and ruthless vengeance soon earned the full respect of his comrades. He was given the nickname "Ruthless Reny" because he'd do any job, no matter what, no matter who.

"Bets on you, Jules," said Lonan.

He pitched a black chip into the pot. "Fifty."

Warren called Julian's bet.

Lonan tossed in his chips and flipped the river card. King of hearts.

A knock sounded on the door. "It's me, Kiki. I've got the food you ordered."

Julian jumped up to open it.

Warren flicked his cigarette ash. "Better slow down, Jules. Kiki will think you're gonna flatten her."

Julian cast him a dirty look as he turned the knob.

"Here's the food, fellas." Kiki carried in a tray of fried ham sandwiches, golden fries, and a jar of pickles.

"Thanks, Kiki." Lonan gave her a polite smile.

She set the tray on the table. "Anytime, boss." With a twist of her hips, she strolled from the room.

Wolfing down the sandwiches, the gang wrapped up the first round with Lonan's full house beating out Julian's trip tens and Warren's straight.

"Could have sworn yous were bluffin'," said Julian.

"Bluff or not," Warren lifted his sandwich, "in the end, you always lose."

"May you be afflicted with an itch and have no nails to scratch it."

"I could always find a lady to scratch it for me."

Julian shook his head. "Eejit."

"Game's just begun. Don't get yer scunders in a twist." Lonan lit another cigar. "Yesterday, I got the skinny on a new plan that Zanneti is cookin' up."

Warren noticed Big Mel slink down in his chair at the mention of Vincenzo Zanneti, their biggest Italian rival.

"Zanneti is teamin' up with a couple other mobs in order to get the upper hand on us. But he's got another thing comin'. We're not about to lose our hold."

Warren drained his glass of scotch. Controlling lower Manhattan, or as the underworld called it, Hell's Kitchen, wasn't easy. It required constant bloodshed in order to keep opponents contained.

"Zanneti is puttin' the heat on O'Brien," said Red. "He told me that they made him a better offer."

Lonan's eyes darkened.

Warren knew that Patrick O'Brien's laundry was one of the many businesses in the McKenna racket. Racketeering was a novel concept. It meant that a gang managed a collection of businesses and profited from them without having to actually put in the work. Businesses like clubs, speakeasies, taxicab services, laundries, and cigarette shops paid fees in exchange for "protection" of the store, its employees, and from other local mobs. If the fees were not paid, the business and its owner would suffer a severe penalty, oftentimes a fatal one.

"If O'Brien doesn't want to do business with us," said Lonan. "Then he ain't gonna do business at all. Red, I want ya to handle that. It's time we make some new partners ourselves. Every one of Zanneti's rackets need to be visited. If they won't switch, take 'em out."

The guys nodded.

Three hours later, the poker game ended with Warren taking the whole pot.

"All right," Lonan clapped his hands, "let's get to work."

The guys dispersed from the room.

When Warren rose, Lonan shook his head. He stayed beside the door until the gang had departed and then took a seat next to his boss.

"I need ya to do another job." Lonan leaned closer. "Ya need to take down Big Mel."

Warren's forehead creased. "Mel Muldoon?"

"That's right. My source saw him go into Zanneti's club. He's makin' plans on the side. He do be playin' us fer a fool. Now he's gotta go. It's got to be out of town."

"I do my checks on Coney this Wednesday. How about then?"

"Good. Keep it to yerself. Don't need Mel gettin' jumpy."

"I'll take care of it.

"That's what I like to hear."

CHAPTER ELEVEN

Sunday, 12:30 PM

Hugh hesitated outside the front entrance to Belle Vue Manor. Upon returning, alone, from the train station, he had shown his parents Eliza's letter. They were saddened that she had been treated like a pawn and appalled by the manipulation, doubtless enforced by Hector. Though his parents felt slightly rebuffed by her ending the engagement, they still respected her honesty. Hugh, too, couldn't fathom her reservations about marrying him. Sure, she had her dreams of singing for audiences, but for pity's sake, they were the perfect couple. Everyone else could see that. He would help her see that, too. For now, he was determined to set Hector straight. He knocked hard on the door.

It swung open to reveal a well-dressed butler. "Good afternoon, Master Whitmore. Didn't know we were expecting a visit from you today."

"Sorry to arrive unannounced, but there is a matter I must address with Hector. Could you please let him know that I am here?"

"Right away." The butler gestured for him to come inside. "Would you mind waiting in the parlor while I inform Sir Hector of your arrival?"

"Very well." He pulled off his hat, walking into the formal living area. He heard low voices coming from a door heading out the back of the room into a hall. It sounded like Lady Katherine's voice, but had a sharper, anxious tone. Unable to restrain his curiosity, he drew closer.

"My daughter is missing. I know that the two of you are close." Katherine paused. "Last night, you delivered a note to Eliza during the dinner party. What did it say?"

"A note?" asked a second voice (which sounded much like the maid who'd come to see him this morning). "Amn't sure I recall."

"Of course you do. You handed it to her last night in the dining room. What was on it?"

No response.

"You helped her, didn't you? You helped her run away."

A longer pause.

"Answer me this minute, Neville."

The maid replied in a soft whisper, "Indeed, Lady Katherine. I did."

"How could you? After all we've done for you? Did the note contain train departures for New York City?"

"It did."

"You realize that your actions demonstrate insubordination toward my husband and myself, and in light of this, I should dismiss you without the rest of this month's wages."

"I understand."

"Have you nothing to say for yourself?"

"I knew the consequences." Her voice trembled like she was on the verge of tears. "But I felt obligated to help Lady Eliza. I'm sorry. I didn't know what else to do."

Katherine remained silent for what seemed a week and then sighed. "Eliza is strong. Do you think she'll contact you once she's arrived?"

"She said she would write to me."

"That is good. We need a means for communication with

her. While you deserve to be dismissed, I will keep you at Belle Vue as long as you inform me as soon as you receive any contact. Do we have an agreement?"

"Yes, me lady."

"Does anyone else know of your involvement in assisting Eliza?"

"None of the Belle Vue staff know…." She drew in a shallow breath. "I went—"

Hugh knocked a vase off a table. It shattered on the wood floor.

A gasp erupted from the hall. Katherine hurried into the room. Her face blushed when she saw him. "Mr. Whitmore, I didn't know you were here."

"Forgive me, I didn't mean to bump the table. I will assuredly replace the vase."

"Don't trouble yourself. It's of no importance." Katherine waved her hand in dismissal. "Neville," she called out.

The maid rushed into the room. Her eyes widened at the sight of him.

Katherine gestured to the broken pieces of pottery. "Please, clean this up immediately. We don't need someone cutting themselves."

"Yes, me lady." She hurried to leave, catching Hugh's eye one more time before departing.

He felt sorry for the maid. She had only done Eliza's bidding and now had earned Katherine's reproach. "I've come to speak with your husband, and you as well, if you'd be so kind to join us."

"I'd be delighted. What news have—" Her question halted when Hector strode into the room.

"Mr. Whitmore." He extended his hand. "A pleasure to see you this fine afternoon."

Hugh ignored the handshake. "If it is fine has yet to be seen. I've asked Lady Katherine to join us as well."

Hector's forehead creased. "Of course. Please, follow me."

Entering his office, he gestured for Hugh to take a chair. He and Katherine sat opposite on the sofa. "It appears you have come with a troubling matter. Do tell me what it is?"

"It's in regard to this." Hugh produced an envelope from his pocket and handed it to Hector.

Hector pulled out a sheet of paper. His eyes scanned the black font. Katherine leaned close, reading over his arm. Hugh watched their expressions morph from horror to anger to dismay.

Refolding the letter, Hector tucked it into the envelope, set in on the coffee table, and released a slow breath. "We, too, received a letter from our daughter. It has come as a rather sharp blow. We are most sorry for her rash behavior. I am determined to send my head butler to New York City to retrieve her. She will follow through on her commitment to you. That I can guarantee. I won't have her creating a scandal. Both your family and ours have a reputation to maintain." He folded his hands. "How did you come into possession of this letter?"

"My butler heard knocking outside Rosemont's front entry. He discovered the note and wedding ring. I assumed Eliza would take the train, hence I hurried to Broad Street Station."

"Did you see her there?"

"I did."

"But you didn't stop her?" Hector strained to rein in his agitation.

"I chose not to."

Katherine's mouth gaped. "Then why did you go to the station?"

"I needed to see for myself if she would leave. Unfortunately, I watched her board the train."

Hector gripped the armrest. "So you let her go."

"I would never force a woman to marry me."

"Nonsense. Eliza agreed to your proposal and that settled it. You should have demanded that she see it through."

"No, you *forced* her to agree to my proposal. I love your

daughter. I had hoped for nothing more than to marry her, but I am too much of a gentlemen to push her to do something against her will."

Katherine's eyes widened with worry. "Does that mean you won't have her anymore?"

"It appears that she doesn't want a marriage."

"How are we to tell everyone this news?" She clasped her rosary as though she were holding on for dear life. "This is simply unacceptable. She has to return. What are we going to do?"

"Admit the truth: it's done, the engagement is off. On Tuesday morning, I will be traveling to New York City. If I find her, I will check to see that she is well, but she is not my reason for going."

Hector's thick brows pinched together. "What do you mean?"

"My father is sending me to New York to conduct research for a new steel business."

"He hasn't informed me of his plans."

"That's because they don't include you."

Hector shifted on the sofa cushion, noticeably trying to restrain his frustration. "Are you saying that Daniel is going to dissolve our partnership and start his own company?"

"You should ask him yourself."

Hector thumped his hand on the armrest. "This is Eliza's fault."

"You did this to yourself. She has nothing to do with it." He stood up. "I can see my way out." He felt their eyes boring into his back as he strode from the room. He could have put them at ease, telling them that he had every intention of winning her heart and bringing her back to Pennsylvania, but they didn't deserve that peace of mind.

On his way out, he spotted Neville polishing the banister. He stopped beside her and spoke in a low voice. "I told the Belcourts that my butler found Eliza's note and wedding ring at our entrance. You were never there."

She looked at him with astonished eyes. "Why would ya do that fer me?"

"Because your loyalty to Eliza should not go unnoticed. Thank you for helping her." With an appreciative nod, he departed.

CHAPTER TWELVE

Sunday, 12:35 PM

Eliza caught a taxi to the City Diner. It certainly didn't look special. The exterior was an old steel railcar. Maybe the food drew the customers? Bells chimed as she entered. Breathing in the aroma of fresh coffee and rolls, she looked around the small space. Not bad. It possessed a level of charm with its red vinyl seats and checkered floor. Her seat squeaked as she slid into a booth.

Waitresses bounded from table to table, filling mugs, delivering plates, and chatting with customers.

A proud smile lifted her lips as she surveyed the lively atmosphere around her. She had done it. The train ride. Checking into the Gregorian Hotel. Sitting in a diner in Manhattan. Soon her parents would find her note and realize that she was gone. Pulling off her crocheted gloves, she watched a curvy red-haired waitress sway to a tune playing on the diner's radio.

The waitress wiped off a section of the bar, tossed the rag over her shoulder, and faced two mid-aged gentlemen who sat on stools behind the counter. "Afternoon fellas, what can I get ya today?"

"What do you recommend?" asked one of the men.

"You want lunch or breakfast? We're serving both."

"Probably lunch."

"Get the pork chops or cheeseburger. Can't go wrong with either."

"Could I add onions on the burger?"

"Abso-lute-ly."

"Then I'll take that along with French fries."

She jotted his order down and looked at the other man. "And for you?"

"How're the hot cakes?"

"They're ducky, especially with our homemade maple syrup."

"Sounds too sweet."

"I'm sure they're not sweeter than you." She winked at him.

"Aww, you're throwing me a line." He waved off the compliment. "Guess I'll try those hot cakes, bacon, and coffee."

She scribbled it down.

The first man added. "Bring me a cup of joe, too."

"You got it." She spun toward the kitchen's window. Tearing the orders off her pad, she clipped it to the line and hollered, "Two cups of mud, burger with breath, fries, and a stack with a grunt."

Another waitress pinned her order. "Flirting for tips again?"

The redhead grinned. "Who's gonna pay for all my bad habits if I don't?"

"You're such a vamp."

"Perhaps you should try it. Then you wouldn't be walking to work every day."

Eliza found the waitresses' open banter surprising. She wondered if all city girls talked so frankly. Scanning her table, she discovered there wasn't a menu, only salt and pepper shakers and four crumbs. With a quick wave of her hand, she dusted the crumbs off the edge of the tabletop.

"What can I get you today?"

Looking up, she found the redhead waitress beside her. "Hello."

"Hi-ya, doll. Know what you want to order?"

"You didn't bring me a menu."

"It's on the wall." She pointed to a board hanging behind the counter.

"Oh, I didn't see that." She released a nervous chuckle. "What a lot of options."

"You never been to a diner before have you, baby?"

Her cheeks blossomed a shade of pink. "Is it that noticeable?"

"Like a swollen thumb."

She blushed darker.

"Listen, it's simple: you choose something off the board and ask for it. So what'll it be?"

"I guess I'll try the pork chops, vegetable soup, and a chocolate shake."

"Got it." Gliding to the counter, the redhead clipped the order to the line and swept a few coins off the bar into her hand. She called out a thank-you to the man exiting.

He nodded to her. "You're welcome, Mattie-girl."

She blew him a kiss and dumped the pennies into the pocket of her powder blue uniform. With habitual ease, she moved from table to table, topping off coffee mugs, bantering with customers, and snapping her fingers in rhythm to the radio.

Did that man call her Mattie? Might she be the one Warren had mentioned?

When her order came up, the redhead returned, set down her meal, and slipped into the opposite seat. "Here's your grub. Where you from?"

Eliza's eyebrows rose in shock.

"What? Did I breach some kind of etiquette?"

"I'm not used to staff being so friendly with the customers."

"I'm not your staff. I'm your waitress."

She blinked, feeling taken aback. "Right, of course."

"What's a gal like you doing in a place like Manhattan anyway?"

"I'm pursuing a singing career."

"A singing career? Didn't expect that. Are you any good?"

"I believe so. People have complimented me on my voice."

"Well then, that's berries."

"Is berries a good thing?"

"Yeah. It means wonderful. Like the bee's knees or the cat's meow and all that." She extended her hand. "Name's Mattie O'Keefe. What's yours?"

"It's you! You're the Mattie I came to find. This is amazing." Her eyes widened in emphatic amazement. "Warren sent me to find you."

"*Warren* sent *you*?" A boisterous laugh erupted from her red lips. "Now doesn't that beat all. What's your name?"

"Eliza Belcourt."

"Belcourt. Sounds expensive. If ya don't mind me asking, how'd you meet Warren?"

"He was on the train. He joined my compartment in New Jersey."

"Ah, Jersey. Sounds 'bout right. Bet you enjoyed that half of your train ride." Mattie wiggled her eyebrows.

She tried to act nonchalant. "He was good company."

"He's not bad on the eyes either, am I right?"

"I—well—yes, I suppose so."

"So does every other girl in Manhattan."

Eliza felt a pang of jealousy. She dabbed her mouth with her napkin. "If you don't mind me asking, what is your accent called?"

"I don't have an accent. This is New York City. How else we supposed to sound?"

"I guess I don't know. I just arrived."

"Where ya staying? Got any connections?"

"Not exactly. I'm staying at The Gregorian, but that's

temporary. Warren said you might be able to help me."

"The Gregorian?" Mattie crossed her arms on the table. "That's a swanky place. I heard it's four bucks a night. How can you afford to stay there on your own?"

Her face flushed. "Without a parlor its three dollars a night, and…Warren actually paid for my room. I told him no, but he insisted. I promise I'm not the kind of girl who goes around—"

"Whoa, baby. It's fine. You don't have to explain nothing to me. The truth is, a girl has to take a hand out when she can. Things don't come cheap you know."

"They don't?"

Mattie chuckled. "You're used to Daddy paying for everything, right?"

She stared at her fork. "I want to be self-sufficient, but I don't know where to begin. Everything's always been done for me."

"You can learn. Every girl has to grow up. Tell you what, I might be able to help you find a place."

"Really? Where?"

"Thing is, my flat mate is moving out. I need to find someone to move in and help with the rent. I have an apartment at Hotel Griffin on West 35th. You wanna come by and see the place?"

She put a hand to her heart. "That would be wonderful."

"I get off today at 8:00. Come by the diner around that time, and I'll take you there. If you like it, we can talk more details. Enjoy your food." Mattie winked and strolled away.

CHAPTER THIRTEEN

Sunday, 8:15 PM

"It ain't far from here," said Mattie.

Eliza watched buildings pass her cab's window. "Did you choose your apartment because it's close to the diner?"

"Nah, I chose it because it's cheap."

"I see." A smidgen of worry set in.

The taxi parked in front of a three-story Gothic building. Cracks snaked along the red brick walls while unkempt hedges clustered around its foundation. A sign by the main entrance read, Hotel Griffin.

"We're here." Mattie swung open her cab door. "My apartment is on the second floor."

They entered a lobby shrouded in cherry oak paneling. Faded oriental rugs lay on the floor. Two potted plants sat at the base of the front desk. Both appeared to be dead.

Eliza's palms grew clammy. She glanced at the exit and then at the desk clerk, hoping for a friendly greeting.

He didn't lift his eyes from his newspaper.

"Come on. The stairs are over here." Mattie ambled up the staircase. Every board creaked and groaned. She stopped at a door with a bronze number Twenty-One hanging on a precarious nail. Jimmying her key in the knob, she gave it a shove. The room number clanged each time she pushed against the door. "It's stubborn sometimes." She thrust her hip into it; it popped open. She waved her hand in a sweeping gesture as they entered the small parlor. "Home sweet home."

Eliza entered into the welcoming scent of musty carpet and shriveled cigarettes. An overstuffed ashtray lay on the coffee table. Varnished peony blossom wallpaper bubbled on the walls and curled like potato rinds at the corners of the ceiling. Its sophistication matched that of the shabby velour loveseat.

Mattie kicked off her heels and tossed her handbag onto a floral chair next to the sofa. "Now for the grand tour." She headed down a narrow hallway off the living room. "Here's the bathroom," she gestured to the first door on the left.

It was the smallest room Eliza had ever seen. A white claw-foot tub pressed against the back wall with the toilet nearly smooching its side. She looked between the toilet lid and the sink with unease. She could do her business and wash her hands at the same time. Maybe the layout was meant to be a time-saver?

In one stride, they crossed the hall into a bedroom.

"We'd share this room," said Mattie. "Most apartments are one bedroom. If you want two, you'll pay double."

"I understand. It's just…"

"Just what?"

She fidgeted with her handbag.

"Spill it, doll. You won't hurt my feelings."

"We only met this morning. It seems a bit personal."

"I've been in a lot more personal situations than this. At least here there are two beds." Mattie grinned. "The way I see it, life's an adventure and change adds spice to it. Let's take a seat in the parlor and talk details."

"Isn't there a kitchen?"

"Course not. If you want food, you have to buy it in the hotel's restaurant. But personally, I wouldn't recommend it.

Maybe for a cuppa joe, but definitely not meat. Trust me, I've learned the hard way. You're better off walking a block to Hotel Elise. They have great food. Who wants to cook anyway?" Sauntering into the parlor, Mattie flopped on the sofa. "Sit, baby. Take a load off."

Cigarette burns dotted the cushions. The likelihood that Mattie ever cleaned was slim. Eliza swallowed her knotting revulsion and lowered herself to the farthest edge.

"Rent here beats every other hotel in the city, especially since we have this living room. It's fifteen a month, and we'd split that. You would have to come up with seven dollars and fifty cents per month. How does that sound?"

"I honestly wouldn't know since I haven't rented before."

"True, but I can assure you it's the best you'll find for the price."

She scanned the untidy parlor. How could this be the best? At Belle Vue Manor, the floors were polished, the upholstery spotless, and each room smelled like lavender. Here, the sofa had questionable stains, crumbs littered the carpet, and the air made her wish she didn't need to breathe. How was she supposed to live here? She studied the coffee table's overflowing ashtray with disgust. It was in complete disorder and without proper amenities. She should remain at The Gregorian. That hotel made her comfortable. Besides, she knew nothing about Mattie. There wasn't a single picture in the whole apartment. No family photos or artwork. The walls were bare. "The problem is that I don't have a job and without an income, I can't pay a monthly rent."

"I bet you could waitress." Mattie looked her over. "I might be able to get you a job at the diner if you'd like?"

"Really?" She chewed on her lip, not daring to admit that she had never lifted a finger to serve anyone in her life and didn't wish to start. Unfortunately, her father's money would run out. If she didn't land a singing contract quickly, she would need a source of income. Besides singing and playing the piano, she didn't possess any skills. She never learned to sew or cook or clean like typical girls. Fear caused her hands to clench. She couldn't fail this time. Even if it meant waiting tables like a common house servant, she was determined to make a life for herself in New York.

"Waitresses get free meals during their shifts. That's a big cost saver," said Mattie. "My roommate moves out on Thursday. You could move in then. Did Warren give you enough to afford The Gregorian three more nights?"

"Yes." She looked at her hands folded in her lap.

"Are you ashamed of that?"

"Not exactly."

"Then what's eating ya, doll?"

"I could have afforded a short stay at The Gregorian without his help." She already felt guilty about stealing the money, but having to confess her shame aloud was even harder. "Before I ran away, I took my father's spare cash from his office."

Mattie slapped her thigh. "Ain't that berries. My new flat-mate is a thief."

She shook her head emphatically. "I promise I'm not. I don't have a record of this type of behavior."

"I believe you, baby. Truth be told, I'm glad you did something wrong. Every reputation needs a touch of scarlet."

This response surprised her. No rebuke. No correction. Instead, admiration?

Leaning over, Mattie picked up her cigarette tin and Wonderlite off the table. "Tell me about yourself."

Eliza paused, contemplating what she should divulge. If Mattie was to become her roommate, she might as well give it to her straight. "I'm from Elkins Park, Pennsylvania. My family is deeply rooted there. I was expected to marry well and stay in the area, especially since I am the only child. As you can see, I didn't obey. My parents are probably livid right now, as I'm sure they've found my letter which stated that I am not marrying Hugh and that I've gone to New York instead."

Mattie's mouth gaped. "That's...something. Do you think your parents will try to find you?"

"I don't know. It's possible that they'll send our butler to search for me, but I don't care. I'm not leaving." She swallowed against her angst. Though she might have rushed into this, mercy, she was determined to make it work. Even if they came for her, she wasn't leaving. She refused to lose her new freedom. "What about you? Is your family in New York?"

Mattie averted her eyes to the green tin in her hand. She extracted a cigarette. "My brother lives here."

"And your parents?"

A muscle clenched in her jawline. "My parents are both dead. I don't have any other siblings."

"I'm sorry to hear that."

"It happened a long time ago. I'm fine with it." Striking the metal match against the flint strip on her Wonderlite, she sparked a flame and lit the end of her cigarette. She held the tin out to Eliza.

"No thank you."

"Have you smoked before?"

"No."

"Ever drink?"

"I've tasted wine before, but it's illegal now."

"That doesn't mean it's not available." Mattie exhaled a stream of smoke. "There are plenty of underground nightclubs and speakeasies, and some folks brew their own gin. Instead of making the country dry, the government's amendment has made people drink even more. Fact is that nobody cares about the law. We live by a simple code: 'Eat, Drink, and Be Merry...For Tomorrow We Die.' You can thank Uncle Sam and the war for that one." She snorted with disdain. "You ever read *This Side of Paradise*?"

"Definitely. I adore F. Scott Fitzgerald."

"Who doesn't? He's a total sheik."

She nodded.

"Do you remember in the book when Amory Blaine says that he's grown up to find all gods dead, all wars fought, and all faith in man shaken?"

She hadn't liked that sentence. It was sad and cynical. "I remember it."

"I think he's right." Mattie took another drag and rested her head on the back of the sofa. "That's why it's best to live for today. No one can say what tomorrow will bring. So why worry about it." She turned to Eliza. "Do you agree?"

Staring into the kohl-lined eyes of Mattie, she sighed. "To say there's no God, no person to trust, and nothing to fight for is a sad statement, and a very lonely one at that."

"In my life, Amory's words have proved true. That's why I live for the next rush. It's all I've found to live for."

Eliza's forehead furrowed. Mattie's view on life appeared much like the walls of her home, barren. "Are you okay?"

"Course, baby. I'm the cat's pajamas." Mattie donned a flirty grin and held up the tin of cigarettes. "I think it's time for your first lesson."

"I doubt I will like smoking."

"You'll get used to it. Besides, these are Lucky Strikes. They're a terrific blend. Just watch me." She demonstrated the process step by step, and then handed Eliza the lighter. "Now you try."

She looked at the Wonderlite in her palm. Ladies of her caliber never smoked and she'd hate to smell like this forsaken room.

Mattie held out a cigarette.

If her father saw her smoke, he would be outraged. But she didn't have to heed his rules anymore. Taking the Lucky, she placed it between her lips and struck the Wonderlite's match. She pressed the flame to the end of the cigarette.

"Good, now inhale."

She breathed in, the ashy smoke pouring into her mouth and

down her throat. It smoldered inside her chest. Her throat itched, and she tried to clear it with saliva.

"It may take a while, but you'll get the hang of it."

She grimaced. "I'm not sure I want to."

"Sure you do. It's part of showing men we're equals. We can vote, cut our hair, smoke, and drink like all the rest of them. Grasp your freedom, baby. It's time to discard your old traditions and embrace your new life. You're not in Pennsylvania anymore. You're in New York City."

Freedom. Eliza stared at the thin cigarette between her fingers. Inhaling another puff, she released gray vapors and a bit of her innocence into the air.

CHAPTER FOURTEEN

July 14
Tuesday, 9:00 AM

Warren and his gang sat around a couple of tables in the rear wing of the City Diner filling up on fried eggs, bacon, and toast.

Finn dumped a gallon of milk into his coffee before taking a swig. "Heard a new one the other day."

A smile curved Warren's mouth. The lankiest member of the McKennas was Finnegan Hennessy. Out of all the gang, Warren liked Finn the most. "Let's have it."

"So a lad goes to the chemist and the druggist asks him, 'Did that mudpack I gave ya improve yer wife's appearance?' The lad nods, 'It surely did, but there's a wee problem.' The druggist is confused by this. 'What's the problem, lad?' The lad sighs, 'It keeps fallin' off.'"

Chuckles filtered around the table.

"By any chance, do ya know the location of that druggist?" asked Lonan.

Finn shrugged. "Can't say I do so."

"That's a fret." Lonan shook his head. "Better luck next time, Red."

"For him or his wife?"

"Both."

"Ye bunch of hoors," grumbled Red.

"Don't ya worry," Finn patted his shoulder, "Yer wife ain't so bad." He paused. "Now yer cousin on the other hand," he whistled, "she's so ugly even the tide wouldn't take her out."

Even Red laughed at that. "She's on me father's side. Never liked that side much."

Mattie strolled up to the table with a fresh pot of coffee. "Any refills, fellas?"

Finn lifted his mug. "Ah go on so."

She tilted the pot. It flowed into the cup and splashed over the side. "Ah rhatz! Let me get that." As she leaned over to wipe the spill, her size-too-small uniform emphasized her none-too-small bosom.

Finn's face lit up like a neon sign.

"There ya go." She stood upright. "All better."

"Much, my dear. Bless yer little Irish heart and every other Irish part."

She gave Finn a playful shove. "Anybody else need a refill?"

Eight more mugs rose in excitement.

"We're all set fer now," said Julian, shooting an angry glare around the table.

"I'll be at the counter if you need me." Pivoting on her high heel, Mattie tucked her tray under her arm and swung her hips back to the kitchen.

"Jules, yer sister is a fine bit of stuff, and her legs," Finn tilted his head back and whistled, "they're long as a mile."

Red nodded. "Every inch grand perfection."

Julian's face darkened.

Finn stuffed another forkful of sausage into his mouth. "But her blouse holds the grandest set of all." He gestured with his hands like he held a pair of melons.

Julian sprang to his feet with his hands balled into fists. "Outside, Finn. I swear I be knocking yer lips off yer stupid face."

"Ah now, I was only jokin'."

Julian remained standing. "Outside."

"Sit down, ya crazy Irish bastard." Warren gave him a friendly thump on the back. "No one's makin' a pass at Mattie. Relax and eat your eggs."

Julian lowered into his seat. "Ya can have yer fun with any woman ya want, but not her."

"Ya don't have to worry, Jules," said Lonan, uncapping a silver flask. He poured a hefty portion of bourbon into his coffee and looked down at his morning paper. "Looks like we made the front page of the New York Times. Says here, 'Suspected Mob Attack. Crime on the Rise in Manhattan. Patrick O'Brien was found dead Sunday mornin' in a ditch by Murphy's Drugstore. His body contained two bullet wounds: one in the back and another in his forehead. The police also found O'Brien's laundry shop ransacked. The police are continuin' to investigate the crime, but it is believed that mob involvement may be behind the assault.'" He turned to Red and Finn. "Good work, lads. This is the publicity we need. It will send a message to our other rackets that nobody leaves us for Zanneti or any other boss."

Julian leaned toward Red. "Did O'Brien scream like a litt'l girl before ya shot him?"

Red grinned. "He didn't, but he ran like one."

The guys laughed.

Lonan set the newspaper aside. "I got another call from my source. She overheard that Zanneti is expectin' two convoys from Canada in eleven days through Niagara Falls. She says it's gonna be a heavy load."

"What kind of shipment?" asked Warren.

"Whiskey and wine." Lonan folded his thick fingers. "We'll need heavy ammo. I'll need more Tommys. Keep yer ears open and let me know if ya hear any other news. I want to stay on top of Zanneti and the others."

———

Hugh's cab stopped in front of a restaurant that resembled a railroad car. Atop the roof, a red neon sign boasted the words CITY DINER. Before he reached the main entrance, a group of men in jackets and fedoras breezed past him.

"Excuse us, lad." A man with a scruffy red beard nodded.

"No trouble at all." Out of the corner of his eye, he noticed one guy's face in particular. Was that...Frederick? He glanced again, but he could only see the man's back. It couldn't have been him. The doors chimed as he entered the restaurant. He approached a counter lined with bar stools.

A waitress turned around with a tray of food. "Hey handsome, wanna have a seat at the bar or a booth?"

"A booth would be nice."

"Go on and take a seat. I'll be right with you."

Pulling off his hat, he tossed it on the seat and scooted across the bright red vinyl. Car horns beeped outside the window. Cabs sputtered down the street, leaving a trail of sooty exhaust in their wake. Two ladies in bell-shaped hats strutted down the sidewalk. A man in wide bottomed trousers snuck up behind one of the gals and swept her into his arms. She screamed until he laid a kiss on her cheek.

He sighed. Where was Eliza now? Would she be surprised to know he was in Manhattan? All his life, he could get anything he wanted. Nothing was out of reach. Nothing except for her. His shoulders slouched as he stared at the tabletop. The last customer had left today's issue of the New York Times. The headline drew his attention.

Suspected Mob Attack. Crime on the Rise in Manhattan.

As he read the excerpt, his brow creased. Mob involvement? He read it again, feeling a slight chill. Was this article accurate? Did Manhattan have a problem with these types of criminals?

"Why so perplexed, gorgeous?" The waitress from earlier stood at his table.

His eyes widened. He hadn't seen her approach.

"What can I get ya this morning? Some pancakes, coffee, my phone number?" Her grin held a suggestive slant.

His eyebrows rose. The girls in Pennsylvania were never so bold. He didn't know what to say.

She leaned against the table and her hem inched higher. "What's wrong, baby? Forget how to talk?"

He cleared his throat. "Pancakes, please."

"You got it." She slid a little closer. "How 'bout a cup of java?"

"That would be nice. Thank you."

Her thick, mascara-globbed eyelashes lowered halfway over her green eyes. "My name's Mattie. Give me a holler if you need *anything* else."

He couldn't help but watch her stroll to the counter. She had a tall frame with plenty of legs, hips, and curves. He looked away. She wasn't Eliza.

———

The owner of the City Diner, Mr. Smeeth, eyeballed Eliza over his desk. They sat in the back corner of the kitchen. The din of pots and pans sounded behind them. She squeezed her knees together to try to keep them from shaking. "I know I haven't got much experience, but—"

"You don't have any."

"Right." She swallowed. "But I can learn. I guarantee that I'll do my best."

Mr. Smeeth shifted in his chair. "If I were to hire you, and I'm not saying I will, I would start you out at fifteen cents an hour. You haven't got the work experience like the other girls, but after a couple months, if you do a good job, I'll consider raising your pay."

"How many days a week would I be working?"

"Five."

"How many hours would I get?"

"30 hours to start."

She looked down at the table, calculating the figures. Her years of tutoring had paid off after all. She'd make $4.50 a week, not including tips. It didn't sound like much, but she was certain she could make it work. With an authoritative nod of her head, she looked at the bug-eyed Mr. Smeeth. "That sounds fair."

"Fine. You can start training on Saturday."

"Thank you, sir." A rush of relief shot through her veins. She shook the pudgy hand of her boss. "It will be a pleasure to work for you." Pushing open the metal kitchen doors, she stepped into the heart of her new place of employment.

"So?" Mattie shimmied over to her. "What'd ol' Smeeth say?"

"I got the job."

"That's the bee's knees! I knew he'd hire you."

"I don't know what I would have done without your help."

"No trouble, doll. When do you start?"

"Saturday."

"That's copacetic. Welcome to the diner." She waved her hand across the expanse of the restaurant.

Soon she would be waiting on these very tables. Her gaze paused on one of the booths where a young gentleman sat alone eating his breakfast. His profile had a distinct familiarity.

"Checking out booth four, huh?" Mattie whistled. "I'd like to take a champagne bath with him." She shoved the coffee pot into Eliza's hand. "Ask him if he'd like a refill and get a better look."

"But I'm not in uniform."

"Don't worry about it. He is as gorgeous as Rudolph Valentino." She gave her a light push forward. "You'll thank me later."

She hoped Mr. Smeeth wouldn't catch her. He might not like seeing her serve a customer out of uniform. Stepping up to the table, she asked in her most professional tone. "Would you like a refill, sir?"

The man looked up from his pancakes. His mouth dropped open. "Eliza?"

"Hugh?" She blinked several times, struck by disbelief. "What are you doing here?"

"Do you work here?"

"I was just hired."

"I never thought I'd run into you this quickly." He shook his head. "I got off the train not more than an hour ago."

Heat filtered into her cheeks. A rush of nervousness made her perspire. "Did my parents send you?"

"No, I'm here on business for my father. He has decided to start a steel branch in Manhattan. I'm his representative."

"Why didn't you tell me that you had planned to come to New York? You knew I wanted to come here."

"Would it have made a difference in your decision to marry me?"

His honesty startled her. She looked away, embarrassed. "I wasn't looking for a marriage. I'm sorry that I gave you the wrong impression. You've always been a good friend to me. I never expected you to propose."

"I assumed you knew that a kiss implies the intention of marriage."

"I got caught up in the moment and..." Her voice trailed off.

He sighed. "I wish you would have talked to me in person instead of having your maid deliver a note."

The truth stung. She knew her actions appeared cowardly, running away in the middle of the night and ending an engagement with a letter, but she was afraid. She didn't know how he would respond. She feared that he would be like her father. "I didn't know what else to do." Tears pushed toward the surface. "I have to go." Hurrying to the counter, she thrust the coffee pot on the burner and snatched up her handbag.

"What's wrong?" Mattie's brows pinched together.

"Nothing." She hurried to the door, hearing Hugh call after

her. Jogging to a cab parked along the curb, she scrambled into the backseat. "The Gregorian, please."

The driver dropped her off at the front entrance.

Paying her fare, she breezed into the magnificent lobby.

The doorman nodded to her. "Welcome back, ma'am."

"Thank you." She managed a steady voice, but inside her heart raced. Walking toward the hall, she extracted the room key from her handbag.

"Eliza!"

She nearly dropped the key when she heard Hugh's voice. Glancing behind her, she saw him enter the lobby. She hurried down the hall, stopped at her room, and jammed it into the lock. The knob didn't open. "Come on." She jimmied the key. It still didn't open. Casting a peek over her shoulder, she jolted. Hugh stood six feet from her.

"I'm glad I caught up with you."

"You followed me?"

"Yes and no. I also have a room at this hotel, but I left the restaurant to follow you."

"I thought my departure made it obvious that I didn't wish to talk." She turned the key and drove her hip into the door.

"I didn't want to end things on a sour note. Can we please discuss the ending of our engagement?"

"What is there to say?"

"More than you've said so far." He gestured to her hand. "You are trying to open the wrong door."

"I think I know which room I am in, thank you very much."

"But you're trying to unlock room 17, and your key says 11."

She looked at the numbers. Sure enough, it said eleven. "I can't even get my room right," she muttered. Trudging up the hall, she looked for her door.

Hugh followed alongside of her. "Your letter stated that your parents had pressured you to say yes to save their business. You seem like a confident woman, so why didn't you stand up for yourself? Why did you accept my proposal?"

She stopped at room eleven. "Because I had to."

"What do you mean?"

She paused, looking at the key. "My father wanted a son, but my mother couldn't have more children after my birth. I thought if I married you then maybe, for once, my father would be proud that he had a daughter." She sighed. "But a marriage isn't the solution. That's why I had to run away. If I can succeed, maybe he'll see my worth."

He shook his head. "When will you realize that you don't have to prove anything?"

"See," She threw a hand up, "you don't understand me."

"I regret that you feel that way." His tone held an underlying note of hurt.

A wave of heat floated up her spine when she noticed the sincerity in his gaze. "I am sorry for leaving the way I did, but I have to chase my destiny. You might think that we make a good match, but we don't. We are too different. It's probably best if you and I go our separate ways."

"It's not that easy."

"Why?"

The muscle beside his jaw twitched. "Because I still love you."

Her mouth gaped. Where was his anger? Where were his vows to never speak to her again? He was supposed to be arrogant and aloof. He wasn't supposed to confess his love in a hotel hallway. He wasn't supposed to be here at all, looking at her with those intense brown eyes that made her forget reason. Turning abruptly, she placed the key in the knob. She paused before she entered and met his gaze. "You shouldn't." Then, she stepped inside and closed it behind her. Pressing her ear against the door, she listened to him walk away.

CHAPTER FIFTEEN

July 15
Wednesday, 9:00 AM

Something scuffed under Eliza's hotel door. Sitting upright in bed, she saw a folded paper. She slipped her feet to the carpet and walked over to the note.

Dearest Eliza,

We can both agree that yesterday was not ideal. Though we find ourselves in an unusual position, once being engaged and all, I believe that as mature adults, we can move beyond that. Since we are both new to this big city, it would behoove us now more than ever to maintain our friendship and have someone to trust. I have known you for four years and value your friendship above all else. To lose it would be a great tragedy. That is why I propose that we do not go our separate ways as you suggested last evening. I would like to continue our friendship on a purely amiable basis, if you would do me this honor. Today, I am planning on having a little fun before diving into business. I am taking a trip to Coney Island. I'm told it's a lovely place filled with shows, rides, games, and a magnificent view of the ocean.

If you would care to accompany me, as I truly hope you will, meet me in the Gregorian's lobby at 11:00. All expenses are on me.

Sincerely,
Hugh Whitmore

"Go to Coney Island?" She said aloud. "I reject him last night, and today, he invites me on a trip." She shook her head. Hugh Whitmore was the most confident and long-suffering individual she had ever met. Though she had to admit, he did present an excellent argument. It would be wise to have someone she trusted in this city. So far, New York City seemed safe and friendly, but she couldn't erase Neville's words from her mind...*it has a dark side*. If her maid was right, then she ought to keep Hugh close. Besides, she deserved a bit of fun. Her father had suppressed her for the last eighteen years; it was time to live a little.

At eleven sharp, she walked into the lobby and saw Hugh reclined in a chair reading a newspaper. "Does this Coney Island have music?"

He tipped up the rim of his boater hat. "I believe there is a singing bearded lady."

"A bearded lady?"

"Indeed. Quite a sight, I'm told. They say she's ugly as sin but sings like an angel."

Her mouth gaped. "You can't be serious."

"Won't know until we get there." He snapped up his paper and offered his arm. "Shall we?"

"I dare say we must."

He ushered her to a taxi that waited outside. Opening the door, he helped her into the back seat and lowered beside her.

The driver spun around. "Where to?"

"57th Street Subway Station," said Hugh.

The driver pulled into the fast flow of traffic. "Goin' on a trip today?"

"We're visiting Coney Island."

"A grand choice. I done been there many a time. Me favorite part is those side shows with all the freaks of nature. Craziest bunch of folks I ever laid me eyes on. I done seen a pair of conjoined twins who could dance a fierce jig and a woman with the skin of an elephant. There was also a lad who could twist himself inta a human knot."

"I've never heard of such a thing." Eliza leaned forward. "Did you see the bearded lady?"

The driver chuckled. "I saw her. She had a beard, black as night and so long, she could braid it like a rope."

"Incredible. And she sings?"

"Like a nightingale." He cast a glance over his shoulder and grinned. "Course, I had ta close me eyes. It didn't seem right, a voice like that coming out of a she-man. But if you're lookin' for a real thrill, I'd suggest ye try out the coasters. The Giant Racer will make yer stomach plunge inta yer throat and lodge there fer a good three minutes. Best not eat b'fore that ride."

She looked at Hugh. "I've never ridden a roller coaster before. Have you?"

"Lots of times. We had the greatest amusement park near Pittsburgh called Kennywood. We would go every summer weekend with a handful of nickels. Spent all day there, just hot dogs and rides. Our favorite was the Jack Rabbit. It had a great first drop."

"Whom did you go with?"

He blinked. "What do you mean?"

"You said *we*. Did you go with a childhood friend?"

His lighthearted expression dimmed. "You could say that." He gestured to a sign outside as the cabdriver slowed to a stop. "Looks like we're here."

She detected something in his gaze. Was it pain, sadness, or regret? She wondered who his friend was, but didn't dare pry. Following him from the taxi, they walked to a set of stairs that led from the sidewalk down to the lower level subway station.

"I'll need to make change," he said. "Almost all rides and food carts take nickels or dimes."

"I did bring some cash with me. I don't expect you to pay for me."

"That wasn't the agreement. I asked you to join me and in return I would pay all expenses." He approached the change booth, pulling out a crisp five-dollar bill. Making the exchange, the teller gave him enough nickels and dimes to ensure a day of fun. "When does the next train leave for Coney Island?"

The teller looked at his pocket watch. "In five minutes. Head through that archway and wait at platform two."

"Thank you." Hugh directed her to a turnstile and handed her a nickel.

She placed it into the machine and pushed open the metal bar.

Paying his fare, he followed behind her. "It's about an hour's journey from here."

Her eyebrows shot up. Oh dear. What was she going to do, trapped in a subway car with him for an hour? What if he brought up the past? She chewed the inside of her lip.

He put a hand to his jacket lapel. "I've come prepared to pass the time." Extracting a magazine from the inside pocket of his suit jacket, he handed it to her. "I give you, the latest edition of Crossword Puzzle Magazine."

A relieved smile curved her mouth. "I love crosswords." She flipped through the pages. "It looks like an exciting issue."

A horn honked as a train rumbled into the station. It squealed to a halt in front of their platform. The door slid open, and he offered his hand to help her inside the olive green railcar furnished with rattan benches, warm incandescent lighting, and overhead fans. White porcelain poles staggered down the middle of the aisle for those who wished to stand.

She selected a woven seat midway through the car. "I suppose we should start with the first puzzle and work our way through." Pointing to number one on the horizontal list, she read aloud. "Provides mirth or amusement."

"How many spaces?" He asked, sitting beside her.

"Three. Could it be ART?"

"I don't know." He leaned over to look at the magazine. "What's the word down from it?"

"Number two down is to govern. Four blanks."

"That could be RULE, which would mean art wouldn't work."

She considered that. "If two down is rule, then perhaps one across is FUN?"

Hugh nodded. "I believe you have it."

A tiny giggle escaped her lips. "Have you a pen?"

He handed her one from his pocket.

She wrote in the two answers. Raising her head, she lifted the pen in triumph. "We're off to a great start."

"You do like crosswords," he chuckled.

The subway's horn honked as it pulled through the tunnel.

"I enjoy the challenge of making words fit together. It's like composing a song, really. Every word builds on the other."

"I never thought of it that way. I didn't realize how much you love music."

"It's my utmost passion. I've dreamed of singing my own songs since I was six years old. What about you? What's your dream?"

He folded his hands. "My dream is a simple one. Take over my father's business and have a family."

"Ah." She dropped her gaze to the magazine, mentally elbowing herself for asking that question. That should have been obvious. A marriage to him would have meant a step closer to achieving his dream, but not her own. At their engagement party, she could tell he wouldn't support her singing career, so she had left. In doing so, she had hindered his dream. This should have upset him, and yet, here he was on a subway with her. It seemed abnormal. "Aren't you at all angry with me?"

He studied her from below the rim of his hat. "I admit that when I received your letter, it stung. I had wanted to…I had thought we were…" He cleared his throat. "Life goes on. My ego was hurt more than anything."

She saw his Adam's apple bob with a forced swallow. "The ladies of Elkins Park will be ecstatic to hear that you're back on the market."

"I believe they will. I am the talk of the town, you know."

"Mostly in your mind."

"My mind is fond of me, I can't lie. Nevertheless, I suppose once business is settled, I shall begin the arduous task of finding another hand to put that hefty diamond on. I hope she has some arm strength."

She rolled her eyes, pretending to read the next question on the puzzle. The words floated in front of her eyes, but all she could picture was Hugh on bended knee, proposing to another woman. "If she's too weak, why would you want her?"

His eyebrows rose.

Hearing the edge in her own tone, she blushed and riddled off three across. "A feeling, disposition, state, or mood. Seven letters."

"JEALOUS."

"I beg your pardon?" Her cheeks reddened more.

"The answer. It's jealous, I believe."

She read number three again. "I suppose you're correct. That does work with the "L" in RULE." She wrote the word into the crossword, not enjoying the small smirk on his face.

They finished the puzzle as the subway slowed into Stillwell Avenue station.

"Mind your step." He offered his hand as she stepped from the car to the platform.

She descended to the pavement and tipped up the brim of her garden hat, feeling the July sun radiate on her cheeks.

They followed the flow of people out of the station. The smell of French fries and shrieks from a nearby roller coaster welcomed them to Coney Island. To their right, a man in a striped vest hollered, "Step right up. The game's High Strikers. Test your strength."

She paused to look at the tall tower with a bell suspended on the top.

"This is the game that separates the men from the boys," said the game operator. "How about you, young man?" He pointed the long-handled mallet toward Hugh. "Price is two wallops for a nickel, five for a dime. Strike the lever and make the puck hit the bell. Win your lady a prize."

Hugh looked up at the high bell. "Perhaps later."

"Is the dashing Hugh Whitmore turning down a chance to show off?" She crossed her arms. "Could it be that you're afraid to take the challenge?"

"Never. I can easily hit the bell."

"Then by all means, let's see."

He handed the operator a nickel and took the mallet. With a look over his shoulder, he said to her. "You might want to stand back. My strength might demolish this lever." Holding the mallet like a sledgehammer, he brought it down on the lever. The puck barely moved.

"The lever seems to be intact." She called to him. "Should I still be in fear for my life?"

"It takes a practice swing to get accustomed." He widened his stance. Raising it over his shoulder, he brought it down harder. The puck leapt halfway up the tower and dropped back down. He gawked at it in shock. "How didn't that reach the top?" He turned to the operator. "Is this some kind of trick? Is this tower fixed?"

The operator lifted his hands in surrender. "I promise there's no trick. It's all about strength and timing. For another nickel, you can try again."

"Forget it." He handed the man the mallet. "Come on, Eliza. I'm famished. I think my strength is being affected by my hunger."

"I'm sure that's all it is." She held out her palm. "Might I have a nickel? I'd like to give it a try."

His forehead furrowed. "This is a man's game."

She looked at the operator. "Are ladies allowed to play?"

"Absolutely, darling."

"Excellent, I'd like to try."

Hugh paid her fee. "I promise you, it's very hard."

When the operator handed her the mallet, her shoulders pulled downward from its heaviness. "Goodness, I didn't expect this to weigh so much."

"Like I said, it's a man's game." He folded his arms with a dose of smugness.

Hefting it onto her shoulder, she narrowed her eyes. "We'll see about that." With a grunt, she bounced it off her shoulder onto the lever. The puck jumped three inches and fell back down.

He chuckled. "What did I tell you?"

"It's a practice swing, remember?" Planting her feet with determination, she swung the mallet up in one fluid motion and walloped it against the lever.

The puck shot all the way to the top, hit the bell, and chimed loud enough for those nearby to stare. Seeing it was a woman, they applauded.

She turned to the onlookers and bowed.

"Congratulations, darling." The operator gave her a little Kewpie doll dressed like a sailor. "You're a High Striking champion."

"Thank you." She turned to Hugh holding her prize. "I guess it's not fixed after all."

The muscle along his jaw tightened. "Perhaps not. I see a hot dog stand up ahead. Would you like to eat?"

"Definitely, I'm famished after hitting that bell." She watched his jaw clench again. She hadn't seen his competitive side before. It amused her.

Grabbing a couple frankfurters and ice-cold sodas, they

continued down Surf Avenue. Sideshow attractions and amusements flanked the road.

"Look at that." She hastened to a woman completely covered in tattoos. Intricate details of ink cloaked the lady's skin. Every inch, from her ankles to her throat, was covered in illustrations. Among them were a bald eagle grasping the American flag in its talons, faces of the presidents in the heart of rosettes, the wonders of the world, the virgin Mary, and cherubs. "Such artistry."

"If you head into the tent behind me, you can get your own," said the tattooed woman.

Hugh choked on a sip of soda. "A tattoo?"

"It doesn't have to show like mine." The lady glanced at Eliza's ring-less fingers. "You could conceal it for a later time." She winked in Hugh's direction.

His expression morphed from shock to contemplation.

The latter caused her to blush. "Thank you for the offer, but I think I'll decline." She walked ahead, noticing him pause to look at the woman's tattoos and back at the tent. He never struck her as the type to like such a thing. It made her wonder how well she knew him.

Falling into step with her, he shook his head. "That was something."

"Do you think they're pretty?"

"Tattoos?"

She nodded.

"Not particularly, no."

"Your curiosity seemed piqued at the mention of me getting one. Do you think I should?"

The question caught him off guard. "I don't think—unless you wanted— anything on you—though I'm sure your skin is lovely without—not that I'm pondering what your skin looks like." He looked away, clearing his throat.

She chuckled at his obvious discomfort. "Is that a yes?"

"Goodness, Eliza." He looked utterly perplexed. "Are you being serious with me?"

"Maybe."

He stared at her in silence.

The steadiness of his gaze gave her goose bumps. "Tell me what you're thinking."

"It's not right for me to say." He shifted his stance, breaking eye contact. "We're only friends."

She blinked. It was the truth of course. Yet the acknowledgment felt almost like a reprimand.

"Sounds like an amusement park ahead." He pointed down the street. "Let's find out, shall we?"

They entered through an arched entrance with tall Oriental spires and paid twenty cents to a female cashier wearing a bright kimono robe. She bent at the waist in a deep bow. "Welcome to Luna Park."

Walking along a broad pathway, Eliza marveled at the surrounding sculptures, Japanese gardens, and fantastical buildings. "It feels like we've left New York and entered a magical place." The main path opened out to a boulevard with benches and pergolas that overlooked a small lagoon. A boatload of screaming passengers descended a slide into the small lake and skipped across the water like a pebble. A man at the rear guided the craft to a dockside landing. "That looks fun," she said with wide eyes. "Can we do it?"

"That's why we're here."

Like a couple of children, they scurried from ride to ride. Shute-the-Chutes. Ferris Wheel. Carousel. Tumblebug. Aerial swings. Fun house. Even a ride on an elephant named Gyp.

"Look." He pointed to an enormous steel beast with a sign that read *The Devil's Racer*.

"Is that a roller coaster?"

"Yeah, you want to ride it?"

"Are you sure it's safe?"

"Absolutely." His voice held the enthusiasm of a kid on Christmas morning.

"Very well." She inhaled a deep breath.

After a tedious wait in line, it was their turn.

He pointed to a car second from the front. "How about this one?"

"It's so close to the front."

"That's the best. Come on."

They settled into the seat together, pulling a metal bar down against their laps.

Once everyone was seated, the roller coaster slowly clinked forward on the track climbing the high slope.

As it climbed, her heart sped up.

The Devil's Racer paused at the top of the first slope, edging forward.

"Isn't this great?" He looked over the side of the car. "People look like the size of your Kewpie doll from up here."

Her eyes bulged at the huge drop in front of them. Then it plunged. A piercing scream erupted from her mouth. She held a hand over her hat and with the other arm she clutched herself against Hugh. They sailed down the steep first drop, zipped up the next slope, and took a tight turn only to drop again. Her eyes squeezed shut. "Is it almost over?"

"Not yet. Open your eyes, you're missing it." He laughed like a young boy. "This is fantastic!"

The car turned a figure eight on the track and raced through more ups and downs before slowing to a stop.

She didn't open her eyes or let go of him, unsure if it was over.

"Eliza, it's done."

She pried open one lid. They were stopped. She turned her face to find his only inches from her mouth. Oh dear.

"Hello, there." He grinned.

Her cheeks blushed. She let go.

Standing, he offered his hand.

"I can manage." She stepped out of the car onto the platform. Her legs trembled a bit. Holding tight to the rail, she descended the steps.

Following behind her, he asked, "What did you think of it?"

"Whoever named it The Devil's Racer had keen awareness."

"Want to do it again?"

"Are you kidding?" She reached the path and faced him. "I felt like I was hanging on for dear life."

Dimples surfaced on his cheeks. "I know."

Her cheeks reddened again. "I—I couldn't help it."

"Don't feel embarrassed. If it takes a coaster to bring you close, I'll take it."

She smiled in spite of herself. Why did he have to be so darn likeable? Giving him a playful push, she upturned her chin. "We're only friends, remember?"

CHAPTER SIXTEEN

Wednesday, 5:30 PM

Hugh assisted Eliza into a small two-passenger boat on The Old Mill ride. Settling into the raft, they sailed down a simulated river through a wooden tunnel, illuminated with twinkle lights. He hadn't thought that she would come to Coney Island with him, but here she was. Though she had trouble admitting it, he knew that she liked him.

"I'll take this over The Devil's Racer any day," she said. "No big drops or feeling of imminent death."

"There wasn't any real danger." He leaned against the cushioned seat. "But this ride does have a peaceful quality that the other lacks."

She draped an arm over the side of the boat, touching the cool water. "I like Coney Island so far. Thank you for taking me here."

"Thank you for coming."

"I almost didn't. I thought it would be too strange, but you've made it easy." She looked over to him with a pondering tilt to her head. "I'm not sure how you've managed that."

"It's easy to be with you, that's all."

"You're too generous."

It wasn't generosity that made him speak the way he did. Flattery wasn't his style. He meant what he said. She was the woman he loved, and she was the woman he would marry. They were the perfect match. He was certain of that.

She noticed him staring. "What are you looking at?"

"You."

Her eyes widened, then she followed up teasingly. "Should you tell a *friend* that?"

"I shouldn't. But mere friendship seems an impossible feat when I look at you."

"Hugh, you shouldn't talk like this to me."

He stroked her cheek. "I know."

"We have to stay focused on the goals at hand."

He leaned closer. "What are those again?"

"Your business endeavor. My singing career."

He noted the slight tremble in her tone. "Ah, those." He tipped up the brim of her hat. "Who says we can't have it all?"

She swallowed again. "I don't know."

"Then let's try." He lowered his mouth to hers.

A loud boom outside the tunnel made her jolt. She knocked her nose against his. "Ouch," she winced.

He rubbed his bridge. "Are you okay?"

"Yes. Are you?"

"No harm done."

"Merciful heavens, what was that?"

Another boom sounded.

"There must be a shooting gallery nearby." He touched her hand, hoping to salvage the moment. "No cause to worry."

A ray of daylight filtered into the tunnel. A ride operator waited two feet away to help them out.

"Looks like our ride has come to an end," she said. "It's for the best. This dark tunnel has altered our sensible thinking." She gave him a shuttered look and exited the boat. "I think we've seen everything in Luna Park. Are you ready to see the other sights around the island?"

"Sure." He squelched his frustration at the missed opportunity.

They entered a congested street called The Bowery. It was lined with penny arcades, game booths, food stands, and thrill rides. The waft of fresh waffle cones hung in the air with the melody of mechanical pianos and barkers competing to take the crowd's nickels.

Hugh purchased two chocolate ice cream cones.

"Perhaps this ice cream will give you strength to win me a prize," she said. "My doll could use a friend."

"By the end of today, your arms won't be able to contain the amount of prizes I will win."

They wove through a thick mass of people. Wolfing down his cone, he stopped at a ball throwing game.

"Step right up," said the barker. "Hit down the pyramid of bottles and win."

Hugh took the ball in hand and lined up to hit the center of the six bottles. With a quick flick of his wrist, the ball sailed straight. It struck the glass with a ping. Like dominoes, all the bottles fell.

"Congratulations, sir." The barker handed him another Kewpie doll.

He gave it to her. "Now your doll has a friend."

"Impressive." She slid the miniature doll into her handbag next to the other. "Where did you learn to throw like that?"

"I played baseball all through grade school. I was the pitcher."

"I'm learning all sorts of new things about you today."

"I've gleaned some firsts about you as well."

She glanced at him. "Like what?"

He smiled. "I prefer to think on them a while longer."

"Insufferable." She rolled her eyes. "Why do I put up with you?"

"Because deep down inside," he paused, meeting her gaze, "you want to." He stepped up to the next game.

———

Wednesday 7:45 pm

Warren despised what he had to do, but it had to be him. When a man's card came up, they always sent a friend.

He liked Big Mel. Sure, he was loud and had terrible breath, but all in all, Mel was a good guy. Trouble was that he double-dipped. Tried to make an extra dollar and got sloppy.

He knocked twice on Mel's front door.

Voices arose inside.

The door swung open to reveal Fae, Big Mel's sweetly plump wife.

"Reny, darlin'. Come in, come in," she declared in her hearty Irish accent. "Mel's in the livin' room. Make yerself comfurtable."

"Thanks, Fae." He found Mel in his chair listening to the radio.

"Reny!" Mel's cheeks widened with his smile. "Grand to see ya."

"Same to you."

"How 'bout a cuppa joe so?"

"Nah, we better head out. It's a long drive to Coney."

"First, we'll have a quick cup then be on our way. Fae! Fix us some coffee, will ya?"

From the sound of the clanking pots and shuffling in the kitchen, Warren knew Fae was on it. His heart sank. Fae was a good woman. She loved her husband and happily served him. Tomorrow, she would be devastated.

Mel turned the radio down a notch. "How many companies we gotta check on?"

"About seven." He sat on the sofa, checking his pocket watch.

Mel craned his neck toward the kitchen. "Fae, where's that coffee?"

She hurried around the wall with mugs in hand. "Here 'tis. Good-niss. Where's the fire?"

114

"We haven't got much time, dear. Reny and I be heading to Coney Island."

Her shoulders drooped.

Warren knew Fae didn't like Mel's involvement with the gang. He stared at the dark liquid in his cup. If only Mel hadn't mixed deals.

Chugging his coffee, Mel switched off the radio. "Let's go." They exited the living room into a narrow hall.

"Wait a minute." Fae rushed around the corner. "Ya gonna leave without so much as a goodbye?"

"I'm still here." He opened his arms.

She hugged him tightly. "I wish ya didn't have to go."

He laid his chin on her head. "Ah now, luv."

"Promise me ya be careful."

"As always, Fae, me lovely Fae." A grin lit his eyes.

She gave him a soft push. "Oh, get on with it."

He cupped her face. "Don't ya worry. I'll be back in a hurry, just as soon as day." He placed a kiss on her mouth. "Good night."

Warren cleared his throat. "Night, Fae. Thanks for the coffee."

"Anytime, Reny. Make sure me Mel makes it home safely."

He tipped his hat and departed. Swinging open his car door, he sank into the driver's seat. His heart pounded.

Mel joined him in the car. As always, he held up the conversation solely by himself. "Ya know Reny, I've been doin' a lot of thinkin'. It might be time to head back to the old country. It's what Fae wants. She's been askin' fer years. I'd do anythin' fer her. She's me best thing in life."

Warren clutched the wheel tighter. "She's a good woman."

"That she is."

Mel continued to talk about Ireland for the next thirty minutes until Warren parked on a dimly lit street called Neptune Avenue.

He stepped from the car. "There's a speak down this way."

Mel followed him into an alley. "Looks abandoned down here. Which door is it?"

"A little further down. That one on the right."

"Bet a peeler never comes down here. Wouldn't have guessed a speakeasy be in this alley."

"Guess that's the idea. Make it hard to notice."

"What's the password so?"

Warren reached under his jacket, extracting his pistol. He sucked in a breath. "Times up."

"Huh, odd sort of—" Mel looked at him and froze.

"We know that you've been making plans with Zanneti."

"Reny, please. It's a small job. Nothin' that conflicts with our gang. I was tryin' to get some extra cash so I could take Fae home. She deserves it. That's all. I swear."

"You know the rules, Mel. You don't mix business. Especially with Zanneti."

"Don't do this." Mel lifted his hands, pleading. "Let me take Fae to Ireland. Ya won't ever see us again. Please, please don't do this. Not to Fae. Don't make her a widow."

"I wish I could let you run, but then it'll be on my head." Warren tried to keep the emotion out of his voice. "You know the rules. You know I gotta do this."

"No ya don't." Mel's voice cracked under the strain of grief. "Every man has a choice. Let me go home to me wife. Please, I be begging, lad."

Warren stood motionless. He watched the beads of perspiration slip down Mel's brow. Was there another way? Some way to spare his friend? His hand trembled. He had to decide. Now.

CHAPTER SEVENTEEN

Wednesday, 8:15 PM

Game after game, Hugh won her prizes, living up to his promise. At the end of the street, a barker gestured for him to come closer. "Step right up. Hit the bullseye and win. Best prizes here."

He handed the man a nickel.

"Sorry this game costs a dime, but the prizes are worth it."

"Seems a bit steep for a game of darts. Eliza, anything worth a dime to you?"

Her eyes fixed on an object.

He drew closer, noticing a gold necklace with a music note pendant. That was the item she desired. Handing the man another nickel, he received three darts. The game board was a set of descending circles with the biggest on the outside worth ten points and the smallest worth one hundred. Pinching a dart, he launched it forward. It struck the board on the ring worth 25. He threw the second dart; it landed in the 50. He inhaled a breath and threw the last one. It hit the bullseye and bounced off the board. "Wait, does that count? I hit it."

"Sorry, lad. The dart must stick. For another dime, you can try again."

"Very well." He dug in his pocket. He threw all darts and missed the bullseye again.

"Don't worry about it." She touched his arm. "It's getting late; we should go."

"I'm going to win you that necklace." He paid the barker a third dime. Pinching the first dart tight between his fingers, he threw it. It hit the fifty. He inhaled a slow breath. Lining up the next one, he snapped his wrist. The dart sailed straight and sank into the center circle.

"You did it!" She clapped her hands.

He did a small bow and spun to the game operator. "I'd like the gold necklace with the music note, please." Taking the necklace, he presented it to her. "Shall I put it on you?"

"Please."

Standing behind her, he hung it around her slender neck and hooked the clasp.

She brushed her fingers over the music note. Happiness settled on her face. "Thank you."

The expression she wore made his whole day a success. "The best for last." He popped open his pocket watch. "We'd better make our way back to the train station. It's nearly half past eight."

"Aren't we going to see the ocean?"

"We'll take the boardwalk and then make our way to the subway."

They climbed the steps to the boardwalk as the sun lowered in the sky. A few bathers sat on the sandy beach below, watching the waves crash against the shore.

"Do you hear that music," she asked.

He strained to listen, but didn't hear any. "No, I don't."

She closed her eyes, lifting her chin toward the ocean. "When the water rolls in, the shells clink together, making a tinkling melody. Isn't it lovely?"

He glanced at her profile. "Very lovely." Today had been blissfully painful. Her companionship reminded him of why he loved her and that she wasn't his to love, at least not yet. Grasping the rail, he cleared his throat. "I have an idea. Since we are both at The Gregorian, I wondered if you'd like to have breakfast with me tomorrow?"

"I'm leaving the hotel in the morning. I'm moving into an apartment with a waitress from the City Diner."

He straightened. "Is that safe? How well do you know this woman?"

"She seems very nice, and I can't afford to continue living at The Gregorian. It's too expensive."

"Maybe I could help—"

She held up her hand. "I'm not your responsibility. You don't have to take care of me."

"Your parents would want me to look out for you."

"You don't owe them anything, and you don't owe me anything. I need to learn to live on my own. Today has been fun and I have appreciated your generosity, but I will pay for myself from now on, in order to keep things in perspective."

"What perspective am I lacking?"

"The proper guidelines for friendship."

"I didn't know such a manual existed. Do tell me where I might buy it so that I can be enlightened."

"There's no need to get offended."

"I ask for a bit of literature and get accused of an offense. I fail to see the connection."

"I know very well that you are being sarcastic, Hugh Whitmore."

He stared at her, perplexed by her reinstated resistance, but he wouldn't allow that to deter him. "I merely want to abide by the proper guidelines. But seeing that a manual doesn't exist, you will have to do the educating." He stepped closer. "Or I fear I will continue to breach your etiquette."

She moved back a brisk step. "Rule One: I pay for myself if and when we go places. Rule Two: You will respect my decisions, even if you don't agree with them. Rule Three: No improper touching."

He grinned. "Define improper."

"Put it this way, conduct yourself as if you were a priest."

"I have heard of a priest giving a holy kiss."

She propped a hand on her hip. "No touching whatsoever unless it's assisting me into a vehicle. And your lips will obviously never need to contribute to that."

"That's unfortunate, but as your *friend*, I will respect these wishes." He gestured to the boardwalk. "It's getting late. We should be going."

"I agree."

They exited the bridge and wandered through Steeplechase Park, now lit for the night.

"Do you remember what street the subway station was on?" she asked.

"It was somewhere between here and Luna Park. I think it might be down this way." He pointed to a street just off Surf Avenue. They walked a couple blocks north but didn't see the station.

"I don't recognize any of these buildings. Are you sure this is the right street?"

"Let's head up to the next cross street and then go one over."

They turned right onto Neptune Avenue. The lampposts burned low, and the bright lights of Steeplechase Park didn't reach this street. The buildings no longer looked elegant. Most seemed abandoned or neglected at best. With the sun gone, the air grew cool. A brisk breeze blew in.

Eliza hugged her arms. "Do you think we should ask someone for directions?"

"I don't see anyone to ask." He pulled off his suit coat, draping it around her shoulders. "Don't worry, we'll find it."

"I think I hear voices up ahead."

He listened, but the wind made it difficult to distinguish.

She stopped by the mouth of a dark alley. "The voices are coming from down there."

He saw two shadowed figures down the narrow backstreet.

She hugged the coat closer. "Maybe we should ask them if we're close to the station?"

"I'm not walking down a dark alley to ask for directions."

"Please, I'm freezing. I'm sure they're harmless."

He huffed. "Fine." Inching into the alley, he stuck close to the bordering buildings. The moon cast eerie shadows on the brick walls. His palms grew clammy. Given the darkness in the alley, he couldn't distinguish more than the outline of the people. He wondered if he had made a terrible decision by listening to Eliza. Who in their right mind would enter a dark alley to ask for directions? The wind howled through the narrow passage allowing him to hear only fragments of conversation.

"—wouldn't have guessed a speakeasy—in this alley."

"Guess that's the idea—hard to notice."

"—what's the password?"

The second man outstretched his arm toward the other. Moonlight reflected against a pistol's barrel. "Times up."

Sweet merciful heavens. Hugh pressed himself against the wall. He had to get out of here. He had to get Eliza on the subway.

"It's small—nothin' that conflicts—I swear."

"—know the rules—don't mix business—with Zanneti."

"Don't please—think of Fae—a widow."

Hugh's pulse picked up. He shuffled to his right, praying the men didn't see him.

"—be on my head. I gotta do this." A loud boom thundered.

Eliza screamed.

Hugh sprinted up the alley, grabbed her arm and pulled her with him. As they ran, he looked over his shoulder. The shooter appeared in the street, watching them depart. Rounding the corner, they turned onto Stillwell Avenue.

"I recognize this street name," she said. "It has to be down here."

They jogged until they saw lights up ahead and a sign for the subway.

Hurrying into station, they dropped their nickels into the turnstiles and found a bench in the train car. Several moments passed in silence while they worked to catch their breath.

When the horn honked and the train moved out of the station, she spoke the first words. "Was that a gunshot?"

He stared at his clenched hands. "I think so."

"Those people in the alley…" Her voice trailed off, unable to finish the sentence.

He looked into her round, fear-filled eyes and knew the truth wasn't an option. "There must have been a shooting gallery nearby." He patted her trembling hands. "I think I overreacted."

"Then why didn't you talk to the men in the alley?"

"When I heard the gun, my instincts took over. But we weren't in any real danger."

Her shoulders relaxed. "You sure had me scared."

"Sorry about that."

A little grin lifted her mouth. "At least I'm not cold anymore."

"That was my real intention. Nothing like a healthy jog to warm up the body." He tipped his hat. "You're most welcome."

She rolled her eyes. "Only you would twist a blunder into benevolence."

"Why thank you. It's a gift, really." He pretended to brush a crumb off his shoulder. The act made her chuckle. She mumbled something about him being a show-off. He inhaled a shallow breath, glad he could divert her mind from the incident that had unfolded. If only she knew the truth. He had witnessed a murder. It made him wonder if New York City was a good idea after all, but as long as Eliza remained here, he would too.

———

The gun shook in Warren's hand. He had to get out of here. That couple would go straight to the police. He looked at Mel's body slumped on the gravel.

He had to do it. If he hadn't killed Mel, he would be the one to die. Lonan had strict rules.

Holstering his gun, he dragged Mel's body behind the nearest dumpster. Then he ran to his car. Sinking into the driver's seat, he scanned the road. No lights. No police yet. Throwing open the glove box under his seat, he reached for his flask. He twisted off the cap. He never wanted this.

The liquid flowed down his throat.

As a child, he had sat in a church pew, then he became an angry teenager who had left home. Now, he had veered so far from good and ethical behavior that he had shot his own friend.

It took a lot of scotch to numb the pain from his first kills, but he quickly learned to rationalize his actions. Bad guys deserve to die. He was doing the world a favor. He had to protect the rights of his gang, his family.

But tonight was different. Big Mel was family. He had trusted Warren, even up to the moment he pulled the trigger.

CHAPTER EIGHTEEN

July 16
Thursday, 9:00 AM

Eliza waved goodbye to the refinement of the Gregorian Hotel, hoping she had made the right decision to move in with Mattie. On the way, she had her cab stop at a five and dime store. The salesman helped her pick out a variety of cleaning supplies. Though she resented the idea of cleaning, she loathed the filth of Mattie's apartment more.

When she arrived at Hotel Griffin, the taxi driver helped her carry her luggage and purchases to her second-floor apartment. After tipping him for his assistance, she knocked on room twenty-one. A couple minutes passed with no answer. She knocked again.

It swung open. Mattie stood in the gap dressed in her silk pajamas with a cigarette burning between her fingers. "Eliza, baby. You're here. Come in, come in." She strolled to the sofa and flopped down. "I didn't expect you this early."

Eliza looked down at her many belongings. Couldn't Mattie have helped her bring something in? With a sigh of frustration, she hefted in her paper bags, followed by her two suitcases and hatbox. "I had to check out of my hotel room."

"I didn't think of that. Just set your stuff wherever. The bed on the left, side table, and two bottom dresser drawers are for you. Good luck squeezing your dresses into the closet."

"Okay." She carried her belongings into the bedroom and looked around. Every surface had a layer of dust. She wondered when her bed linens were last washed. At home, the staff put crisp sheets on her bed every week. They were fresh and smelled of lilac. All she could smell here was musty carpet and stale cigarettes. She cupped a hand over her nose, breathing in her lotion. She could do this. After it was clean, it would be better. Swallowing past her revulsion, she reached into her paper bags. Like she'd seen Neville do many times, she poured a cleaner on the towel and wiped the dresser, end table, headboard, closet doors, walls, and basically anything her hands would touch. After she completed the bedroom, she moved onto the bathroom with a can of Boraxo and a fresh towel. When she entered the living room, Mattie looked up from her magazine. "A deb who knows how to clean. Now I've seen everything." Chuckling, she returned to her reading. The comment grated Eliza's nerves. If Mattie weren't such a slob, she wouldn't have to clean. Never in all her days did she imagine she'd be washing furniture in an apartment. When the last drop in the bottle was gone, she trudged into the bedroom to unpack her luggage.

Unclasping the leather case, she pulled out the treasures Hugh had won for her the day before at Coney Island. With care, she set down her two Kewpie dolls, a glass bowl, an embroidered change purse, two bracelets, and an Oriental fan on her bedside table. The trinkets might have cost less than anything she had owned at Belle Vue, but they made her happy. Having something of her own made the room feel less lonely.

Turning to the closet, she rummaged through the crowded space for empty hangers. It proved to be another arduous task. Neville had always hung her clothes, starched and pressed on bright gold hangers. Now, she was forced to hang her dresses on thin hangers in a sliver of a closet, knowing full well her garments would become wrinkled. She wiped a droplet of sweat off her brow. It appeared that at any moment the garments would burst forth like confetti.

"Impressive." Mattie entered the room. "You managed to squeeze them in."

"They're in, yes. If they remain so is yet to be seen."

Mattie stretched out on her own bed. "Are you all unpacked?"

"Almost." With a slow exhale, she sat on the edge of her hand-me-down bedspread. She would have to go out today to buy new linens. There was no way she could sleep on these.

"I've been wanting to ask you who that guy was in the diner the other day." Mattie rolled onto her stomach, propping her hands under her chin. "You raced out pretty fast."

She hesitated to answer as she straightened her dolls on the table. "That was Hugh, the guy who proposed to me in Pennsylvania."

"That's him?" Mattie exhaled a surprised breath. "That gorgeous man is your ex-fiancé?"

"The very one."

Suddenly more interested, Mattie sat upright. "What's wrong with him? Is he a flat tire?"

"Pardon?"

"Is he dull?"

"Oh…no, he has a sense of humor."

"Is he rude?"

"Not too much. He can be arrogant."

"Is he rich?"

"His family is, so he'll inherit it."

"You mean to tell me that you *chose* not to marry Mr. Masterpiece?"

Eliza studied her trinkets and sighed. "He's a good friend, but—he doesn't understand the things I need most. It would be better if he simply moved on."

"So you're saying that *I* should help him?" Mattie's lips stretched into a devious smile.

"Good luck."

"I don't need luck, only my short black dress and red lipstick."

Jealousy pricked Eliza's heart, but she assured herself that he would never be interested in a girl like Mattie. "Go ahead; see what happens."

"I might. Say, you wanna go downtown? We could visit a couple of stores. Maybe buy you some new clothes. What do you think?"

"I do need a few things, but not any clothes."

"You sure? I think some new clothes would be a good choice."

"I promise you, they're not old. My mother recently had them imported from Paris."

"Ah! That explains it. Your mother picks out your clothes."

"In Elkins Park, I am the epitome of fashion."

"Maybe there, but here you look like you stepped out of a *Good Housekeeping* magazine."

Her mouth dropped open. How could someone deem her old-fashioned? It came as a swift slap. "I disagree."

"Listen doll, if you hope to land a studio producer, you're going to have to change to the modern fashions. Wide bonnets and barrel skirts don't fit this city."

Her words echoed Warren's aboard the train. She hadn't liked hearing his opinion, and she didn't like hearing Mattie's now. "You truly think producers will dismiss me based on my appearance?"

Mattie nodded. "So what d'ya say?"

"Can I make a call first?"

"Sure, doll. To who?"

"My lady's maid."

"Your maid? I can't even begin to fathom the life you've led." Mattie shook her head. "The phone is on the end table in the parlor."

Entering the living room, she picked up the brass candlestick telephone and asked the operator to connect her to Elkins Park 7759. She waited for the number to be plugged in. The line started ringing. She pressed the cone to her ear, listening for an answer on the other side.

"Hello. Belcourt residence."

She brought the tulip mouthpiece close to her lips. "Neville, is that you?"

"Jaysus, Mary, Joseph and the wee donkey!" gasped Neville. "I didn't expect to hear yer voice on the other line. Are ya okay?"

"I'm perfectly safe. How are things there?"

"It's been heated waters, me lady," she said in a quiet tone. "Nearly lost me job."

"Merciful heavens. What happened?"

"Yer mother pinned me on that note I gave ya at yer engagement party, but she's made me a deal in order fer me to stay employed here."

"What kind of deal?"

"I have to tell her anytime ya contact me or write letters."

Her upper lip curled in disgust. "My parents love to lord their power."

"It's not for me to decide. I need this job. Have ya called to talk to yer mother?"

"No, I called for you. I wanted to thank you for helping me and let you know I'm safe."

"For that, I'm most glad."

There was a rustle in the background and then a frantic voice. "Neville, who're you talking to? Is that her? Is that Eliza?"

Neville didn't have a chance to answer before Katherine's voice came on the line. "Eliza? Is this you?"

She drew in a slow breath. "Yes mother, it's me."

"Where are you? Have you been hurt or robbed?"

"I'm in Manhattan. I'm doing fine."

"Do you know how worried I've been? What you're putting us through? It has been five days! Why haven't you called sooner?" Her voice was hitting octaves only dogs could hear.

"I've been getting settled."

"Settled? What do you mean settled?"

"I found an apartment and a job. If I'm going to pursue a career in singing, I'm going to need to live here for awhile."

No response. She wasn't sure if her mother had hung up or dropped dead.

"Listen to me." Katherine's tone was firm. "I understand that you have dreams. You want to sing, but you can sing here. This is where you belong: with your family."

"Not anymore. I have to do this for me; I'm not coming home."

"If you don't come home now, you might never be welcome back." She paused. "How are we supposed to explain your behavior to everyone? Do you know what this will do to our reputation in the community? What this will do to your father's business?"

"I'm sorry that your reputation might be damaged. How terrible that must be for you. At least you have enough money to live comfortably; my inheritance paved the way for that."

"How dare you. This is foolishness, Eliza. You come home right now and stick to your commitments. You are a Belcourt. You have a duty to uphold."

"Those duties have ended. I'm not living for you anymore. Goodbye, Mother."

"Don't you hang up this phone. I'm not finished—"

She pushed the earpiece into the stem's clasp. She clenched her bottom lip between her teeth to keep it from trembling. Her parents were wrong. She wasn't foolish. She would show them. She would show everyone. She was going to be great. Taking a deep breath, she stepped into the hall. "Mattie, let's go shopping."

―――

Hugh sat on a bench outside the hotel with a newspaper in hand. He skimmed each headline hoping for closure. Last night, he had barely slept a wink. After he saw Eliza to her room, he caught a cab to the nearest police station and told them everything he had witnessed. The police guaranteed him they would contact the Brooklyn station to investigate it further.

He turned to the newspaper's last page. There weren't any articles about a man found dead in Coney Island. Did they find the body or did the shooter dispose of it before the police arrived? What kind of man would kill another in the middle of an alley? He remembered Eliza's maid warning him that New York City had a dangerous side. He wondered what that might mean for his business.

A checkered cab pulled to the curb in front of him. He climbed into the backseat. "I'd like to take a drive around the city to locate a good area to start a business."

"What kind of business?" The driver looked into the rearview mirror.

"A steel company."

"I'd recommend Midtown East. It's the best district in the city."

"Perfect. Let's take a drive around that area."

They wove through the streets, and the driver threw him facts along the way. As they rounded down Sixth Avenue, Hugh asked about businesses along the west coast of Manhattan.

"There ain't anything special on that side."

"Are the buildings residential or commercial?"

"Somewhat both. I doubt it's the kind of location you're looking for."

"I'd like to be the judge of that."

"Suit yourself." The driver drove up Ninth Avenue and turned onto 45th Street. They came across a large brick building bearing a sign, *Real Estate Brokerage Services.*

"A brokerage company." He straightened in his seat, excited by his good fortune. "Stop here, please."

The driver glanced back. "I don't think this is the kind of place you're looking for."

He squared his shoulders. "Correction: it's exactly what I need. Professionals that can help me investigate the real estate of this city."

"They're professionals, all right," he muttered, pulling into the parking lot.

"Please wait here. I'll only be a few minutes."

"It'll cost you extra."

"I'm not worried about the price." Exiting the taxi, he entered into a small lobby.

A pretty blonde receptionist looked up from her magazine. "Hello, sir. How may I help you today?"

"I saw your sign out front. Can I set up an appointment with one of your brokers? I'm new to the area, and I need help with finding a building and property."

"I see. Well right now, our brokers are out assisting other clients." As the receptionist reached for a business card, the door opened. "Hi-ya, Finn. Perfect timing." She gestured a hand to Hugh. "This gentleman's new to the area. He's wanting to set up an appointment with one of our brokers."

"Welcome to New York City." Finn offered him a friendly smile, extending his hand. "My name's Finnegan Hennessy. What's yer name?"

He shook his hand. "My name is Hugh Whitmore."

"Where are ya from, Mr. Whitmore?"

"Elkins Park, Pennsylvania."

"Ah, that's grand so. What brings ya to this fine city?"

"I'm looking to start up a separate branch of business for my family's steel company."

Finn's eyes widened. "Good, good. This is a great location fer a new business. What kind of property would ya be needin'?"

The attentive attention from Finn made Hugh feel rather important. He quite liked being the main man in charge. In Pennsylvania, his father led each discussion of business. But here, he made the decisions. "I'd say a sizeable building with some land around it. It'll need space for parking and shipments."

"Sure, sure." Finn nodded like he had a location already in mind. "So, when ya wantin' to start up this business?"

"It depends on how soon I can get everything arranged."

"It'll be an extension ya say?"

"Perhaps, but if it goes well, we might make New York City our primary location."

"Hope we can make that happen fer ya. I don't be our main broker, but my boss is just the man ya'd need. His name is Lonan McKenna, but he's not in the office today. Would ya be able to stop by later this week fer an appointment?"

"Most certainly."

"All right. Have ya got a phone number where ya can be reached?"

"I'm staying at The Gregorian hotel. You can ring me there."

"Sounds good. Why don't ya write yer name down here?" Finn handed him a piece of paper and a pen.

Leaning over the secretary's desk, Hugh wrote down his information. He held the pen firmer, writing his name with a stronger edge. As the man now calling the shots, he felt more alive. More determined. More ready to build a business and a life with the woman he loved.

A breeze suddenly blew in as the door swung open. A man in a tweed cap stepped inside. "Finn, amn't I glad to see ya. I done got some real trouble. Zanneti busted me tires 'cuz I refused to give him ear and now he's threaten' to—"

"Whoa there, Walsh." Finn held up a steadying hand. "No reason to get heated in front of me other customers. Whatever's the worry, we'll get it sorted."

Hugh recognized the man. It was the cab driver that took Eliza and him to the subway station yesterday.

"Sorted, ya say? Tell that to me tires. They're blown with bullet holes."

Finn gestured to the secretary. "Kiki, could ya take Walsh to me office while I finish up here?"

"Yes, sir." She led the driver out of the lobby.

"Is everything okay with that man?" Hugh motioned toward the departing cabbie.

"Ah yeah, just some business trouble. We'll help him get it figured out." Finn glanced over the information written on the paper. "In case we try to call ya and yer not there, I'll give ya our business card."

"Thank you. I appreciate your help." He shook Finn's hand.

"Anytime. Look forward to workin' with ya."

He exited the building, enlivened by finding the brokerage and troubled by the driver's dilemma. Who would shoot a man's tires? How could a real estate broker be able to solve that problem? Did that man say the name Zanneti? He opened the door to his taxi. Didn't he hear that same name last night in the alley?

The driver looked at him. "Ya get what ya needed?"

"I did. Let's continue on."

"Sure thing."

He sighed. Zanneti. He was sure that was the name he heard.

CHAPTER NINETEEN

Thursday, 1:00 PM

Three department stores later, Eliza still remained empty-handed.

Herding her into Fifth Avenue Department Store, Mattie pulled several gowns off a rack and ushered her into a dressing room.

Donning a lavender dress, she stepped out and looked into the mirror. She cringed. "I can't wear this. I told you I want them to be longer. You can almost see my knees."

"That's the idea."

"I have never shown this much skin in all my life."

"You need to start. It's beautifully smooth."

Heat poured up her neck. "I'm not ready for this."

"Yes you are."

"I don't like the style. It looks like I'm wearing a potato sack. How can this be considered attractive?"

"It's called a frock, and it's sleek. You look like a hotsy-totsy in that lavender crepe."

Eliza returned her gaze to the mirror. The dress was simple. It looked like a skinny, short-sleeved rectangle covered in small, white polka dots. The best part was the belted ribbon that ran below her hips. "It's a straight tunic. I look like I have a boy's figure. At least with formed dresses and corsets, I have some curves."

"Nowadays, girls don't want curves. The goal is to achieve a trim, lean figure. Girls are buying corsets to flatten big breasts and constrict wide hips, and you barely have boobs or hips. You've got the perfect body for the modern look."

"I'm thrilled," she said in a flat tone.

"You should be." Mattie gave her a soft pinch on the arm. "It's perfect on you. Besides, you need to start a new wardrobe. Try on the black evening gown next."

Sighing, she reentered the fitting room. When she emerged wearing the dress, Mattie whistled. She turned to look into a floor length mirror, and her cheeks reddened to a shade of ketchup. "This isn't appropriate in public."

"You kidding? You're the cat's pajamas."

She stared at her reflection in the sleeveless, black lace gown. So much skin. The other dress at least came below her knee. This one cut at knee-level and hung in soft drapes edged with beads. Its neckline scooped into a U-shape both in the front and back. If that wasn't enough, her legs appeared naked in flesh colored stockings. She had only ever worn white, ivory, or black, which granted complete leg coverage. She swallowed, feeling completely exposed. "Perhaps a different one."

"We're going to Club Fianna tonight. This one is perfect."

"I'll wear one of my own." She jutted her chin with indignation.

With both hands on her hips, Mattie expelled an irritated huff. And then, as if on second thought, a sneaky glimmer crossed her eyes. "Did I mention that Warren would probably be there?"

Eliza's posture straightened. Would he remember her from the train? If he did, he'd certainly be surprised to see her in this. She studied her reflection. "Maybe I will buy this one."

"Good decision. I'm sure Warren will agree."

In addition to three frocks and the black evening gown, she purchased a long strand of fake pearls and a gray cloche hat with a white bow.

"The way you tie your ribbon gives a message," said Mattie. "For example, an arrow-like bow indicates that you're single but you've already given your heart to someone. A firm knot signals that you're married, but a flamboyant bow indicates that you're single and interested in mingling."

"What kind of bow says, 'I'm unsure'?"

Mattie tied the ribbon into a large rabbit-eared bow. "Cloche hats are worn low on the forehead and hug your head to keep your bob nice and neat."

"I don't have bobbed hair."

"In a few minutes you will."

"Excuse me?"

"Ever read Fitzgerald's article in the *Post* called, 'Bernice Bobs Her Hair'?"

"I'm not going to do it. Absolutely not."

"You have to. It's the completion of the modern look. You have to cut your hair."

"My hair is all I have left. It's my crowning glory."

"It will be a glorious bob."

"It will be hideous."

"If Bernice could do it, so can you."

"Bernice was tricked into cutting her hair."

"True, but afterwards she felt liberated."

"I don't want to."

"If you're going to be modern, you need to go all the way. We're going to the barber. That's the end of it."

Eliza contemplated slapping the pushy broad. Instead, she let out an exasperated breath. "I don't want to. That's the end of it."

Mattie crossed her arms. "Do you wanna be a singer or not?"

"What does that have to do with my hair?"

"It has everything to do with it. You look like an old maid."

"I despise you for saying that."

"That's okay." Mattie hailed a cab. "You'll thank me later."

They traveled to a small barbershop near the diner. She looked around the small, sterile room. It smelled like bleach and hair oils. Three black chairs sat open for the next brave customers. A few unswept curls littered the floor. Her heart pumped faster. Taking a step backward, she peeked at the door. It wasn't too late to make an escape; just a couple quick steps and she'd be out.

"Eliza, sit over here." Mattie ushered her to an open chair.

Sitting rigid in the cold chair, she glanced at the exit. "I'm not sure that I'm ready."

"Trust me on this." Mattie touched her shoulder. "Image is everything. You have to look the part to be the part."

"Good afternoon, ladies." The barber approached. "What can I do for you today?"

She stared at him from the reflection in the mirror, unable to reply.

"She wants it bobbed," said Mattie. "A short bob."

The barber studied Eliza. "Are you sure you want to cut off your long, beautiful hair?"

She swallowed. "I've been considering it."

"Of course she wants it cut." Mattie rolled her eyes. "Why else would she be here?"

"Sure thing, ma'am." He picked up a pair of sharp, silver shears. A flicker of light glistened across the shiny surface.

Her heart pumped faster. She tried to take even breaths, but her throat constricted, limiting the flow of oxygen.

His hand gripped one of her ebony locks. Slowly, he opened the shears.

Her eyes bulged at the horrid sight of the pointy blades extended for the kill. She attempted to inhale. The scissors closed upon the defenseless curl. Her chest squeezed. Lightness filled her head. A slow agonizing crunch resounded in her ears. Then the fatal snip swished a single strand to the floor. She slumped forward, fainting on the tile.

———

Thanking the bellhop, Hugh picked up the phone at The Gregorian's front desk. "Hello, this is Mr. Whitmore."

"Mr. Whitmore, this is Kiki from Real Estate Brokerage Services. I'm calling on behalf of our business director, Lonan McKenna. He wondered if you were available for an appointment tonight?"

He was surprised by the company's promptness. It showed good management. "Yes, tonight would be fine."

"Wonderful. Lonan asked if you'd join him this evening at half past eight. The first appointment is a casual assessment to discuss your business needs."

"Where should I meet him?"

"Lonan owns a nightclub in the back of our building. It's a ritzy club reserved for special guests on a password only basis."

"A nightclub?" His forehead crinkled in confusion. "He owns a nightclub too?"

"It's merely a side business, and only open in the evenings."

"Do they sell alcohol?"

She expelled a sweet, melodic laugh. "Mr. Whitmore, this is New York City. There are numerous nightclubs, and they *all* sell alcohol."

"But with the prohibition…what if the police find out?"

"They already know. Listen Mr. Whitmore, one of the first things you need to learn about this demographic is that it's not Elkins Park. New York City is the place where everything goes."

He fell silent, pondering the situation.

"Are you okay with having the meeting at the club?"

While he found it odd, he reasoned that things were bound to be different. He pulled his jacket straighter and squared his shoulders. "Yes Ms. Jones, that will be fine."

"Terrific. Remember this password: Hardly Wet. You'll need to give that to our door attendant. We look forward to assisting you, Mr. Whitmore."

"Thank you, Ms. Jones. I'll be there at eight-thirty."

CHAPTER TWENTY

Thursday, 8:00 PM

"I'd like a scotch, neat," said Warren.

"You got it, Mr. Moore." Club Fianna's bartender turned to pour the drink.

Resting an elbow on the counter, he glanced over the crowd. The night was young and already over a hundred people filtered around tables while others swayed on the dance floor to a band playing on the stage. A hand rubbed against his arm. He turned to face a pretty blonde.

"Hello, Warren. I had fun the other night."

The bartender slid Warren's scotch to him. He lifted the glass. "I liked it too."

"We should do it again sometime."

"We just might. Enjoy your evening." Brushing a hand against her hip, he approached a corner booth where Julian and Finn sat. "Evening, lads. Checking out the talent?"

"Plenty to see." Finn surveyed the groups of women. "That blonde is a sugary litt'l lass."

Warren gave an approving nod. "She is…and was."

Finn whistled.

"Don't encourage him," said Julian.

"What's the matter, Jules?" He leaned back with a grin. "You jealous?"

"Not a chance." Julian took a puff of his cigarette. "'Member the time we went down to Chicago?"

Warren rubbed a hand over his chin, remembering the evening. "Four flappers, a bottle of bourbon, and a questionable container of chicken."

"That was quite a night."

"Indeed. I think it may be time for another trip."

"Sounds good to me."

"Why haven't ya invited me on one of these trips?" Finn set down his drink. "Don't ya think I'd like to come?"

"Trouble is, Finn, I don't think ya could handle it," said Julian. "Yer brain would probably explode out yer nose from the excitement."

"Yer off yer nut. I done had loads of girls. Just last week, I had two mollys show up at me 'partment."

Warren inclined his head. "And how are your sisters?"

"Ask me arse won't ya?"

"So I'm wrong?"

Finn frowned. "They're doing well." He threw back a gulp of beer. "C'mere till I tell ya, but there's a rich lad come by the office yesterday, wantin' property fer a steel company so."

"I heard. Got a meeting with him tomorrow."

"Ya gotta land this one, Reny. I told Lonan he's a big fish. If we can reel him in, we're gonna be sittin' pretty."

"We'll see." He drained his glass of scotch.

"Evenin', lads." Lonan ambled up to their table, wearing a pinstripe suit.

Warren nodded to him. "Looking dapper, as usual."

Lonan brushed a hand over his front lapel. "The wife bought me this suit yesterday."

"She did good."

"I thought so. Fianna's not crazy 'bout it, but hey, she's not crazy 'bout my wife either."

Warren liked Lonan McKenna. The man had style. Every night, he came to the Fianna dressed in a suit and a starched collared shirt.

Bending over, Lonan placed a hand on the table. "Gonna have us a meetin' later. I'll keep ya posted."

———

Eliza stared out the window at a plain brick building. "I thought we were going to a ritzy nightclub."

"It is, I promise. Don't worry about the outside. It's the inside that counts." Mattie handed the taxi driver thirty cents. "Come on."

She followed behind, feeling naked in her slinky dress and bobbed hair. It had been an unpleasant afternoon trying to tame her short springy curls with hair tonic and bobbie pins. She'd been suffering haircut remorse ever since.

Mattie stopped in front of a wooden door. A sign hung on the brick wall beside it that read "Real Estate Brokerage Services." Lifting a fist, she knocked.

Glancing behind her, Eliza noticed more people approaching. "Why does the sign say this is a brokerage?"

Mattie flicked her wrist in dismissal. "Never mind that."

A slot in the door opened, revealing a pair of eyes and nose. "Who's there?" The voice was accented with a thick Irish brogue.

"Hardly Wet sent me," said Mattie.

The slot closed, and the door opened. A burly, redheaded man allowed them inside a small lobby furnished with an oak desk, chair, sofa, and a coffee table bearing a couple of magazines. "Mattie, darlin'. I thought that was yer pretty face."

"Good to see ya, Red."

"Who's this pretty lass ya got with ya?"

"This is Eliza. She's my new flat mate."

He tipped his hat to her. "Grand to meet ya."

"Nice to meet you." Eliza dipped into a small curtsy.

His eyebrows lifted. "Well aren't ya fancy. A litt'l curtsy and all. Not used to seein' those anymore."

Another knock resounded on the door.

"Best get back to work. Have yerselves a good time."

"Will do." Mattie led her down a hall. "Just a tip, I'd probably lose the dip."

"You mean the curtsy?"

"Exactly."

Two black steel doors loomed ahead of them. A man in a tuxedo stood left of the entrance. "Welcome to Club Fianna." When he opened a door, the soothing sound of a saxophone and the warmth of yellow lights washed over her. The smell of sweet tobacco and vanilla twirled around her nose as they entered the enormous room. Dotted across the space were people dressed in sparkling gowns and shimmering suits…all drinking, smoking, laughing, and dancing. She soaked in the electric atmosphere, feeling dizzy from the haze of smoke and the dazzle of the room.

Mattie steered her toward a bar that extended the length of the back wall with stools tucked beneath it. Behind the counter, three bartenders plucked bottles from the floor to ceiling shelves and poured amber, brown, red and gold liquids into glasses. "They have everything here. Customers can name their poison and have it served up in a shiny glass or teacup for the sophisticated ladies." Mattie winked. "You might like that."

"Welcome ta the Fianna," said the bartender. "What can I get ye ladies this evenin'?"

"Two cocktails, please," said Mattie.

"Comin' right up."

"It's lovely in here." Eliza scanned the room. Pristine white linens and flickering candles decorated the tables, which surrounded a large dance floor. A mahogany stage featured a shiny grand piano.

"I know, baby. It's the bee's knees and the cat's pajamas all rolled into one. The owner, Lonan McKenna, knows how to run a swanky club."

"When we arrived, why did you say Hardly Wet sent us?"

"That's the password. You can't get in without it."

"What does it mean?"

"It means you're looking for a drink. Because if you ain't dry then you must be wet." Mattie handed her a cocktail. "Dive in."

Peering into the skinny glass, she watched tiny bubbles float through the glistening gold.

"Go on, baby, taste it."

She lifted the glass to her pink lips. It poured down her throat and into her chest like a thick wave of heat. She squeezed her eyes. "Ugh, that's strong."

"That's how you know it's good."

"What's in it?"

"Gin, lime, mint, sugar and seltzer water. It has a little woodsy taste because of the juniper berries in the gin. Don't you think?"

"I think it tastes awful."

Mattie laughed. "Try it again."

The second time wasn't better. It smoldered all the way down. "It burns."

"You'll get used to it. Sometimes change isn't easy, but once you get the hang of it, you will love being a flapper. Soon you won't even remember the old you." Mattie lifted her cocktail. "To us. May we live for the moment." She clinked her glass against Eliza's and drained it dry.

If her parents could see her now, they would begin paying penance for her soul. The muscle lining her jaw clenched as she remembered the conversation she'd had with her mother earlier. She watched the bubbles bob inside her glass. She'd never been good enough for them anyway. Why start now?

———

A slot in the door opened. "Who's there?"

Hugh stepped closer. "Uh...Hardly Wet?"

"Are ya posin' a question or statin' an answer?"

"No, well, I don't believe so. You see, I received a call from a Ms. Kiki Jones, and she told me to say that."

The door attendant grumbled under his breath.

His forehead furrowed. Did he get it wrong? Even if he did, they invited him here. What kind of establishment required a client to give a password? He didn't need this aggravation. He turned to leave, when he heard a female voice in the background yelling, "That's him! Let him in! Let him in!"

The door immediately opened to reveal a scruffy man and the receptionist.

"I'm terribly sorry for the confusion, Mr. Whitmore." Kiki stepped forward with an apologetic smile.

He straightened his jacket. "It's a good thing you arrived when you did." He gave the doorman a disapproving look.

"Sorry 'bout that. Hope I didn't offend ya."

He turned to Kiki. "If there is a next time, I hope the door attendant will be better prepared."

"Yes, Mr. Whitmore." She motioned for him to follow her. "I'll take you into the club now."

Hugh couldn't be sure but he thought the doorman said 'arsehole' under his breath, whatever that meant. "I'm looking forward to meeting Mr. McKenna."

"He's looking forward to meeting you as well."

As she ushered him down the dim hallway toward the large steel doors of the club, he couldn't help but wonder why a man who owned a real estate business would also own a club located in the same building. It struck him as odd. He needed to find out more about this Lonan McKenna and contact a few other brokerages. It would be good to weigh all his options.

CHAPTER TWENTY-ONE

Thursday, 9:00 PM

A woman in a long satin dress stepped onto the stage of Club Fianna, wrapping her hands around the microphone. As the piano played a somber tune, the woman sang. It sounded like the lyrics were spun from silk. Enchanted, Eliza stepped from her stool, drawing closer to the stage. She forgot about Mattie and the tables surrounding her. As she watched the woman sing, she longed for a chance to do the same.

"You seem to enjoy the song."

She spun toward the familiar voice. "Warren."

"Hello, Eliza."

Hearing him say her name made her head feel light. She took a deep breath. She didn't want to have another barbershop episode.

"I never dreamed I'd see you here," his gaze slid down her body, "wearing that."

"I took your advice and found Mattie O'Keefe. She's been helping me out. She took me shopping."

"I'll thank her later. I saw you enter, but it took me a moment to realize it was you."

She breathed in a wave of his spiced cologne. Goodness, he

smelled good. "You remembered me?"

"You're hard to forget." He stroked the edge of her jet black bob; his finger brushed her cheek. "I see you've cut your curls."

The skin on her face tingled. He had an uncanny way of stirring her. "I did."

"It suits you well. Not to say I didn't enjoy your long hair, but this is bold. You look stunning."

"Thank you."

"Would you like to join me at my table?"

"I would, but first I should find Mattie."

"She's already at my table." He extended his arm. "Shall we?"

As they walked across the room, she glanced up at her handsome escort. It felt like a dream. "This is a beautiful club. Do you come here often?"

"I do." He smiled down at her. "How do you like the city so far?"

"It's amazing, but there's a lot to get used to."

"Soon it will be normal. Have you made it to any studios yet?"

"No. I honestly don't know where to begin."

"How would you like to sing here?"

She stopped walking. "You could arrange that?"

"I know the coordinator. I could pull a few strings and get you an audition if you'd like?"

"Would I?" She put a hand over hear heart. "I wouldn't know how to thank you."

"I might be able to think of a few ways."

A soft gasp escaped her lips.

"I'm teasing, doll. I'll have a word with him in a couple of moments, but first let's have a seat so you can finish your drink." He ushered her to a far corner of the club where several men in fedoras and black suits lounged, drinking with Mattie.

"Looks like you've been reunited with your train companion." Mattie winked.

Eliza's cheeks flushed. "Warren remembered me."

"With an angel face like yers, how could he forget ya?" A lanky man with blondish hair stood up. "Name's Finnegan Hennessy. And what might yer name be, lass?"

"Eliza Belcourt." She extended her hand.

He clasped it. "A lovely name to match yer lovely face." He lowered his mouth to her hand for a kiss.

Warren shoved him back. "Don't even think it. These here are some friends of mine," he said to Eliza. "Next to this fool," he gestured to Finn, "is Mattie's brother, Julian O'Keefe, but we call him Jules."

Eliza studied Julian. He had the same defined chin, red hair, and green eyes as his sister.

"This is Sully O'Leary," Warren gestured to the next man. "Aidan MacSween and Owen Bray."

"Yeah, yeah," said Mattie. "Enough already. Have a seat."

Warren pulled out a chair for her next to Mattie. "Do you like your cocktail?"

"It's different."

"A good different?"

"I haven't decided yet."

"Keep drinking them and your decision will be made for you."

Finn donned a solemn expression. "I done found in life that all great things tend to end…except fer one."

"Really?" Her eyes grew with interest. "And what is that?"

He leaned forward. "Ya can always get more pints."

Her forehead furrowed. Definitely not the answer she expected.

"Spoken like a true Irishman," said Julian.

"Ah, but a true Irishman would give a toast." Finn stood, beer in hand. "I propose a toast to Eliza, our newly added friend and drinkin' companion. May the lilt of Irish laughter lighten every load. May the mist of Irish magic shorten every road. May all yer friends remember all the favors ya are owed.

I drink to yer health when I'm with ya. I drink to yer health when I'm alone. I drink to yer health so often. I'm startin' to worry about me own. But alas, here's to long life and a merry one. A quick death and an easy one. A pretty girl and an honest one. A cold pint—and another one! Sláinte!"

"Sláinte!" The men lifted their glasses.

"Cheers." Eliza clanked her glass against Mattie's.

Warren pulled a cigarette from his suit pocket. "Where are you staying?"

Mattie piped up. "She's my new roommate. I'm helping her get accustomed to the city. I even got her a job at the City Diner."

Julian folded his hands. "Yer livin' the diner dream as well, eh?"

"I need the job," said Eliza. "My training begins on Saturday."

"Perhaps I'll stop in and you can practice on me," said Warren.

"That might make me too nervous."

"In that case, I'll wait. Excuse me for a moment, I'm gonna walk over to our coordinator and have a word."

"Of course. Thank you." Leaning close to Mattie, she whispered. "Warren is going to ask the coordinator to audition me."

"That's berries. I hope you get it."

"Thank you for everything. If it weren't for you, I'd probably still be sitting in The Gregorian, spending my Father's money."

"Don't mention it, doll."

"Can I ask you a question?"

"Sure, baby."

"I've heard a lot of Irish accents since we've been here. Is this an Irish club?"

"Sort of. The owner is Irish and lots of his Irish friends come here, but there's a lot of Americans too. Like Reny, for example. He's Irish-American. His father is American and his mother's Irish."

"Who's Reny?"

"That's Warren's nickname."

"Oh. That explains why he doesn't talk like the other guys."

"Rumor has it that he came from a ritzy family." Mattie snickered. "In his home, he probably had to talk like a proper American."

"What about you? Your accent doesn't sound as strong as Julian's."

Mattie shrugged. "I know my roots, but I'm a New Yorker now. How'd you know the accent was Irish anyhow?"

"Most of my staff came from Ireland so I'm familiar with it."

"How nice of your rich daddy to hire all of us poor Irish immigrants to wait on your family hand and foot."

"They are all paid fair wages." Eliza defended. "And one of my dearest friends is my lady's maid."

"*Your* lady's maid?" Mattie released a derisive chuckle. "You say that like you own her."

"Merciful heavens, that's not what I meant at all."

"What's the name of your dear friend?"

"Neville."

"Is that her first name or her last?"

Heat rose into her cheeks. "It's her last because…because that's all I know."

"You never asked your *friend* what her first name is?"

She dropped her gaze to the table. "I never thought to ask."

"Because she's your *maid*, right?"

Her throat tightened with hurt. "You've made your point, Mattie." She spun her chair toward the dance floor, effectively ending the conversation. She had never considered asking Neville about herself. While she had treated the staff with respect, she had viewed them through the lens of their position. Servants were employed to serve. When she had wanted to talk, Neville listened. When she had cried, Neville brought a handkerchief. When she had needed help to run away, Neville put her job on the line. She inhaled a slow breath. It would seem that the only one who had been a friend in their relationship was Neville. "Do you think I'm a bad person?"

Mattie arched a thin brow. "Do you?"

"I always thought myself to be good."

"We all got skeletons, but they'll stay hidden if they're locked up, right?"

She blinked. "What do you mean?"

"Forget about it. You ever do the Charleston?"

Eliza hesitated, wondering if she should feel relieved or convicted by Mattie's answer. She chose to push it aside.

On the dance floor, couples jived to an energetic tune. Girls flapped around with their arms swinging and feet kicking. Beads bounced and bracelets jangled with their crazy gyrating movements.

The dancing looked positively immoral. Her forehead creased. Some of the couples' chests touched as they danced. She gasped as one of the ladies kicked up her leg, exposing the ruffle of her undergarment. Never would she dance in such a fashion. As couples shifted on the dance floor, she glimpsed Warren surrounded by a trio of women. She watched him talk and flirt with cool, collected poise. A jealous sensation churned in her stomach. That must be his game. He flirts with all the ladies. She turned to Mattie. "I'd like to freshen up. Where's the restroom?"

"Over there." She pointed to a hallway close to the bar.

Once inside, Eliza turned the sink's knob and dabbed water on her face. She told herself that Warren wasn't important. She only needed him to get her an audition. A few breaths later, she collected herself and exited the bathroom.

Warren stood at the end of the hall. "Care to dance?"

"No, thank you." She proceeded to their table.

"Have you ever done the Charleston?" He fell in step beside her.

"No."

"It's not as crazy as it looks. Once you get the main steps down, it becomes relatively easy."

"I don't feel like dancing. Especially *that* dance. Besides, you seem plenty popular, I'm sure you can find a partner."

"I could. But I'd rather dance with you."

"I only know ballroom."

"That's no problem; I'm a great teacher. I promise not to laugh, or at least I'll try not to." He winked, extending an open hand.

She hated the fact that his smile gave her goosebumps. Developing a will of its own, her hand lifted from her side and slipped into his grasp.

He led her onto the dance floor. His right palm pressed against the exposed skin of her back.

She flinched at his touch.

"Sorry to startle you."

"I'm not used to someone touching my naked back—I mean my bare skin—I mean…"

His aqua eyes filled with laughter. "The fact that your back is indeed bare only adds to the fun of this dance." Grinning, he continued with his instruction. "Now place your left hand on my shoulder."

Swallowing her embarrassment, she did as he instructed, feeling the firmness of his arm beneath the suit coat.

He scooped her free hand into his grasp, holding it level with his shoulder. "Partners can dance with space between them or with their torsos touching."

Her black eyelashes flew up in shock.

"But for training purposes, I think it's best to leave some space."

She nodded.

"The Charleston is a fast-paced dance. The music determines our pace. Try to stay loose and keep a hop in your step. First, I'll tap my left foot behind me. Mirror my movement by touching your right foot in front. When you step, swing your leg around like this." He demonstrated the movement, kicking his heel outward while keeping his knees bent in time to the music. "Then repeat this step with the opposite foot." He demonstrated again. "Let's try it."

She rocked forward, her footwork awkward. She thought she saw his lips twitch.

"Not bad. Let's keep going, you'll get the hang of it."

As they danced, she stepped on his feet multiple times, but he never complained. "I'm doing terribly."

"It'll come." He held her closer. "Relax. Feel the music."

In his confident arms, her body found the beat of the song. Forgetting her modest pride, she twirled. Her hem lifted as she spun, revealing more of her legs, but she didn't care. She was having fun.

The trumpet's outro signaled the end of the tune.

"You did it. You got the basic steps."

At this proximity, she could smell alcohol and a hint of mint upon his breath. "I guess I did."

He continued to hold her. "Do you want to keep dancing?"

"If you'd like to."

They completed one spin before Julian tapped Warren's shoulder. "Lonan would like us to join him."

He nodded. "I've enjoyed dancing with you, Eliza. I've got some business to attend to. Before I forget, you have an audition here at four o'clock on Tuesday. Enjoy the rest of your night." He strolled away.

She stood alone on the dance floor, staring after him.

CHAPTER TWENTY-TWO

Thursday 9:45 PM

Hugh folded his hands atop the boardroom's table, considering the broker, Lonan McKenna. Not only was he knowledgeable about the city, he also possessed a certain business savvy that Hugh found admirable. "When I arrived tonight, I had planned to hear your suggestions and then interview other brokers before settling. However, your expertise on the city and business management has thoroughly impressed me. My intuition tells me you will be the right broker to assist my family's steel company. I would be pleased to hire you."

"I be mighty glad to hear that, Mr. Whitmore. It will be our pleasure." Lonan leaned over the table to shake his hand.

A knock sounded on the door.

"I wanted to introduce ya to our other brokers," said Lonan. "Come on in, lads."

Several gentlemen filtered inside. The last man closed the door and turned toward the table.

Hugh's breath caught in his chest. It couldn't be. He stared at the man he had presumed dead. Five years had passed without a single word or letter. But now Frederick Warren Whitmore, his estranged brother, stood before him, alive and well.

"And last but not least, this here is Warren Moore," Lonan gestured with his hand. "We'll all be available to ya in whatever way we can. Let me assure ya, we will find ya the perfect property and building for yer venture."

"Thank you." He mechanically shook the hands of each employee. When he came to his brother, they paused, looking at one another in stunned silence.

Freddie lifted his hand. "Glad to have you on board." His voice sounded emotionless.

Hugh hesitated, seeing his brother felt like being reunited with a stranger. All he could manage was a thank you.

Lonan looked between them. "How 'bout we go into the club and celebrate with a drink?"

"Actually, I'd like to head back to my hotel. It's been a long day."

"That's understandable." Lonan opened the boardroom door. "We'll be in contact."

"Would you like me to escort Mr. Whitmore to the lobby and call him a cab?" asked Frederick, or as he now called himself, Warren.

"That would be grand."

Hugh followed his brother out of the boardroom and into the crowded club. Neither said a word as they wove through the sea of people. Exiting through the large steel doors, they entered the lobby.

Kiki sat at the desk smoking a cigarette.

"I need you to call a cab," Freddie told her, "for Mr. Whitmore."

"Sure thing." She picked up the phone.

"I think I'll get some fresh air while I wait," said Hugh. "Care to join me?"

"After you." Frederick opened the door.

The brisk night air greeted him as he departed the building. With a soft creak, the door swung closed. He shook his head, trying to overcome the shock. "I can't believe it's you. We all thought you were…" The last word stuck in his throat.

"Guess I'm not."

"We've worried these last five years. Why didn't you call, write, anything? You could have at least let us know you were okay."

Frederick scuffed the sole of his shoe on the pavement. "What are you doing here?"

His brow creased in confusion. Five years and this was the answer he received. "Starting a business, which is why I hired the company you work for. You didn't answer my question, Freddie."

He glanced behind him, and then at road. "I don't go by that name anymore."

"Your birth certificate says Frederick Warren Whitmore."

"Here it's Warren Moore."

"Why?"

"A new name for a new life."

"Technically, it's not entirely new, just abbreviated."

Freddie's lips pressed into a thin line. "Then call me by the abbreviation. This is my life. You can't come barging into it."

Hugh threw up his hands. "You're my brother."

"We've never been close."

"We used to be." He released a heavy sigh. "Regardless, we're family. A certain respect should come with that."

Frederick rubbed a hand against the back of his neck. "In New York, your rules of etiquette don't apply."

"Does family not apply here either?"

"I moved on. Things are different now."

"Moved on?" Frustration sharpened Hugh's tone. "You can't cast aside our family like a female fling. I thought by now you would have gotten over your anger. Whether you acknowledge it or not, you're a member of our family."

"The fact that it has taken five years for you to come to New York says you're doing fine without me."

"Our parents tried to find you. They hired someone to

search, but it didn't avail anything. We hoped you would call, but you never did. Mother has grieved over you the last five years. We didn't know if you were alive."

Frederick shoved his hands into his pockets. "The person I once was *is* dead. Time changes things."

"It doesn't erase bloodlines. Our parents will want to see you."

Freddie's expression hardened. "I don't want to see them."

"Why?"

"Don't you get it? I left." Frederick stressed the last word. "I was tired of our parents' impossible standards and sick of living in your shadow. But now you're here, ruining things for me again."

"Ruining things?" His eyes lit with anger. He stepped closer, his chin raised. "I hired your brokerage. Our family is giving your company business."

Frederick gritted his teeth; he moved forward so his face was inches from Hugh's. "Should I thank you?"

"Certainly not. Gratitude would be out of character for you."

"Grateful?" He uttered a coarse laugh. "For what? Our parents carried on about everything you did. How well behaved you were. How well you did in school. How helpful you were. They'd tell me to be more like you."

"That was years ago." Hugh scoffed. "Get over it."

Frederick grabbed him by the collar of his jacket. "Don't tell me what to do."

"Get your hands off me." He shoved him backward.

"You don't belong in Manhattan. This city will eat you alive."

"I can handle myself." He turned toward the cab as it pulled to the curb.

Frederick halted him, by clutching his arm. "Trust me, you can't. You're in over your head. Go home, Hugh. That's where you belong."

"I decide where I belong." He stepped into the cab, shutting the door. "To the Gregorian," he directed the driver. Five years with no word from his brother, and this was how they reunited. His hands fisted in frustration. He never understood Freddie. What would his parents say now that the prodigal had been found? No doubt they'd rush here to see him. And then what? Beg him to return? Ask him take his place as the rightful heir? Where would that leave Hugh? He scowled. Frederick didn't deserve it. Perhaps he should go along with Frederick's request and pretend he didn't know him. It would solve everything. If he wanted to be Warren Moore the broker, so be it. He was never much of a brother anyway.

CHAPTER TWENTY-THREE

July 18
Saturday, 6:00 AM

Sunlight streamed through the rectangle windows, highlighting the diner's faded ivory and black checkered linoleum. The air smelled of lemon floor polish and sausage frying on the range.

Eliza breathed in the aroma of her new workplace and swiveled on a vinyl-padded barstool. Today was her first day of training, and her first time having a job.

Mattie sat on a stool beside her, sipping a morning cup of joe.

The other two waitresses, Hazel and Fern, stood behind the counter stocking cream and sugar. Fern was eighteen years old, but her keen brown eyes made her seem older. Hazel had to be close to sixty, but she clung to her youth. Her shiny, butterscotch hair bobbed below her chin, and bright shades of pink rouge painted her cheeks and lips. Her eyes were accentuated with black eyeliner and mascara. Stuffed inside her uniform was a voluptuous pair of bosoms and hips. Beneath the layers of makeup, she supposed that Hazel had a rather nice face, even pretty.

At ten minutes past six, Mr. Smeeth ambled through the door. "Morning, gals." He parked himself next to Eliza. "I'd like to introduce our newest recruit." He placed his hand on her shoulder. "This here is Ellie Bridgeport."

"Uh Mr. Smeeth, it's Eliza. Eliza Belcourt."

"Oh, yeah." He rubbed his pudgy finger across the tip of his chin.

"I made introductions ten minutes ago." Mattie gave a dismissing flick of her wrist.

"Ah good. Then let's get down to business." He pulled a pale blue dress and white apron from his briefcase, extending the garments to Eliza. "I have some business to attend to, so I won't be giving the orientation. Hazel will give you the tour of the diner and conduct your training."

"Why Hazel?" Mattie crossed her arms.

Mr. Smeeth's broad forehead creased with annoyance. "Who else would I choose? You?"

"Why not? I know this diner as good as anyone else. I've been working here for five years."

"That's a miracle in itself. It's a good thing you're pretty." Turning his attention to Eliza, he continued, "Hazel is our longest standing waitress and the best one I have. She'll teach you well. After you put on your uniform in the bathroom, you can begin training."

Proudly clutching the garments between her hands, she thanked her new boss.

He responded with a grunt that sounded like "welcome."

Hurrying to the bathroom, she slipped off her frock and pulled the collared uniform over her head. She threaded her arms into the cuffed sleeves before tugging the dress down. It required a rather forceful jerk, to say the least. Fastening the top buttons, she turned to the mirror and gasped. The dress squeezed the lines of her figure all the way until it cut across her kneecap. Above her left breast were the words *City Diner* stitched in black thread. Merciful heavens, she needed a bigger size. She tied the apron around her waist, folded her frock, and walked into the diner.

Hazel smiled in appreciation. "Looking good, doll. You can

place your belongings in the cupboard under the register, and we'll get started."

She did as instructed.

"Here," Hazel held out a notepad and pencil. "These are for you. Come with me. I'll give you the grand tour." She steered Eliza through the restaurant, explaining things as they went.

Information streamed through her head: how to make coffee, the rules of table washing, sweeping, and additional clean up, how to take down an order and clip it to the line, how to ring in a purchase, how to stock the cream and sugar, how to make a salad, how to starch your uniform.

"Speaking of uniform, my dress seems a little small. Do you think I could get a bigger size?"

Hazel looked her over. "It fits you perfectly. Truth is, the pay here is crap. And Smeeth doesn't give raises none too quick, which means we're working for tips. My philosophy is the tighter and shorter, the better." With a nod of her head, she continued the training. "For our first customer, I'll do the talking as a demonstration, but after that, you'll do the talking."

The doorbell dinged, signaling the arrival of customers.

Trailing like a faithful apprentice, she attempted to jot down every word, including Hazel's hello and the specials for the day. While the couple perused the menu, they went to the kitchen to fetch the coffees.

"What have you been scribbling on that pad of yours?" asked Hazel. "I swear you're gonna start a fire writing so fast."

Eliza lips curved into a sheepish grin. "I'm trying to write down everything you say so that I can copy it."

"You're such a silly nilly. You don't have to say things exactly like me. You only need to welcome the customer, give the specials, get their drinks, and take their food order."

"You make it sound simple."

"It becomes simple. Practice," she snapped her fingers, "that's the key. As you get used to the drill, you'll begin to add your own flair."

"Flair?"

"Yeah, your signature. Your personal touch. For example, I have a warm, southern charm. I moved from Virginia to come to New York when I was 15. So I say hearty hellos and friendly goodbyes to every customer. That way I hope they'll come back to see me. Returning customers mean returning tips."

She nodded in understanding. "What about the other girls? What do they do?"

"Fern writes her name on a napkin for each table she waits on. And Mattie," Hazel shook her head, "does a lot of winking, kiss blowing, and hip swaying."

"It works every time," Mattie called from a nearby booth. "The guys love me."

Hazel propped a hand on her hip. "Yeah? What about the girls?"

Mattie grinned. "They like me too."

"Ha," snorted Hazel. "Your brassiere is cutting off the air to your brain."

"It's white with lace." Mattie batted her long lashes.

"Go cook a radish." Hazel rejected her with a wave. "Eliza, I'm sure Mattie's neurotic behavior won't be your type of flare."

Mattie snapped up her cleaning rag, sauntering closer. "Don't be so sure. You should have seen her last night at Club Fianna. She danced a pretty mean Charleston."

"That right?" Hazel's eyebrows lifted with surprise. "How'd ya like it?"

"I guess I liked it fine, but the dance didn't like me very much. I fumbled all over myself."

"Baloney," said Mattie. "You were a regular Oliver Twist."

Eliza laughed. "The only thing twisting was my legs around Warren's."

"I'm sure he didn't mind."

"Warren?" Hazel drummed her fingers on her chin. "Is that the friend of your brother Jules?"

"That's the one."

Hazel's eyes twinkled with mischief. "Is Warren the really tall, terrifically handsome one with a body that looks like it has been carved from stone?"

"You got it."

"Well done, honey." Hazel patted Eliza on the arm. "Every girl deserves a bit of fun. But one thing's for sure. The fellas that run in that circle are nice for dancing but heartbreakers in romancing."

She didn't understand this comment. Before she could ask for clarification, the doorbell chimed.

"Okay, it's your turn." Hazel steered her toward a booth.

Then she saw the customer. A surge of dread pumped through her veins. "Hazel, could I do the next one? You see, that man and I, well he's, I just don't think—"

"I'll take him," Mattie announced with a hungry smile.

"No, Eliza will do it," said Hazel. "Baby, there'll always be customers you'd rather not wait on, but it's part of the job. Let's go."

She looked down at her snug uniform and swallowed. Clutching the notepad in her hands, she strode up to the booth. Her greeting poured from her mouth in a single breath. "Good morning, welcome to the City Diner, today's breakfast special is bacon, fried eggs, and toast for twenty-five cents. Can I get you something to drink while you look over the menu?"

Hazel whispered softly in her ear. "Good job honey, but slow down a bit."

"Eliza?" Hugh stared at her, stunned. "You look so…different."

"I thought a change would be good. New look for a new city."

"I've never seen your hair short. Or down for that matter." Taking in her appearance, his eyes lingered a little too long on her short hem and legs.

She crossed a leg over the other to cover a shin. "They gave me the uniform. It's part of the job."

"It's really waitress-like." He smiled. "You look beautiful."

She blushed. "Thank you."

"Any time."

Hazel cleared her throat.

He startled, as if seeing Hazel there for the first time.

"Listen Christopher Columbus, Eliza isn't the New World. Can we bring you a cup of coffee while you look over the *menu?*"

"Coffee, yes, please."

"Be back in a minute." Hazel steered her toward the counter. "Who is that?"

She winced. "It's a long story."

"That bad, eh?"

"It's a strange situation."

"Would you rather not wait on him?"

"It might be better."

"I don't normally do this, but today I'll let Mattie take him. Lover boy can't seem to focus, anyway, with you standing in front of him." She waved her hand at Mattie who was ringing up a purchase. "It's your lucky day. You can wait on handsome in booth five. He needs coffee."

"My pleasure." Mattie sounded much too eager.

"Eliza, you can fill the salt and pepper shakers." Hazel pointed to the glass jars sitting on the counter.

While she opened the shakers, she couldn't help but notice Mattie's extra sway in her step as she strolled over to Hugh. The smile on her lips looked sweeter than the sugar she carried.

"Hello, handsome. Here's your coffee." Mattie set the cup in front of him.

"Thank you." He glanced toward the kitchen. "Isn't Eliza my waitress?"

"She's training and has to do multiple tasks. But I'm more than happy to help you. Anything look appetizing today?" Her eyebrow arched a bit on the word appetizing.

"Ah, I think I'll have the special."

"Good choice. I'll put that in for you right away." She gave him a playful wink as she strode away. Clipping his order to the line, she stopped beside Eliza. "Hey Liza, 'member when you said you wanted Hugh to move on?"

"Yeah."

"So you don't mind if I go for him, right?"

"I guess not."

"Great." Spinning on her heel, she wheeled to the kitchen, picking up a few plates. She distributed the meals table by table. As she crossed by Hugh, she cast him a sultry glance.

What a flirt.

When Hugh's order came up, Mattie swung his plate atop her tray and sashayed to his side. "Here you go. Anything else you need?"

He snapped his fingers. "I remember you."

"You do?" She leaned closer.

"Yes, you waited on me the last time I was here. Your name is…" He snapped his fingers again, "Mattie. Right?"

She expelled a merry laugh.

Eliza's eyes narrowed from behind the counter.

"That's right. I can't believe you remembered."

"You're the kind of gal a guy doesn't easily forget."

Eliza's eyebrows shot up. Did she hear him correctly? Was he flirting? In a swift hurry, she loaded the shakers onto a tray and moved into the seating area. She stopped at a booth close to where he sat, lifting one set of shakers onto the table.

"Thank you," Mattie beamed. "You're the kind of guy a girl doesn't easily forget, either."

His shoulders broadened. "Why thank you."

"Say, I have an idea." Mattie slipped into the other side of his booth. "You're new to this area right?"

"Yes, I got into town a few days ago."

"I thought I could show you around, help you get to know the city. What'd ya think?"

Picking up her tray, Eliza moved a table closer.

"I'm here to start up a business. I already have a broker to help me."

"He'll help you find a location for your company, but he's not going to explain the ins and outs of the city. I know Manhattan, and I'd be happy to give you a personal tour."

Eliza stifled the urge to snicker.

"Well…I am new."

What? He was falling for her ploy? She moved to the table directly across from the booth in which Hugh and Mattie sat.

"Trust me," Mattie touched his hand, "I'm a great guide. I could show you all the hot spots, the best restaurants, clubs, movies, my apartment…"

Anger rushed through her veins. She snapped up her tray. A saltshaker tipped off it, shattering on the floor. "Oh no!"

Hugh and Mattie turned to see the broken glass and pile of salt.

She dropped to her knees with her tray and napkins.

"Eliza, are you all right?" he asked.

She nodded vigorously.

"It's fine," Mattie flicked her wrist dismissively. "She'll get it cleaned up. So, how about tomorrow night? I'm off at five."

Hugh looked back at Eliza, who shifted to hide her embarrassment. "I have some responsibilities to attend to this week. My real estate broker, Mr. McKenna is showing me some properties for a business venture. But I could be open on Wednesday."

"That's berries! There's a restaurant overlooking the river…"

Brushing the mess onto her tray, Eliza stormed for the kitchen, but was halted by a customer at the bar.

"Hey little lady, I need a warm up on my coffee." He held up the mug.

She huffed. "You will have to be patient. I'm in the middle of cleaning up a spill." As she pushed open the swinging metal door to enter the kitchen, she heard him say loudly to his friend,

"Awful high and mighty for a *waitress*. That broad won't be getting a tip." Humiliation and anger strained her muscles. Every part of her wanted to throw down her apron and quit. She wasn't supposed to be a waitress; this was never part of the plan. She inhaled a deep breath to keep herself from tears.

The cook granted her a sympathetic smile as he flipped a pancake. "Don't worry, everyone gets first day jitters. You'll be okay."

"Thanks." Dumping the broken jar and salt, she sighed. Though she needed this job, she doubted that she would ever like serving. She pictured Neville, working day and night around Belle Vue. How many times had she wanted to quit but couldn't because she needed the money? And how many of those times had been because of her? She stared at the tray in her hands. Neville was a good person. She should have taken note of that sooner.

———

"See ya tomorrow, Kiki." Warren tossed on his fedora as he head outside. Halfway to his Ford, he heard Lonan call out.

"Reny, wait a minute." Lonan walked over to him. "Haven't had a chance to talk with ya about our newest client yet. Wanted to see what ya thought."

Warren shrugged. "Seems like he'll be a good customer once we help him get settled."

"Ya seemed a bit tense at the meetin' with him. Ever meet that Whitmore lad before?"

"Not that I recall. It seemed like he knew me from somewhere, but I honestly don't know how."

"He did seem to know ya. But yer sure ya never met the guy?"

"Positive, but I'm gonna dig in to it. I didn't like how he looked at me."

"I didn't like it either." Lonan's tone was sharp. "He could be a promisin' client. I don't want anythin' to mess that up. Ya understand?"

"Course."

"Good. If ya learn anythin' about him, let me know." Lonan weighed him with a critical look. "Loyalty means everythin' to me. Without that, what have ya got?"

"Nothing."

"That's right." Lonan gripped his shoulder. "Yer a good lad, Reny. I trust ya with me life. Yer like a son to me."

The words struck him. He had always longed for his own father's approval, but it was never granted. Lonan had taken the time to mentor him. He made him a part of his family. Warren didn't want to disappoint him. "Thank you."

Lonan patted him on the back. "See ya tomorrow."

He sank into his front seat, hands gripping the steering wheel. This wasn't supposed to happen. His old life was supposed to be done. If Lonan uncovered the truth about him and Hugh, the worlds he'd tried to separate would crash into each other. The outcome would be grave. The mob used families as leverage when they wanted something, and his family had wealth. If an individual or family refused to comply with the mob, they were taught a lesson, usually a deadly one.

If he racketed his brother, he would be putting his whole family at risk. If he didn't, his life would be on the line. He hoped that after their argument, Hugh would go home. There wasn't anything here for him anyway.

CHAPTER TWENTY-FOUR

July 19
Sunday, 3:30 PM

Hugh should have called home by now. He should have told his parents that he had found his ingrate brother, who he had changed his name to Warren Moore, and mentioned that he had found a brokerage for their business. Instead, he went to a car shop.

Since it was Sunday, he also should have found a church and attended like he had every other Sabbath since birth. But instead, he went to a car shop.

He should have rented a practical car, like a Model T, which would have cost 15 cents per mile. But instead, he drove out of the sales lot in a 70-horsepower, inline six-cylinder engine, deep red Pierce-Arrow Runabout.

Next on the day's agenda should have been locating a permanent apartment to rent, but instead, he headed to the City Diner to show off his new mode of transportation. Maybe Eliza would be done with her shift soon and he could take her for a drive. Maybe they could park near the river and watch the boats pass. Maybe they could replay the moment they shared in the tunnel ride at Coney Island. Today, he felt like anything was possible. He had a Pierce-Arrow.

Parking outside the diner, he entered the door with a smile.

Eliza stood behind the bar wiping the counter.

He walked, maybe strutted, up to her. He couldn't help it. "How are you this fine day?"

"Splendid. I love cleaning up after people."

He paused, absorbing her sarcasm. "I think you need a break. I have the perfect idea. How would you like to take a drive in my new car along the Hudson River?"

"When did you get a car?"

"Today." He pointed out the front window. "See that red Pierce-Arrow?"

Her eyebrows lifted. "You bought that?"

"Rented actually. But yes, it's mine until I bring it back. When do you get done working?"

She glanced at the wall clock. "Thirty minutes."

"Would you like to head out when you're done?"

She tossed the wet rag into the sink behind her. "Actually, I would."

"Great. I'll have a bite to eat while I wait." He noticed a shine of gold by her throat. "Are you wearing the necklace from Coney Island?"

She lifted up the music note pendant. "Yes, it's my favorite."

"It looks good on you." He liked that she wore it. Maybe next he could get her to wear a ring.

When her shift ended, she changed out of her uniform, and they walked to his car. He opened the door for her.

"This certainly is a nice car." She ran a hand over the warm leather upholstery.

"That's why I rented it." He crossed to the driver's side, started the engine, and drove west on 29th street. "How do you like New York City so far?"

"It has its ups and downs. I like the freedom I have here, but I'm not keen on working as a waitress. Nevertheless, I think my big break is coming. On Tuesday, I have an audition at a nightclub. If it goes well and they schedule me, my performances could attract a studio producer."

"What club is it?"

"Club Fianna."

"You don't say. I know the owner of that club, his name is Lonan McKenna. I just hired his brokerage to help me find a property for our steel company." He waited for her to comment on the sheer coincidence, but she didn't respond. He glanced at her from the corner of his eye. Her eyebrows were pinched as she stared at her clasped hands. "Is something wrong?"

She exhaled a slow breath. "When your father severs the partnership, will my father's company fail?"

His stupidity struck him dead in the face. What was he thinking, bringing this topic up? Of course her father's business was going to fail. Hector didn't have a clue how to run a proper company. Without Daniel to help him, he would run it into the ground. But he couldn't tell her that. That would ruin the evening for sure. "Your father ran his business on his own before, he can do it again."

"The only place he ran it was toward bankruptcy."

He flinched. "How do you know that?"

"My parents told me. Right before they told me to marry you. They said I had no dowry because my inheritance paid to keep the Belcourt Steel Company afloat." Her jaw twitched with emotion. "Did you know that? Did you know that I didn't have a dowry?"

He turned north onto 12th Avenue, glancing at the Hudson River out his window. It should have been a calming view, but, his muscles tensed. He didn't care a whit that she didn't have a dime to her name, but how dare Hector strip her of that comfort, all for the sake of his own pride. "I didn't know about the dowry, but it wouldn't have mattered. I would have married you regardless."

She studied him with quiet scrutiny.

He waited, hoping she would voice the thoughts she processed.

She didn't. Instead, she motioned toward the river. "I didn't expect to see so many boats."

Though questions brewed inside him, he welcomed the subject change. "It's a large river, which lends itself to easy importing and exporting. That's why New York City is a good place for business." He pulled up beside another vehicle in a gravel parking lot that overlooked the river. "Shall we sit awhile and watch?"

"Why not."

They sat in silence, watching ships dock and others depart.

"I recognize those men." She pointed to a group of fellas unloading boxes from a two-toned boat about fifty feet from them.

Hugh studied the men. They exited down a ramp onto the pier, approaching a truck parked in the landing. One face in particular stood out. What was his brother doing at this pier? "How do you know them?"

"Mattie took me to Club Fianna on Thursday evening. See that man in the white shirt and suspenders? That's her brother, Julian. The one with the beard is named Red, and the guy over there in the black fedora," she paused, gazing at the man, "that's Warren."

A slight chill crept into his bones. He didn't like the way she said his brother's new name. It had a ring of familiarity. "I met them on Thursday night, too. They work for Lonan McKenna. They're brokers in his business."

"Really? I didn't see you there."

He noticed a look of surprise on her face along with something else. Was it guilt? He thought of his brother and the way she said his name. "I didn't see you either. I had a meeting in their boardroom. Did you enjoy yourself?"

Her features smoothed, perhaps with relief. "I did. It was different, but enjoyable."

He opened his mouth to pry when a police patrol vehicle whipped into the landing in front of the truck where Warren loaded another box.

The officer exited his vehicle, pointing an angry finger at the truck.

Lifting a hand in surrender, Warren motioned toward the boat.

Red and Julian stopped short on the pier, seeing the officer. They set down their boxes and walked over.

Hugh rolled down his window to eavesdrop. Eliza leaned close to him, curious as well.

The officer pointed again to the truck's back doors. "Open them now."

Warren did as he was told.

The policeman leaned into the truck, extracting a green glass bottle with a shiny gold label. His expression grew indignant. "This is wine."

"Only the best." Warren grinned. "Would you like a taste?"

"The importing and exporting of all alcoholic beverages is against the law. You gentlemen are in violation. I am confiscating all of these boxes and fining you $400.00."

"We understand that as an officer of the law, it's your duty to fine us, which we'll happily pay. But I'm afraid you won't be taking our merchandise. We have a business to run, and there's no need for anyone to get hurt over a few bottles of wine. So this is what's going to happen. We're going to pay the fine and make a substantial donation to you personally for your consideration. Then you'll go on your way, and we'll be on ours." Warren pulled out his wallet, extracting several bills.

The officer looked between the three men. With a begrudging sigh, he accepted the money. "I'll let it go this time." The officer reentered his patrol car and sped away.

The three men finished loading their last packages from the boat, closed up the back doors, and left.

Hugh's stomach churned. How could his brother dare to

bribe an officer, and how could that officer accept it?

"What just happened?" she asked.

"They were unloading a shipment of imported wine, probably for Lonan McKenna's club, which is illegal. The policeman either didn't care enough to uphold the law or he was too afraid."

"Afraid? Of what?"

He was wondering that same thing. Would Warren have hurt the police officer if he hadn't accepted the cash? "I don't know, but it sounded like Warren's words held a threat."

"I doubt that."

"Why? How well do you know him?"

She shifted in her seat, looking uncomfortable. "Not well, but I didn't sense that he was dangerous. I think you might be overreacting. Remember Coney Island?"

Yes, that's exactly what he remembered. "Have you read any of the newspapers since you've been here?"

"No, why?"

"The headlines talk about organized crime here in this city. One article mentioned the mob."

"The mob? Like gangsters?"

He nodded.

"You don't really believe in all that, do you?"

"Maybe. It's a big city, it might be real."

"Marion Harris got her break here, so if it's safe enough for her then it's safe enough for me."

"You don't know Marion personally. Maybe it hasn't been safe. Besides, you only arrived in this city a week ago. How much can you possibly know?"

"I know that I need to be here. It's the only way to accomplish my dreams."

"What if you're wrong? What worked for one singer might not work for you."

"Rule number two."

"I beg your pardon?"

"You're breaking it. You agreed to respect my decisions even if you don't agree with them."

"So I should idly stand by?"

"I'm not in any trouble."

"I hope you're right." He rolled up his window. There wouldn't be any reasoning with her. She had made up her mind. He didn't know if the mob was real or not, but one thing was for sure, he didn't want to work with those kinds of men. He doubted that Lonan McKenna and his employees were anything of the sort, but he couldn't shake an uneasy sensation. "Let's continue our drive."

CHAPTER TWENTY-FIVE

July 21
Tuesday, 5:30 AM

Eliza yanked a brush through her wild curls. *Wretched bob.* She released an exasperated harrumph. Her hair was easier to manage when it was long. She paused. Or was it? Neville had always brushed it, washed it, and arranged it. Before New York, her maid had done almost everything for her. Yet Neville never complained, never griped, never scowled. She always wore a smile. Eliza couldn't say the same for herself. It had been only three days that she'd been at the diner, and she already grumbled about serving customers.

Pouring a handful of La Creole tonic into her palm, she focused on taming the animal atop her head. The onyx strands now hung in wavy folds around her cheeks. Today was her audition. With a nod of determination, she walked out of the bathroom. Since the audition was scheduled for four, she would go straight from the diner to Club Fianna. Now was her last chance to practice her song, *There'll Be Some Changes Made.* It was by her heroine, Marion Harris. The song couldn't have been more apt considering all the changes she had made since her arrival to New York.

In the living room, she snapped her fingers to the rhythm in her head and sang the song for what must have been the fiftieth time. As she finished the last stanza, she heard Mattie's voice pipe up from the hall.

"You're singing about making changes and strutting your stuff, but that performance wasn't at all convincing."

"I'm only rehearsing. When I perform, I'll dress it up more."

"How do you plan to do that?"

"I'll smile and snap and…" She trailed off, reaching for a better answer.

"My point exactly," Mattie frowned. "The coordinator isn't gonna give you a spot simply because you can sing. You've got the voice, but you need the appeal. You look like a turtle afraid to come out of her shell. Nobody wants a dull act. If you want this spot, you gotta prove that you're worthy."

She threw up a hand. "I don't know what else to do."

"What I'm trying to say is that you can sing. Now, you need to start performing." Her mouth parted into a sly smile. "That, I can teach you. But first, we're gonna need to free up some time." She picked up the phone and asked the operator to connect her to the City Diner. When the other line answered, she affected a weak, scratchy voice. "Hey Hazel, this is Mattie." She coughed a couple times. "Got some bad news. Liza and I are sick. We better not come in today. No one wants a waitress hacking on their food. Know what I mean?"

Eliza didn't hear Hazel's response, but from the grin on Mattie's face, she knew Hazel bought it.

Setting the phone down, Mattie turned to her. "That's called performing."

———

At 3:45pm, Eliza and Mattie entered Club Fianna.

A man in a gray blazer and flannel trousers waited for them. "Hello. Which of yous is auditionin'?"

"That would be me. I'm Eliza Belcourt." She extended her

hand. "But my stage name is Eliza Adrienne."

"Pleasure to meet ya, Eliza. I'm Jack Mullane."

She gestured to Mattie. "This is my friend Mattie O'Keefe."

"Might ya be related to Julian O'Keefe?"

"He's my brother," said Mattie.

"What a grand surprise. Jules is a swell lad." He waved his hand in a wide arc gesturing to the large empty room. "I coordinate the entertainment for this club. So Eliza, what song ya be doin' for me?"

"*There'll Be Some Changes Made,* by Marion Harris."

"Okay, why don't ya hop on the stage, and we'll get started."

She climbed the steps while Jack and Mattie took a seat at a nearby table. With each step, her heart pumped against her chest. She attempted to calm her rattled nerves with some deep breaths. Mattie's words on the ride over looped through her mind. *You have what it takes. Convince yourself, and you can convince anyone else.*

"Start whenever yer ready," Jack called from the table.

She looked down at the polished mahogany platform and inhaled one last, slow breath. When she lifted her chin, she shone with poised confidence. Swishing back and forth, her hips kept time to the beat of her snapping. In a low, husky voice she sang a cappella.

> *For there's a change in the weather*
> *There's a change in the sea*
> *So from now on there'll be a change in me*

Her feet glided across the stage, her eyes fixated on Mr. Mullane's face.

> *My walk will be diff'rent, my talk and my name*
> *Nothin' about me is goin' to be the same*
> *I'm goin' to change my way of livin' if that ain't enough*

Pausing for a moment, she placed a hand on her hip and grinned deviously.

Then I'll change the way that I strut my stuff

With a tap of her toe, she spun her hips around in a slow, rhythmic circle.

'Cause nobody wants you when you're old and gray
Baby, there'll be some changes made

Wagging her finger, she narrowed her eyes like a scolding teacher.

They say the old time things are the best
That may be very good for all the rest
But I'm goin' to let the old things be
'Cause they are certainly not suited for me

With a playful pout, she put her hand under her chin and swayed back and forth.

There was a time when I thought that way
That's why I'm all alone here today
Since ev'ry one of these days seeks something new
From now on I'm goin' to seek some new things too

With a whoop, she kicked her foot so high she wondered if Mattie and Mr. Mullane saw the frill of her chemise. Swinging her arms and throwing out her heels, she danced the Charleston around the stage.

For there's a change in the weather
There's a change in the sea
So from now on there'll be a change in me

She tapped her toes in front of her as she jived to the end of the stage.

Why, my walk will be be different, and my talk and my name
Nothing about me gonna be the same
I'm gonna change my way of livin', and that ain't no shock
Why, I'm thinking of changin' the way I gotta set my clock

She plopped down draping her legs over the edge of the stage. Laying down on her side, she placed her head in her hand.

Because nobody wants you when you're old and gray
I guarantee you…there'll be some changes made

With a playful grin, she nodded and winked.

Mattie bolted to her feet, clapping loudly. Mr. Mullane also stood, bearing a large smile.

Eliza stood, took a bow, and walked off the stage. As she descended the stairs, she also heard applause from the back of the club.

A man in a suit walked toward her. "That was brilliant, doll."

Jack turned to see the man. "Lonan, I'd like to introduce ya to Eliza Adrienne."

Lonan grasped her hand. "It's mighty grand to meet ya." Lifting her hand to his lips, he placed a soft kiss on her creamy skin. "This is my club, and I want ya singin' on my stage. Yer voice is fresh and has a unique style."

"Thank you." Her smile illuminated her whole face. "I'd be so happy to perform here."

"We be most happy to have ya." He turned to Jack. "She'll be a hit. Let's make it happen soon so." Lonan noticed Mattie standing beside Jack. "Mattie darlin, are ya the one who brought Eliza to the audition?"

"Sure did. She's my new roommate. Just moved here from Pennsylvania."

Lonan nodded in approval. "Eliza, there's not a finer gal to show ya the ropes of city life than Mattie. Listen, tomorrow night I do be havin' an exclusive party at me house to celebrate some new business mergers. I'd be honored to have ya both come. What'd ya say?"

They readily agreed.

"It starts at eight," said Lonan. "There'll be hors d'oeuvres and a live band, plus all you can drink. We'll see ya then." He tipped the brim of his fedora and strolled away.

Jack opened up his pocket calendar. "How'd ya like to do yer debut performance next Wednesday at nine o'clock?"

Eliza nodded. "That's wonderful. Thank you so much, Mr. Mullane."

"It's no trouble at all." Jack patted her arm. "Ya got a mighty fine voice. Most glad to have ya perform on our stage."

"This means so much to me." She placed a hand over her heart.

"Yer very welcome, dear."

She couldn't stop smiling. Joy welled in the place of worry. They liked her.

Mattie steered her toward the door.

CHAPTER TWENTY-SIX

July 22
Wednesday, 7:45 PM

"Mattie, weren't you supposed to go out with Hugh tonight?" Eliza looked out the window as Hotel Griffin faded in the distance.

"I wouldn't miss a party at Lonan's for anything or anyone." She applied another coat of lipstick. "I told Hugh that we'd have to reschedule. He said he needed to do the same because of a business meeting."

"Is that right? Did he reschedule with you?"

"Net yet. He said he needed to see what his week was going to look like first."

For some reason, she felt glad. She didn't want Hugh for herself, but she also didn't want him with Mattie. He was too good for Mattie.

The cab turned onto Riverside Drive, which bordered the Hudson River. Heading north, they passed several piers, boats, and the place where she and Hugh had witnessed the transaction between Warren and the police officer. The occurrence seemed odd, but she chose to shrug it off. There were bigger things at stake, like her career.

Slowing, the cab pulled into a gated estate. A long driveway led to a magnificent three-story granite mansion with gothic roofs and spires.

She blinked in amazement. "This is Lonan's house?"

"Something, ain't it?" Mattie looked ahead at the illuminated fountain in the middle the drive's circular end. "It has 20 bedrooms, 10 bathrooms, a swimming pool, library, art gallery, ballroom, and plenty else. Lonan hired a French architect to design it and another to decorate the inside. He has only the best of the best."

This intrigued her. Belle Vue Manor also had a French emphasis in accordance with the Belcourt heritage. Her father hadn't spared any expense. Her family's estate surpassed this mansion, but her parents both came from money. How could Mr. McKenna afford a place like this? Could a club and a real estate business be this prosperous?

"He's practically famous in Manhattan," said Mattie.

Her brows lifted. "How?"

"You'll see."

The cab stopped.

A man in a tuxedo opened their door. They walked up tiered stairs that led to a pair of steel doors. A doorman bowed. "Welcome to The Morrigan."

Eliza entered behind Mattie into a grand foyer with potted palms, flowers, and a marble statue of a war goddess. An attendant collected their shawls, then escorted them through a hall of tapestries and copper plaques of mythological beings. The hall had several offshoots that led to other wings of the house. At the foot of the hall, they entered a two-story ballroom with an ornamental plaster ceiling. Light from chandeliers glittered onto the marble floor, where people milled around carrying crystal goblets. Pivoting on her heel, she surveyed the entire room. "Lonan has impeccable taste."

"He certainly does," said Mattie. "And plenty of charm to go with it. I suppose that's how he hangs onto both his wife and his mistress."

"What? Does his wife know?"

"Of course, but she doesn't care. Why would she when she gets all this?" Mattie waved her hand in a wide arc.

"I hardly think a house makes up for infidelity."

Mattie shook her head. "Your innocence never ceases to amaze me. Like I said before, this is New York City. Things are different here; nobody's faithful. And if you are, your man probably isn't."

"That can't possibly be true."

"Trust me, baby, it is." She pointed to a divided stairway that led to the second-floor. "There's the man of the hour now."

Lonan McKenna descended the marble staircase and waved at them. He looked dashing in a shiny black tuxedo. He shook hands with several guests before heading toward them. "Lovely to see yous ladies tonight." He kissed Mattie's hand, then placed a kiss above Eliza's knuckles. "How ya like me home?"

"It's exquisite. Thank you for inviting me."

"The pleasure's all mine."

"And mine as well," said a husky voice from behind.

She spun to see Warren smiling at her. The temperature inside her body heightened several degrees. Sweet mercy, he was a gorgeous man.

"Didn't know I'd be seeing you ladies here this evening," said Warren. "What a treat."

"Lonan invited us at Eliza's audition," said Mattie.

"Is that right?" He looked to Lonan with arched eyebrows. "It must have gone well."

"It did," said Lonan. "Mighty fierce voice she has." His eyes skimmed her figure with appreciation. "A fine dancer too. She'll be performin' on our stage next week."

"This calls for celebration," said Warren. "I'll get us a few drinks for a toast."

"My apologies, but I regret that I must excuse myself." Lonan gestured to the crowd, "A host has to welcome his guests."

"Of course. Thank you again for inviting me to your home, Mr. McKenna. It's beautiful."

"Yer most welcome. Reny will see that ya have yerself a marvelous time."

"That I will." Warren gestured to the bar at the far end of the ballroom. "Shall we get some drinks?"

"You two go on without me," said Mattie. "I have people to meet." Spinning on her heel, she sashayed to a gentleman in a suit.

Warren ushered her through the crowded ballroom until they reached Lonan's luxurious bar. With liquids of every color, it looked a lot like his club. "What would you like?"

"Surprise me," she said.

"Do you like wine?"

"Is it bitter?"

"No, this one is on the sweeter side. Trust me, it's the best. You'll love it." He gestured to the tuxedoed bartender. "A glass of the house special for the lady, and a scotch for me."

The man nodded, pulling a green bottle with a shiny gold label off of the shelf.

She immediately recognized it as one of the bottles that the police officer was going to confiscate, until he took the bribe. She wished Warren hadn't chosen this particular wine for her, drinking it felt like she would be tied to the misconduct, but she didn't dare tell him no.

Leaning an arm on the bar, Warren looked around the room with an air of appreciation. "Lonan knows how to throw a party."

She watched couples dancing in time with the pianist and jazz quintet. "It seems like it."

Receiving their drinks, he handed her a goblet of wine. "Would you like to sit outside on the patio?"

"Lead the way." She took his extended arm.

The sweet melodies of the saxophone, clarinet, and flute followed them through a set of doors that led outside.

Wrought-iron tables dotted Lonan's expansive cobblestone patio. Lanterns along the perimeter of the courtyard wrapped it in a soft yellow glow.

Warren escorted her to a table, pulling out a chair. She settled into it. "Now for a toast," he said, scooting his chair closer to hers. "'Course, I'm no Finn Hennessy, but I'll do my best." He lifted his glass. "To you, Eliza, for leaving home to chase your dreams. Though it might come with hardships, if you persevere, your dreams will come true. To you."

They chimed their glasses. He threw back half of his scotch.

She stared at her goblet of wine, struggling to bring it to her lips.

"Is something wrong?"

Yes, this wine was tainted with crime. But she couldn't tell him that. Although, she had to admit, she had already broken the prohibition law; she had drunk a cocktail at the club. The alcohol in that drink was probably obtained the very same way as this wine. The pressure of his gaze made her uncomfortable. If the policeman didn't object, why should she? "Nothing's wrong." She sipped the red wine. It was sweet, better than anything she'd tried before. "It's delicious."

"I knew you'd like it." He finished the rest of his scotch. "I'm looking forward to hearing you sing."

"It wouldn't have happened without you. It means more than you could ever know." In her high society world, none of the men believed in her dreams and none wanted to help her achieve them, including Hugh. But Warren was different. He wanted to help her. For that, she liked him all the more.

"I'm glad I could be of service. When did Jack schedule you?"

"Next Wednesday."

"What time?"

"Nine."

"Good slot. He must have liked you."

"I guess so."

"It's no surprise. I couldn't imagine anyone not liking you." He smiled. "Even with the modern updates, you still stand out. I mean that in the best way."

"How do I stand out?"

"You have this way about you. The way you move, the way you talk. You have an elegant innocence. No one in New York City has that. But you," he placed his hand on the back of her chair, inclining his head close enough that his lips could erase the gap in a second, "you are one of kind."

She stared at his mouth. "I'm glad you think so."

"Could I take you to dinner sometime?"

"I'd love that."

His smile broadened. "I hoped you'd say that."

A curvy waitress in a short dress and apron interrupted them. "I'm making my last round. Would you like another hors d'oeuvre from my tray?" She looked straight at Warren as she asked the question.

Eliza thought she saw his gaze skim down the waitress before it landed on her tray.

"I'd like that." He lifted a miniature skewer. "Thank you."

"My pleasure." The waitress smiled at him. She inattentively offered the tray to Eliza. "And you, miss?"

How dare this lady flirt with Warren in front of her. "No thank you."

Shrugging, the waitress left, casting one glance over her shoulder.

He ate his appetizer and stood. "It's getting chilly. We'd better head inside." He offered his arm.

"All right."

Before they reentered ballroom, Mattie stepped outside, linked arm in arm with Hugh. "Eliza! Look who I found. Guess we're having our date after all."

Eliza's bottom lip dropped open. She hadn't expected to see Hugh, here, looking exceptionally handsome in a black tuxedo.

"I didn't know you'd be here." Hugh looked from Eliza to Warren and back to her.

"I didn't know you would be either."

"Lonan invited me, since he's my real estate broker."

"Lonan invited me also. I'm going to be singing at his club next Wednesday."

"That's wonderful." His dimples surfaced. "I knew they'd like you."

"Thank you." She felt Warren's eyes on her, but she didn't offer any explanation.

"Hugh and I were just coming out for some fresh air. Looks like you were about to head inside. Don't let us intrude on your evening," said Mattie, giving Hugh's arm a slight tug away from Eliza.

"You can join us if you'd like," said Hugh, looking directly at Eliza.

She noticed Mattie frown. "Well…" She glanced at Warren.

"We were about to dance." He placed his hand on her back. "Shall we?"

Hugh's eyebrows pinched. His displeasure with Warren's closeness was palpable. "Maybe she'd rather not."

A corner of Warren's mouth twitched. "I think she would."

Eliza looked between their faces with confusion.

"Hugh, let her dance. Come on." Mattie gave his arm another pull.

He didn't move.

Though he said they were only friends, she had the feeling that Hugh still wanted more. She looked up at Warren. "Actually, I would like to dance."

Hugh's hopeful expression fell into a frown.

Warren cast him a triumphant smirk.

Mattie's irritation was transparent.

"Excuse us," said Warren.

As he led her into the ballroom, she stole a peek behind her. She met Hugh's eyes. Feeling a spark of guilt, she looked away. She shouldn't feel bad. They were only friends. Nothing more.

CHAPTER TWENTY-SEVEN

July 23
Thursday, 8:00 AM

The diner's telephone rang several times before Mattie finally picked it up. "Hello, this is Mattie."

"It's Warren. Is Eliza there with you?"

"Nah, she has off today. Visiting some studio. Want me to give her a message?"

"Actually I called to speak with you."

"What'd ya need?"

"Does Eliza know what I do for a living? Does she know about the McKennas?"

Mattie stopped twirling. "I don't think so. I haven't told her."

"Good. I don't want her knowing. At least not yet."

"That's fine and all, but what about Hugh? He's gonna know soon enough." Her tone contained a bite.

"What do you mean?"

"Don't play dumb with me, Reny. I know how it works. A new guy comes to town. He's wealthy and looking to start a business. You guys sweep in all nice. He thinks a real estate brokerage is helping him, but he ain't got a clue. He don't know that soon he's going to be helping you. Hugh's the next one you're gonna racket, am I right?"

He paused. "Seems you already know the answer."

"Seems I do," she sighed. "I understand the way things work, but sometimes I wish Jules never got into it. We needed the money after…" she stopped short. "Tell me, what is this I hear about you asking out my roommate?"

"Last I knew, it was okay to ask a single lady out for dinner."

"It is, but Eliza's not another single lady. She ain't like the other girls you date. I don't want you hurting her."

"I have no intentions of hurting her."

"Keep it that way."

"I will, but don't tell her."

"I'll keep it sealed as long as you treat her right."

"Always. And Mattie…it's best if you don't let on to Hugh about the McKennas either."

She huffed. "Oh I know."

"Yeah, okay. How does Eliza know Hugh anyhow?"

"Ask her yourself. I got customers waiting." She hung up the phone.

———

The door clanged behind Eliza as she stepped into Feran's Studio. She approached the receptionist. "Hello, my name is Eliza Belcourt. I'd like to speak with the manager here."

The middle-aged receptionist peered over the rim of her glasses. "Do you have an appointment?"

"I do not." She spoke in a bright voice. "But I'd be happy to set one up."

The receptionist flopped open a notebook and turned pages. September, October, and then November passed.

She bit the inside of her lip. He sure was busy.

Down the hall, two male voices boomed with laughter. "Yeah George, that sounds terrific. We'll pencil you in for next week." The men emerged into the lobby. A stubby man with a pointy nose and small onyx eyes walked to the receptionist, asking what he had available on the calendar.

She thumbed back to September. "You could do Wednesday at two."

"How's that sound, George?"

"Sounds like a go. We'll talk more then. Thanks." He nodded and exited the building.

Eliza wondered if the man beside the receptionist was the manager. If his schedule was open next week for George, why did she have to wait until December? She took a deep breath and turned to the man. "Hello, my name's Eliza Belcourt. Are you the manager of this studio?"

He exhaled an irritated breath. "Yes I am."

"I couldn't help but overhear that you're available next week to speak with George," she motioned toward the door. "But for me, there's no available dates until December. I wondered if there was a way I could speak with you sooner?"

The manager stepped around the desk, measuring her with his gaze. "What would you like to speak with me about?"

"I wanted to discuss a potential record. I'm a singer, and I've already written several original pieces. I thought maybe I could show them to you."

"Well…" He checked his watch. "Tell ya what. How'd you like to have lunch with me today? I know a great place a few blocks away."

"That would be great. Thank you very much."

"My name's Harris Feran." He shook her hand. "Come with me. My car is parked around back."

Walking onto the sunny sidewalk, Feran led her to a long, burgundy Chevrolet. He opened the door and helped her inside. His fingers brushed the top of her thigh as he released her hand.

The touch surprised her, but she assured herself it was an accident. Feran's crazy driving also shocked her. She clung to her seat as he steered between cars and whipped into the restaurant's parking lot. Feeling slightly seasick, she climbed out of the car.

Throwing his door shut, Feran saddled up next to her. "Cars and gals. Both can give a smooth ride."

Her stomach churned. She drew in a deep breath.

"Come on, honey. I haven't got all day." He opened the door for himself and breezed inside.

She caught the door before it closed in her face.

After a hostess showed them to a table, he brushed an oily strand of hair off his brow. "Tell me about yourself."

Determined to prevail, she launched into her story about moving from Pennsylvania in pursuit of a singing career. "I'd love to show you my songs."

His tongue brushed against the front of his teeth. "We might be able to work something out."

Her smile faltered.

The waiter arrived with two glasses of ice water and menus.

As Eliza perused her choices, she felt Feran perusing her. She looked up. "What's good here?"

"Everything's fine, but I'm sure nothing on the menu would be as satisfying as you." He reached under the table, glided a hand over her knee, and grabbed her thigh.

She gasped, shoving his hand aside.

Her resistance didn't faze him. "I have an apartment not far from here. Why don't we skip lunch and talk more there? Perhaps we could come to an arrangement."

Springing to her feet in horror, she flung her glass of water onto his lap. "Arrange this, you vile man!"

He howled as it soaked through his trousers.

Racing out of the restaurant, she ran down the sidewalk, shaking with anger and fear. She didn't see any taxis. Glancing backward, she darted around the corner. As she continued to sprint, her heel slipped into a hole. Her ankle swiveled, and she crashed to the cement. Pain shot up her calf. Looking at her ankle, she found it swelling and her shoe heel broken. Cringing, she scanned the street. Not a single cab. She pulled off both shoes and struggled to stand. Her twisted ankle throbbed under the weight of her body. Straining against the pain, she limped forward.

A car pulled onto the street. She turned to see if it was a taxi. Her heart lurched in panic; Feran's monstrous car sped toward her. She limped faster and faster, terror masking the pain.

He drove alongside her. Pointing his stubby finger, he yelled through his open window, "You made a big mistake, you little broad! You'll never have a singing career, I can promise you that." Stomping on the gas, he left her in a cloud of exhaust.

"I will, you repulsive jerk! I can promise you that!" She threw her shoes after him, screaming. Turning around, she hobbled back toward the restaurant in order to use the phone to call a cab. Nearly reaching the corner, she paused as a Ford roadster pulled up to the curb. Wearily, she faced it.

Lonan McKenna rolled down his window. "Eliza?"

"Mr. McKenna?"

"What in heaven's name are ya doin' out here by yerself? Please get in the car 'n let me drive ya home." Not waiting for a response, he stepped out of his vehicle and offered his arm.

She took it, relieved to be saved. Tears suddenly filled her eyes.

"Don't ya worry now, lass." Helping her to the passenger side, he noted her limp and snagged stockings. "What happened to ya? Where're yer shoes?" He opened the door.

She sank into the seat, whimpering. "I threw them."

"Why?"

"Because he threatened me, chased me, and there were no cabs." Tears rolled down her cheeks. She tucked her face into her hands.

Lonan patted her shoulder. "Now, now. Calm down, darlin'. How 'bout ya first tell me where to take ya."

"M-my ap-partment. Is 502 W-west 35th Street. Hotel Griffin."

"Okay, doll." He closed her door, walked around the back, and climbed into his seat. Driving down the road, he turned the corner. "Now, who threatened ya?"

"Harris Feran." She wiped her face with her palms. "I went to his studio today because I want to make an album. Harris said he would like to talk to me over lunch, but all he really wanted to do was…" Her voice caught in her throat. "I felt humiliated and violated. I poured my glass of water on his lap, ran out of the diner, and twisted my ankle. He came after me, threatened me, and I threw my shoes."

His compassionate expression morphed into anger. "That scum had no right to treat ya like that. I'll have Red pay him a visit. Feran needs to be reminded of how we treat ladies."

"I doubt anyone can teach him manners."

"Trust me. Red's deadly convincin'."

She wondered what Red would do to Feran, and how Lonan had the power to assign such a task. Whatever the answer, she hoped Feran learned what it felt like to be scared.

Lonan pulled into the lot of her apartment and turned off the car. "I be friends with the owner of Swift's Music Studio. Gonna tell him to come to the Fianna and watch ya perform next Wednesday. If he likes what he sees, maybe we can get ya a contract."

"Really?" Light reentered her eyes. "You're my knight in shining armor."

"Thank ya lass, but I don't be no knight. I do be a businessman. I think ya got what it takes to be a real hit. I'd like to be a part of that."

"I'd like that too."

"Then I make the arrangements." He helped her from the car into her apartment.

CHAPTER TWENTY-EIGHT

July 24
Friday, 3:00 PM

Hugh paced the floor of his hotel room. How dare his brother mess up his plans? Eliza was meant to be with him, not Frederick. The image of her dancing in the arms of his lousy brother looped in his mind. He cringed, recalling Frederick's stupid hand on her bare back. In Elkins Park, she never would have worn such a revealing dress or permitted a man to touch her in such a fashion. He assumed she was caving to the pressures of this modern city. Eliza possessed a wholesome and honorable character, unlike his brother. His hands clenched into fists. Frederick didn't deserve her. In all the years of rivalry between them, this was a competition he refused to lose. Luckily, he had a wrench to throw into his brother's wheel of schemes. With swift steps, he proceeded to the lobby, picked up a phone, and said, "Elkins Park 7761."

Several rings later, a voice answered, "Hello, Whitmore residence."

"It's Hugh. I need to speak with my father. It's urgent."

"Of course, Master Hugh. I'll fetch him straight away."

The line went silent until a winded Daniel came onto the line. "Son, what is it?"

"I found him. He's here in Manhattan."

———

Mattie strolled out of the diner's kitchen. "Liza, you done cleaning the tables?"

"I'm done." Eliza wringed out a rag in the sink. "What's the rush?"

"Our shift is over. My brother and Warren are coming to get us. There's a dance marathon happening at Madison Square Park. It started 28 days ago with 50 couples. Now it's down to five pairs."

"28 days? How can they keep moving without sleep and food?" She draped the rag over the faucet.

"They get a fifteen minute break every hour. Contestants are fed meals while they dance. Sometimes men carry their gals on their backs so they can sleep. I've even seen women carry their men to keep dancing. It's a sight."

"Why would anyone do such a thing?"

"The winner gets $1,500 at the end."

"Hardly seems worth it to me."

"It's worth it when you're desperate." Mattie grabbed her handbag and change of clothes from under the counter. "Come on, let's get ready to have some fun." With their uniforms off and dresses on, they exited the diner to find Warren's black Ford beside the curb.

"Afternoon, ladies." He tipped his fedora. "How was another day at the diner?"

"Awful," said Mattie. "That's why we live for the after-party. Where's my brother?"

"He'll be here any second. Eliza, have you ever witnessed a dance marathon before?"

"No. Mattie's been informing me."

"There ain't nothing like it. The promoters are running a

final grind today to push for eliminations, which means the next twelve hours will have no rest periods. The couples have to dance continuously."

Her eyebrows rose. "That sounds cruel."

"For the dancers it is, but for the watchers it's quality entertainment." He smirked. "On grind days, things get interesting. Dancers collapse. Some get hysterical. Others talk to imaginary companions. I even saw a lady once pick apples off of an invisible tree."

"Those poor people."

He waved off her concern. "They know what they signed up for."

A yellow Cadillac sped to a halt behind Warren's car. Julian stepped out, flinging his door closed. "Who's ready fer some fun?"

"Always." Mattie led Eliza toward her brother's car. "Wait until you ride in this. It's the fastest car I've ever been in. Way better than Warren's tin Lizzie."

"Jules's car isn't any faster than mine."

Julian scoffed. "Yer mad as a box of frogs. Me breezer can do circles around yers."

"I passed ya on 10th Avenue yesterday. I can do it again."

"Care to make it interesting?"

Warren crossed his arms. "Hundred dollars says I outrun you to Madison Square Park."

"Yer on." Julian shook Warren's hand. "May the best car win."

Warren grabbed Eliza by the arm. "Come on." She barely closed her door before he raced his car into the street. Julian roared past, blowing a cloud of exhaust through their open windows.

She coughed, waving the haze away.

"Hang on." Warren swerved between cars on the street, nearly clipping a pedestrian.

Adrenaline coursed through her veins. She clung to the leather seat cushion.

Speeding through a cross street, another vehicle appeared from around the corner. He wrenched the wheel left, to swerve around them. The momentum flung her head against the car's frame. She winced, pressing fingers to her temple. Blood bubbled from a small cut.

Passing a slow driver, Warren pulled into the oncoming lane. A blue roadster headed toward them.

"Warren, get over!"

He didn't budge.

"We're going to hit them."

"Then they better get out of my way."

She screamed as the roadster came within a cars length before it squealed onto the sidewalk, crashing into a bench. "Are you crazy? Those people are probably hurt."

"They should have gotten over sooner." He pulled up hubcap to hubcap with Julian's Caddy. "Now I've got him." At the corner of Madison Avenue, he turned a sharp right, forcing Julian to brake or crash into Eliza's passenger door. His car slowed down. Warren flew ahead, leaving Julian in his dust. They screeched to a halt in a parking lot. "We did it." He slapped the dashboard. "I can't wait to get a load of his face." He patted her shoulder. "We did good, huh?"

She glared at him. "Does this look good to you?" She pointed to the cut on her face.

He pulled a handkerchief from his pocket. "It's only a little scratch," he dabbed at the blood, "no real harm done."

"Don't you care at all that we could have been hit?"

"I knew that other car would turn. We were perfectly safe."

"I didn't like it."

He sighed. "Sorry, doll. I forget that you're not used to how we do things in this city."

Julian roared into the space next to them. He and Mattie exited his Cadillac, laughing like a couple of kids.

Warren hopped out of his car. "What did I tell you?"

"I can't believe ya beat me." Julian shook his head.

"On my last turn, I thought you were going to hit us."

"Ya piece of cac, I almost did! I had to slam on me break. Can't believe ya pulled that off. Say, how'd ya like to go double or nothing? I bet three couples drop."

"Nah. The stakes need to be higher…"

Eliza stopped listening to their banter. She didn't care. For the first time, she doubted Warren. He might support her dreams, but would he protect her? Hugh would never risk her safety, no matter what.

CHAPTER TWENTY-NINE

July 25
Saturday, 3:00 AM

The Lower Arch Bridge loomed like a steel ghost in the thick mist of the Niagara rapids. It emerged through the forests of the Canadian border and disappeared back into the impenetrable green of New York territory. Like phantoms among the trees, the McKennas hid inside the shadows.

Warren, Julian, Red, and Lonan were on the left embankment. The other lads were staggered along the right. All was black except for the silver gleam of their Thompson submachine guns. Apart from the water thrashing below, all was silent. Minutes ticked by.

Finally, the rumble of Zanneti's two convoy trucks ascended the large steel bridge from the Canadian border. They rolled into New York and were greeted with a downpour of .45 caliber automatic bullets.

The first driver accelerated in an attempt to outrun the ambush.

Warren aimed the barrel of his gun at the driver and pulled the trigger. His bullet sliced through both the windshield and the man's skull. The truck swerved off the road, careening into an unyielding oak.

The second convoy's front tires blew. Rims shrieked across the pavement, skidding to a halt. Red's bullet sealed the driver's fate.

Warren ran to the truck wedged around the tree. Prying the doors open, he looked inside. Streams of whiskey ran between toppled crates and broken shards of glass. "Bottles are broken," he hollered, "the whiskey's ruined." He slammed the door shut, kicking the side of the truck.

Red stepped inside the second convoy. "Everythin's good in here."

"Load it up," said Lonan.

The gang transferred the crates into their trucks.

"We gonna head back to the warehouse and unload this. Jules and Reny, burn the evidence." Lonan climbed into a truck with Red, and they left.

"How ya wanna do it?" Julian asked, looking at Vincenzo Zanneti's once shiny trucks.

"We'll have to blow 'em up." Warren reached under one of the trucks, cutting its gas line. Gasoline bled on the ground.

Julian grabbed an oilcan from his car and dashed fuel on the trucks.

After Warren cut the other truck's line, he jogged twenty feet out. He and Julian unloaded a round across the inky mess. Sparks jumped out of the liquid and died.

They looked at one another.

"That should have worked," said Julian.

"Plan B." Warren pulled a box of matches from his jacket. Striking one, he threw it into the gasoline. A hiss shot up from fuel followed by yellow and orange flames.

"That's more like it." Julian grinned.

A wave of fire snaked around the trucks licking up the fuel. The heat intensified. A growing shriek rose from the inferno.

"Run!" Warren bolted for the ditch. Julian tore after him. They felt the increasing warmth against the back of their jackets. Their heels dug into the gravel. A shrill quake sounded in their ears, followed by a loud explosion. "Holy mother!" He dove to the ground. Julian landed beside him. Pieces of glowing metal and sizzling debris flew through the air. He glanced at the cloud of smoke and the horde of flames. Bits of ash swam in the sky.

"Think my arse is burnt," said Julian.

"It probably needed a tan."

Julian chuckled, followed by Warren's eruption of laughter. "That was fierce."

"Let's get outta here." Gravel kicked up behind Warren's Ford.

Hours later, they squealed to a halt by their gang's warehouse.

Lonan exited the building. "How'd it go, lads?"

"Not a trace left." He closed his car door. "The evidence is effectively incinerated."

"That's what I like to hear. Come over and help us finish unloadin' the whiskey."

Red stood inside the truck hoisting up a crate. "Jules, step up here and give us a hand."

Julian took the opposite end. "Shite in a bucket, I think this crate is 'bout as heavy as yer wife."

Red's mouth twitched with a grin before he gave him a hard glare. "Talk 'bout me wife again, and I'll knock ya into next Tuesday."

"I like me a woman with some meat." Finn lifted a crate behind them with the help of Warren. "There's nothin' like the warmth of a woman or the pie that she's cookin'."

"Or the weight she's now gainin' from the pie she's retainin'," said Lonan.

Red nodded. "But the pie is so good, her melons so round, and with that combination, why would I frown?"

"That be the truth of it," said Finn.

Once all the crates of wine and whiskey were stacked inside the warehouse, the gang gathered for a toast.

Red snapped off the caps and passed a drink to each member.

"Today, we made a big move," said Lonan. "Takin' this shipment is a statement of purpose, power, and war. These are the risks that must be made in order to maintain control of the Kitchen. I does know that together, we're up fer it. I be mighty proud to work alongside ye fine and fearless men. Those Italian maggots don't stand a chance against us. We're the McKennas. We're Irish. We're not afraid of a fight. Fortune favors the brave, and I do be fortunate to have nine brave men with me." He raised his bottle high. "May those that love us, love us, and those that don't love us, may God turn their hearts. And if he doesn't turn their hearts, may he turn their ankles so we'll know them by their limping. Sláinte!"

Grunts, cheers, and the chimes of glass bottles resounded through the room. The warm slosh of whiskey filled their bellies. Today was a success. And tomorrow, they'd see.

CHAPTER THIRTY

Saturday, 6:00 AM

Vivian Whitmore sat beside her husband in the back of a taxi. She watched cars swerve around them, scarcely missing the occasional pedestrian. "Manhattan is busy for six in the morning."

"It's a big city." Daniel gave her a reassuring smile.

Her throat tightened with emotion. "I still can't believe Frederick is here, in this city." She shook her head. "For five years, I worried that I wouldn't see him again, and now I'm worried that he won't want to see us."

"It'll be all right."

She leaned her head against his shoulder. "Where did we go wrong? What could we have done differently?"

"We did the best we could. Truth is, the boys were so different it was hard not to raise them differently. Frederick was impetuous, Hugh was studious. Hugh listened to the rules, Freddie broke them. It was hard not to show favoritism to Hugh because he was easy to handle, unlike Freddie, who challenged us on everything."

"Frederick received a bigger dose of my fiery Irish heritage." A soft smile touched her lips. "I liked his gumption. If only he could have channeled his determination into the right choices."

"Nothing worked with him. Rewards, punishments, even bribery. What were we to do?"

She looked out the window, remembering how the dominoes had fallen. Freddie had failed a class in school. He received a black eye from a fight on the playground. She found a tin of cigarettes under his bed. He started showing up drunk on their doorstep. Then she found a girl in his bedroom. At age 15, he had spent a night in jail for stealing a watch they could have easily purchased. She closed her eyes. "I don't know why Frederick made the wrong decisions, but at least he had spirit. Hugh could use a little of more that."

"What do you mean?" Daniel studied her. "I thinks it's good that Hugh doesn't act irresponsible. He is wise and follows orders well. Someday, he will carry on our family business. That's why I've sent him to New York. I know he can handle it. The boy is steady. The only hasty thing he's ever done is propose to Eliza, which didn't work out well for him."

"At least he took a risk and followed his heart. I was proud of him for that." She suspected the reason Hugh tried so hard was to please Daniel. His elevated expectations were almost unreachable. He had set near-impossible standards like his father. When the boys had failed to meet them, strict consequences followed. They had worked for Hugh but aggravated Frederick. She hated the power struggle that raged between Daniel and Freddie. While Frederick had grown worse, Hugh had excelled. He climbed the academic ladder in school, receiving awards and praise. Daniel and she glowed with pride. They encouraged Freddie to be more like Hugh, but he despised their words. He had no interest in studies. He wanted to have fun. He loved excitement, which usually meant trouble, resulting in more arguments.

By Freddie's 16th birthday, she was out of ideas and weary of the fight. One year later, he had disappeared. The pain of his departure caused her to spiral into depression. She begged

Daniel to move somewhere new; she wanted to flee Pittsburgh and all the memories. They had moved eastward to Elkins Park. Daniel went into business with Hector Belcourt, and that had become another episode of trouble.

The taxi stopped in front of an elegant white hotel called The Gregorian.

"Here we are," said the cabdriver.

"Here we go," said Vivian.

———

The first gleam of dawn shone through the window, illuminating the velour sofa. A tired Eliza trudged into the bathroom, splashing water on her face. Yesterday had been an adventure she didn't wish to repeat. She entered the living room, flipped on the light switch, and grabbed her stationary off the side table. Staring at the blank sheet, she contemplated what to write her mother. Her ankle still ached from running from filthy Feran, and she had to wait tables in one hour, but she couldn't tell her mother that. It would justify her parents' opinion that she was foolish for leaving. She had to prove them wrong. Uncapping a pen, she placed its point to the sheet.

Dear Mother,

As you know, I have been in Manhattan for 14 days now. Everything is clicking into place exactly as I had hoped. In addition to finding a roommate and a job at the City Diner, I have begun my pursuit of a career in singing. I auditioned for a distinguished club, and they loved me. They have scheduled me to sing this Wednesday at nine. I am one step closer to accomplishing my dream. Someday, you'll be hearing my voice on the radio.

She stopped writing. While the letter sounded good, she knew it wasn't honest. The truth was that she had gotten lucky with her small successes, and she wouldn't be here now if it weren't for Neville's sacrifice.

Mattie's previous words at the club taunted her. *"You never asked your friend what her first name is? Because she's your maid, right?"* The reproach stung because it exposed the truth, a truth Eliza hadn't seen before. All this time, she had judged her parents for acting like they were superior. They expected everyone to bow to their whims, but was she not like them? Didn't she think herself better too? Even though she had forced herself to succumb to the lesser-privileged life of New York City, in her heart, she thought herself better than the apartment she lived in, the job she held, and the roommate she kept. She couldn't blame her parents for the environment in which she was raised, because she had liked it. Their wealth and community position had made her feel valuable. She enjoyed her privileged existence. She liked lording her station. She chose to look down on others, and she chose to view Neville as a mere servant. Why? Because she believed herself to be better.

Her shoulders hunched under the shame of her inward ugliness. Tears trickled down her face. She didn't want to be this way. Crumpling the letter, she pulled out a fresh sheet and scribbled through blurry eyes.

Dear Mother,

I've been in New York City for 14 days now. It has come with challenges, but those challenges are shaping me into a better person. I'm sorry for hurting you, but I had to be true to my heart. I need to sing. I hope you and father will forgive me for leaving. Also, I beg that you wouldn't place any blame on Neville for my departure. I pressured her to help me. She is not at fault. I take full responsibility for my actions.

In case you'd like to call, write, or perhaps come visit me, here is my information:

Hotel Griffin
502 West 35th Street Apt. 5
New York, NY 10001
(Clinton) 4437

Your Daughter,
Eliza

Folding the letter, she slipped it into an envelope. She clasped it between trembling hands, knowing a response would be unlikely. With the back of her hand, she wiped her cheeks. There was one last thing she had to do. Unhooking the telephone's earpiece, she requested her home number. It rang several times before a voice switched onto the line.

"Hello, Belcourt residence."

She thought it sounded like the cook. "May I speak with Neville, please?"

"She's busy with her morning chores. Might I take a message?"

"Please, it's important. I must speak with her. This is Eliza."

"Oh. Lady Eliza! I'll retrieve her this minute."

The silence didn't last long before Neville came on the line. "Me lady?"

"Neville." She inhaled a shaky breath. "I need to ask you an important question. What is your first name?"

"I beg yer pardon, me lady?"

"I never asked you, and I should have. What is your first name?"

She paused, and then said in a soft voice. "Aisling."

"Aisling. That's a lovely name."

"Thanks, me lady."

"I'd like for you to call me Eliza."

"I couldn't do that. It wouldn't be right."

"It's my fault that you feel that way. You were always a friend to me, but I never returned the kindness. I took and took without a second thought, thinking it was acceptable because you were my servant, as if that made me superior. Living in New York has opened my eyes. A job isn't who we are; it's just what we do. I've learned that since I've become a waitress at a diner. The truth is that it's been humbling, and I needed it. I know that I have made life hard for you, and I'm sorry. Will you forgive me?"

Another pause silenced the line. "Ya don't know what yer words mean to me. Thank ya ever so. I forgive ya."

"I wish I had spoken them sooner."

"Not a better a time than now."

"Thank you for all your help. I'm truly grateful. Would you...would you be my friend, Aisling?"

"I'd like that, Eliza."

CHAPTER THIRTY-ONE

Saturday, 12:00 PM

"Still no answer." Hugh hung up the phone.

"How can a legitimate real estate business not have a receptionist answering calls?" asked Daniel.

"Father, it is completely legitimate. Freddie's employed with the company. They must be having trouble with the phones today."

"I'm sure there's a reasonable explanation." Vivian touched Daniel's arm. "Maybe we should go to the company and ask for him?"

"I think we ought to make sure Freddie is in the office before we drive there."

"Could we reach him at another phone?" asked Daniel.

"This is the only number I have."

"He didn't give you his home number?"

"Hardly. Like I said before, he wasn't happy to see me, but I thought you deserved to know that I had found him." He exhaled. "There is one other thing I didn't mention on the phone. He's not exactly going by the same name anymore. He calls himself Warren Moore. He said he wanted a new name for a new life." He watched his parents' faces as they absorbed his words.

"That boy." Daniel shook his head. "Call up that receptionist again. I don't care if Frederick...Warren...whatever he calls himself wants to see us or not. He's still my son, and we're not leaving until we've spoken with him."

He picked up the phone.

By the fifth ring, Kiki's voice came onto the other line. "Real Estate Brokerage Services. How may I help you?"

"Hello, this is Hugh Whitmore."

"Mr. Whitmore, so nice to hear from you. What can I do for you today?"

"I've tried to call numerous times over the last hour and no one has answered. Is there a problem with the phones?"

"There's no problem. It's been a hectic morning. I'm sorry for the inconvenience. What can I do for you?"

"I hoped to set up an appointment with Warren Moore today. Lonan said he'd be helping me with my real estate needs."

"I'd be glad to set up a meeting, but it will have to wait until later Sunday or Monday. All of our brokers are gone this weekend for a conference in Canada."

He huffed. "The earlier the better. Could he meet us tomorrow for a late lunch at The Gregorian's restaurant?"

Kiki paused, "I'm not sure. That might be possible. When Warren returns, I'll have him give you a call."

"Very well. Thank you for your help."

"No trouble at all, Mr. Whitmore. Have a great day."

"You, too." He hung up. "He's at a conference in Canada. He might be able meet us tomorrow, later in the afternoon. In the meantime, how about we get some lunch? There's a hot spot called the City Diner."

Vivian looked disappointed. "I guess so."

Hugh ushered his parents out of the hotel to where the red Pierce-Arrow sat proudly.

"This is your rental car?" Daniel lifted a brow. "A bit excessive, don't you think?"

"Not at all. This car says I'm a serious businessman with serious goals."

"Or that you're paying a serious price out of my wallet."

"Father, we both know we can afford it, right?"

"A good businessman doesn't spend frivolously. We are here to make money, not spend the money we haven't yet made."

He brushed an agitated hand through his hair. "What are you saying? Do you want me to take the car back?"

"What do you think?"

"I think I'd like to keep it."

Daniel sighed. "I need a cup of coffee. And some food."

As they drove to the diner, Hugh tried to covertly slip into conversation, "Eliza may be working. She's a waitress there now."

Vivian didn't bat at eyelash. "Is that why you chose it?"

Goodness, she was quick. "Not at all. I would take you there regardless. I merely wanted to let you know that she might be working."

"It might be a bit awkward considering that she broke off your engagement and ran away from home. Lord knows Katherine's been an emotional wreck ever since."

"We've already discussed this," he said. "Eliza wasn't ready for a marriage proposal, but her parents forced her to say yes. She felt she had no other option but to run away."

"I still think she made a terrible decision." Vivian folded her hands. "She won't find a better husband than you."

"Thanks, mother. I know that Eliza has feelings for me, even though she's afraid to admit them. I won't give up until I help her see that we're meant to be together."

"All right darling. Good luck." Vivian patted his knee.

"Thanks." He'd probably need it. They were almost to the diner. "Did either of you ever tell the Belcourts about Freddie?"

"Of course we did," said Vivian.

"What did you tell them?"

"We told them we had two sons, but one of them left home at the age of 17."

"Did you tell them his name?"

"Yes, we said Frederick."

"So the Belcourts don't know that Freddie's in New York? Or that his middle name is Warren?"

Vivian sized up her youngest son. "Eliza's met Frederick, hasn't she?"

His eyes widened in astonishment. How did she get that so fast? "Actually, she has, but I didn't tell her that he was my brother. I suspect *Warren* hasn't claimed me either. He seems pretty adamant about keeping his new life separate from his past."

Daniel crossed his arms. "Is there a reason you withheld that information?"

"I didn't withhold anything." He shifted. "There hasn't been a proper time to tell her."

"Hugh, don't be evasive."

"I am not being evasive. I truly haven't had a good opportunity to explain it, and I think something of that magnitude should be handled delicately."

"What makes it a delicate situation?" asked Daniel.

He shrugged. "Eliza's important to me, that's all."

Vivian sighed. "I know you and Freddie had your differences. It seemed the two of you were always trying to beat the other at some challenge. I don't want Eliza to become another one of those competitions."

"I couldn't agree more."

Vivian met his eye with a firm look. "Then tell her soon. She deserves to know that he's your brother."

"Okay, but can we at least keep it quiet until I've personally spoken with her? If she asks you why you're in New York, can we say it's to discuss the new business?"

"Today, we'll say that's our reason for the visit," said Daniel.

"But we're not hiding the truth. Frederick is your brother. Even if he wants to change his name and pretend to be someone else, that doesn't mean we're going to do the same."

He nodded. "We're all in agreement then."

———

The tune of Vaughn De Leath's *Banana Oil* flowed from the speakers of the diner's radio. Eliza whistled along as she wiped off another table.

The doorbell announced more customers.

She looked over her shoulder and froze. Dressed to the hilt in tailored ensembles of worsted wool, silk, and tweed stood Daniel, Vivian, and Hugh Whitmore.

"Morning, Eliza," said Hugh.

She pushed out a stunned reply. "Morning." Perspiration formed under her arms as she watched Daniel and Vivian behold her new and improved appearance. She could only imagine what they were thinking. Hugh ushered his speechless parents to a booth. It was one of Hazel's tables. She breathed a sigh of relief.

"Looks like lover boy brought his entourage," said Hazel.

"Those are his parents."

"Doesn't the poor fella have any friends?"

She chuckled in spite of her nervousness. "I believe so, but they're all in Pennsylvania. His parents must be visiting."

"They sure look high and mighty for the likes of our diner."

The corners of her mouth turned down. "They're not. They just dress nice." She used to dress as dapper as the Whitmores, but now she had succumbed to the fashions of the city, which in her mind didn't hold a candle to her former ensembles.

"Well, no matter," Hazel shrugged. "They're at my booth. Be right back. I gotta make a quick stop to the ladies' room." She walked around the corner to the rear wing of the diner and gasped. "What on earth happened here?"

Eliza heard a door clang, followed by sounds of disgust.

Hastening into the hall, she saw a stream of water seeping under the men's bathroom door.

Hazel stepped out of the men's room, shaking her head. "The toilet's backed up. Looks like somebody's colon exploded in there. My guess is some fella ate too many pancakes this morning."

"That's going to stink up the whole diner." Her face scrunched in repulsion. "What do we do?"

"I'm gonna fetch the plunger and a mop, but I need you to wait on my tables."

"Of course." She nodded.

"Thanks, baby. It may be awhile. You'd better get back out there."

"Right." Heading behind the diner's counter, she stretched the hem of her snug uniform as far down as it would go. With each step toward the Whitmores, she felt the dress inch a little higher. Her heart pounded inside her chest. Stupid uniform. Why did they have to show up at the diner? She plastered a smile on her lips and greeted them. "It's so good to see all of you." She hoped they didn't detect the shakiness in her voice. "You must be visiting Hugh."

"We are," said Vivian. "He said we might see you today. Do you like it here?"

She met her steady gaze, seeing that the question went deeper than the diner. "I do." Ending the engagement and running away must have disgraced them, but she had to do it. With an apologetic expression, she added, "It's a good thing for me."

"I'm glad for that," said Vivian.

"It appears you've made some changes." Concern interlaced Daniel's words. "I hardly recognized you."

She clutched her notepad tighter. "New York styles are definitely different. It's taking a while to get used to them."

Hugh took a brief glimpse at her hem.

Her cheeks reddened. "Can I get you something to drink

while you look over the menu board, or are you ready to order?"

"I think we're ready," said Daniel.

She jotted down their orders. "I'll put these in right away." She clipped it to the line and circled the diner, topping off coffee and distributing meals. When the Whitmores' order came up, she collected their plates and managed a confident stride to their table. She set down their meals. "What do you plan on doing while you're in New York?"

Daniel picked up his fork. "We're here to talk over some business plans with Hugh."

"Oh." The folly of her question resonated in her head. Of course that was why they were here. To talk about the new business they were starting without her father because she didn't marry Hugh. She swallowed past the guilt. "I hope you enjoy your visit."

"Thank you."

Nodding, she retreated behind the counter and through the kitchen's swinging metal doors. Her father's business was going to fail. She leaned against the wall, hugging her arms against her chest. Hector hadn't been a warm father, but she still loved him. She hadn't wanted to hurt her parents, but she had to leave. It was the only way she could succeed. Soon, she'd have a record deal and become the next Marion Harris. Then, they would see that she made the right choice and hopefully forgive her.

Hazel pushed through the doors. "Is something wrong, baby?"

"No." She shook her head. "Just taking a minute. Guess I better check on the customers." Before Hazel could ask more questions, she exited the kitchen.

Finishing their meals, the Whitmores approached the counter.

She rang in their purchase at the register. "Your total is $1.85." Daniel handed her a five-dollar bill. She counted his change into his hand and gave him the receipt. She made to hurry away, but Vivian reached out to her.

"Eliza, wait. I imagine that serving us today wasn't easy, but you did a good job. Thank you."

"I appreciate that." She dropped her gaze to the counter. "I'm sorry. For everything."

"All is forgiven."

She looked at Vivian, amazed.

Daniel nodded in agreement. "We would have loved to have you as our daughter-in-law, but we hold no hard feelings for the ended engagement. I'm happy that things are coming together for you. We wish you the best."

"You don't know what that means to me." Her throat knotted with emotion. She wished it had been her own father instead of Hugh's that had spoken those very words. In a meek voice, she asked, "Vivian, do you still meet every Wednesday morning for bridge group with my mother?"

"Yes I do."

"Do you think you could give her a letter for me?"

"Of course. Do you have it with you?"

"Actually, I do." She extracted her handbag from below the counter. "I planned to mail it after work, but perhaps you could give it to her. Maybe let her know that I miss her, and she's always welcome to come visit."

"I'll do that, dear." Vivian took the envelope.

Hugh silently followed his parents out of the diner.

Walking to the sink, Eliza kept her back to the customers seated at the counter and blinked back the tears.

Hazel appeared at her side. "So you were engaged to him?"

She wiped away a sneaky tear. "You can't always believe what you hear."

Hazel gave her a light hug.

CHAPTER THIRTY-TWO

Saturday, 1:15 PM

Hugh exited the steps of the City Diner onto the brick sidewalk. His parents followed him to the parking lot. A black Model T raced into the lot, parking three spots down. "Crazy Manhattan drivers," he muttered, unlocking the door to his Pierce-Arrow. A familiar laugh sounded from the black car.

"Did you hear that?" Vivian spun toward it. "It's him."

Hugh looked up. Oh, for crying out loud. What was his brother doing here? He was supposed to be in Canada. Eliza couldn't find out that Freddie was his brother. If things went sour in Manhattan, she might see him as her second chance to save her family's business. Then, Frederick would reclaim his right as heir and marry her. Frederick would be the hero, robbing him of everything he deserved.

"Freder–" Vivian began to call out.

"Warren and Julian," Hugh effectively interrupted as he physically stepped in front of his parents.

Warren's shoulders tensed as his parents' eyes fixed on him.

"Mr. Whitmore, grand to see ya." Julian crossed in front of the cars, extending his hand.

"Good to see you, as well." Hugh returned a firm handshake.

"Looks like ya are enjoyin' an afternoon out. Who might these fine folks be?" Julian turned to Mr. and Mrs. Whitmore.

"These are my parents, Daniel and Vivian."

"A pleasure to meet ya both." Julian shook their hands. "I'm Julian O'Keefe."

Hugh gestured between Julian and Warren. "These men are brokers from the real estate company helping us find a property."

Vivian pulled her gaze off her long lost son to address Julian. "O'Keefe. I thought your accent was Irish. My maiden name was Cleary."

"Ain't that a grand surprise," said Julian. "Yer son didn't tell me that he was part Irish."

"Really?" Vivian looked back at Warren. "He always seemed to like that part of his heritage the most."

Hugh touched his mother's arm. "Of course, I love being Irish, but it's not something I commonly mention in a business meeting."

Vivian appeared confused. "I didn't mean—"

"Though," interjected Hugh, "I do find it nice doing business with other fellow Irishmen."

"It's a pleasure, indeed." Julian patted Warren on the back. "Me colleague hasn't had a chance to introduce himself." He paused. "Unless yous have met already?"

"Of course we have," said Vivian with an adoring smile.

Warren opened his mouth to interject.

"Over the phone," said Hugh.

Daniel studied Hugh with a shrewd expression. He turned to Warren, extending his hand. "It's good to meet you in person."

"Likewise."

Hugh noted the puzzled expression on his mother's face, and yet, she lifted her gloved hand to shake his brother's. He gave it a light squeeze and let go. She reluctantly dropped her hand to her side. The look on her face said she was likely to throw her arms around the prodigal. For goodness sake, Hugh had to wrap up this interaction. Wrong place. Wrong time.

"Our receptionist tells me that you would like to meet tomorrow," said Warren. "How about we do a one o'clock lunch at The Gregorian's restaurant?"

Vivian's face fell. "But you're back today. Must we wait until then?"

Julian threw a sideways glance at Warren. "It's fine with me if yous would like to join us fer lunch."

Her face cheered up. "I think that would be—"

"They're clearly on their way out," said Warren. "It would be rude to intrude upon their day. We'll stick with tomorrow's meeting."

Hugh gestured to the diner. "We have already eaten."

"Ah, very well," said Julian. "Lovely to meet ya, Mr. and Mrs. Whitmore. Look forward to seein' ya again."

"Jules, go ahead and get us a table," said Warren. "I'll be there in a moment."

The Whitmore family stared at one another for a moment in tentative silence.

"It's so good to see you, Frederick." Vivian stepped forward with her arms open.

"This isn't the proper place or time for what looks to be a reunion. I'll see you all tomorrow. We'll speak there." He didn't wait for a reply.

Vivian rocked back a step, stunned.

Daniel put an arm around her shoulders.

Hugh needed to get his parents away from here. "How about a drive past the river?"

———

When Warren entered the diner, Eliza felt a mixture of irritation and uncertainty.

Lonan's house party had been one of the greatest nights of her life. Warren's charm had left her breathless. As they danced, he had whispered silly musings and flirtatious compliments in her ear. Everything around her faded when she was with him. She felt herself falling under his spell, and she liked it. The whole night was perfect except for one thing: he never actually proposed a day for their first date.

She had expected him to call the next day once he had checked his schedule, but no call came. When she saw him Friday night, she thought he would mention it. But he didn't. In fact, Friday hadn't been one of her better experiences with Warren. Perhaps today would be different. He could apologize; she would forgive him. Then they could discuss a day for that date. Approaching Julian and Warren, she asked what they would like to order.

"A burger, fries, and cola for me," said Julian.

Turning to Warren, she waited for his grand apology and order, but instead he focused on something outside the window. She pushed a curl behind her ear. "What would you like, Warren?"

He didn't respond.

Julian swatted him. "Reny, she's askin' ya a question."

He blinked as if hearing them for the first time. "Oh, ah, coffee."

"Anything else?"

"Just coffee."

Julian raised a brow but didn't say anything.

"I'll put these orders in." Spinning on her heel, she headed to the kitchen. Her jaw clenched. He didn't even acknowledge her. Where was her apology? What happened to the enchanting man she had danced with? Didn't he mean anything he had said before?

Outside the diner's front windows, she noticed a man hobbling down the sidewalk. His face appeared bruised, his lip swollen. Harris Feran? She hurried closer for a better view. Despite his banged up condition, she recognized his stubby frame and rat face. He looked terrible. Did Red to do that to him? A touch of guilt pricked her heart. She disregarded it. Harris deserved whatever happened to him. Scooping plates onto her tray, she delivered meals to a table. As she headed back to the kitchen, she noticed Julian say something to Warren. With her curiosity piqued, she fetched a dishrag and slid into a booth two behind them, wiping down the table.

Julian took another bite of his burger. "Is it me or are those Whitmore folks kinda strange?"

"Yeah I'd say they are," said Warren.

Whitmores? They must be talking about Hugh and his parents.

Julian studied his friend. "Have ya met them before?"

"Don't think so." Warren took a swig of his water. "But that woman acted like she knew me or better yet…like she wanted to *know* me."

Her eyebrows leapt into her hairline. How dare he say that about Vivian!

"That's exactly what I thought. The way she looked at ya and shook yer hand, I thought she was gonna throw her arms around ya right then and there."

"What can I say, Jules? I have that way with women."

She narrowed her eyes.

"And right in front of the old man, too." Julian shook his head. "I think ya could've handed her yer address, and she'd have taken it. Did ya see how happy she got when I asked them to join us fer lunch?"

Her fingers choked the rag. Not only was Vivian a married woman, she was a respectable one. She never would have flirted with Warren. But apparently he thought rather highly of himself. Ladies had surrounded him at the club; he might be used to women falling all over him. So what did that make her? Just another gal?

Warren nodded. "Should be an interesting meeting tomorrow."

"Better not wear yer cologne. We don't want ya upsettin' ol' money bags because his wife is gettin' sweet on ya."

Stupid cologne. She grimaced. If only the Whitmores knew how he talked behind their backs. He was their real estate broker. How dare he disrespect them?

"Unless, of course, she controls his wallet," Warren chuckled.

Her sapphire eyes darkened to cobalt. That must be his game. Wooing women for their money. She came from a wealthy family. He probably wanted her for her inheritance. She scooted out of the booth. Too bad for him, she didn't have one.

CHAPTER THIRTY-THREE

July 26
Sunday, 10:00 AM

Julian stood waiting in Lonan's parlor. He felt like a snake in the grass, but he had to do it. Something was off with Warren.

Lonan entered, smoking a cigar. "What'd ya find out?"

"I been watchin' Reny like ya asked." Julian brushed a hand over the back of his neck. "Noticin' strange things between him and those Whitmores. Reny is sayin' all the right things, but somethins not addin' up. Yesterday, we went to the diner to get a bite. We ran into Hugh Whitmore and his folks. There was odd tension between Reny and Whitmore's parents."

"Why'd there be tension between Reny and that lad's folks?"

"That's what me be wonderin'. I done thought maybe the woman was sweet on Reny, ya know how the ladies flock to him. But there be somethin' else in the way she looked at him. The old man looked at him strange, too. As if they were in awe at seein' him. Reny was real reserved with them. He hid it well, but he seemed uneasy, so."

Lonan released a heavy sigh. "I done asked him if he knew Whitmore. He swears he don't."

"I know," said Julian. "Can't figure it out."

Lonan tapped his foot. "Somethin's not right. I have a feelin' that Reny's not bein' honest with us. I think he knows these people. I do be wonderin' what the connection is. Keep followin' him and let me know what else ya find."

"Will do, boss."

———

Hugh sat beside his parents in a wooden pew of Grace Church. Sunlight poured through the stained glass windows, casting colorful patterns upon the reverend's white robe.

"In conclusion," said the reverend, "I would like to invite you to join me in standing as we recite the Apostles' Creed."

The congregation stood to their feet.

He chimed in with everyone else in the recitation of the creed. "I believe in God, the Father Almighty..." The words rolled off his tongue out of habit. He figured even Frederick would still remember it, despite how little he had paid attention in church.

Freddie always found church boring. He had devised creative schemes to pass the time. He executed one of his most ingenious plans when he was fourteen. On this particular Sunday, 15-year-old Cynthia Nelson had worn a flouncy white dress. She was the prettiest girl in church and had the longest legs. During the Apostles' Creed, Frederick donned a solemn expression, bending down upon the kneeling bench. Their parents thought him awfully spiritual, but Hugh didn't buy it. He watched as his brother pulled a small mirror from his pocket. Leaning closer to the ground, he angled the mirror below Cynthia's skirt. A naughty smirk brightened his brother's face as he stood and whispered, "Her panties are pink."

Hugh grinned at the memory. The reminiscence followed by a pang of remorse. When they were young boys, Freddie and he had spent every day chasing the next amusement. Freddie would devise elaborate schemes, convincing him to carry out the worst of each, until Hugh grew old enough to know better. Then he chose to focus on school and sports, but not Frederick. Division followed as they pursued separate interests. They might have been brothers, but oftentimes he didn't think they were friends.

His father elbowed him. "...the communion of saints, the forgiveness of sins, the resurrection of the body, and the life everlasting. Amen."

The reverend gave the benediction and dismissed the congregation.

Families shuffled out the tall double doors.

Daniel shook the minister's hand as they exited the church. "Fine sermon today."

"Thank you, sir. God bless."

"You as well." Daniel nodded.

As they walked to the parking lot, Daniel popped open his pocket watch. "It's nearly noon. Frederick will be arriving to our hotel shortly."

Hugh unlocked the door of his car. "He'll probably be late."

Vivian sighed. "I hope he comes."

"He'll come," said Daniel, helping his wife into the back seat.

"But yesterday he was so distant."

"I know dear, but what did you expect? The boy hasn't called in five years."

She nodded sadly. "He didn't even acknowledge us or claim us as his parents. Hugh introduced us like we were meeting for the first time. Frederick never corrected him. He played right along. Why? Why did he do that?"

Hugh sat in the front seat, starting the car. "I told you Mother, no one knows his past life. He's changed his name, for crying out loud."

Daniel closed his passenger door. "And you happily played along. But enough, we've already hashed this topic to death."

"You're right," said Vivian. "We need to be hopeful. Today is a new day."

They entered The Gregorian's lavish restaurant, known as The English Room, at ten to one. Light from the crystal chandeliers sparkled over the floors.

A waiter showed them to a table.

"We'll be expecting one more," said Vivian.

The waiter nodded.

As Hugh predicted, Warren arrived fifteen minutes late. He watched his brother's hesitant stride. Warren halted behind an empty chair next to him.

"Son, I'm so glad you came." Daniel spoke in a tender voice.

"We apologize for the awkward situation yesterday." Vivian opened her hands as a plea. "It wasn't our intention to meet that way."

"I would have been surprised to find you in New York, regardless." Warren brushed a hand over the five 'o clock shadow covering his chin. "Hugh never told Kiki the real reason for this appointment. It wasn't for business; it was to ambush me."

Daniel's brows raised a fraction. "We're not trying to ambush you. We miss you. It's been five years. Did you think Hugh wouldn't call us?"

"That was my hope." Warren's voice was flat.

Vivian put a hand over her heart. "Why would you hope that?"

"Why do you think? I wanted to get away and live my life. Under your roof, I couldn't do that."

The muscle in Daniel's jaw tightened. "Are you saying we stifled you?"

"Exactly. I couldn't reach your standards. But luckily, you had good ol' Hugh." He patted his brother on the shoulder.

"That's not true at all." Tears surfaced in Vivian's eyes.

"It's not? As I recall, your favorite sayings growing up were, 'Freddie, see how polite Hugh is? Freddie, see how Hugh's doing his homework? See how he's always on time, he always listens, he always—'"

"Enough," said Daniel.

"But the best one was, 'Freddie if only you could be more like Hugh.'"

Vivian pressed a hand to her mouth, looking down at the table.

"Have you no respect?" Hugh bolted to his feet, only inches from Warren.

"I told you to mind your own business, but you didn't listen."

"I am free to make my own choices."

"Have they been any good?"

Daniel swung around the table, pressing his sons apart with his palms. "Calm down, both of you." He looked behind his back. The patrons by the window stared. "You're drawing attention to yourselves."

Warren's eyes darted around the room. He took a step back.

"This isn't how I wanted this to go," said Daniel.

"You're right, Frederick," said Vivian softly. "I have done many things wrong. I have anguished over those very words these last five years. I am sorry for the past. You are my firstborn child and no one could ever replace you." Her voice cracked. "Please, please can we all sit down as a family and talk?"

Warren remained standing.

"Please, Freddie," she beseeched.

Reluctantly, he sat.

"I know we've never seen eye to eye," said Daniel. "But I want you to know that your mother and I have always loved you. We can't change the past mistakes, but we can control what happens in the future. We want to make amends. We want to be a part of your life." He paused. "Will you forgive us?"

Warren released a long sigh. "A lot of time has passed. I'm not the same person I once was." He stood to his feet. "I think it's best if you go back home. Keep your business in Pennsylvania. It's better there."

Vivian hastened to his side, grabbing his hand between her

own. "Please, son. I love you more than words can say. Please don't cut us out of your life."

Warren stared at his mother's pleading face. He spoke more gently to her. "Too many things have changed in my life. You couldn't understand the things I've had to do. I'm not the same person, Mother."

"You're still my son."

"I wish…" His voice faltered. He throat strained with a forced swallow. He pushed away her hands. "I have to go." He made a sharp turn, leaving the restaurant.

CHAPTER THIRTY-FOUR

July 29
Wednesday, 9:30 AM

The trip to New York City seemed almost a failure. And yet, Vivian held onto a small piece of hope that the words she had spoken to her son would eventually take root. Frederick Warren would always be her son, and she would never give up on him. Someday, they would be reunited as a family. Until then, she had to press on.

A maid escorted her into the Belcourts' elegant parlor. Today was Bridge group. She hadn't seen Katherine since their children's ended engagement. She wondered how it would go.

Katherine looked up from the table where she counted cards. "Vivian, I thought you were in New York. I didn't think you would be coming." Her voice trembled.

"I hate to miss bridge group."

"I'm glad of that." Katherine stood from the chair. "How are you?"

"I am well. We had a nice trip."

"And how is Hugh?"

The corners of her eyes creased in a soft smile. "He is getting adjusted to city life and working hard."

"That's good."

"We also saw Eliza while we were there."

Katherine's breath exhaled in one gush. "You saw her?"

"Yes, she's doing well. She asked me to give you this." She pulled an envelope from her handbag.

Taking it, Katherine sank back in her chair. She gazed at the rectangle, and then traced her finger over the small, curvy penmanship on the front.

"She was going to mail it, but when we saw her at the diner, she asked me to deliver it personally." She sat in another chair at the card table.

"At the diner? Did you have lunch together?"

"No. She was our waitress."

"A waitress?" Katherine's eyes widened in surprise. "In a diner?"

"She appeared to enjoy it. She seemed so grown up. You would be proud of her."

"I still can't believe she's gone."

"She misses you. She specifically asked me to tell you that. And she wants you to come visit her."

"She said that?"

Vivian nodded. "I think it would be great if you and Hector went to Manhattan."

"Hector would never go." Katherine's shoulders sagged in sadness.

"Then go without him."

"I wouldn't dare go alone, and Hector wouldn't allow it."

"But she's your daughter, and she needs your support."

Katherine stiffened. "She's the one who left."

"I know. I saw the heartbreak on my son's face when he told us the news," the muscle in Vivian's jaw twitched, "but I also saw the guilt and sorrow on Eliza's in the diner. She didn't mean to hurt anyone. She simply chose to follow her heart instead of someone else's." She studied her friend. "I have known you for years, but there is something I never told you.

When I was younger, I longed to go to France and study art, but my Irish family was poor, so I married instead. I love Daniel, don't misunderstand, but oh, the things I gave up." She paused. "Did you have dreams that you never pursued?"

Katherine gazed toward the piano sitting beautifully in the corner. "That was a long time ago. It doesn't matter anymore."

"I, for one, am proud of Eliza. Hugh told me that she left to become a singer. She had the courage that I never did."

"I know she's talented, but I want her to have a good life." Katherine spread her hands in plea. "I wanted her to marry Hugh because I knew they would be a good match. That's the best a woman can hope for. Women in our social sphere don't have dreams, they marry. They take care of their husbands and homes. That's our role. I do not understand why she can't accept this."

Vivian released a sympathetic sigh. "Maybe it's you that needs to accept that Eliza isn't like us."

Katherine's cheeks reddened. "Hector said if she chose to leave then she was on her own. Now, she is." She stood abruptly. "The other guests will be here any moment. Please excuse me." She strode out of the parlor, clutching the envelope in her hand.

———

Tonight was her big night.

Eliza took a deep breath as she gazed at her reflection in the bathroom mirror of Club Fianna. She stroked a finger over the strand of pearls that dangled below her collarbone. A new scarlet silk gown wrapped her ivory body in smooth, sensual lines. Pulling a tube of lipstick out of her handbag, she snapped off the cap. While she applied a fresh coat of crimson, Mattie's past words flittered through her mind. *Sometimes change isn't easy, but once you get the hang of it, you will love being a flapper. Soon you won't even remember the old Eliza.*

Mattie was right. The image that stared back at her looked

nothing like her former self. She swallowed past her uneasiness. It was the only way to achieve her dream. Exiting the restroom, she walked to a table beside the platform's stairs. She looked at the clock. *8:35 PM. Twenty-five more minutes.*

"How ya doing?" Mattie sauntered to her.

She fidgeted. "Nervous."

"You nailed it at your audition. You'll do it again."

"The producer for Swifts Music is here. I have to impress him. I've dreamed of being a singer for so long. I can't tell you the number of hours I've spent writing and singing in my parents' parlor, hoping that one day I'd be able to share my music with the world." She sighed. "This is my first real step in making my dreams come true, and I don't want to mess up."

"Eliza, I believe in you. I don't believe in much, but I believe in you. You have what it takes. You are meant to perform. Let yourself go and kick your feet up high." Mattie gave her a small wink. "I better take my seat."

"Wait."

Mattie spun around. "Yeah?"

Eliza threw her arms around her shoulders. "Thank you."

"Don't mention it." Mattie patted her back, hastening out of the embrace.

At five minutes to nine, Lonan McKenna ascended the steps onto the stage and tapped the microphone. "Evenin', ladies and gentleman. I hope ya are all enjoyin' yerselves."

Several whoops and hollers answered him.

"Tonight we have a special treat fer ya. Her name is Eliza Adrienne. She's singin' a song called *There'll Be Some Changes Made.* Please put yer hands together fer her." He clapped his hands as she came onto the stage. "Knock 'em dead, doll."

She struck a pose with one hand on her hip. The lights gleamed upon the silk of her dress. The pianist's fingers danced across the keys and his shoulders bobbed along with the beat of her hopping tune. She swished her hips back and forth while she snapped her fingers. A couple men cheered. She felt her shoulders relax. In a low sultry voice, she sang:

> *For there's a change in the weather*
> *There's a change in the sea*
> *So from now on there'll be a change in me*

She swayed across the stage like she'd done in the audition. With each line she sang, she came more alive. The crowd cheered and laughed at her playful facial expressions during the verses. When she reached the climactic chorus and kicked up her leg, she heard several men whistle. Swinging her arms and kicking out her heels, Eliza danced the Charleston around the stage. She sashayed to the end of the platform as she sang the last verse.

> *Because nobody wants you when you're old and gray*
> *I guarantee you...there'll be some changes made*

On the last note, she knelt to her knees, placed her head in her hand and cast a mischievous wink at Lonan McKenna who sat at the front table.

He clapped his hands.

The room erupted in applause.

She stood to her full height, beaming with happiness. Crossing one arm around her waist, she bowed. When she straightened, the room still clapped, so she blew a kiss and bowed again. In all her dreaming, she had never expected this response. She scanned the crowd for her parents' faces, but they weren't present. It was silly of her to think they would come. As she walked off the stage, Jack stopped her.

"Darlin', ya gave a deadly performance. Goes without sayin' that we want ya to sing again so."

Her mouth spread into a wide smile. "I'd love to."

"How 'bout next week Thursday, same time?"

"I'll be here."

"Thanks, doll. Yer a real gem. Look forward to hearin' more from ya." Jack smiled as he walked away.

She felt giddy.

"What a swell job ya did." Lonan gave her a hearty pat on the back. "Simply grand. Don't ya agree, Clarence?" He looked at the man beside him.

The man nodded. "Sensational. You got some real talent." He offered his hand. "My name's Clarence Fitzpatrick. I own Swifts Music Studio on West 53rd Street."

Her eyes grew with understanding. "It's a pleasure to meet you, Mr. Fitzpatrick."

"Please, call me Clarence. Say, I liked what I heard tonight. How'd you like to come by the studio and show me some more songs?"

Her heart leapt with excitement. "I'd be honored."

"How about this Saturday morning at eleven?"

"I'll be there." Her smile extended from cheek to cheek.

"Looking forward to it." He shook her hand again and strolled away, talking business with Lonan.

She inhaled deeper. If only her parents could see her now.

Mattie strode up. "You were berries!"

"You think so?"

"I know so. Didn't you hear the crowd? They loved you."

"And they're not the only ones," interjected a smoky voice.

She turned to see Warren in a black suit, looking more handsome than humanly possible. His words at the diner still played fresh in her mind. What a weasel.

"You were amazing," he said.

She exerted a nonchalant shrug. "I have a lot to work on, but it felt good being up there."

"Trust me," he stepped closer, "it was a perfect performance. You're a natural."

Taking a step backward, she replied, "I do love to sing."

"Fitzpatrick was impressed."

"I'm going to show him some songs on Saturday."

Mattie's green eyes grew. "That's copacetic, baby. It's exactly what you hoped for."

The corners of her mouth edged into a smile. "I know."

"I liked when you blew a kiss at the end," said Mattie.

"It came out of nowhere."

"Sounds like we've got some things to celebrate," said Warren. "How about you ladies join me at my table? I'll have the waitress bring you whatever drinks you'd like, on me, of course." He extended his arms to them.

Mattie cheerfully linked her arm with his. "I'm always in for free drinks."

She hesitated.

"Something wrong?" He inclined his head.

He didn't know that she had overheard his conversation at the diner, and it wasn't worth discussing right now. Why ruin a good night? She took his arm. "Not at all. I'm the bee's knees."

"That you are." He steered them to the back corner where some of his friends were seated.

When Finn saw her, he shot to his feet. "Eliza, my dear, ya were absolutely grand."

"Thank you, Finn." She enjoyed Finn Hennessy; he had an irresistible quality.

"I must propose a toast." Finn lifted his beer.

"The evenin' wouldn't be complete if Finn didn't give a toast so," said Julian in a wry voice.

She lifted her chin. "It would honor me greatly, Finn."

"Why thank you. Everyone lift yer glasses." Finn raised his own, ready to make a speech.

She looked down at her empty hands.

"Hold your horses, Finny boy," said Warren. "The ladies haven't got a glass yet." He looked over his shoulder and snapped his fingers.

A waitress hustled to their table. "Yes, Mr. Moore?"

"I'd like to order a couple of drinks please." He motioned to Mattie and Eliza.

Mattie didn't miss a beat. "I'd like an orange cocktail."

Eliza asked for the same.

The waitress returned lickety-split with their drinks.

"Let us try this again." Finn made a big to-do of clearing his throat. "Our dearest Eliza, may yer heart be light and happy, may yer smile be big and wide, and may yer pockets always have a coin or two inside. Always remember to forget the troubles that have passed away, but never forget to remember the blessings that come each day. May the luck of the Irish lead to happiest heights and the highway ya travel be lined with green lights. Wherever ya go and whatever ya do, may the luck of the Irish be there too. I have known many and liked not a few. But have loved only one, and this toast is to ya!" He bowed his head to her. "To Eliza."

"To Eliza!" The rest of the group cheered as they toasted their glasses.

Warren clinked his scotch against her glass. "To you."

Tipping back her head, she took a drink. To her surprise, it tasted sweet, almost like an orange soda with a punch.

Mattie drank her cocktail dry in four gulps.

Julian gestured to her empty glass. "That's how we know she's Irish."

"Ah now, I'm not as bad as some Patties." Mattie wiped her mouth with the back of her hand. "Take Finn for example, he'd step over ten naked women to get at a pint."

"'Tis true. Drink is the curse of the land. It makes ya fight with yer neighbor. Makes ya shoot at yer landlord. And worse, it makes ya miss him."

Mattie ran her finger along the rim of her glass. "I need another. How 'bout it, Warren?"

"As many as you like." He shifted his focus to Eliza. "How about a dance?" He stood from his chair.

She mused at his confidence. What if she said no? Would he sit back down? She decided not to test the theory. She felt like dancing. "All right."

"Have fun, Ms. Oliver Twist." Mattie wiggled her eyebrows. She rolled her eyes. "Fly a kite, will ya?"

"Spoken like a true flapper."

Warren led her to the dance floor. "You know, we still haven't gone on an official date. I believe we need to remedy that."

"I would agree." His words grated her. That's it? No apology? No explanation? "There is much to be remedied."

His eyebrows arched as he took her into his arms, swaying back and forth. "I beg your pardon?"

"Well since you've begged for it, I guess I will pardon you."

"For that I'm glad," he pulled her closer to his chest, "because I'd like to get to know you."

She opened her mouth to give him what-for about his conversation with Julian, when she noticed Hugh standing on the edge of the dance floor. She stopped moving.

Warren followed her eyes to see what had suddenly grabbed her attention.

Hugh strode directly to her; his eyes never left her face. "You were astounding tonight."

"Thank you." She stepped out of Warren's embrace. "Did you come to hear me?"

"Of course."

Her parents didn't come, but Hugh did. She had rejected him, but he still came. He was always there for her. His unwavering loyalty spoke to her soul and pulled her closer to him. "That means a lot."

"Excuse me Mr. Whitmore, but we were in the middle of a dance," said Warren.

"If it pleases Eliza, I'd like to cut in." Hugh extended his hand.

She smiled and then looked at Warren. She noticed an edgy annoyance on his face; it gave her a great deal of joy. She turned her body toward Hugh and put her hand in his. "I'd like that."

Warren gave an agitated sniff. "What?"

"So long, Warren." Hugh pulled her into his arms, whisking her across the floor. "Does this dance qualify as breaking rule three?"

"You are holding me a bit close."

"Is it improper?"

"I'll let it slide."

"Excellent." He nodded toward her neck. "I see you're wearing the music necklace again."

"I wear it everyday. It's my good luck charm."

"Is it lucky because I won it for you?"

"Maybe."

CHAPTER THIRTY-FIVE

July 30
Thursday, 8:35 AM

Eliza sat on the sofa reading a *Radio Stars* magazine. She had today off and relished the quiet. A knock sounded on the door, interrupting the silence. "Who is it?"

"It's Warren," called the muffled voice. "Can I come in?"

Her pulse jumped. What was he doing here? "Just a minute." Darting into the bathroom, she checked her reflection. Her hair was a fluffy mess. Grabbing a brush, she yanked it through her thick bob. She squeezed some paste onto her toothbrush, managing a speedy scrub on her teeth. Three pinches on her cheeks gave them a pop of color. Luckily, she wasn't in her bathrobe. Zipping down the hall, she unlocked the deadbolt and swung open the door. "Hello." Her voice sounded slightly winded.

"Hello." Warren smiled.

Planting herself in the doorway, she crossed her arms. He held silent, as if waiting for an invitation inside. She had no intention of granting that.

After a painstaking minute, he pressed on. "I've come by to sweep you away for that date."

"What makes you think I don't already have plans?" Her expression was so matter-of-fact that his poised confidence teetered.

"Do you?"

"No, but I could have."

"I get the distinct feeling that you are angry with me."

"I overheard your conversation with Julian at the diner."

His eyebrows pinched together in confusion. "What conversation?"

"You think you can get any woman you want, even if they're married. From the sounds of it, you only like the ones who have money." Her brows dipped in an accusing slant. "I guess that's why you chose me, isn't it?" When he didn't give an immediate answer, she proceeded to close the door.

He caught it with his hand. "Let me explain something." His tone was slow and direct. "First of all, you have no clue what you think you overheard. I have had my share of dates, but so far, none of them have been married. I don't date women for their money. I have enough of my own. The truth is that you're not like the women I normally date. Manhattan dames aren't innocent like you. It's hard to find anyone in New York who is." He released a long sigh. "I told myself that I shouldn't date a gal like you because I'm no good for you. The trouble is, I can't resist. I hope you'll give me a chance to take you on that date."

She blinked. She hadn't bargained for that speech. "I…uh…" Under the heat of his gaze, she felt her stony resolve melt. "Okay."

"Okay." His shoulders relaxed.

She continued to stare at him, unsure of what to say next.

"Are you going to keep me in the hall?"

She flinched. "Oh, right. Please come in."

He pulled off his white fedora as he entered the parlor. "Have you ever been to a horse race?"

"I don't believe I have."

"Would you like to go to one with me today?"

"Will I be safe? Last time I went somewhere with you, my

life flashed before my eyes."

He looked at his hat in his hands. "I might have gotten carried away that night. It won't happen again."

"Then I forgive you, and yes, I'll go to the race."

His posture straightened. "You're in for a real treat. I'm going to take you to the Saratoga Races. It's a three-hour ride by train and the race begins at 1:00 PM. We have to catch the 9:30 train out of Penn Station."

She noticed that he was dressed in a gray suit. "What is a woman supposed to wear to a horse race?"

"It's a swanky event. A cocktail dress would do the trick."

"Why don't you have a seat on the sofa while I change." After donning a blue cocktail dress and heels, she hastened to the bathroom to flatten her curls with tonic. Emerging, she slipped her handbag on her wrist. "I'm ready."

At 9:14, they breezed into Penn Station. Warren stopped at a ticket booth. "First class to Saratoga, please." He handed the clerk a ten.

The clerk gave him the tickets and change.

As they walked toward the boarding platform, she studied him. "First class. I didn't know that working as a broker could pay so well."

"I might be more fortunate than others. Our brokerage does great business." He helped her into the train. "I wanted to tell you again what an amazing performance you gave at the club. You blew me away."

"Thank you. It was the best night of my life."

"I'm glad." He rested his arm on the back of her seat. "But I hope you'll have more nights that can be added to the category of best if not better."

"Last night will be tough to beat. How do you suppose there'll be *better* nights ahead?"

He tipped his head so that his face was only inches from hers. "Because you're dating me."

"We'll have to see how today goes first." She grinned.

———

Hugh couldn't erase his smile. The previous night replayed in his mind. Eliza had chosen him over Frederick. His brother had lost. He crossed through the hotel lobby to a telephone. Tonight, he would take her to a ritzy restaurant. They could celebrate her performance and—his smile widened—their budding relationship. Dialing, he waited.

The diner's line rang four times before someone answered. "Hello."

He winced, recognizing Mattie's voice. He had pretended interest only to incite Eliza's jealousy. Mattie probably still hoped for a date with him. He'd break the news to her at a later time. "Hello, is Eliza there?"

"You just missed her," she replied in a distracted tone. "She stopped in for a coffee before heading to the races with Warren."

"With who?"

"With Warren Moore."

He froze. It couldn't be true. Why would she do that? She chose him last night. This didn't make sense. "Do you know when she'll be home?"

"No. Why? Is this Hugh?"

He hung up.

———

Strolling into the clubhouse, Warren steered her to a teller window. "Let's place our bet, then we'll take our seats."

"Bet on what?"

"The horse we think is going to win today. There are six horses racing. I've studied up on each of their averages and odds. The horses most favored to win are Soothsayer and Mo'Mentum. Soothsayer is fast and keeps a steady pace. Mo'Mentum has a lagged start but ends strong. He's lost twice, but those were the jockey's fault."

Her eyebrows rose with interest. "Which are you betting on?"

"I'm placing our bet on Mo'Mentum."

"Our bet?"

"That's right. Even though I'm supplying the funds, we're in this together." He gave a wink.

"What if he loses?"

"I lose my money." He turned to the teller's window. He dropped two twenties on the counter. "$40.00 on horse number four, Mo'Mentum."

"Sure thing, sir." The teller scooped up the money without hesitation.

She took a step closer to him. "Are you sure you want to bet that much?"

"Trust me, money isn't an issue." Taking the ticket from the teller, he extended his arm. "Shall we?"

They wove through a crowded clubhouse into a covered section of stands. He ushered her to a seat three rows from the rail. The sun poured over the large dirt track.

She couldn't help but smile as she breathed in the air. It smelled sweet with a hint of hay and freshly cut grass.

He pointed to a row of metal gates. "When the gates open, the horses will race around the track once. It's about a mile long, and the first horse to cross the finish line wins."

A loud bell rang over the speakers.

"What's that?" she asked.

"The final call for all jockeys to report to the paddock. The race will begin soon."

"What's the paddock?"

"It's the area where the jockeys saddle up and mount their horses."

"My, there's a lot to learn about a horse race."

"True, but mostly, you learn through the experience. Are you ready?"

She straightened her back. "I believe I am."

"You think we're gonna win?"

"I hope so. I'd hate to see you lose all that money."

"The way I see it, a person can never advance in life without taking some risks. Take you, for example. You took a risk by coming to New York. Now, you're one step closer to a singing career. If you hadn't come, you wouldn't have met Clarence Fitzpatrick. See what I mean?"

"You're absolutely right."

"I don't sweat risks because more times than not, I'll get ahead. It's good to keep that in mind." He tipped his hat a little further to keep the sun out of his eyes. "I wondered if I could ask you a question?"

"Of course."

"Seems like you know my client, Hugh Whitmore, fairly well." The question rolled off his tongue with supreme nonchalance. "How did you meet him?"

Her eyebrows lifted. She hadn't expected this question. "That's a long story."

"Did you meet before you came to Manhattan?"

She smoothed her palms over the front of her dress, thinking back to the Piersons' ball. Hugh had been such a show off, dancing with all the ladies, but she had caught him staring at her. After that, he became a regular around the Belcourt house, usually under the guise of business. But he spent more time with her than with her father. Not that she minded his company; they had become good friends. Despite their kiss, she told herself that friendship was all she wanted from him. However, when he came to the club last night, something had sparked inside of her. Something she didn't fully understand or want to admit. "We met at—" A horn's cry interrupted her sentence.

Horses bolted out of the gates like rocks from a slingshot.

An announcer's voice came over the clubhouse speakers. "And they're off! Soothsayer goes for the lead. Lord Gaffney moving up quickly now, taking the lead by a head. Out in the middle of the track, Black Knight moves up to third. Mo'Mentum fourth with Lady Laude on the outside as fifth followed by Expropriate sixth."

A cloud of dust kicked up behind the thoroughbreds' hooves as they raced around the oval dirt track. Jockeys in checkered polos clung to the backs of galloping steeds, determined not to fall off as the horses rounded the clubhouse turn. The large chestnut thoroughbred named Soothsayer slipped through the stampede to pass Lord Gaffney. Behind Gaffney, the tall red horse known as Mo'Mentum passed Black Knight as they continued down the backstretch.

Eliza could hardly sit with the adrenaline coursing through her body. "Hurry up, Mo'Mentum!"

The announcer continued illustrating the play-by-play in a voice mounting with excitement. "The leaders are still heads apart. It's Soothsayer now showing the way by a head, Lord Gaffney in second with Mo'Mentum a close third. On the outside is Lady Laude now in fourth with Black Knight in fifth. Expropriate three lengths back in sixth."

The horses rounded to the final stretch of the track. Soothsayer commanded the lead by a length. Mo'Mentum's thick muscles rippled as he pulled up beside Lord Gaffney.

The crowd bolted to their feet, cheering, yelling, and clapping.

Eliza stood, too, clutching her handbag in anxious anticipation. "Come on, Mo'Mentum!"

The horses now neared the yellow finish line. Mo'Mentum's nostrils flared as he steamed closer to Soothsayer.

The announcer's voice bellowed over the speakers. "One furlong left to the finish line. Soothsayer still in the lead. Mo'Mentum coming up on the outside. He's passing Soothsayer on the rail!" His voice reached an even higher pitch. His words spilled out in a quick, croaky yell. "They're heads apart. Finish line is only a length away. Mo'Mentum now a length ahead of Soothsayer. Soothsayer fighting to re-challenge. Mo'Mentum pushes forward, crossing the line a length before Soothsayer. Mo'Mentum is the winner! What a hero!"

The stands erupted in applause.

"We did it." Eliza threw her hands up. "We won!"

Warren whistled.

"I can't believe we won!"

"We sure did, doll." Warren lifted her at the waist, spinning her around.

She was so overcome by the rush of winning that she didn't object to his boldness. "Our horse won." She yelled at the top of her lungs.

"Now we get to claim our winnings, which is almost double what we put in."

"You mean you'll be taking back almost eighty dollars?" Her mouth gaped.

"Not bad, eh?" He wrapped his arm around the back of her shoulders and steered her down the row.

They were about to turn into the aisle when a man dressed in a suit stepped in their path. Two men flanked his side.

She felt Warren's arm tense.

"How'd your horse do, Warren? Did you win?" The man asked in a harsh Italian accent.

Warren squared his shoulders. "As a matter of fact, we did."

The man sniffed. "Mo'Mentum's a risky choice. He got lucky this time. Soothsayer's the real prize."

"Says you."

"Says the majority."

Eliza looked between Warren and the Italian man. A wave of apprehension rolled over her.

"Too bad I never follow the majority." Warren motioned for him to step aside. "If you'll excuse us, we have a ticket to cash in."

The man moved to the side.

Warren protectively steered her past the three men, but he was halted by an iron grip on his shoulder. "Get your hand off me."

"I know it was you guys. I know who snitched the information to Lonan. I ain't lying down for it. Better watch your back." He looked at her. "Take it from me, litt'l miss. You're spending time with the wrong crowd." He walked away, followed by his colleagues.

Her throat knotted in fear. Why was this man threatening Warren? And why was he telling her to stay away from him? She recalled Hazel's words, *the fellas that run in that circle are nice for dancing but heartbreakers in romancing.* She swallowed. What kind of circle was Warren in? She peered at him under her heavy lashes. "Who was that?"

"Vincenzo Zanneti. He's got his own real estate business and recently lost a big deal to our company."

"He acts like he hates you," she said in a soft voice. "Why'd he be that angry over a business deal?"

"It was worth over three thousand dollars."

A considerable amount of money, to be sure. She tilted her head to the side. "Then who's the snitch?"

"A gal who gave us a tip on how to land the client. She normally works with Zanneti but she helped out Lonan with this particular one."

"She doesn't sound like an honest person."

"She's not."

"Why would Lonan want to work with someone like that?"

"A three thousand dollar deal doesn't come every day. Business is business. Don't worry about it."

She looked down at her pointy-toed pumps, trying to piece her thoughts together. "That man threatened you and Lonan. You should tell the police."

"I'll think about it, but for now, we're not going to let him ruin our day."

She crossed her arms. "What did he mean when he said I'm hanging with the wrong crowd?"

"He's jealous, doll. He's mad about the deal, and he's mad that his company's failing. He wants to make my life as miserable as his. So he doesn't want a beautiful woman like you to be with me."

"You think I'm beautiful?"

"I think you're very beautiful." He bent his head, placing a soft kiss on her cheek.

Her mind turned to mush. *He thinks I'm very beautiful.*

CHAPTER THIRTY-SIX

Eliza lay in the drowsy warmth of her bed. Yesterday was extraordinary…

The race in Saratoga. A train ride to Albany. Shopping. Eateries. Dancing. Smoking. Laughing. Drinking.

She had been completely swept away by a freedom she had never known in the company of a man she was sure she would like to know better. They had ended their date with a train ride home. Warren carried bags of gifts he had bought for her. For the next two hours, in the shadows of their compartment, they had done the unthinkable.

They had talked.

She had expected a little romance, but in the quiet of the car he had set his head back and closed his eyes. She had thought him asleep until he whispered a question, "Are you happy?" The inquiry caught her by surprise. She echoed it aloud, "Am I happy?"

He opened his eyes. "Are you?"

"I think so."

He leaned closer to her. "What makes you happy?"

"For once, I'm not relying on my parents. I've gotten myself a place to live, a job, and soon I might have a contract with Swifts Music Studio. All those things make me happy."

He looked disappointed. "That's good."

Did he expect to hear something else?

In a faint voice he said, "Do you believe in God?"

She bit the inside of her lip, feeling uncomfortable by the turn in their conversation. Why was he asking that? What did that have to do with anything? "I'm not sure what I believe. Do you?"

He sighed. "I don't think so."

She shifted in her seat, feeling uneasy. Did he want her to be religious? "Please, tell me what you're thinking."

"I only asked because you remind me of someone."

She saw sadness cross the sphere of his eyes.

"It's nothing, really." He offered a weak smile. "I'm glad you're happy."

Guilt crept inside her chest, expanding like a balloon. She hadn't attended mass since moving to New York. If she was honest with herself, it wasn't because she was too busy; it was because she didn't want to go. And how could she go now? She would be in confessional for hours. He never struck her as the religious type. Who did she remind him of?

A loud crash jolted Eliza from her reverie. She looked around her bedroom, disoriented. "What's going on? What was that?" she said aloud. Pushing her quilt forward, she climbed out of bed and opened the blinds. Mattie's bed was empty. "Now what has she done?" Sliding her feet into a pair of silk slippers, she pulled on her housecoat and walked down the hall into the parlor.

Mattie slumped on the carpet with the table lamp shattered beside her. The black kohl that once nicely outlined her eyes was now smeared down her cheeks. Her bottom lip was cracked and a sheen of dried blood painted the gap. Her eyes looked hollow as she stared blindly at the broken pieces of porcelain.

She gasped. "Are you okay?"

"I tripped," mumbled Mattie. "Sorry about the lamp."

"What happened to your face?"

"An accident."

She sank to the ground beside her. "What kind of accident?"

"Went for a drive with some fella. We swerved to miss a car and went into a ditch." She shrugged. "Nothing major."

"Was he drunk?"

"Probably. I can't remember."

"Are you in pain?"

"No."

She rose to her feet. "I'll get the trash can." It was the same story with Mattie most nights. Clubs. Parties. Excessive drinking. When she came home, or if she came home, she would cling to the walls as she stumbled to her bed. She would wake the next morning, moaning from the stupidity of excess. Usually she suffered a headache, but this time it was worse. Eliza didn't understand why she chose to live this way. With can in hand, she knelt to pick pieces of the lamp off the rug. "Why do you do this?"

"What do you mean?" Mattie looked at her through bleary eyes.

"This?" She gestured to her deflated posture. "The drinking, the partying. It's too much. If you keep living like this, someday you won't be lucky enough to be alive."

"Don't worry your pretty little head about it." Mattie crawled over to her purse and dug out a cigarette. "I'm the cat's meow." Her hands shook as she lit it. She took a shallow drag.

"No, you're not." Anger sharpened her tone. "You're a mess. You're destroying your life."

Mattie's top lip curled back. "Someone like you could never understand someone like me."

"What's that supposed to mean?"

"Just look at you, in your housecoat and slippers. You're a rich girl playing house. You haven't a clue about real life and real problems. You've lived in endless sunshine."

"Money doesn't equal happiness. You don't know what my life has been like, so don't pretend that you've got me all figured out."

"Yeah? Maybe I don't, but you sure don't know me either."

"You're right. Probably no one does. You hide behind a happy-go-lucky façade, but if you were carefree you wouldn't need to numb yourself with cigarettes and alcohol."

"Listen to Miss Education." Mattie snickered. "Think you have me all figured out, huh? You wanna know the truth? I'm the daughter of a no-good Irish drunk who cheated on my ma and beat her. When he tired of hitting her, he'd start on Jules and me. Finally, when I was seven, he left. He left us without a dime. My mother cried for days." Her voice cracked. "Two years later, Jules found her strung up by a rope in the bathroom shower. They dumped us on my aunt in Queens. She couldn't afford us, and who'd want two miserable, hopeless kids?"

Eliza sat in stunned silence.

"Jules and I ran away to Manhattan. We scraped by until he got wise and picked up a job working for Lonan McKenna. Things got better after that."

Her shoulders sank. "Oh Mattie, I'm sorry."

The cigarette shook in Mattie's hand as she brought it back to her mouth. "You didn't know."

She swallowed. "I judged you. I had no idea."

"Yeah, well, life happens."

"That's true. We can't control the past. It's already done. But what about the future? If you put your mind to it, I believe you can make a good life for yourself." She paused. "I'm worried about you. Maybe you could at least try to drink less."

Mattie released a cynical chuckle. "I gotta drink, doll. I'd wanna kill myself if I didn't."

"Oh." She sucked in a quick breath.

"What, is that too honest for you? Everyone wants to live in ignorant bliss. Pretend all is well. It's easier to live that way.

That's why I told you from the beginning, live for the moment. Eat, drink and be merry…for tomorrow we die." She pushed herself up and ambled to the bedroom.

———

Hugh breezed into the Real Estate lobby. "Ms. Jones, I'd like to speak to Warren Moore, please."

"Good morning, Mr. Whitmore," said Kiki. "Do you have an appointment?"

"No, but it's important."

"Have a seat. I'll see if he's available." She walked out of the room.

Hugh remained standing and tapped his foot.

When Kiki reappeared, Warren was with her.

"Warren, I need to speak with you," he said. "Can we go for lunch?"

"I suppose we could do that." Warren grabbed his coat. "Follow me." Once they were outside, he said in a low voice, "Wait until we're in the car."

Hugh yanked the door shut behind him. "What are your intentions with Eliza?"

Warren relaxed his shoulders against the back of his seat. Starting the car, he pulled out of the parking lot.

"Well?" A vein bulged in Hugh's right temple.

A smirk developed on his brother's mouth. "You haven't changed a bit."

"Neither have you. You're still playing the same old games to drive me crazy."

Warren took his hand off the steering wheel and placed it on his shoulder. "I've gotta make up for lost time."

"You can be such a moron."

"That may be true, but it's worth it for the joy of seeing that vein in your head look like it's gonna explode."

"Don't patronize me. Where are we going?"

"My house."

"I thought we were going for lunch?"

"There's food in my refrigerator."

He huffed. "Are you going to answer my question?"

"What question?"

"What are your intentions with Eliza?"

"What's it to you?"

"It's everything to me. She's meant to be with me."

Warren's eyebrow arched with surprise. "Does she agree with that?"

"I thought she did that night at the club, but then you can't accept second place, can you?"

"What makes you think I'm second?" Warren shrugged. "Maybe you haven't a clue."

"No, you haven't a clue. I've known her for a whole lot longer."

"And how long is that?"

"Four years," he said with a proud jut of his chin.

"How did you meet?"

"Her father is partners with ours."

This caught Warren off guard. "What kind of business?"

"They co-own a Steel Company in Elkins Park."

"Elkins Park? You don't live in Pittsburgh anymore?"

"No."

"Why?"

"Mother wanted to move." He exhaled a slow breath. "Once you left, she was devastated. She begged Father to move someplace where she wouldn't be reminded of you. It's been good for them. For all of us."

Warren drove along Fifth Avenue, passing brownstone mansions and ornate lampposts. Turning onto a side street, he parked alongside a black gate that surrounded a magnificent three-story house.

"This is yours?" he asked.

Warren nodded.

"Business must be good." He exited the car.

"I do well for myself." Warren opened the gate and walked the red brick path to the front entrance.

He followed him into a grand foyer with glistening marble tiles. "It's clean. Do you have a maid?"

Warren hung his jacket on a coat rack. "Yes."

"A cook?"

"I have meals delivered or I go out."

"Who does your laundry?"

"The maid."

"Do you live alone?"

"At the moment. Next question?" Sarcasm laced Warren's tone.

He walked through the foyer into the living room. "Ritzy." He crossed his arms. "Has Eliza been here?"

"You're not going to quit with that, are you?" Warren relaxed onto the sofa. "Here's the thing I don't understand. If you're so certain that she's the gal for you, why after all this time, is she still Eliza Belcourt and not Eliza Whitmore?"

"We almost did marry." He brushed a hand over the back of his neck. "But she needed time to pursue her music career."

"Doesn't sound like she loves you."

"She does. She's just confused right now."

"Maybe she's not confused at all. Maybe it's you who is confused." Warren leaned forward, his hands on his knees. "Face it, Eliza's moving on. You should too."

"That's not true. We're going to be married. She simply needs more time."

Warren shook his head. "She didn't seem like she needed time yesterday on the train. In fact, she seemed happy to seize the moment with me."

"What?" His face reddened with anger. "Did you kiss her?"

Warren opened his hands. "I don't think Eliza would want me to discuss her personal business with you."

"Did you kiss her?"

"No, but I plan to."

He grabbed his brother by the jacket, wrenching him off the sofa. "Stay away from her."

Warren shoved him back. "She doesn't want you. She wants someone who excites her, makes her feel alive. She wants me, and I'm going to have her."

He socked Warren in his gut, then received a retaliated punch. Blood trickled from Hugh's lip. He pressed a hand to his mouth. "Why can't you bow out?"

"Why would I do that?"

"Because I love her. Can't you be a big brother to me for once?"

"We were never close. Why start now?"

"That's not true. We once were." He paused. "Will you stop seeing her?"

"No."

"Then I'll have to find another real estate company to help me with my purchase for Father's new branch."

Warren's eyebrows pinched together. "You've already made an agreement with Lonan."

"Nothing's been signed. I'm free to choose whomever I want."

"You don't understand. You've made a verbal contract. You have to stick with our company."

"Stay away from Eliza, and I'll stick with your company."

A look of disgust washed over Warren's face. "Fine."

"Then I'll continue to work with Lonan's brokerage." He headed for the door. "Though today, I'll pass on lunch. I've lost my appetite."

CHAPTER THIRTY-SEVEN

August 1
Saturday, 10:00 AM

Eliza came to a tan concrete building. A sign above the door read Swifts Music. She inhaled a nervous breath. Clasping a black iron handle, she opened the door into a spacious lobby.

A receptionist looked up from her desk. "Welcome to Swifts Music."

"Thank you. I'm here to meet with Mr. Fitzpatrick. My name is Eliza Belcourt."

"Yes, he's expecting you. I'll tell him you're here." The receptionist left her post and headed down a hall.

She heard muffled voices.

Heels clicked up the wooden hallway as the receptionist reappeared. "Eliza, you can follow me. Mr. Fitzpatrick is ready for you."

They entered a room with microphones, stands, recording equipment, guitars, and a polished grand piano. Her eyes widened in wonder. So this was a recording room. Clarence Fitzpatrick and Lonan McKenna stood at the back of the room talking, which surprised her. She didn't know Lonan would be present.

"Eliza!" Clarence walked to her. "So glad you're here. I hope you don't mind, but I asked Lonan to come today as well."

"That's fine with me." She gave Lonan a warm smile. "He's the one who arranged the showcase."

"I'm certainly glad that I did."

"Let's talk for a minute." Clarence gestured to a table. "Would you like anything to drink? Water, coffee, soda?"

"Thank you, but I'm fine for now."

"Very well." Clarence folded his hands atop the table. "Tell me Eliza, how long have you been singing?"

"I've always loved music." She released a dreamy sigh. "Before I could crawl, I was singing. Granted, no one understood the lyrics, but there was a melody. Rhythms and tunes play in my head, and I write songs to them. I've brought several originals with me today." She opened her handbag, extracting music sheets. "I hoped to show them to you."

"So not only do you sing and dance, but you also write?" asked Clarence.

"And I play the piano."

"Janey Mack." Lonan slapped his hand on the table. "I done knew she was somethin'."

"It sounds that way." Clarence smiled. "Do you have any songs written with piano?"

"I have a few. Would you like to hear them?"

"Absolutely." He gestured to the grand. "Set up and we'll hear what you've prepared."

Scooping her charts, she settled onto the piano bench.

"What's the name of the song you're going to play?"

She selected a sheet from the pile and set it on the rack. "*If Only You'd Love Me.*"

"Great. Take it away."

Her fingers glided over the keys, playing a sweet, somber tune. "If only you'd love me. If only you'd see. If only you'd open your eyes and recognize the pain in me. If only you'd listen. If only you'd care. I could make you proud instead of doubt, but you're unaware." She reached the second stanza when Clarence held up his hand. A note froze upon her tongue.

"I'd like to hear something with more beat. This song is depressing. Folks wanna hear something fun. Catchy. Like you did on Wednesday. Have you got something like that?"

She fought the immediate sting of his disapproval. Mattie was right. People don't want to hear about her brokenness. They want to be excited. "I have upbeat songs." She thumbed through her song sheets. "This one's called, 'Sweet Jazz.'" She managed to keep her fingers from shaking as she played the next tune.

The thumping beat made Lonan whistle. He nodded to Clarence.

At the end, Clarence clapped his hands. "That's more like it. I think you've got some real talent. Let's hear another one."

"Sweet Jaysus, Mary, and Joseph. What more ya need to hear before ya snatch her up?" Lonan's forehead creased. "She's a hit. That be a great song."

"I think so, too. But as a producer, we need to know she's got more than one song."

"Can't ya see her stack of music? Course she's got more."

She looked between the men, feeling confused. "I'll gladly play another."

"There shudn't be any need fer that." Lonan crossed his arms. "He's heard ya, lass. Are ya gonna make her an offer or are ya wastin' our time?"

Clarence's lips pinched in a thin line. "I wouldn't dream of it." His expression softened as he faced her. "I think you're exactly what the radio needs. I'm going to put together some figures, then we'll meet again to discuss a contract."

She looked dumbfounded. "Are you saying that you're going to record me?"

"That's right."

"Yer voice is going to be everywhere." Lonan beamed with satisfaction. "New York City will be breakin' down the doors of Club Fianna to see ya sing. Me couldn't be prouder."

"This is incredible." Her head felt light. "I can hardly believe it. I've dreamed of this moment so many times. Thank you, Mr. Fitzpatrick."

"I look forward to working with you. Once I write up the contract, you can review it and ask any questions. After you sign the agreement, we'll begin recording. I'll have my receptionist take down your information so we can contact you."

She nodded.

Lonan slapped Clarence on the back. "This is going to be a great deal."

"It looks that way." Clarence walked her to the front desk. "Thanks again. We'll be in touch."

Lonan winked at her. "Don't ya worry. I'll make sure ya get a great contract."

"Thank you, for everything Mr. McKenna." She clasped his hand. "I don't know how to thank you for taking a chance on me."

"I only take a chance on people who show great potential. Yer one of those people. Yer gonna be big. I look forward to being a part of it."

"So do I." She felt like she was soaring in the clouds. Her time had come. Touching the music pendant hanging at her throat, she smiled. Finally, her time had come. Soon, her parents would hear her on the radio.

———

Hugh climbed the steps to the second floor of Hotel Griffin. He rapped twice on the door.

It swung open. Eliza's eyebrows rose with surprise. "Hugh? What brings you by?"

"Are you alone or is Mattie here?"

"She's at the diner. Did you come to see her?"

"No, I came to speak with you. Can I come in?"

"Sure." Stepping back, she allowed him to enter.

He took a seat on the sofa. "Sit with me." He gestured to the spot beside him.

"What do you want to talk about?" She sat, folding her hands in her lap.

"I know that you went on a date with Warren."

She stared at him. "So?"

"I'm confused. You danced Wednesday night with me, and yet, the next day you're off with another guy. What am I supposed to think about that?"

"I don't know. He showed up at my door, and I went."

"That's it? What if I had been the first to show up at your door, would you have gone with me?"

"Maybe."

"Did he pay for you?"

She shrugged. "Of course."

"What happened to rule number one?"

"It doesn't apply to Warren. I set up rules with you to preserve our friendship."

He brushed an agitated hand through his hair. "I don't get it. I thought we had connected at the club. Didn't you feel something when we danced?"

She fidgeted with a ribbon on her dress.

"I need to know. Do you feel something for me?"

She hesitated. "Yes."

"I knew it." He scooped her hands into his own. "I saw the look in your eyes. I saw it the night we kissed in the library too. You care for me like I care for you."

"It's not that simple." She pulled away. "I agree that we have shared some special moments, but you and I can never be. In the end, we are not meant for each other."

His face colored with frustration. "That's not true. I see it when you look at me. I feel it in your kiss. You like me, Eliza Belcourt. Why can't you give us a chance?"

"Because what you want and what I need are two different things."

"I love you, that's all that matters. I don't care about anything else. All I want is you."

"You might say that, but I know that you'll have expectations of me. My father had expectations for what kind of daughter I should be. My mother had expectations for what kind of woman I should be. You'll have expectations for what kind of wife I should be." She lifted her chin. "I'm tired of everyone's expectations. It's time for me to decide who *I* want to be."

"And who is that?"

"A singer whose name will shine in electric lights."

"You truly think fame can make you happy?"

"You will never understand. I have moved on with my life. It would be best if you did as well."

"As you wish." He walked to the door, yanking it open.

"Hugh, I'm sorry that it has to—"

The door slammed shut.

He stormed down the hall, descended the steps, and nearly collided with Mattie.

"Whoa," she grabbed the banister, "what's the hurry?"

"I'm sorry. Are you okay?"

"I'm fine, baby." She lifted a brow. "Are you?"

He scowled at the stairs behind him. "You should ask your lovely roommate."

"I knew this was coming." She shook her head.

"What do you mean?"

"Eliza has been stringing you along, but it seems she has finally made up her mind."

"She says that we're not meant for each other, but I see the way she looks at me. The night she sang, we had shared something special."

Mattie crossed her arms. "Did she tell you she likes you?"

"She said she felt something."

"Did she say what she felt?"

"Not exactly but the look she gave me said—"

Mattie held up a hand. "That night, she enjoyed your

company, so her face said, 'I like this.' But that's not the same as, 'I like you.'"

As he processed her words, his shoulders sank.

She squeezed his arm. "You need to stop dwelling on what you can't have and start focusing on what you can have. You're in New York City, the land of opportunity. Everything is right at your fingertips. Why not enjoy it?"

He rubbed a hand over his mouth. Mattie was right. Why waste his energy on someone who was set on rejecting him? He had everything a woman could want. He was Hugh Whitmore, for pity's sake. Any woman would be privileged to have his affection. His eyes shifted over Mattie's curvy frame; he knew one woman right now who'd love for nothing more than that. "I feel like having some fun. Are you busy?"

Her lips spread into a playful smile. "My schedule just opened up."

"Can you give me that tour you had mentioned before?"

"It would be my pleasure."

He tucked her arm under his own. "My car's parked outside." He led her to his Pierce-Arrow.

Her eyes widened in wonder. "This is your car?"

"It is."

"I can't fathom the money you must have."

He chuckled. "It's considerable."

"Let's consider spending some, shall we?"

"Yes, we shall."

———

Warren rebuttoned his collar and reached for his jacket lying on the floor next to two pairs of scattered shoes.

"What's the rush, baby?"

He cast a casual glance to a brunette lounging on his bed with a sheet clutched to her chest. "I have work." Scooping her dress off the back of a chair, he tossed it onto her toes. "If you don't mind."

"Work can wait." Dropping the sheet, she swung her feet onto the floor. "Play is much more fun."

"Usually it is." He pulled on his hat without a second look at her. "I'll call you a cab."

He felt a shoe fling past him. Jogging down the stairs, he hollered for his maid to ring up a taxicab. As he exited the house and crossed to the front gate, he heard yelling from his third floor window. He shook his head. Some dames couldn't handle rejection. Lunch at the diner had been pleasant until he'd taken the dessert to go. Too bad it wasn't as sweet as he had expected.

By the time he arrived at the club, Red had divvied cards around a table. The whole crew was seated except for Lonan. "Afternoon, lads."

"Reny," Red tipped his beer to him, "ya see Lonan on yer way in?"

"No, figured I'd be the last here."

"Ya usually are." Red motioned to the pot. "Ante in."

As Warren looked at his cards, the double doors flung open.

Lonan burst into the room, his face ashen. "She's dead. My Fianna is dead."

The gang clamored to their feet.

"Who did it?" asked Warren.

"Zanneti." Lonan pulled a crumpled business card from his pocket. "Me found her this afternoon. He shot her while she lay in her bed. He left his card on her pillow so I'd know it was him." His expression twisted with pain.

"He's not gonna get away with this," said Red. "We'll make him pay."

Lonan's normally broad shoulders sagged under the weight of grief. "Why Fianna? What kind of man takes the life of an innocent woman?"

"He's trying to make a point," said Warren.

Lonan turned to him. "What'd ya mean?"

"I saw Zanneti at the races. He said he knew it was us and

wasn't lying down for it. This is his way of striking back."

Lonan's hands fisted. "He went too far. I done gonna make him bleed. Zanneti wants war, and now, he done got it."

CHAPTER THIRTY-EIGHT

August 2
Sunday, 12:30 PM

Hugh never thought he could enjoy the company of any woman besides Eliza, but Mattie O'Keefe opened his mind. Her wild, carefree nature amused him. Chasing the wake of her crazy momentum and sugary perfume caused his head to swim. She impressed him with her witty humor and shocked him to the point of blushing with her blatant forwardness.

Throughout their date, they zigzagged through a maze of attractions, restaurants, and shops. As the hours ticked by, passing midnight and reaching toward sunrise, the city continued to roar with life. At half past three, he stood exhausted outside Mattie's apartment.

Her green eyes glistened as she stared into his face. "I guess this is goodnight?"

"I'd say it's morning."

"The day is young," she took a step closer, "if you want it to be." Her lashes lowered in a suggestive stroke.

His heart skipped. "I'm not sure I understand, but it's definitely late."

She flattened her palm upon his chest. "I'd be happy to

come to your apartment."

His eyes widened. He had never been propositioned before. "This doesn't have to be hard. Just invite me." Her voice touched his ear as smooth as a silk petal.

A battle raged inside his mind. He shouldn't. It was wrong. Her hand felt warm on his shirt. A part of him wanted to simply forget. Movement from above caught his eye. A curtain pulled back from the window, and he caught a quick glimpse of her face. *Eliza*. His breath stuck in his lungs. Taking Mattie's hand off his chest, he held it. "Goodnight, Mattie." He placed a light kiss above her knuckles.

Her hand dropped to her side. She looked stunned. "Why?"

"Because a man should commit to you first."

"It's not like that in Manhattan."

"That's a shame. Perhaps I can take you out again sometime?"

Her forehead crinkled. "Okay."

He strode to his car. It was a weary drive to the hotel. By the time he entered his room, his body collapsed on the bed. He wondered how he had kept up with her all day, and if he actually desired to do it again. Mattie was a whirlwind.

He wasn't sure how long he had been asleep when he finally pried his eyelids open. He popped his watch: 12:30 PM. Shoving back the bedspread, he pushed himself into a seated position. He groaned. "I need coffee."

After a cold shower, four cups of coffee, and a full breakfast, his brain once again functioned. A thought looped through this mind on a cycling wheel. He had to get another real estate company.

A peculiar conversation with Mattie had finalized his decision. On their date, she had asked how Lonan's company had been treating him. He replied that it was going smoothly; they had located a property on the corner of 12th and West 41st street, near the river.

"He would choose Hell's Kitchen," she mumbled.

He didn't know if he heard her correctly. "What did you say?"

"Upper Manhattan would be a better place for your business."

He crossed his arms. "What's Hell's Kitchen?"

"Just a nickname for Lower Manhattan." She flicked her wrist. "No big deal."

"If Lonan is a professional, wouldn't he direct me to the best locale?"

"I like Lonan McKenna. Heck, my brother works for him. But sometimes, he's more interested in his interests than his clients."

"Do you think I should switch to a different brokerage?"

"I don't know if you can." Her expression sobered. "I can tell that you're good guy. Manhattan isn't nice to good guys."

Before he could question her further, she flipped a switch. Smiling once again, she pulled him to the next craze of the evening.

Hugh rubbed his temples. He had to sever ties with Lonan. He couldn't do business with a man who dealt in illegal activities. Besides, he didn't want to work with his intolerable brother. He picked up a phone in the lobby, asking the operator to connect him.

"Hello," his mother's voice answered.

"Hello, it's Hugh."

"Darling! How are you?"

He squeezed his eyes shut. His mother's usually pleasant tone rang like a bell in his ears. "Good. Busy. I'm calling to propose a new idea to father. Is he home?"

"Yes he is. How're things coming along in New York?"

He stuck one of his fingers inside his ear. "Fine enough, but I think we may need to go another direction. Can you put Father on?"

"Oh, yes of course." She sounded a little wounded. "I'll put him on."

"Hello, son." Daniel's strong voice came onto the line. "Do you have some news?"

"I'm calling because I think we need to pursue another real estate company."

"Why is that?"

"I'm not sure about the integrity of Lonan McKenna's company. Oftentimes, the brokers aren't in the office when I call. Lonan only shows me properties in Lower Manhattan, which I'm told isn't ideal. Furthermore, his brokerage is housed in the same building as his nightclub, which sells alcoholic beverages. Customers have to give a password in order to get inside. It's their way of keeping the police in the dark."

He listened to his father's steady breath as he processed the news.

"That certainly doesn't sound good. Does Frederick attend the meetings with Lonan?"

"Most of the time."

"Have you ever visited this nightclub when a meeting wasn't planned?"

"I attended the night that Eliza sang. It's a ritzy establishment, but there's something about it that doesn't sit well with me."

"Did you see your brother there that night?"

"I did."

"Who was he with?"

"A lot of the other real estate brokers. That's another thing. Some of these so-called agents that work for Lonan don't fit the part. They look too rough."

"I think you're right. Lonan's brokerage might not be the best fit for us. We should look into other possibilities."

"I'll start today."

"First, talk with your brother and explain our decision. I don't want this to further complicate our relationship."

"Absolutely." He agreed, even though he had no intention of seeing that conversation through.

———

10:00 PM

Warren crossed through the alley onto 28th Street with a jar of gasoline, a towel, and his gun. Under the shadows of the stone buildings, he and the McKennas drifted toward The Black Velvet. They were a group of reckoning.

Lonan motioned for his men to gather around. "You each know what ya are supposed to do. Tonight, Zanneti dies." The men circled the club, careful to remain unseen. Warren uncorked the gasoline, twisted the towel, and shoved it into the bottle's mouth. Red neared the club's brick walls, dousing it with gasoline. Other McKennas disappeared around the sides of the building with jugs of fuel. Lonan struck a match.

Warren watched the small splinter of light between Lonan's fingers. With a flick of his wrist, he flung it against the drenched wall. A writhing serpent of fire snaked along the trail of gas. It gulped the fuel and multiplied into roiling tongues of heat.

Julian aligned the barrel of his Thompson with a window. Bullets collided with glass, causing it to shatter into daggers.

A second round of gunfire echoed from the opposite side of the building.

Horrified screams erupted inside the club.

Warren struck a match, lighting the soaked towel. He chucked it through the open window, yelling to Julian, "To the back door!"

Vincenzo's white Cadillac sat in the parking lot, not twelve feet from the exit.

"He be comin' out any moment, boys," Lonan hollered as he glanced around the wall toward the club's back entrance. The door flew open. Five armed men rushed from the club, encircling Vincenzo and his family.

Vincenzo clutched his revolver in one hand while the other held firmly to the elbow of his wife. His son and daughter followed closely behind.

Lonan, Warren, and Julian moved beyond the cover of the wall and fired shots. The daughter's scream rang out above the volley of bullets. Two of Zanneti's crew fell. Return fire forced Warren to leap backward. Lonan aimed again. "He's to the car."

Vincenzo swung open the rear door while his men shot back at the McKennas.

Sweat poured down Warren's brow from the heat of the flames.

Another bodyguard fell to the ground, clearing a window to Vincenzo. Lonan leveled his rifle. As Vincenzo shoved his daughter into the backseat, a bullet sliced the side of his neck. Blood sprayed from the wound. The daughter shrieked. Vincenzo's wife pushed her wounded husband into the backseat beside their daughter and son.

Warren trained his gun on the wife. Lonan ordered him to shoot, but his finger froze on the trigger. She reached for the door's handle. Lonan fired. A curdled cry escaped her lips as the bullet pierced below her shoulder blade.

The Cadillac's tires spun, kicking up dust and gravel. Vincenzo grabbed his wife as her body sagged toward the open door.

Julian unloaded on the rear window of the car as it squealed from the lot.

Warren's eyes burned from smoke and the image of terror on the wife's face.

CHAPTER THIRTY-NINE

August 17
Monday, 6:00 AM

Eliza thumbed through a stack of mail on the coffee table, thinking. It had been 36 days since she had established New York City as her home. So far, she had sung at Club Fianna four times and had recorded one song at Swifts Music Studio. She asked Clarence to send the song to the radio, but he told her they had to finish the record first. It frustrated her. Why not create interest before releasing the entire album? She considered speaking to Lonan about it, since he had taken the position as her manager. If only a music career could whisk her away from waiting tables. Working at the diner proved to be hard work with little pay. A raise wasn't likely due to the tight Mr. Smeeth.

She tossed another piece of mail on the table. After their heated talk two weeks ago, Hugh avoided her. He didn't lunch at the diner anymore. He didn't come to Club Fianna. He came a week ago to pick up Mattie for a date, but he waited in the hall. Never in her wildest dreams had she anticipated him dating Mattie O'Keefe. In part, she wondered if it was to spite her. Mattie liked to brag about things Hugh said or did, which grated her nerves. She wanted to tell her to take her remarks and share them with someone who cared. But like a good friend, she smiled and only thought the things she wished she could voice aloud. Luckily, Hugh's business venture for his father didn't allot him much time for dates.

In all honesty, she missed Hugh. She wished things hadn't fallen apart, but she didn't know how to repair the breach. Mattie said he was going to head home for a visit. She thought it might be nice to do the same, but she doubted a warm welcome. Her parents hadn't called or replied to any of her letters. As she flipped over the last piece of mail, she discovered that today was no different. A sigh pulled her shoulders down. At least she had Warren. Sure he could be reckless, but he was thrilling. He also supported her passion to become a jazz singer. That was all she needed. At least, that's what she told herself.

———

After weeks of hard work, planning, and dodging calls from Lonan and Warren, Hugh returned home. The staff carted off his luggage as he joined his parents in the parlor for morning coffee. They were eager to hear an update on business and his brother.

"I found a new brokerage who has showed me several properties in upper Manhattan. There's a particular one on the river which I think will suit us best for shipments." He sipped his coffee. "As for Freddie, I haven't seen him. I guess he hasn't the time for me or chooses not to make the time."

This had a sobering effect on his parents.

"And how is Eliza?" asked Vivian.

"Good, I suppose. We're not speaking much as of late. She made it clear that she's too busy chasing her dream—and likely Freddie—to spare a smidge of time for me."

Vivian set her cup on a saucer. "I'm sorry, dear."

He crossed a foot over his knee. "Don't be. I've moved on."

"Does she know that he's your brother?"

"Not yet."

"I thought you were going to tell her."

He sighed with annoyance. "As I said before, we're not speaking much." Reaching for the bound sheets of paper beside his chair, he handed them to his father. "Moving on to more important matters. Here are the details for our new branch."

Daniel thumbed through the papers. "It might need some adjustments, but it's a solid place to start."

"I agree. All I need are the funds to solidify our property and your signature on the purchase agreement."

"Very well. If you'll excuse us darling, we're gong to finish up in my office." They walked down the hall. As they entered Daniel's office, he asked, "How did Frederick respond to the news that we are using a different company?"

Hugh hesitated. "He doesn't exactly know."

"I told you to speak with him first."

"I had to move forward. I don't need his permission to do so."

Daniel took a seat behind his desk. "Your mother and I want to mend our relationship with Frederick; this could hinder that if handled poorly. Besides, Lonan deserves to know that we've decided to use another company so his agents aren't wasting their time."

"If they are agents." Hugh settled into a cushioned chair.

"Nevertheless, they deserve to know."

"Okay. I'll call Freddie."

"Thank you." Daniel slipped on his spectacles and flipped through the pages. "This looks good. I think you've found a good location. Is the building suitable for setting up assembly lines?"

"Absolutely. The building is sufficient to begin operations. In the future, we might need to expand, but we'll have the land to do so."

"Then let's proceed." He scribbled his signature on the final page. Setting down his pen, he folded his hands. "I have another important matter to discuss with you. I realize that we wrote you into the will as the legal heir, but now that Frederick has been found, I think we'll need to adjust those documents."

His body stiffened. He wondered if this would happen. "Are you saying you're giving everything to him?"

"No, but he is our firstborn, and as such, he should be included."

"He's hasn't been around for the last five years. He doesn't even claim us as his family. Why would you entrust anything to him?"

"I know that he left, but he deserves a second chance. If he decides he would like to return to his place as a Whitmore, then I will need to reassess the allocation of assets."

"I'm the one who stayed. I've been the faithful son. I'm your representative in Manhattan. I found us property and a building for the new branch. Me," he pointed to himself, "not Frederick. I've tried to please you in every way, but apparently that doesn't matter. Goodness, if only I had known that sooner. My whole life I've striven to meet your insurmountable standards. Freddie didn't care, but I did. Lord knows I have wanted to give up, but I didn't. But now that Freddie's been found, all my hard work means nothing. All is forgiven for the wayward child while the faithful one is cheated."

Pain creased Daniel's forehead. "I know you've worked hard. I realize that I've made mistakes while raising you boys. Perhaps I was too tough on you, but my father raised me the same way. He told me that the higher the bar is set, the higher a man will achieve. I thought higher expectations would set you boys up for success. That's all I meant to do. I saw your strength and determination. I knew you were capable of achieving anything." He paused. "You've grown into a fine man. I'm proud of you."

The words surprised him. His father had never been one to

admit his failings or feelings. He struggled to absorb the compliment. "Thank you."

"I'm proud of Frederick too. He's grown into a successful young man. I know the relationship between you boys has been strained for years, but he's your only brother. Perhaps that counts for something?"

"I doubt anything can bridge the divide between Freddie and me."

"Forgiveness might be a start."

"I'll forgive him when he apologizes."

"It doesn't work like that. Forgiveness isn't based on whether it's earned, it's offered before. It's a lot like love that way: it's given regardless if it will be returned."

His fingers tightened on the armrests of his chair. "I'm not sure how to process this conversation, and frankly, I can't. I have to go." He stood.

"Go where?"

"Back to New York."

"I thought you were going to stay a few days."

"I've changed my mind. You can send the funds once I finalize the paperwork. Goodbye, Father."

CHAPTER FORTY

Monday, 8:00 PM

Eliza stared out the window of a fancy restaurant. Below, city lights cast a glowing pattern on the Hudson River. "What a beautiful view."

"Not as beautiful as the one I'm looking at." Warren studied her from across the table.

"Thank you." A shy smile curved her lips. "I happen to like this view as well."

"Lucky me."

Halfway through their steaks, Eliza noticed Finn enter the restaurant with a rather voluptuous gal. She waved at him.

Leaving his date in the waiting area, he shuffled to their table. "Fancy runnin' into ya here. What're the odds?"

Warren shrugged. "It's a popular place."

"A valid point." Finn laid his hand on the back of her chair. "Eliza my dear, yer lookin' radiant this eve. My greatest failure in life is not spyin' ya before this plonker." He nodded toward Warren. "But if ya want a real Irishman, I'll show ya the life of shamrock green and make ya my darlin' Colleen."

Warren dismissed him with his fork. "In your dreams, Finny-boy."

"Can't fault a Patty for tryin'. My Da always said, 'Tis better to have fought and lost than never to have fought at all.'"

"Your father gave you good advice," she said.

"On that maybe. He also said, 'Cheaters never prosper, unless they get away with it.'"

She chuckled. "You make me smile. The world would be a darker place without you, Finnegan Hennessy."

Finn put a hand to his heart. "I appreciate that, lass. I best be gettin' back to my date. Enjoy yer evenin'." He nodded to Warren. "Be seein' ya in the morn."

"Is there a meeting?"

"Didn't Lonan tell ya?" Finn stepped closer to his side. His jovial expression grew serious. "We need to discuss movin' the warehouse. Zanneti's been sniffin' around now that his health is on the mend. May need another job to put him down for good."

Warren threw a furtive glance at her. "We'll talk more in the office."

"Got ya. Enjoy yer meal."

She watched Finn walk away. "What's he talking about?"

"Office details. Nothing to worry about."

There was something strange about Lonan's real estate company. "Zanneti is the man who threatened you at the races, right?"

He nodded.

"Then why would you want to further upset him? Sounds like you guys are digging up trouble."

"Maybe, but it's something we've got to do."

She frowned. "I don't like it, especially after the way he spoke to you in Saratoga."

"Listen doll, business is business. Sometimes companies feud and things get difficult, but it will all blow over." He gave her a reassuring smile. "How's your meal?"

She wished she believed him, but she sensed it wasn't the truth. "My dinner is wonderful. Thank you for taking me here."

"You're welcome."

After they finished eating, they exited the restaurant into the city lights.

"I'm not ready for the evening to be over," he said.

"Would you like to come to my apartment? We could bring up a couple of coffees from Griffin's restaurant."

"I'd like that."

Opening the passenger door, he helped her inside his Ford. Twenty minutes later, they entered her apartment, coffee in hand.

She hung up her coat and handbag on the rack beside the door. "Mattie?"

No answer.

"I guess she's gone."

"Does that surprise you?"

"Not really." She settled onto the velvety sofa beside Warren. Taking a sip from her Styrofoam cup, she grimaced. "I'm not going to lie, this tastes awful."

"Well, we did get it from your hotel's restaurant."

"Good point." She set the cup on the table. "Thanks again for dinner. It was an elegant place."

"Glad you liked it." He placed an arm behind her shoulders. "You're amazing, you know that?"

"I do now."

Cupping her face, he lowered his lips to her mouth.

The firm press of his kiss formed goose bumps on her arms. She leaned closer to him. Butterflies danced in her stomach at the touch of his warm palm upon her knee. It wasn't right. She should tell him to remove his hand, but she didn't want to. Everything about him enticed her. If temptation had a scent, it would smell like Warren.

He moved his hand below the hem of her dress.

Her conscience called out, but she shoved her inhibitions aside as his mouth descended to her ear.

Lowering her back on the sofa, his kiss traced the expanse of her neck.

She sighed, ready to give up the fight of being good, when the door swung open.

Mattie strolled inside, laughing. Hugh followed behind her.

Eliza bolted into an upright position, sending Warren backwards.

"Oh," Mattie blinked. "I didn't know you were here. Sorry to intrude."

Heat flooded her veins. Eliza felt her face blush.

Hugh's eyes betrayed his apparent shock.

"If I had known you had company, we could have gone back to Hugh's for coffee," said Mattie. "Of course, we still can if you'd like?"

"N–no, that's fine." Eliza rose to her feet. "We were just having coffee ourselves."

Mattie chuckled. "Is that what people are calling it these days?"

The blush in her cheeks spread across her face and down her neck. Sweat formed on the inside of her palms.

Hugh stared at Warren. His eyes burned with anger.

Warren stood, his face cool and aloof. "I best get going."

"You don't have to go," said Mattie. "I was only teasing."

"No, I should." He turned to her. "I'll call you later." With that, he swept around Hugh and out the door.

Mattie offered her an apologetic look.

Retreating to the bedroom, she shut the bedroom door behind her. She couldn't believe Hugh had caught her on the couch with Warren. She pressed her hands against her chest to still her breathing. It was only a kiss. There wasn't anything to be ashamed of. She didn't do anything wrong.

Breathing deeply, she looked into the mirror mounted above her dresser. Her mouth dropped open. Her hair was slightly disheveled. The top button of her dress had been undone. Mortified, she fell onto the edge of her bed. Did Hugh notice? How could she be so dumb? How would she ever face him again? She flopped facedown into her pillow. "How could

I be so stupid?" She drove a fist into her mattress, angry that Warren had been able to seduce her. Angry that he had taken advantage of her. But even more angry that Hugh had seen her in Warren's arms.

CHAPTER FORTY-ONE

August 18
Tuesday, 7:30 AM

Hugh squealed to a stop in front of Warren's house. Storming to the front entrance, he jabbed the doorbell. After ten seconds, he rang it again.

Ten rings later, Warren stumbled to the door, wiping sleep out of his eyes. "What are you doing here?"

"We had a deal." He shoved past his brother into the entryway. "You said you would stay away from her."

"What can I say? It didn't work out."

"You never intended to keep up your end of the bargain, did you?"

"Turn it down a notch, Hugh. It's way too early to be yourself."

"You promised you wouldn't see her again."

"Why do you care? Aren't you seeing Mattie?"

His angry front faltered. It wasn't that he was dating Mattie, he just needed a way to keep tabs on Eliza. "Sort of, but that's not the point. We had an agreement."

"I actually tried to keep the deal, but she pursued me."

"Don't blame her for what I saw last night." He pointed a

finger at him. "That was your doing. Eliza isn't some tramp. She's not the kind of girl who kisses men on couches. You pushed her into that situation."

"I didn't have to push at all. She wanted it."

"Liar!"

"I ain't lying. Eliza wants a man, not a boy. Go home, Hugh."

He grabbed Warren by the collar. "If you lay a hand on her ever again, I swear I will—"

"You'll what?"

He shoved Warren backward. "The deal's off. I've contacted another real estate brokerage. They found me a property. I returned yesterday from showing the details to Father. He signed the contract."

Fear washed over Warren's face. "You can't use another company."

"It's too late. The contract is signed. I have a meeting with the company today."

"You don't get it. This isn't some kind of game. Lonan's a shrewd man; he hates to lose a business deal."

"That's your problem, not mine."

"It is your problem. He'll be gunning for you."

"What kind of businessman does that? I'm allowed to change my mind."

"You don't understand," Warren shook his head, "There's more to it."

"Tell me what I don't understand. What's Lonan really up to? He's not into real estate at all, is he?"

Warren's eyes shifted to the floor. "I can't explain."

"I don't know what kind of business you're a part of, but it doesn't matter. I've changed companies. Lonan's going to have to deal with it." Sidestepping his brother, he walked out the door.

———

Turning on the faucet, Eliza wrung a dirty rag under the hot water. Another day at the diner. She thumped it inside the sink over and over, freeing it from crumbs.

A throat cleared behind her.

She flinched. Spinning around, she found Hazel watching her.

"You okay, kiddo?"

"Yes, I'm fine."

"I'm sure that rag would agree." Hazel propped a hand on her hip. "I think it's time for a break." Looking over her shoulder, she called to the other waitress. "Hey Fern, Liza and I are taking ten."

Fern nodded as she poured another cup of coffee.

Draping her arm around Eliza's shoulders, Hazel steered her out the backdoor. She tugged a cigarette and match from her uniform's pocket. Lighting it, she inhaled. "Want a smoke?"

"No thanks."

"You wanna tell me what's eating you?"

"Life just isn't easy."

"It's giving you lemons, huh? It usually does. So what's your dilemma?"

"I guess I'm confused about men and love."

"Oh, baby." Hazel shook her head. "Truth is that I'm no expert on either. I'm divorced, haven't had a decent relationship since. But I will tell you this," she looked at Eliza with an intent pinch of her brows, "I still believe in love. A woman deserves to have someone who will be faithful to her until death." She shrugged. "I just haven't found that person yet."

"Was your husband," she paused, "unfaithful?"

Hazel took another puff. "Yeah. He liked to cheat."

"I'm sorry to hear that."

"It's been ten years since the divorce. Took a long time to get over it. I had to come to the realization that I deserve to be loved." Sadness shifted in her eyes. "For a long time, I didn't think I was worthy. That's a bad place to be." She paused. "I don't know what's happened to you in the past, but I see pain in your eyes. You left home to become a famous singer. I'm wondering why? What makes that dream important to you?"

She lowered her head. "Music is the only thing I'm good at. It's all I have."

"That's not true." Hazel touched her shoulder. "You are more than your music. Your worth isn't contingent upon your talent. Worth doesn't have to be proven, simply accepted. Someone somewhere is going to be better at something than you. Does that mean they have more value? Absolutely not. You are the only Eliza Adrienne Belcourt. That makes you special."

"If only it were that simple."

"It is that simple. All you have to do is accept the truth."

"My last 18 years have taught me something different."

"Then you were taught wrong. No one can replace you, sweetheart. You're special because God himself dreamed you up. That's the real truth."

"What if I don't believe in God?"

Hazel inhaled a slow draft. "I think you do, but you're scared. You're afraid that you've failed him, or that he won't approve of you. But you can't fail him. His love isn't determined by our performance."

"You talk about God like you know him."

"I do." Hazel smiled. "I might be rough around the edges, but He loves me just the same."

Fern stuck her head out the door. "Hey you two, it's bananas in here. Quit your gabbing and come inside."

"We're coming, Fern." Hazel put her cigarette out on the cement. She patted Eliza's cheek. "Don't worry, baby. It'll come to you."

CHAPTER FORTY-TWO

August 20
Thursday, 10:00 PM

A roll of thunder rumbled through the evening sky. Dusk hugged the McKenna warehouse like an eerie cloak. Warren and Red hoisted another crate of whiskey into a truck. A light rain tapped their hats. From under the brim of his hat, Warren studied the clouds. "They're gonna break soon."

Red nodded.

A jagged strand of lightning illuminated the sky for a second. A loud boom sounded above, and the clouds opened, letting forth streams of rain.

Warren and Red ran into the warehouse, already drenched.

Lonan rubbed a hand across his chin, appraising the sky. "Doesn't look like it's goin' to let up. We need to get everythin' to the new location tonight. We've got no choice but to work in the rain."

Warren wiped a wet hand over his face. "How many more crates we got?"

Finn scanned the stack. "Ten."

"It shouldn't take long if we—" Lonan's sentence dropped off as Vincenzo Zanneti and nine of his men entered the building with pistols ready. The thunder in the sky and whoosh of rain had concealed their approaching tires.

Without time for cover, the McKennas met them head on.

Warren ripped out his Export, firing at a man in front of him. A return bullet sliced the sleeve of his jacket. He slammed his pistol into an opponents face before shooting another man in the chest. Beside him, Lonan emptied his last round and pulled out his knife. Lonan slipped on the wet floor. As his balance faltered, a bullet cut below his shoulder. Before his challenger could seal his fate, Julian hooked the man's jaw with bloody knuckles. The Italian stumbled, falling to his knees. Lonan swiped the blade of his knife across the man's neck. Julian buckled as a bullet tore his calf. Warren caught a punch to his jaw, reeled back a step, and unloaded his last round. "Reny, behind you!" bellowed Lonan. As Warren turned, Finn leapt forward, shoving him aside. He heard the crack of a pistol, but felt no bullet. Red fired at Zanneti and the last of his men as they retreated. He made contact with one, but the rest escaped.

Despite the thunder and rain, the warehouse grew silent. Mud and bodies painted the floor. Finn lay in the middle, sputtering for air.

Warren stared at the large spot of blood darkening Finn's chest. He ripped off a piece of his shirt and pressed it against the wound. "Hold on, Finn. I'll get you to the hospital."

Finn coughed. "I ain't gonna make it."

"Sure you will, Finny," said Warren. "We still got to take that trip to Chicago. Think of all those Mollys you'll meet."

Lonan knelt by them. "Ya got to fight it, Finn. Don't ya give up."

"Dying is…" Finn strained to pull in a breath. "A thing that can be done." He coughed.

Warren placed an arm under his head. "Breathe."

In a voice above a whisper, Finn added, "As easy as lying down."

"No, Finny boy." Warren shook his head. "It's not your time. Not today."

Finn offered a weak smile. Blood trickled out of the corner of his mouth as his eyes rolled back. His head sagged against Warren's arm.

This wasn't supposed to happen. Not to Finn. Warren stared at his friend, fighting back tears.

———

A loud bang sounded on the door. Eliza jolted upright in bed. She glanced around the dark room, disoriented. The knock came again, more persistent this time. She scrambled to her feet. "Who's there?"

"It's Warren and Jules. Please, let us in."

Throwing on her housecoat, she rushed down the hall. She flung the door wide to find Warren supporting Julian under his arm. She gasped at the sight of them. Their clothes were torn and bloodied. Warren's jaw displayed dark bruises. Julian's face bore similar marks. His left pant leg was ripped off at the knee, exposing a blood-drenched bandage around his calf. "What happened?"

"An attack." Warren assisted Julian to the bathroom. "Get Mattie." He lowered him on the toilet seat.

She ran to the bedroom, yanking the covers off Mattie's sedated form. "Get up! Your brother's hurt."

Mattie rubbed her face.

"Julian is in the bathroom. He's bleeding."

When Mattie saw Julian's bloody bandage, she rebuked Warren in a high pitch. "Why didn't you take him to the hospital?"

"He wouldn't go. He demanded that I take him here. He said you'd know what to do."

Mattie swore. "Reny, you're—"

"Whiskey," Julian moaned.

"Get it for him. It's in the cabinet." Turning the faucet to hot, Mattie knelt by Julian's feet. "Eliza, don't just stand there. Grab my sewing kit from the bedroom."

Running to the bedroom, she snatched the wooden box from the dresser. Her heart raced in her chest. Was that a bullet wound in Julian's leg? How did it happen? Why wouldn't he go to the hospital? She unclasped the latches and placed it on the bathroom floor.

Mattie inspected the wound. "Looks like the bullet made a clean pass." She pressed a hot cloth to the wound.

Julian cringed as he drank from a bottle of Jack Daniels.

"How many times am I gonna have to do this?" Mattie shook her head as new blood seeped out.

"You always manage," said Julian.

"There's gonna come a time when I won't be able to fix you." Mattie washed the wound, ran the rag under the steaming water, and wrung it out. "Warren, take this and apply pressure." After she sanitized her needle under the hot water, she proceeded to thread it.

When the needle pierced Julian's skin, Eliza's head grew dizzy. She looked away sucking in a deep breath.

Mattie worked swiftly as though she'd had plenty of experience. Finishing the stiches, she tied off the end. "Was anyone else hurt?"

"Lonan and some of the guys have some nasty wounds." Warren rubbed the back of his neck. "Finn didn't..." He shook his head, unable to finish the sentence.

Mattie rose to her feet. "What about Finn?"

"He's dead," Julian whispered.

Eliza's hand flew to her mouth.

Mattie looked between her brother and Warren, her eyes lit with horror. She thrust her fist against the wall, cursing. "I knew this would happen. It always happens."

"He's in a better place," said Julian.

Tears filled her eyes. "I hate this life."

"It should have been me." A glazed look of despair spread over Warren's face.

"What do you mean?" Eliza asked.

"He chose to do it, Reny," said Julian. "Ya couldn't have stopped him."

"What's going on? Who killed Finn?"

Mattie's upper lip curled. She shook her head with contempt. "Naïve Eliza. You still don't get it, do you?"

"Not now," said Warren, almost beseeching her.

Mattie glared through her tears. "People are dying, and she's oblivious." Hysteria amplified her tone. "Open your eyes, Liza. Your precious Warren isn't a real estate agent. Neither is Jules. None of them are. That's just a cover."

"Mattie, please," said Warren.

She steamrolled on. "They're the most powerful mob in Manhattan run by Lonan McKenna. Finn's a causality of war."

Eliza blinked, completely stunned.

Warren sighed. "I'm sorry this is how you had to find out."

"What would have been better, Reny? If you had taken her to a fancy meal and told her?" Mattie sneered. "You should've been straight from the start."

Eliza faced her. "Why didn't you tell me?"

"Because Warren told me not to."

Julian wobbled on the stool. "I need to lie down."

Warren caught him under the arm and Mattie swept under the other. They supported him into the parlor. Warren glanced at Eliza as he left the room.

Confusion muddled her mind. Who were these people? Everything she knew was based on a lie. A shiver rolled through her. Mattie. Warren. Lonan. All of them were part of the mob, and she was connected to them. The truth squeezed her lungs like a vice. She pressed her palms onto the sink counter.

A footstep sounded in the doorway.

Her body tensed.

Warren spoke in a tender voice. "Eliza, you don't have to be afraid. You're not in any danger."

Anger sharpened her reasoning. "Not in danger? Look at you. Look at Julian. What happened tonight?"

"The man from the races, Vincenzo Zanneti, is a boss of a rival gang. Tonight, his crew attacked us at Lonan's warehouse. It's like Mattie said, it's a war and certain things must be done in order to stay in control."

"Control of what?"

"Lower Manhattan businesses."

"So you don't do real estate at all?"

"We do whatever pays the most. We manage a collection of companies. They pay us in exchange for protection from other local mobs."

"What if a business doesn't want your help? What if they don't pay?"

"There are penalties."

"Have you…killed people?"

He avoided her gaze. "I've done whatever has been asked of me."

"Meaning whatever Lonan asks of you, right?"

He nodded.

"Can't you get out?"

"Once you're in, you don't get out."

"I can't believe this." A tremor reverberated through her body. "I don't know you. I don't know any of you. All I know are lies."

"You do know me. I'm the same person."

"No, you're not. You tricked me. I can't fathom the things you've done."

His jaw clenched. "Go ahead. Blame me. Blame all of us. But the truth is that you would have nothing without us. I directed you to Mattie. She gave you a place to stay and helped you get a job. I arranged your audition at the club. Lonan set up your recording project. You say you've been tricked, but all we've done is help you."

Sweat formed inside her shaky palms. "I didn't know who was helping me."

"Yeah, well now you do. So what? You gonna stop singing at the club? You gonna give up your contract?"

She looked at the floor.

"No, I don't think you will. And you know why?" He stepped closer. "Because just like me, you like the benefits."

Her lip quivered.

"It's okay," he lifted her chin with his finger. "You don't need to give them up. You deserve what you've worked for. It doesn't matter how you got it."

She should get as far from him as possible, but he was right. She didn't want to give up her success. She had worked hard for it. It wasn't fair to walk away from everything now. How would she accomplish her dreams if she did?

Warren took her into his arms.

She caved. Sobs shook her body.

He held her tightly against his chest, racked with his own grief.

CHAPTER FORTY-THREE

August 24
Monday, 10:15 AM

Hugh unlocked the building for his family's new steel company. Flipping a switch, the overhead bulbs brightened with a low whirr. He looked around the room with a proud smile. His father would be impressed when he saw this. Boxes of equipment rested against the back wall. He had a crew coming in two days to assemble the factory lines. Yesterday, he placed a help wanted ad in the local paper. His father planned to join him for the interviews in five days. Crossing his arms, he nodded to himself. He had done well.

"See ya got yerself a building."

He spun around to see Lonan and one of his colleagues enter. A slight shiver ran through his bones.

"Looks like the right choice fer yer company." Lonan nodded in approval. "So when's the grand openin'?"

"In a few months. We have hiring and training first."

"Of course. Too bad we couldn't have helped ya find the place, but I'm glad ya got it settled just the same."

"Thank you. I appreciate that you understand my decision."

"No trouble at all. I'm a businessman. One thing I

understand is that a lad's gotta make choices that best suit him."
Lonan drew closer. "That's why I've come by. Though we
weren't able to help ya get started, we'd like to help ya get
properly established. I been runnin' businesses in this city since
I was a young lad. I know the ins and outs. So I tell ya what I'm
gonna do. I'm gonna help ya. I'll become yer partner." He
offered a grand smile.

Hugh's brow furrowed. "I'm not looking for a partner. I
have the financing and management taken care of."

"Right, but have ya got yerself the proper security? Ya know,
protection?"

"I don't think I understand what you mean."

"As a partner in yer company, I be ensuring that everythin'
remains safe and sound. This bustlin' city can be dangerous,
'specially for new owners like yerself. So in exchange for a
commission, I'll see to it that yer buildin' and property don't
have any accidents."

"What if I don't accept your partnership?"

Lonan narrowed his eyes. "Then ya'd be riskin' the safety of
yer business and yer workers. Of course, managers like yerself
usually get it the worst. This city's filled with all sorts of
unpleasant folks."

"I'm not one to be bullied." He planted his feet. "I'm not
looking for a partner. Kindly see yourself out."

"I can respect that." Lonan turned to his colleague. "Red, I
guess we best be on our way."

"Such a pity," said Red. In three swift steps, he came toward
Hugh. He rammed a punch into his abdomen, then sent
another blow across his jaw.

Lonan caught Red's arm as he prepared to punch again.

Hugh wiped blood from his lip. "Who are you people?"

"We're the most powerful men in Manhattan," said Lonan.

"You're not a real estate company?"

"We are when it's convenient. We'll be back in a couple of
days to collect our first installment as your partner. Three

hundred should be sufficient." He turned to leave.

"Does Warren know about this?"

Lonan stopped. "What's Warren gotta do with it?"

"He hasn't told you who I am?"

"He says he hasn't met ya before."

"It's hard to believe he wouldn't know me when we were raised under the same roof for 17 years."

"Ya sayin' he's yer brother?"

"That's right. His birth certificate says, *Frederick Warren Whitmore*. He's my blood, even if he won't claim it."

Lonan's face darkened. He knocked Hugh to the ground with a fist to his face. "You have two days to pay up or get out."

———

Eliza clocked out of the diner, depleted. Days ago, she learned the truth about Lonan and his gang and attended a funeral to bury Finn, a casualty of mob life. Though she felt trapped in their mob world, she couldn't leave. She refused to lose everything she had built. Her taxi stopped outside Swifts Music. At least here she found happiness. As she stepped out, the cab's door snagged her necklace. It snapped. The music note slipped off the broken chain, clanging on the pavement. "My necklace!" She knelt down to scoop the pieces into her hand. It was a cheap carnival trinket, not worth the price of fixing, and yet it saddened her. Such emotion seemed completely irrational. There were other necklaces she could purchase. Better ones. She stopped at a trashcan beside the entrance to the studio. Stretching her clenched hand over the can, she paused. She should let it go. It was fake gold anyway. Her arm trembled. Why did she care about this? It didn't have any value. It was broken. With a huff, she stuffed the pieces into her purse. She didn't know why, but she couldn't part with it. As she entered the lobby, she found stacks of boxes and equipment.

Clarence scurried around the room, spouting directions to

the receptionist. She jotted notes at a feverish pace.

"What's going on?" she asked.

His head popped up. "Eliza, what are you doing here?"

"Our recording appointment."

"Appointment? Oh, yes. That's going to be a problem." He walked through the maze of boxes and pointed to one. Turning, he shouted to his receptionist, "This needs a label." He continued his walk. "As of today, we're relocating."

"To where?"

"Anywhere but New York City."

Dread knotted her stomach. "Will I have to commute?"

He glanced in her direction, his expression disbelieving. "That's not what I'm saying. Swifts Music is finished. New management moved in yesterday. I'm through with it."

"Will this new management be taking over my contract?" She stared at him with pleading eyes.

Sighing, he came to her. "Sorry, doll." He placed a hand on her shoulder. "I've got nothing for you. I can't handle the charade anymore. I'm tired of paying for nothing and getting nowhere. This city's out of control. The studio ain't worth my life. I'm moving to a less crazy place. You're a sweet girl; you really do have talent. I wish ya the best." Turning his back, he hurried away and spouted more directions.

She left the building in a daze. Rain pattered on her hat. Her contract was over. She wouldn't be completing the record. How could this happen? It didn't seem right. There had to be another option. Maybe Lonan could help her? It troubled her to be tied to gangsters, but she didn't know whom else to turn to. She caught a cab to Club Fianna.

Kiki reclined at her desk, enthralled in another edition of Vogue.

"Hello, Kiki."

Kiki glanced up. "Hi, Eliza."

She twisted her gloves between trembling hands. "Is Lonan in today?"

"He's in the club. Go on in."

She stepped into the hallway when the clubs' double doors swung open. Lonan emerged from them, looking perplexed. "Hello, Lonan. Do you have a moment?"

"Eliza, dear. I do have an important meetin' to get to. Could ya make it quick?"

"Yes, of course. I just came from Swifts Music." She paused, holding back a sob. "Clarence told me that he is ending my contract. He said new management has moved in. He's relocating. Is there anything you can do to help me? I've come so far. It's not fair for it to be over."

"New management, eh?" Lonan swore under his breath. "I work and work to ensure the businesses of Lower Manhattan and fer what? To have spineless men like Clarence buckle under pressure and filthy Italians overrun me streets." He shook his head. "Life's not fair, lass. I don't have more studio contacts. Me plate is too full to worry about yer record deal. Yer on yer own. I wish ya the best of luck." He breezed past her.

She stood alone in the hall, feeling like she'd been slapped. "Is Warren here?" she called to Kiki.

"In the club," she hollered back.

Pushing through the doors, she scanned the room. Warren sat at the bar with a scotch and a slender blonde draped over his shoulder, whispering in his ear. He chuckled. Eliza's eyebrows pinched together. Warren slid a hand down the woman's back, pulling her close. "Let's go to your place," said the blonde, kissing his neck. "No one is here right now," he said laying a hand on the bar, "this counter is sturdy." Eliza gasped.

Warren's head snapped in her direction. "Eliza." He rose from the barstool.

Bolting from the room, she hastened through the hall, past Kiki's desk, and out the lobby doors. Her heart raced in her chest. Overhead, the sky had darkened to onyx. Rain fell with fury. Jogging down the sidewalk, she waved her hand hysterically to an approaching cab. It washed up to the curb with a spray from its tires. She threw open the backdoor and fell into the seat, soaked through to her cotton shift.

"Sorry, ma'am. Didn't mean ta splash ya." He spun to face her. "It's rainin' purty hard, eh?"

She glared at him. "502 West 35th Street."

He turned around without another word.

Warren was cheating on her. Squeezing the handle of her purse, her knuckles grew white. How dare he do this to her? How dare they all do this to her? Warren. Lonan. Clarence. Those wretched liars with their silk-lined smiles.

The taxi stopped at Hotel Griffin.

She tossed the driver his fee and trudged up the uneven path. As she plodded through the lobby, the desk clerk said, "Hey, you look like that girl who sang at Club Fianna. Are you Eliza Adrienne?" She kept walking. As usual, the door to her apartment wouldn't budge. "Stupid door." She drove her hip into it. It popped open.

Mattie looked over from the loveseat and exhaled a draw of smoke. "You look terrible."

"I hate this city." She dropped her handbag on the floor. "Everything I've worked for is ruined. The music deal, my relationship, it's all done."

"I'm not following you."

She marched to Mattie, yanked the cigarette from her fingers, took a drag, and shoved it into the ashtray. "I went to Swifts Music today. Clarence told me he's relocating; my recording contract is terminated," she snapped her fingers. "Just like that. I went to Club Fianna to talk with Lonan. He says he can't do anything to help me. Then to make matters worse, I found Warren kissing another girl. That son of a gun is cheating on me."

"That's horrible."

"Horrible?" Her hands balled into fists. "That's all you can say?"

"Life's a gamble, baby." Mattie shrugged. "Sometimes you hit the cards right and other times you come up short. Sure, it's a blow that you lost your contract, but those are the breaks. Find a new studio," she waved her hand in dismissal, "and a new man."

"What?" She stared at her, aghast. "I put my heart on the line, first with Warren, then with the studio. I deserve better than this."

"You really are blind, aren't you?" Mattie gave a cynical snort. "Warren's never been faithful. He doesn't know how to be. Like I said before, no one in this city is."

Her top lip curled back. "I can't believe he'd do this to me."

"Sweet Eliza. You think you're special, don't you? You think somehow you're an exception? That problems won't come to you? Well, I've got news: this is New York City. Your heritage, your social class, they don't mean nothing. Here, you're simply another person. And to Warren, you're just a dame among many."

Fury lit her eyes. Leaning over, she slapped Mattie across the face.

Mattie gasped, cradling her cheek.

Snatching her handbag off the floor, she stomped out of the building. She didn't bother hailing a taxi; there wasn't anywhere to go. Instead, she walked in the drizzling rain, shivering inside her wet clothes. How did it all go so wrong? Manhattan was supposed to offer her a life of promise. It was supposed to solve her problems. It was supposed to make her a star, make her someone great. Make her a person her parents would be proud of. "It wasn't supposed to be like this."

Perhaps she should have listened to Neville. She had warned her about the city's dark side. Heck, even Warren had told her that it wasn't all shimmer and sunshine. It didn't matter. All she heard was her heart's desperation to become someone worthy. She had believed the stories in the magazines that boasted that New York City was a place where glittering hopes and dreams came true. That's why she had chased her chance for fame without caution.

Wise guys like Lonan and Warren had spotted her talent and eager innocence. They had taken advantage of her, played her for the fool. She had shaken hands with the devil, Lonan himself, and dated his sidekick, Warren. In trusting them, she'd been burned.

Sighing, she sank onto a sidewalk bench. Raindrops hit puddles on the street, creating small ripples. She would have to start over from scratch. How would she find another club? Another studio? She recalled the first time she had sung at Shaker's Nightclub in Philadelphia. Her performance would have failed had it not been for the man in the bowler hat, and she wouldn't have sung at Fianna had it not been for Warren. Was she even capable of succeeding on her own? She stared forlornly at her feet. She didn't know if she could do it alone, but whom did she have to help her?

CHAPTER FORTY-FOUR

Monday, 8:30 PM

Eliza knocked on Room 26.

"Who's there?"

"It's Eliza." The sound of a chain jingled; the door opened. When she saw Hugh's bruised face and cut lip, she gasped. "What happened to you?"

He stared at her disheveled appearance. "I could ask you the same question."

"It's been a horrible day."

Peeking into the hall, he pulled her inside. "Same here." He reset the lock.

"Who did that to your face?"

"Lonan."

She sucked in an astonished breath.

"He came to my new building today and offered to become my partner, which means I have to pay him for protection from unfortunate accidents that could happen to myself and my business. When I said I wasn't interested, he and a guy named Red did this," he gestured to his face. "He said he'd be back in a couple days for his first installment. I'm leaving the city tomorrow morning."

She noted a suitcase on the bed. "Heading home?"

"That's right."

"What about the new branch?"

"It's over. I can't do business when I'm being bullied by a mob." He crossed his arms. "Did you know that their so-called real estate company is actually a cover for their gang?"

"I found out days ago. I'm still processing it all."

"I'm not sure how I'm going to explain this to my father." He sank onto the edge of the bed.

"We've been fed lies. I'm sure your parents will understand that." She sat next to him. "I'm sorry they hurt you." She exhaled a slow breath. "I lost my recording contract today. Swifts Music Studio is closing its doors. I'm not sure what to do. I've dreamed of being a singer for too long. Maybe we need to get out of Manhattan and move to a different city in New York?"

"We?" He studied her. "I thought you chose Warren."

Her lips curled in disgust. "He's a liar. I don't ever want to see him again. You are the only one who has been honest with me." She laid her palm over his hand. "I want you to know how sorry I am. I haven't treated you fairly. You're the only real friend I have. Will you forgive me?"

He looked down at the carpet. "Did Warren tell you who he really is?"

"He told me that he's a member of Lonan McKenna's gang."

"But do you know his real name?"

"It's not Warren Moore?"

He shook his head. "His actual name is Frederick Warren Whitmore."

She tilted her head in confusion.

"He's my brother." He paused, watching her register his words. "At 17, he ran away from home. We hired someone to search, but we couldn't find him. I didn't know if he was alive until I saw him at Club Fianna."

"But he…and you…" She rubbed a hand against her throat. "Why didn't you tell me?"

"I was going to, but then when I saw you with him…" He exhaled. "Growing up, he always won out. Every girl liked him more. I wanted to prove that I could beat him. I thought I could. It's childish, I know, but I wanted you to love me and only me. I wanted you to choose me. The night you performed at Club Fianna, I was sure of your feelings. But then you rejected me and picked him." He crossed to a dresser. "Everything changed. I couldn't figure out how to tell you the truth. So I didn't."

She stroked a wet curl behind her ear. The fog inside her brain made it hard to think. "What happens now?"

"I'm going home. My father and I can start a new branch in Philadelphia or Harrisburg, anywhere in Pennsylvania for that matter." He opened a drawer, pulled out a handful of ties, and crossed back to the bed. Lifting the lid of his suitcase, he threw them inside. "I'm through with New York."

She fidgeted with a damp ribbon on her dress. "Are you through with me too?"

"That's impossible." He returned to the dresser. "I can't release what I never had."

She opened her hands in plea. "I didn't want to hurt you. You are my only friend, the only person who has ever supported me. I need you."

His disbelieving expression hardened. "You rejected me, remember? You told me to move on. And now you need me? I can't keep up with you, Eliza."

Before he reached in a drawer, she saw hurt on his face. Her throat knotted. A realization dawned on her: she had treated him the same way she had treated Neville. She had used him when it suited her. He gave her his loyalty, and she gave him nothing in return. "I'm sorry. I haven't been a good friend. I used you. You have every right to be upset with me. I know that I pushed you away, but I made a mistake." She walked to him. "Let me prove to you that I can be a better friend."

"It's not that simple. I saw my brother kiss you. Touch you." His forehead scrunched. "You let him."

"I was naïve. He played me for a fool. Today, I even found out that he hasn't been faithful to me."

A knowing look crossed his face. "Ah, that's why you're here. I'm the fallback plan."

"That's not it. You're the only person I trust. You are my dearest friend. I don't want to lose you."

"I need more than friendship." He crossed to the door. "I think you should go."

"Please, Hugh. Give me a second chance."

"Funny, I asked you to give me another chance, too, and you refused." He turned the knob, pushing it open. "Now you know how it feels."

She drifted out of his room like a ghost. She never thought he would reject her. He had been her only consistency in life. Now, she had lost him, too. Standing in the lobby, she looked around, disoriented. She didn't know where to go or what to do. Her heart ached. If only she could go home. The front desk's telephone caught her eye. Maybe her parents would forgive her. Then she could piece her life back together. As the phone number was plugged in, she waited.

A maid's voice answered. "Hello, Belcourt residence."

"This is Eliza. Is my mother home?"

"No dear, I'm afraid she's out. Your father is in his office. Shall I put him on?"

"Yes, please." Her heart sped up.

"Hello."

"Father, it's Eliza." She hurried on. "I'm sorry for running away. I made a mistake. Can I please come home?"

Silence.

Her voice trembled. "Will you let me come home?"

"The daughter I once had chose to leave and ruin everything I worked to build. I no longer know her."

The line went dead.

Her fingers grew limp. The phone dropped to the floor. His words echoed in her ears, triggering a faint memory.

She peeked inside her father's study; he wasn't there. Her eyes locked on his grand desk. Books with gold bindings and pristine paper sat on top, beckoning her to take a closer look. Hurrying inside, she stared at a cluster of shiny pens. They were lovely. She uncapped one, drawing pictures on papers and envelopes. Her works of art stained her fingers with smudges of black ink. She giggled until she heard a low voice in the doorway.

"Eliza Adrienne Belcourt." Hector entered the room with Katherine behind him. "What are you doing?"

She smiled. "Drawing pictures."

"This is my office, not your playroom." He walked up to his desk, his lips pulled tight. "You are scribbling on my important business documents. Can't you see these papers are not blank?"

"I'm sorry. Please don't be angry, Father."

He shook his head.

"She's just a child, Hector." Katherine placed a hand on his arm. "She didn't mean any harm."

"She has no business coming into my office. She's old enough to know better. I don't understand why God saw fit to give me this extra burden. Instead of having an heir, I have been stuck with a useless little girl." He crossed his arms. "Eliza, you are never to come in here again. Understand?"

Her lower lip trembled. "Yes, sir."

"Come dear, we must wash your hands." Katherine took her by the arm.

A hand tapped Eliza on the shoulder. "Ma'am, are you all right?"

She blinked.

The desk clerk stared at her. "Might I help you with something?"

She exited the building without offering a reply. He couldn't help her; no one could. Her father was right. She was useless.

———

Warren sat in the back corner of Club Fianna. Downing his third round of scotch, he stared into the glass. Twenty-three years of life paraded through his mind in a colorful array of bad decisions. He had seen and done more horrible things than he could count. His conscience was stained. Guilt tightened around his throat, choking him with the image of Finn on the warehouse floor. It should have been him. He should have died, not Finn. In truth, he was glad that Finn had taken the bullet for him. He wasn't ready to die. But in his line of work, death hovered. If only he could escape.

The waitress brought him another scotch.

Maybe he could go someplace far away, where no one would find him. He could start over, become a better person, and make his parents proud. A fresh beginning would be perfect, especially if he had Eliza beside him. Her anguished expression replayed in his mind. He had to convince her to forgive him. Then they would flee and start over together.

Finishing his drink, he shrugged on his jacket and headed for the door.

———

The soles of Eliza's shoes slid upon the sidewalk with every weary step. Her arms hung limp at her sides. It was all meaningless. Dreams. Life. Love. Why would God, if he did exist, want her? She didn't have anything to offer. Wandering up the path to Hotel Griffin, she drifted inside. When she opened the door, Mattie sat upright on the sofa.

"I didn't think you would come back."

Eliza tossed her wet jacket aside. "I didn't plan to."

"What changed your mind?"

"My father said I wasn't welcome home. So I came back here."

"I'm sorry about the things I said earlier. You had every right to slap me."

She shrugged. "Let's forget about it."

"Sounds good to me. Wanna get drunk?"

"Why not."

"Take a load off. I'll pour us some gin." Mattie opened a cabinet. Filling a glass, she handed it to her.

She threw back the full drink. "Ugh. That's awful."

"Careful. You're not used to drinking this stuff."

"I'll be fine. And if I'm not, even better." She lifted her empty glass. "Fill it."

"Suit yourself." Mattie topped it off, handing her the refill. "Where'd you go?"

She stared at the liquid swaying in her glass. "Nowhere."

A knock sounded on the door. Mattie opened it. "What are you doing here?"

She heard a voice in the hall say, "I came to apologize to Eliza." It belonged to Warren.

"She doesn't want to see you." Anger sharpened Mattie's tone.

"I'm not leaving until I speak to her."

Finishing her second drink, Eliza rose to pour herself a third. A swirl of heat swept through her head. She sat back down. "Go ahead, let the cheat in."

Mattie stepped aside with a sneer.

"I came to say that I'm sorry." Warren lowered beside her.

She scooted farther from him. "Words are easy."

"You're right. But I mean them. I'm a fool for hurting you. You are the best thing that has come into my life. I don't want to lose you."

"Why would I trust anything you say?" Her words fell out slightly slurred. "You're a no good cheat."

"I messed up. The girl you saw at the club is nobody to me. I will never be unfaithful to you again. I promise."

"Don't listen to him, Liza." Mattie crossed her arms. "He's a liar."

"You're one to talk." He shot her a glare.

She sighed. "Mattie, it's okay. Give us a moment."

Releasing an infuriated breath, Mattie stomped down the hall. The bedroom door closed with a bang.

"I'm telling you the truth." Warren leaned close, lowering his voice to a whisper. "I want to start over, get out of the mob. I have seen and done more horrible things than I can count. I watched Finn die. He gasped his last breath while I held his head in my hands. It should have been me, not him. Truth is, I'm afraid to die. I don't like the path my life has taken. I want to be a better person, someone my parents can be proud of. I'm going to run away tonight. I want you to come with me. We can go to Canada, start a new life together. What do you say?"

She blinked, trying to clear her muddled mind. "I don't know. You said no one can get out of the mob."

"If we leave now, we'll be gone before they know we're missing. They won't find us." He gently lifted her chin. "It will be different this time, I promise."

Hope rekindled in her heart, warring against her better judgment. She shouldn't believe him, but she wanted to escape. There wasn't anything left for her in Manhattan. She wanted him to fix the aching in her heart. "I'll go with you. I better pack."

"No, you can't bring anything. We have to go now. If Mattie knows, she'll tell Julian, and if he tells Lonan, I'll be dead before the day is done."

"I need clothes."

"I'll buy you new clothes."

"What about my sheets of music?"

"Where are they?"

"The bedroom."

He rubbed a hand against the back of his neck. "All right, get them." Helping her to her feet, he added, "but don't tell Mattie why."

Liquor burned through her veins making her feel unsteady.

She stumbled down the hall into the bedroom. She knelt by her bed.

"What are you doing?" asked Mattie.

She pulled out her suitcase. "I'm going to Warren's house."

"What? Why?"

"Because." Unzipping the bag, she threw in her music, a strand of pearls, undergarments, and two dresses from the closet.

"But he cheated on you."

"I don't care. I have no family, no career, and nothing to live for." She hefted the bag. "Warren's the best I can do."

"You're drunk." Mattie trailed after her as she trudged back to the parlor. "You're not thinking straight."

"It's like what you said," she looped her arm through Warren's, "eat, drink, and be merry, for tomorrow we die."

CHAPTER FORTY-FIVE

Monday, 9:30 PM

Mattie's fingers trembled as she listened to the phone ring.

"Gregorian Hotel," answered a pleasant voice.

"I need to speak with Hugh Whitmore in room 26. It's an emergency."

"Yes, ma'am. Please hold."

The line went silent. Mattie looked out the window. She saw Warren's Ford in the parking lot, which meant he hadn't left the building yet. The stairs were probably proving to be a challenge since Warren had to escort a tipsy Eliza.

"Hello, this is Hugh."

"I need you to hurry to my apartment," said Mattie. "Warren has talked Eliza into running away with him. They are going to leave right now."

"That's her choice. I'm done fighting for her."

"You don't understand. No one can outrun the mob. Warren has a target on his back. He won't make it out of the city alive. Since Eliza is with him, she's in just as much danger. If you want to save her, you better get here. Fast."

———

Eliza stumbled toward Warren's car with his arm around her waist. "I hear your real name's Frederick." She poked his shoulder with her finger. "You lied about that too."

"I had to lie," he opened her passenger door, "in order to protect my family."

She dropped into the seat. "It didn't work."

"What do you mean?"

"Lonan beat up your *brother*."

"What?" His body tensed. "When?"

"Today. Something about being a partner, but Hugh said no."

Warren cursed. "We have to hurry. They'll be coming for me." He scanned the parking lot.

The passenger door slammed shut.

He jumped into his seat, starting the engine. They cruised onto 10th Avenue.

"Who's coming?"

"Red, Julian, maybe Lonan himself. I betrayed the gang's trust. We need to get to Canada before they find us."

A horn honked from behind.

She glanced over her shoulder. A vehicle raced toward them. "Someone is following us. It looks like Hugh's car."

Warren looked into the rearview mirror and pressed harder on the gas.

"Why are you speeding up?"

He didn't answer.

She checked again. "It is Hugh. Pull over."

"I can't do that."

"He might want to tell us something." She shifted in her seat, catching sight of another car speeding up behind Hugh. It swerved around him into the oncoming lane. "Are those the men from—" her eyes widened, "—they have guns!" Deafening bullets peppered the backend of their car. The window shattered. She screamed, cowering down on the leather seat.

Warren stomped on the gas. "Hang on!" A bullet punctured

his shoulder, causing him to swerve. Another bullet cracked his window. Pieces of glass fell into his lap.

As they sped across West 36th Street, she looked around the side of her seat.

Hugh rammed his car into the bumper of the attacking vehicle, causing it to fishtail. He crashed into it again. It hit the curb, rolled, and collided with an oncoming vehicle. Then Hugh's car sped out of control into a lamppost.

Warren pulled off to the side of the road.

"Where are you going?" asked Eliza.

He removed his gun. "To get my brother." He ran out.

As she pulled the door handle, she noticed a trail of blood slither down her right arm. Fear pushed her on. She scrambled after Warren, pausing for a moment to look at the attacker's vehicle. It was crumpled against another car like a metal accordion. There was no way they were alive.

Warren pried open Hugh's car door. His body was slumped forward with his forehead on the steering wheel.

She gasped. "Is he dead?"

Warren felt his neck. "He's got a pulse. Help me get him to our car." Groaning against his own pain, he hoisted his brother up. "We need to get him to the hospital."

She struggled to help carry Hugh to the backseat of Warren's Ford. His face looked like ashen snow. She offered a silent prayer, hoping God might answer.

CHAPTER FORTY-SIX

Eliza sat next to Hugh's bed, watching the slow rise and fall of his chest. He had been asleep for the last 23 hours. The doctor said he had suffered a concussion, fractured ribs, and a collapsed lung. Other than purple bruises, his face appeared pale. The once confident, impervious Hugh Whitmore had been reduced to a motionless man in a hospital bed.

The doctor had advised her to rest in her own room due to a bullet wound in her bicep, but she had pleaded to sit with him. She couldn't rest until she knew he would be okay. He had placed his life on the line for her and Warren. If he hadn't showed up, she would be dead. Guilt pressed heavy on her shoulders. "I'm sorry. It should be me lying here. You don't deserve this. You are an incredible man. I've been too stubborn to acknowledge it." Fresh tears glassed her eyes. "I was scared. I refused to fall for you because I thought I would lose myself and my dreams like my mother did when she married my father." She paused, stroking her fingertips down the side of his cheek. "I was wrong."

Hugh's body stirred.

She straightened. "Hugh? Can you hear me?"

His forehead scrunched before his eyelids opened. He looked at her for a long moment, scanned the room, and returned to her.

"My goodness, you're awake." She leaned close, clutching his hand. "I've been so worried."

"Where am I?"

"At the hospital. You were in a car wreck. Do you remember that?"

"It's a blur."

"You've been asleep since the accident." Her throat tightened. "The doctors have been monitoring you closely. How do you feel?"

He inhaled a slow breath. "Sore."

"I'm sorry." Her eyes fell. "We didn't know if you'd make it. I've never been so frightened."

"Looks like I'm still here." He tried to clear his throat. "May I have some water?"

"Of course." Lurching to her feet, she hurried to a table in the corner with a pitcher.

"Are you hurt?" Concern carried in his voice.

She glanced at the bandage on her arm. "The doctor says I should heal well. It's nothing compared to what you've suffered." She placed a full glass in his hand.

He groaned as he tried to sit up. "I might need help."

Placing her good arm behind his back, she gently leaned him upright and propped a pillow behind him.

He sucked in a sharp breath. "That's enough."

"Are you okay? Should I get the nurse?"

He shook his head. With trembling hands, he brought the glass to his lips.

Guilt hit her anew. "I blame myself for all of this."

"It's not your fault. I would give my life to save you and my brother any day."

"Oh, Hugh." She exhaled a slow breath. "My world wouldn't be the same without you."

"I feel the same way about you." He glanced toward the door, his expression growing worried. "Is my brother okay?"

"He has injuries, but he'll recover."

"Good. As soon as I'm able, I plan to talk with my father. I am going to relinquish my title as heir. I want Warren to be able to care for you well."

Her brow furrowed. "What do you mean?"

"When you're discharged, Warren and you will be able start a new life. I hope you'll have a happy one together."

Despite the love revealed through his generous offer, her shoulders sagged with sadness. Warren wasn't the man she wanted. If only she had admitted that sooner. She loosened her hold on his hand. "I'm sure Warren will be grateful." She rose to her feet, wanting to disappear. "I better get a nurse. They'll want to know that you're awake." Footsteps sounded on the linoleum outside the door. She looked over to see Warren filling the frame. A flush filled her face as she met his eyes, feeling caught and ashamed. Since the accident, she hadn't gone to Warren's room once. Instead, she had been seated beside his brother.

"Eliza." He cleared his throat. "You're in here."

"Yes, well, I felt I should check on Hugh after everything that happened. I wanted to see if he was okay. Luckily, he just woke up. I better tell a nurse. Please excuse me." She brushed past him in a flustered rush.

———

Hugh watched Eliza leave, knowing it would be hard to get over her. His brother was a lucky guy.

Warren sank into a chair beside the bed. "How're you feeling?"

"My best day ever."

"You never were a good liar. You look like hell."

"I didn't know the hospital was hosting a beauty pageant."

The side of Warren's mouth curved. "I wanted to tell

you…thanks. We would have died if you hadn't put your neck on the line."

"I had to. You're my brother."

"You always were the good one." He shook his head. "I guess that's partly why I left. I thought I needed to make a name for myself. When I arrived in New York, I met Julian. He was a part of the McKennas. They had everything: wealth, power, prestige. I craved it. So I did what it took to join them. That decision has been costing me ever since." He released a slow breath. "I've done so many terrible things that haunt me every day. I wanted to be free of the mob, and I tried to take Eliza with me. I should have known better."

"Eliza chose to go with you. Just like I chose to run my vehicle into the other car. We all made our own choices, and we all survived." He met his brother's perplexed expression. "I'm glad you decided to get out of the mob. Eliza's going to need you."

"What do you mean?"

"Aren't you going to marry her?"

"I would, but I'm not sure she loves me. As soon as the doc bandaged her arm, she went to your room."

Hugh blinked. "Why would she do that?"

"Could be guilt. Or facing death opened her eyes."

"But she chose to run away with you. Doesn't that mean something?"

"Desperation can force us to make bad decisions. I think she always liked you best." Warren shrugged. "Besides, she isn't safe with me. I can't escape the mob. It's hopeless."

"There's always hope. It just depends where you're finding it."

Warren raised a brow. "Are you getting religious on me?"

"Definitely not, but I don't believe that we're ever too far gone." He smiled. "Even you."

Warren looked at his hands in silence.

"Mr. Whitmore," a nurse entered his room, "good to see

you awake. I'm going to check your vitals and bandages."

"That's my cue. I'll visit you later." Warren walked to the door.

"Hey Freddie."

Warren halted. "Yeah?"

"You remember that time in church when you pretended to pray and knelt on the bench to look up Cynthia's skirt?"

A knowing grin curved his brother's lips. "They were pink."

He chuckled as Warren exited his room.

CHAPTER FORTY-SEVEN

Tuesday, 10:00 PM

"Sleep, my child, and peace attend thee all through the night. Guardian angels God will send thee, all through the night. Soft the drowsy hours are creeping, hill and dale in slumber sleeping. I my loved ones' watch am keeping, all through the night."

The soft lullaby flowed into Eliza's ears. She remembered the song from when she was very little, those carefree days when life blossomed with opportunity. The humming stopped. A hand rubbed her cheek. She opened her eyes. "Mother?"

"Yes, sweetheart. It's me." Katherine leaned close.

"How did you know I was here?"

"Vivian called me. I boarded the first train available. I've never been so afraid in all my life."

She studied her mother's face, searching for disapproval, but all she saw was concern. "Did Father come too?"

"I'm sorry." Katherine bent her head. "He didn't."

She turned to the window to hide her sadness. He hadn't forgiven her. He probably never would.

"Did you see the vase of lilies? I had them brought to your room." Her mother stroked a curl from her forehead. "They have such a cheerful fragrance."

The vase sat on her bedside table, overflowing with white petals. The smell did nothing to cheer her. "Do you remember when I was six, and I picked all your lilies in the garden?"

"Yes, I remember." Katherine folded her hands. "At the time, it seemed devastating."

"You were furious. I hated myself for disappointing you. Ever since that day, I never liked lilies."

"I didn't know that." Katherine touched a nervous hand to her rosary. "I shouldn't have been cross with you. I overreacted because those lilies were special to me. I had planted them to remind me of…" She paused. "A different time in my life."

"Before Father?"

Her fingers traveled the beads; she nodded. "His name was Philip. I met him when I was 15. He was adventurous and full of life. I would meet with him in secret at the back of my parents' property. Beyond our trees was a field of lilies that grew by the river. We would sit, talking for hours. I wanted to marry him, but my parents forbade it. His family wasn't in our social standing."

"Why didn't you fight for your love?"

"That was unheard of. A woman obeyed her parents, so I did as I was told."

"Your parents wanted you to marry father?"

"Yes. He was a good match for me."

"Do you regret marrying him?"

"Sometimes. But then I wouldn't have you. And I love you."

"Do you wish you had borne a son to carry on the family name?"

"Your father wanted a boy, not me." Katherine grasped her hand. "I should have stood up to your father for speaking harsh words to you and to myself, but I was afraid of his rejection. I spent our whole marriage striving to earn his approval and the acceptance of our community. I thought their praise would make me happy, so I held the best parties, bought the best clothes, furnished our home with the most expensive décor. In the end, I felt unsatisfied. I had lost sight of myself, the girl who used to lie in a field of lilies watching the sunset. It wasn't until I received Vivian's call that I woke up from my slumber. A younger Katherine would have encouraged her daughter to live life to the fullest. She would have told her to marry for love." Her voice cracked with emotion. "My selfishness caused you to run away, but I promise, from this day forward, things will be different. I love you, Eliza Adrienne. Will you forgive me?"

A smile spread across her mouth. "I already have."

Katherine wrapped her arms around her. "Today is a new day for us."

"I like the sound of that."

"I spoke with the doctor. He will discharge you in the morning, if you feel like you're up to it." She loosened her hold, studying the bandage on Eliza's arm. "How is your pain? Do you feel able to leave?"

"It aches but I can handle it."

"Do you want to come back with me?"

"Father made it clear that I wasn't welcome home."

"We're not going to Belle Vue. My parents have agreed to let us stay with them until I can find a more permanent arrangement for us."

"What did you tell them?"

"Only what they needed to know. But they understand your father's ways."

"Will father allow it? Won't that create a stir in the community?"

"I won't allow my decisions to be made for me any longer. Your courage has inspired me." She straightened in her seat. "If your father wants to come for us, he will know where to find us. As for the community gossips, let them talk. You matter more to me than any amount of wealth or reputation. I've made mistakes, but I want to start over." She squeezed Eliza's hand. "Will you come with me?"

"I would like that."

"Then we will go together and see what life has in store for us."

"Mother, I have only one question. If Aisling Neville would like to leave Belle Vue, could she continue as our lady's maid? She has been a faithful friend and employee."

Katherine nodded. "Whatever she chooses, I will see to it."

CHAPTER FORTY-EIGHT

Tuesday, 11:00 pm

Julian snuck into Warren's room like a shadow against the wall.

"How good of you to come visit me," said Warren.

"I've been sent."

The three words settled into Warren's bones like a cold draft. "Lonan sent you?"

Julian nodded. "He says yer a liar. We know ya tried to bail. Since I'm the one who brought ya in, I gotta be the one to take ya out."

They stared at each other in silence. Warren knew this day would come. He had tried to run from it, but he knew it would catch him. A life for a life. "I know. Will you promise me one thing?"

"What's that?"

"Will you leave a message for my parents?"

Julian frowned. "I can't do that."

"Please, Jules. There is something they need to know. I won't be able to tell them personally, so it has to be you."

Julian rubbed the back of his neck. "I hate this."

"It's the life we chose."

"I still hate it," said Julian in a grieved tone. "What do you want me to tell them?"

"That I'm sorry, and I forgive them. Tell them that it's goodbye for now, but I'll see them again."

Julian looked confused by this, but he didn't ask for an explanation. "Okay."

"Make it quick." Warren closed his eyes. All was dark until he heard a click followed by intense heat inside his chest.

———

11:25 pm

Despite the horridness of the accident, Vivian had renewed hope. Both of her sons were alive and recovering. "Before we go to our hotel, let's say goodnight to Frederick."

"I already planned on it," said Daniel. "It's been a rough day, but I think this accident might change things for the better. Frederick was more receptive with us earlier."

"I sensed that, too." She put a hand to her heart. "When I hugged him, he returned it. I felt like I had my son back."

"Maybe now he'll decide to come home."

They walked down the hall into Frederick's room. The light was off. "Son, are you asleep?" asked Daniel.

No response.

He ran a hand along the wall, searching for a light switch. He flipped it on.

Vivian released a piercing scream. Her son lay limp on the hospital bed, drenched in blood. She ran to his side, touching his face, pleading for him to open his eyes. "God, please."

Daniel yelled into the hall. "Help, we need a doctor now!"

She knelt by the bed, noticing a piece of paper on his pillow. Scrawled letters danced before her eyes. *I was sent. I hate what I had to do, but it fell to me. Warren asked me to write down his last words. He's sorry. It's goodbye for now, but he will see you again.* Her vision blurred. Pressing her face against her son's shoulder, she wept horrible racking sobs.

CHAPTER FORTY-NINE

September 25
Friday, 8:45 PM

Eliza returned to Shaker's Nightclub in Philadelphia. The stage was still small, the overhead lights flickered, smoke hung like a cloud in the room, and a lack of airflow caused the patrons to perspire. But she knew this place. The same smiles. The same atmosphere. It was familiar. It wasn't luxurious like the Fianna, but it was home.

Sadness subdued her smile as the events during and after New York replayed in her mind. It had been four weeks since Warren's funeral. The Whitmores had shipped his body to Pennsylvania for the service. Eliza and her mother had attended the wake to pay their condolences. She had laid a single lily on the coffin. As she walked past Hugh, he had nodded to her. She had returned the gesture. That was the last time she had seen Hugh Whitmore.

She and her mother now resided with her grandparents at Woodbridge Hall. Katherine's separation from Hector had come with a price. He had declined them any funds and ceased contact. Not only had the high-society women of Elkins Park ostracized them, they had also trampled on their good names.

Even Geraldine, her supposed bosom friend, had refused to speak to her. Gradually the pain of rejection lessened. The outward conflict had drawn Eliza and Katherine closer. They might have lost status, but they were gaining themselves in the process.

Tonight, she would be performing on stage for the first time since returning to Pennsylvania. In the audience, her mother and Aisling sat waiting with expectant smiles.

Flora Gray patted her on the back. "Looking forward to hearing you sing again."

"Thank you. I'm glad to be back."

"Knock 'em dead, baby."

"You got it." She laid a hand over her music pendant necklace. She had decided to have it fixed after all. It didn't matter that it wasn't luxurious; to her, it had value. She climbed the steps with a peace she hadn't felt before. Somewhere in the chaos, she had discovered that her achievements or failures didn't define her. Her worth couldn't be earned or lost. As a human being created by God, she was born worthy. She didn't need music to prove it. Now she sang because she loved it. She drew close to the microphone. "It's a pleasure to be here with you this evening. I'll be singing an original piece that I call *It Ain't Over*." Her voice carried over the crowd as she sang her lyrics to an energetic tune.

Several patrons cheered, but the loudest came from the back corner.

Despite the foggy air, she made out a familiar black bowler hat with the white ribbon. As soon as the last key played, she watched the man move toward the exit. Bowing, she hurried off the stage, determined to catch him this time. She wove through the crowd, dashed out of the club, and scanned the street. Her heart raced. She didn't see him. She stomped her foot in frustration.

"Looking for someone?"

Spinning around, she came face to face with Hugh. Her eyes

grew wide with shock. "You're wearing the hat."

His dimples surfaced with a smile.

"You're the one who's been cheering me on this whole time?"

"I always was a fan."

"Then why did you run off after my first performance? Why didn't you tell me that it was you?"

"I thought you might find it unsettling that I followed you. I didn't want to scare you off, especially since I had planned to propose. We both know how that ended." He grinned in spite of himself. "Truth is, even though I cheered for you that first night, I still didn't want you to return to Shakers. I cared more about molding you into the person I wanted than supporting your dreams. I was selfish and proud. Sadly, I didn't realize this until it was too late. After my brother's funeral, I didn't know how to approach you, so I stayed away." He stared at her. "But I've missed you."

"I've missed you too." She touched the brim of his hat. "Ever since my first performance at Shakers, I wondered who my mystery man was. Honestly, I never thought it could be you. But tonight, when I saw the black hat again," she paused, "I hoped it would be you wearing it."

His forehead furrowed. "Why did you leave the hospital without saying goodbye?"

"I was ashamed. You were willing to give everything up for me, even your inheritance, so that I could marry your brother. But I didn't want him. When he died, I felt more guilt. I figured you would be better off without me in your life."

"It's hard to live a better life when the person you love isn't in it."

"You still love me?"

"I never stopped."

She stepped closer. "I lied before when I said I didn't feel fireworks. I felt them the night we kissed in my parents' library. I felt them the night we danced at Club Fianna. I feel them every time you're near me. I've been fighting my heart for too long, but I refuse to go another day without telling you the truth." She touched the side of his cheek. "I love you, Hugh Whitmore. I love how your dimples surface when you smile. I love how your trousers are perfectly creased. I love your ego, even when it's excessive, and I love your honesty, even when it's aggravating. I love you, and I don't want to lose you again."

He stood, speechless.

Wrapping her arms around his neck, she kissed him with all the passion she possessed. "What do you say? Do you want to court me?"

"Only on one condition."

She tipped her head to the side. "What's that?"

"Someday, when we do marry, we'll buy an estate with a pond."

Her mouth curved with laughter. "I hope you're a good swimmer."

The story continues in the spirited sequel, Marvel and Mayhem.

Audacious flapper, Mattie O'Keefe must undertake a journey that will drop her in a place she never dreamed of, a farm, in the middle of nowhere. She would rather work her pitiful life away in a crummy diner than be on a forsaken farm, but she's stuck. If she leaves its concealed security, it could mean her death, and she's not ready to die.

Now an Excerpt from Marvel and Mayhem:

The Whitmore's butler glanced in the rearview mirror. "We're nearly there, ma'am. Just up ahead now."

In the last twenty minutes, Mattie had only seen ordinary, unimpressive homes. Wasn't she supposed to be working for a rich aunt? They were reaching a dead-end. A huge river extended north to south, bringing the icy dirt road to a halt. There were only two properties left and both were farms. "Are we lost?"

The Packard Touring slowed as it reached a snowy path leading to a large farm at the end of the road. "No ma'am. This is the place."

Despite her splitting headache, she could tell this was no mansion. The house looked over a hundred years old. Its exterior paint looked like a worn white leather boot, crackled and flaking. The adjacent red barns appeared just as desperate. "I was supposed to be working for Eliza's rich aunt. How can this be the right place?"

The car rolled to a stop. "I'm not sure what Lady Eliza might have said, but this is the place."

Mattie stared in confusion. "But it's a farm."

"Yes ma'am."

How could this aunt be rich if she lived here? The butler opened her door. She exited, staring at the sagging porch. This place looked about as grand as her apartment.

The front door opened. A petite woman in a heavy wool coat stepped onto the porch. "Are you Eliza's friend?"

"Yes." Mattie's forehead creased. "Are you Eliza's rich aunt?"

The woman chuckled. "Indeed, I'm her aunt. Rich? That's debatable." She marched down the steps, extending a pale hand aged with sunspots. "I'm Velma Emery. Welcome to Emery Farm."

"Thanks. I'm Mattie O'…Carroll. Mattie O'Carroll." She shook Velma's hand, inwardly despising Eliza. Eliza knew where she was sending her, but she let Mattie believe it would be a mansion, even though, it was a decrepit farmhouse. The butler handed her a small suitcase filled with Eliza's hand-me-down charity, clothing that was two sizes too small. Her shoulders sagged in a sigh. She couldn't return to Eliza's house, and even if she had money to go back to Manhattan, she'd live looking over her shoulder.

"I'm sorry to hear about your loss," said Velma. "Death is a painful thing. If you need to take things slower at first, we can oblige you."

The muscles lining Mattie's jaw twitched. It wasn't Eliza's place to tell her aunt such a personal thing. She managed an uncertain thank you.

Velma thanked the butler for delivering Mattie, then walked

up the porch steps. "Let's get inside before this cold blows through our bones."

Mattie glanced backward as the Packard rolled out of the driveway. Anxiety constricted her chest. She was in the middle of nowhere. Without a dime. Without a cigarette. Or a bottle of gin. She was doomed.

"I'll first show you to your bedroom so you can set your things down." Velma walked through the kitchen and into the living room. Turning a sharp right toward a narrow staircase, she said, "Your room is up here." She bounded up steep wooden stairs like a teenager.

Mattie felt her chest squeeze after the first five steps.

Reaching the landing, Velma motioned to a door on the left. "That bedroom belongs to my granddaughter, Effie. This one will be yours." She stepped into a small room. "It used to be my sewing area." A cot squeezed against the far wall beside a Singer sewing machine. Stacked baskets of fabric, threads, and quilts covered most of the floor. "Forgive the mess. I only found out about your arrival last evening. I promise to make more space for you this week."

"It's no problem." Mattie's voice came out winded.

Velma noted her apparent strain. "Perhaps you would like to rest after you settle into your room." She shoved a chair aside, opening a built in closet door. "You can hang your clothes in here. I'll call you when it's time to prepare dinner. Is there anything you need right now?"

"Do you have a cigarette?"

The wrinkles around Velma's eyes stretched with shock. "I don't smoke. No one in this house does."

"Seriously?"

"I most certainly am. If you choose to smoke, you will have to do it outside. I keep a clean house."

Mattie set her suitcase on the bed with a frown. "Where's the bathroom?"

"Head down the stairs, go through the living room and out

the back door. You'll see the outhouse."

"Outhouse?"

"We don't have running water in the home. Hence, our toilet is outside. On these winter days, I certainly wish it wasn't. Keep your coat on. It's dreadful cold out there." She turned, exiting the room.

Mattie took a deep breath. The ache in her bladder forced her back down the stairs and out the door. A wooden outhouse with a moon carved on the front door greeted her. Her top lip curled back. "I'm gonna kill Eliza." The door creaked on its hinges as she opened it. She gasped. A wooden bench sat on the floor with a hole cut in its middle. A stack of Sears and Roebuck catalogs sat on the right hand side. She took a step forward, peering in the hole. Her hand flew to her mouth with a scream. She stumbled backward into the snow. "These people are crazy!"

A young girl stepped out from a small barn, holding a wire basket of eggs. "Are you okay?"

Mattie whipped around to see a young brunette eyeing her.

"Are we out of paper in the outhouse?" the girl called.

"There isn't any toilet paper."

The girl walked up to her. "I'm Effie. You must be the new help."

Mattie nodded.

"Glad to meet you," said Effie. "I thought Gram stocked the catalogs yesterday." She opened the outhouse door. "She did stock 'em. The paper is right there. You might want to get your eyes checked."

Mattie stared at the girl in disbelief. "You wipe with catalog pages?"

"Course. What do you use? Corn cobs?"

To her surprise, Mattie didn't think the kid was making a joke. "No. I use Scotts toilet paper. I buy it at the store."

Effie waved her hand in dismissal. "We don't buy that fancy stuff. The trick is to crinkle a page in your hands several times.

It'll make the paper softer and more pliable." She patted Mattie on the arm. "Good luck." With that, she trotted back to the barn.

Cursing, Mattie flung open the outhouse door. She slid the lock into place. Lining the hole with pages of ladies in summer frocks, she pulled down her drawers. Her buttocks rested on the cold paper. She swore again. Icy air circled around her bare thighs and her teeth chattered. Maybe she had died after all.

And now, she was in hell.

CPSIA information can be obtained
at www.ICGtesting.com
Printed in the USA
LVHW091300180319
611023LV00001B/32/P

9 781985 377622